Scripted In Love's Scars

A Phantom of the Opera Novel

Michelle Rodriguez

DEDICATION

To Dr. Jan Bickel for instilling in me a love for music
and singing that is poured into every Phantom story I
write. You are my teacher, my mentor, and an
absolute inspiration in all that I do. I would not be
the person I am today without you in my life. Thank
you!

ACKNOWLEDGEMENTS

A special thank you to Jessica Elizabeth Schwartz for the stunning cover. This was the first shoot where I got to see you work and watch you be inspired, and the finished product is truly gorgeous. This cover will always hold a special place in my heart, and every time I pass the place where it was taken, I will think of hot days in June, a literary tea party, and getting yelled at by a museum worker. Oh, such memories!

And thank you to Erin Marie Brooks and Dan Moran. I feel so lucky to have met you both and to have seen you model and become the characters. You are both amazing!

Chapter One

Erik~

In all my years as a reluctant and unaccepted member of the human race, I've come to learn that life is actually a stagnant existence. *We* do not change, per se. The world changes. It evolves and shifts, and unless *we* follow suit and go along with the tide, we remain the same boring soul, perhaps a little more cynical for wear, but certainly not a spirit in motion, pulled along life's well-cut route. To change and grow, we must *want* to. We must be willing to be secondary in importance to the flow of the universe around us. I have never been a person to live beneath anyone's laws and physics, even God's. No, I *make* my destiny; I do not let destiny make *me*.

As such, when the world spit at me and constantly tried to beat me down at every turn, I rose up from the ashes like the eternal Phoenix and became something new, something untouchable but equally unchangeable. I severed my ties to the world and *chose* to stay the same.

Most people cannot do that. As integral members of earth's shifting patterns, they have no choice but to deal with its mistakes and foibles and Fate's backhanded swing. Connections are weaknesses. Fall in love, tie a heart, and at some point, life will alter without your permission. Either a child will be thrown into the picture, and two will

1

become three; perhaps a pleasant change, but a *change* just the same. Or maybe instead Fate will decide it hates you and take your love without consideration. Death, scandal, altered heartbeats. Pick a path. Every one means *change*, for good or for bad.

But...slice ties, abandon the world's telling trails and *you* control your own existence. And life unavoidably plays by your rules. It stays unaltered, fixed, ...but inevitably, it will seem stale. How could it not? To relive the repetitive routine day to day without hope for some undetermined factor to make a difference. I cannot grow as a person without *other* people, without a world evolving and encouraging me along the path of enlightenment.

What is a worse existence? One full of derision and abhorrence, pain, intolerance, and cruelty, but *moving* in some way? Or one that holds suspended in place, follows its custom-made pattern every single day without fail and without hope for modification?

Years ago, I decided the first choice as my answer and buried *myself* for my persecutors. Death without dying. But as time spun mercilessly onward and healed internal scars when external were permanently molded, I started to wonder if I'd made the right decision.

Cut off from the world.

At first, it was an easy path. I *liked* being alone, and since solitude was achieved by my own doing, I had control in how I spent my time and how I embraced the silence. I could return to the world at least to catch glimpses of day or stars if I wanted; I *chose* not to. It was simple.

Years in the molded niche I'd constructed for myself, and I didn't change, didn't grow. Instead, I started to shut down. Emotions turned off and faded into the deepest recesses of a heart, but when the majority learned in my years had been the ugly and vicious sort, that was no loss.

Apathy overcame the surface, and I never fought its possession. I *wanted* to be apathetic. It made existing tolerable. I believed I'd stay in that blank haze until my eventual death. And why not? What did I have worth existing for?

The music... That was the only detail of the world I knew I'd mourn when I was fully dead and in the crypt. I still *felt* in music's sphere. But...music did not have a cruel tongue full of violent remarks and stinging attacks. Music had no free will as mankind did, and therefore could not forsake me. It was the only thing I considered a *friend*, but what a hollow relationship! I'd die someday, and music wouldn't mourn *my* loss as I'd mourn if it abandoned me instead.

No friend, no foe, no attachments to a life not even worth living. I might as well have been the *corpse* I'd so often been called. To mankind, *corpse* was a derogatory insult; to me, after years living the equivalent of a corpse's future, I found it a new aspiration. *Be* a corpse, but a *real* one this time. Corpses had the advantage of having no thoughts. I was eager for the day my brain would be as turned off as my heart.

But...well, sometimes even the best-laid plans are interrupted, and Fate finds a way to sneak in and change things against our wishes. Such was my case.

For years, I had taken up the role of Opera Ghost, a further push toward the future I wanted where ghost would be an applicable title. Initially, I had created the part for myself because I needed a means to *politely* get my opinions heard.

In theory, severing oneself from the world is doable. *In theory*, I repeat, because if you have foolishly chosen the pits of an *opera house* for your secluded sanctuary, unless deafness is also in the cards, life worms its way inside. It wasn't much with so many floors in between, but I enjoyed the resonant echoes that trickled their way through the catacombs.

When indoors, they were minimal, but music had a siren's call straight to my soul and hypnotized my better sense, drawing me out of my grave to be its eager audience.

Yes, *music*, but what I heard in that opera house was *not* music. It was a far cry from it. Too many egos and not enough talent to back them up.

Rejecting the living world should have meant that I kept my distance, but this felt like a sacrilege to the arts. The managers of the opera were bumbling fools with no taste or ability to do more than cut paychecks. They put their opinions on a scale contingent with the monetary value attached. La Carlotta, famous name, diva. Forget the fact that she sang like a cat being strangled! She was given any role she wanted on reputation alone. It sickened me. She drew crowds because she was known for her attitude and arrogance. Her latest tantrums were leaked through the media outlets, and people came to see if she would sing, if she had gotten her way as she always inevitably did. And then they left the opera without the glory of the music in their ears, but with stories of *seeing* the great La Carlotta. Not *hearing* because how could one associate her voice with the essence of what opera was supposed to be?

I had to do something. Opera Ghost seemed an ideal manner in which to play both sides of the world. A ghost need not interact with the living beyond what it wanted. And I had tactics to make myself a viable threat so as not to be dismissed: notes, accidents that looked like child's play compared to the tricks in my past, the occasional disappearance of a useless stagehand, although only ones truly deserving of such a fate. *Play God.* That was my mantra. Deem who lived or died and which commands must be followed. My role stole my growing ennui, and I felt I'd mastered the point between *living* in the world and *controlling* it.

Now there was one added activity I threw into

my repertoire, and it ended up being the beginning of my inevitable downfall. I believed the best means to keep my pretense alive and menacing was to occasionally make an appearance. Ghosts materialized at times, didn't they? It added the terror factor, and who better to carry my doctrine of fear than the gullible little girls of the *corps de ballet*? Those girls built my entire empire with their exaggerated tales. They were my unknowing allies and fans in our bizarre relationship because for as scared as they genuinely were, they propagated the rumors. Of course that also meant they blamed *everything* on their so-called ghost, but I took the bad with the good in this case.

Some of the ignorant stagehand boys were hopelessly enamored with the ballerinas and often snuck into their dressing room to claim un-given tokens as prizes. Missing ribbons was a rampant sin in the entire department. But fine. Blame the Opera Ghost. Make *me* your lusting, infatuated lover. I didn't care about the petty thievery, and the stories spun so rapidly about the company that if anything, it made me what I'd never in my existence been: a Don Juan lothario. It gave my legend a dangerously seductive edge that it wouldn't have otherwise had.

As I said, my interactions were as the ghost. From time to time, I would 'appear' to one of the ballerinas, finding one alone so as not to cause an uproar and doing no more than popping out of shadows. It was little effort on my part. Seeing a masked man *made me* a ghost because what mortal man would strut about in a mask? They made my image into the Opera Ghost and fabricated story after story of what lay beneath the mask. The consensus was a horror; it was the one detail they ever got right.

I played well with them, but they took my little game and wanted control. Foolish children! It became a new pastime among the tutus to dare each other into the lower cellars. Who could linger the longest in the ghost's domain? Who would travel to the lowest cellar? Who would stand in the center of the deepest floor and call the ghost three times? Idiotic, childish nonsense. Only occasionally did I indulge them, merely as a way to capitalize on my title.

The ballet mistress' young daughter was my favorite target. She was so easy to frighten; I barely had to do more than whisper her name, and she'd scream in this blessed high pitch that resounded through the entire opera house. She was unwittingly my greatest instigator and perpetrator of my existence, and as the daughter of the head mistress, she had more clout and believability than the other ballet rats. When she ran to the management with tears in her big, green eyes, gushing over the ghost, they *listened*. What an asset for me! My demands were met without argument because I scared a bunch of highly anxious, fanatic, hysterical little girls!

My reign went undisturbed from this pattern for a few blissful years. Life was my subservient slave. *I* was in complete control, and even if I'd shut down internally and put myself on a pedestal above the world, I let my love for the music draw me down from time to time, aiding it along and not letting it be squashed and demoralized the way *I* had once been by the world. As much as I could.

There were certain things I could not touch. I abhorred La Carlotta, but no one else in the company could fill her shoes, and the ledgers called for a *diva*. Without her, the opera would have suffered, so though I had to keep her on, I had her working by my rules. I kept her tantrums under control because she wasn't allowed to have them. I gave the management their excuse to leash her. The *Ghost* commanded this or that, and though she argued and insulted in vibrant Italian, she had no option but to obey. I loved it. This proved *I was* a god. Omnipotent, all-powerful. Ghosts had flaws because even dead, they had connections to the living. I had none and therefore saw myself as invincible.

The largest egos fall the hardest and most violent.

Fate backhanded me and tossed me from my throne one unfortunate day with one choice and one action. *One.* And my world shattered.

I woke up that destined day knowing it was the start of rehearsals for the new production. I needed leverage to be certain my opinions were heard loud and clear. As far as I was concerned, the management worked for *me*, but threats and *encouragement* were a part of the job and my unbreakable persona. In the haste of the last show's opening, I'd sat back and observed their triumph due to *my* guidance. There was little need for a ghost's antics during a performance week. Now I had to re-establish my hold. An appearance was necessary, and as usual, the ballerinas were my top choice victims.

A new show meant new recruits. Fresh blood added in, new faces, new means to enhance my reputation and fame. It had become a tradition among the ballerinas to induct new members of their tulle brigade by subjecting them to a good scare. They favored forcing the new girls to take turns wandering the cellars and taunting the Opera Ghost to rise. A juvenile manner of promoting camaraderie and proving self-worth if you asked me, and I usually did not play along. I didn't have to. The idea of ghosts alone left the new recruits a step from hysteria and frightening *themselves*, convinced they heard *something*, saw *something*, were touched on a shoulder or felt a cold breeze along their skin. All ridiculous nonsense when I kept nowhere near this immature display. New ballerinas were too susceptible to gullibility and peer pressure; why would I bother instigating it onward?

Today, however, choices were minimal, and I thought a quick appearance to a new ballet rat would at least stir the pot until I could track down the young Giry alone and truly start the inferno blazing.

Oh, this would be too easy! I barely had to lift a finger. The girls would throw the new ballerina into the first cellar and hold the door closed for a two-minute count. ...It was cruel in the way children were mean to one another. To a man who'd been on the opposite side of *real* torture, it was further proof of immaturity.

As I lingered in the first cellar impatient for the induction to begin, I concluded that I'd wait until the last girl so as to achieve a deceptive level of comfort. Let the others make up their stories of intangible touches and calls, nothing to arouse too much panic. The last girl was my target. I'd make it look like a magical materialization with a lantern she'd never glimpse. No, this glow had to look otherworldly and would illuminate the mask first and foremost; who needed a genuine weapon when a manmade mask caused more trauma than anything?

As I readied myself for my grand entrance, I could already hear the screams I was about to cause. The idea alone swelled a peculiar anticipation. I never liked communicating with the world on *their* level, but like this, as the superior role of ghost, it was a thrill. To cause fear meant *power*. I had it; I adored it. Here was proof that I would never be a fragile, fallible mortal again. Why would I ever put myself on their plane when it was so much better to be a god?

I knew from a glimpse at the ballet roster that there were three new tutus in the bunch. And so I waited.

One, and she spent the whole time clawing at the door to get back out, hyperventilating with *no* reason whatsoever. *Two*, and she was a bit more composed until a spider climbed up her ankle. Then she screamed to the high heavens and claimed the *ghost* tickled her. As if I would ever touch one of the little brats! I took it as an insult.

Finally, *three*, and she was heaved in with a sound of a slammed door and the giggles beyond to accompany her entrance. I was too busy preparing my trick to give her much more than a passing glance, enough to make out the silhouette of another tulle skirt in the dark. Perfect, just what I was after.

In the blackness, the girl would see nothing, not until *I* ignited the light, and I was determined to play this exactly as I saw it in my head. Her gasped breaths echoed about the stone cellar walls. Scared already. This was going to be *simple*. A quick pop in and out, and she'd have stories to cry over with the other rats for the rest of the new production.

In all my extensive planning for this exact moment, I failed. I realized that only after the fact. I performed it with a hardened heart, playing my role as I had for years. What hadn't been anticipated, what had *never* been even a consideration was that a factor outside of myself would sway my stable core. *She* was that factor. Unexpected, unplanned for, and with a power all her own, one she did not realize she possessed. It was strong enough to rip a god from his podium and expose his mortal heart. *Damn her...*

I struck my lantern light, knowing its gradual burn would make it seem as if I slowly faded into view, and then I simply stared and waited for her to turn and regard the growing glow. The hint of a smirk was on my lips. Screams, I expected: horror, terror, all extrinsic and beyond my being, none of it touching me. What I got was only *internal*, and I was suddenly the scared one between us.

I saw dark curls knotted back in a pink ribbon, a tiny build, slender and lithe with willowy limbs. She turned, and my world fell apart.

I was the one who gasped; *I* was the one terrified and horror-stricken...because I felt the full weight of emotions I'd spent years without strike me to my core. Like an earthquake that trembled along its fault line, it cracked my stone shield irreparably, making fractures that raced out to its edge and shattered protection. I felt exposed and vulnerable even in my mask because the figurative armor I'd worn about my heart was suddenly gone, and *she* was to blame.

The girl lost a gasp that echoed mine, blue eyes widening to fill the frames of dark lashes, and porcelain, pale skin blanched. My first thought was *why* if I bore my mask and had not shown my face. Why was I receiving such a response? Then sense caught up and reminded me with a strike to my dazed mind that I was the *ghost*. Of course I'd get this response; I *wanted* this response, didn't I? But...where were the screams or tears? I got nothing but a continued stare, as we both seemed to respond with the same unqualified surprise to each other's existence. I didn't understand and had the strange urge to ask *her* if *she* did.

"Ten more seconds, Christine," came a shout from the opposite side of a closed door, and the countdown began. I knew I had to leave before the other rats came to fish her out, but it took another long second before I could tear my gaze away. It felt ensnared upon her little, pink shape, scrutinizing and memorizing and letting her overwhelm me because it felt so *wonderful*.

Still, she made no sound, nothing beyond that continued wide stare. Could I dub it shock if I saw no other verifying proof of fear? *...She was so beautiful...* I could reason little else, but as the doorknob whined in its turning, I quickly put out the light and drew away.

Darkness was the thing to finally incite the gasp I'd been expecting, laden in her terror, and I had to fist my hands at my sides when they longed to *touch* her, to *comfort* her. It threw me from stable ground: to go from emotionless to reacting with compassion all in one solitary minute and all for *one girl*. I would have called myself pathetic if I weren't so focused on the commotion quickly arising around the girl, ...*Christine*.

Dozens of wide eyes were peering into the shadows, but I kept back and knew I remained unseen. Only *she* would know of my observing presence.

"Christine," the little Giry called, jumping up and down in her place as if half a breath from bolting back through the doorway, "did the Opera Ghost haunt you? Oh, tell us!" Excitement overrode both concern and fear as she grabbed Christine's arm and gave more little leaps.

My attention was solely on Christine, and as she lifted blue eyes back into the shadows, I knew she *wanted* to see me again, but I refused a yearning I equally shared.

"No," she said after a moment, and I shivered merely from the sound of her voice. "There was nothing...only the dark."

Yes, the dark... *I* was the dark, and whether she considered me a true ghost or deciphered me as a mortal man, I could not figure her out. She hid her true emotions so completely that I had no answer. All I could argue of this disconcerting encounter with utter certainty was that I was fascinated by every detail of her. ...More than fascinated. I *felt* my reaction inside and out, and it was so complete and all-encompassing that I wasn't sure whether to call her a blessing or a curse to bring such feelings into my life.

Lurking like the ghost they called me, I listened to a fluster of pink crinoline and tulle scurry out of the cellars, for the first time in my existence *mourning* the loss of other human beings. ...Well, *one* human being. And *why*? I didn't know the girl; I'd never seen her before, and if I chose, I never had to see her again.

But there were heavier thoughts I was afraid to admit because sense called them ludicrous. In that one moment and one shared stare, I'd seen something my right mind told me was improbable; I felt foolish even to ponder it to myself. But...in those blue eyes, I'd read a story; I'd seen beginning to end through one look. *She* was meant to be the inspiration of my greatest triumphs and equally my greatest tragedies. I couldn't say how I knew; I just did. Our existences would be irrevocably intertwined, and she would either be my salvation or my damnation. It was impossible to say which. And I had a choice to make. I could leave now and never return, let ghosts die in infamy and preserve my heart with new armor or...follow the unpredictable pattern of a heartbeat.

No matter the path, I knew I was doomed. I was destined to be haunted forever. A *ghost* haunted... The irony wasn't lost on my cynical outlook. I should have known callous hearts couldn't stay that way forever.

Chapter Two

Christine~

"Christine Daaé, your arabesque is late! Pay attention, girl!"

The shrill sound of Madame Giry's voice went through me like a lance full of disdain and disapproval in every consonant. That alone was a talent unto itself. Inflicting a physical reaction like injury with words, ...or perhaps it was only so bitter and sharp to me because I'd never been on the derogatory end of disappointment before. I was accustomed to praise and affection, being told I was an amazement by an over-proud father. I was beginning to see that his opinion might have been biased.

Skipping a half-beat to catch up with the other ballerinas, I was determined to match them step for step, but determination only went so far. These were girls who'd trained since the age of three, and I was grossly inferior and unprepared in comparison. Ballet was not my specialty. It was last on a list of things I knew *how* to do, but recognizing the basic principles did not make me prima ballerina material. No, at this rate, I'd be fortunate not to be called incompetent and turned out of my job.

Madame Giry beat the next segment with her walking cane, striking it violently to the wooden floor in perfect rhythm and leaving me certain I was again behind the others. I cast her a nervous glance only to

13

find her cold stare locked on my every movement. Cringing again, I hastened to catch up.

Despite the reproach in Madame's eyes, I was well aware that the minute rehearsal was over, it would soften with an affection I didn't feel I deserved. It was only because of a kind heart buried beneath the layers of stern disciplinarian that I was here. She had known my father. That point alone made me the equivalent of her ward after his death. No parents, no family, and if not for her extending wing, I'd have been tossed onto the streets, a pauper starving to death. She was the reason I had a position and a makeshift family among the ballerinas, ...and I felt sure she was now regretting her choice.

"Ah, you are all a hopeless mess!" she suddenly shouted over the group, waving her arms to cease. "Five minutes, and when you return, I expect your heads to be as attentive as your feet!"

She barely finished before I rushed with the other girls in a mass of crinoline offstage. Better to bypass the brunt of her wrath as soon as possible. I was terrified that if I did not stay in the center of the gaggle, I would be singled out for extra attention, and though I knew she would do it with good intention, I could not bear further embarrassment in front of the other girls. I wanted to be their equal, but my limited expertise would always be my downfall.

My first day in the opera house as a cast member, and so far the highlight had nothing to do with fame; it was still seeing a ghost. After all, I couldn't hope for praise for a talent I did not possess, so...yes, the ghost was the best part of my experience thus far.

Ghost... Was that what I'd seen? I had yet to decide. And Madame wondered why I was distracted and half a step behind! How could I focus on dancing when my head was so full that it left no room for choreography? A ghost... I'd been in the presence of a *ghost*. It seemed to be true, but when the ghost had been more surprised and agape than I had been, it contradicted the theory. A ghost in shock... That didn't seem right, not if *he* was supposed to be the one frightening *me*.

"Christine."

Meg Giry abandoned a throng of giggling girls and came to join my solitary stance. Now *Meg* was a trained and true ballerina. She was Madame's daughter and couldn't even walk without grace saturating her footfalls, as if every step were a part of some un-choreographed routine. I did not have that inherent talent, and it left me doubting that I'd ever succeed as a ballerina.

"Are you all right?" Meg asked with a bubbly grin as she tilted her golden head back and forth, more motions in her unrealized dance. "I know it's a lot of dancing on your first day, but you'll get used to it. Well," she shrugged with a little wince, "after the initial soreness wears off. But...don't worry! I promise it will get better!"

She meant to be encouraging and added an overdone grin, but I had a difficult time returning it. Meg saw me as a porcelain doll one step from shattering to pieces. Since my father's death, she'd been eager to play makeshift sister and best friend, and although I appreciated her attempt, it did nothing to heal the wounds in my heart. Sure, I had an ally in a place where I'd otherwise be a stranger, but Meg could not replace the wholehearted adoration I'd always received from my father. He'd have filled my ears with his approval and convinced me that though I was not the best ballerina, I would be in time. Hard work, effort, and heart, he'd have said. Fill the part with passion, and no one would ever pose argument with that. Meg could have said the same words, and yet I wouldn't have believed her.

A giggle suddenly fluttered past Meg's lips, and catching my arm with her little hands, she pushed, "Or are you still traumatized from our lunchtime initiation? Oh, Christine, you know it was all harmless fun, right?"

Harmless? I silently questioned her chosen depiction. Being thrown into a cellar and forced to remain inside as a test of character and courage? Maybe it was harmless when ghosts *didn't* materialize.

"I mean...the ghost *is real*, of course," Meg went on in a flurry of anxiousness, "but he's never hurt one of us. Not the ballerinas anyway. ...Usually only the stagehands."

She spoke it so innocently that it took me a moment to fully grasp her words. So...this ghost *had* hurt others before? I wasn't sure how much I wanted to push the subject with Meg, certain I did not want to share my so-called encounter and have to endure the squealing panic as the story traveled the gossip chain. I didn't want to be known as the girl who saw the ghost, especially on my first day!

"I don't believe in ghosts," I decided as my memory flashed a vision of something that seemed like a *man*. My idea of *ghost* was spirit-like and transparent, and the creature I'd come face to face with had seemed *tangible* and *alive*. Unless it was all part of the illusion.

Meg suddenly clamped her hand over *my* mouth and shook her wide-eyed head. "Don't ever say those words!" Her hysteria darted in frantic glances to the wings and then the rafters above our heads, and she held her breath a long moment before taking her hand from my mouth and concluding, "All right, I think we're safe, and he didn't hear you. But, Christine, watch yourself! If he ever heard such blasphemy, there's no telling what he would do!"

"You just said he doesn't harm the ballerinas-"

"Not usually," she insisted in incredulous terror, "but *we* never question his existence. The ghost is *real*, Christine, and the opera house is his kingdom. We don't argue with that fact, and things stay peaceful. Not holding hands, skipping through the flowers sort of peaceful, but uneventful and without accident or incident. The ghost is *powerful.* We need to be careful not to stir his wrath instead of his tolerance."

In truth, had I come out of the cellar as ignorant as I was making out with no clue or proof that *anything* existed in the dark, I would have thought insanity ran rampant through the opera house. Because this unquestioning belief did not just live in the ballet. Every person in the opera walked around with tentative fear in their eyes, as if constantly on guard. Now after seeing with my own eyes, I understood why, but...the ghost man I'd encountered hadn't posed a threat to me. ...Perhaps I was just lucky that I'd frightened him first.

"Have *you* seen the ghost before, Meg?" I asked, casting my own glances about. How much did this ghost eavesdrop?

Meg nodded proudly as if ghost sightings were a badge of honor. "A few times actually. Once is for amateurs! I am practically a trained professional in dealing with the ghost."

I could not justify the twinge of jealousy I felt, but...in some way, I liked considering I was the only one to actually *see* him. "And what does he look like?"

"Like a man, but that's probably a projection of his once-human body," she replied with exuberance, growing more excited with every detail. Obviously, the ghost was a delightful topic around here... "He wears a mask over his face."

"Mask..."

My memory flickered with pictures of the stark, white shape fading into view. It had seemed so unnatural, peculiar and not at all ordinary, but...masks were costumes. It was unfathomable for a normal person to walk around wearing one: a point to confirm what I had seen *was* indeed a ghost.

"Why?" I demanded, knowing Meg would be only too happy to tell me.

"Well, we don't know *exactly*. Our best guess is that his face is a mangled disaster, probably the very thing that killed him. And being anything of a gentleman, he wouldn't want to wander the opera house with guts and gore hanging out, not with so many pretty girls to impress!"

It shocked me because though she spoke quick and animated, she was serious. A ghost out to impress girls by hiding the deadly wounds that had brought his demise... I had the urge to ask what *he* thought would come of his behavior. Was he looking for a mate to *kill* and spend eternity haunting with him? To think, my only worry the day before had been walking into an established ballet corps and not knowing the steps; now I had masked ghosts to worry about as well!

"So...what does the ghost want if he's so committed to lurking about the opera?" I asked and wondered if a legitimate answer existed.

Meg paused and pondered, golden brows arching and lips pursing as her thin shoulders rose in a shrug. "To be in charge, I suppose. I mean...I've never asked."

"Girls!" Madame Giry's call pierced over every conversation backstage, and with another blameless shrug, Meg grabbed my hand and pulled me back onto the stage.

She could shut off musings of ghosts and return to pliés and pirouettes, but *I*... I had a difficult time even trying. My thoughts were now running deeper with more information gathered as my memory threw random images back into the forefront.

His eyes... They'd pierced me in a look. Their colors were unlike any I'd ever seen. One eye was blue, turquoise and bright, while the other burned in emerald green, both hues so vivid. Never before had I come across a human being with eyes that were not both the same color. Another point favoring ghost over man. A ghost could defy the principles of logic.

And the violent manner in which those brilliant eyes had assaulted me... Eyes were not supposed to be weapons, but *his* had struck deep and vicious even without a threat. They'd hit some spongy, soft spot within my being, a place I'd never realized existed to conceal it from attack. *He* had attacked and hit, firm and undeniable, and left a lasting mark in his wake.

A ghost... I had to remind myself that even if what I'd seen had substance, it *wasn't* a real person, not anymore. Wasn't it best to try to forget the encounter then? When nothing could come from it but being *haunted*, forgetting seemed intelligent.

But...as I moved my body in the same elegant motions as the other ballerinas, I felt that piercing sensation again. It knocked me off balance and made me jolt in my steps as it delved within and found that same unknown soft spot. A look, and it tore me open because I *knew* the Opera Ghost was watching me.

"Christine Daaé, pay attention!"

Madame Giry's screech dragged me back to the present even as I yearned only to *feel* onward. But though my racing heart insisted what I knew to be real, the sensation evaporated away. It bothered me to admit I wanted to feel it again...

Rehearsal passed slowly onward, and though the surface of my skin tingled with anticipation, it went untouched. If the ghost still watched, perhaps he did it invisibly, for I felt nothing but a longing that humiliated me. I *longed* to be the focus of a ghost... Sense dubbed me foolish and immature.

As we were dismissed for the day and ballerinas rushed off to change, the summons I'd dreaded finally arrived. "Mademoiselle Daaé, a word please?"

I halted and cringed in my spot as Meg gave my arm a reassuring pat before escaping. Perhaps I should have considered it fortunate that at least the Madame hadn't belittled me in front of the other girls. One positive in a sea of negatives.

"Yes, Madame?" I bid as I offered a dutiful curtsy before her.

"Christine, don't bob like a servant girl," she insisted, but I caught the hint of fondness in her voice and calmed even if only a little.

"Yes, Madame."

"You know, Christine, when I agreed to take you on in the *corps de ballet*, I was under the impression that you'd been trained, but...that's not the case, is it?"

I knew I couldn't lie, and I ducked an embarrassed blush to be found out. "Not exactly...*trained*, in the formal sense of the word."

"What other sense is there?" Madame pushed with a doubtful shake of her head.

"The woman my father hired to look after me as a child had been a ballerina in her youth, and...she taught me the proper positions and movements. I suppose that is *informal* training." I offered it hopefully when I knew she had every right to berate me for the conclusions I'd let her believe. She'd known my father when she'd been a ballerina at the opera in days when he'd been first chair violinist, but...that was a long time ago. She was not indebted to take care of his daughter.

Madame Giry huffed a heavy breath, and I lifted beseeching eyes as she sought a polite way to say what I knew she must. "Perhaps...the ballet is not the best fit for you, Christine. What about...costumes or backstage work? Or the chorus? I recall your father doting upon your beautiful voice. The cast is set for the next show, of course, but you could audition next season. Would you like to sing, Christine?"

Sing... I quickly shook my head. "No, I don't sing. Please, *please*, Madame, don't dismiss me from the ballet. I...I will keep up with the other girls. *Please*..."

This was about more than dancing. Being employed in the opera meant a roof over my head and a stipend. If I lost my position and had to wait until next season, not even Madame's hospitality would be enough.

"Well..." I could tell she wanted to refuse, and if she did, despite my disappointment, I would understand. I was *not* a ballerina. That was not her fault; it was God's.

"I will do all I must to improve," I promised wholeheartedly.

"Yes, you will," Madame agreed. "You have a rough road ahead, Christine. I expect nothing but perfection, and you will do everything the other girls do at their level. I will not be lenient on you or make allowances for your lack of proper training. You will prove to me that you can and deserve to be here."

"Yes, Madame," I replied with gratitude so thick that it brought tears to my eyes.

Madame looked me over head to toe, and though her sternness softened its rough edges, she was still solemn as she insisted, "Go on to the dormitories and rest. I daresay tomorrow will be a greater challenge than today."

That was all. Madame Giry gave a firm nod and took her leave, disappearing into the wings and leaving me alone on the stage.

I felt my posture drop in a mixture of relief *and* defeat. I was no ballerina, and yet I had to prove myself to equal one. Had any other battle ever seemed so great?

As I lingered with the stage stretched out before my ballet slippers, I heard it for the first time. A voice whispering my name in gentle tones. It was so soft and delicate, ...beautiful, and as I ran tentative eyes over the dark theatre beyond the stage lights, I *prayed* to see *him*.

But I had only shadows and that delicious sensation of his gaze upon me. Another point in favor of ghosts. No body, only a voice and a *feeling*, and it either proved ghosts existed or that I was losing my sanity. Crazy was definitely viable and only reinforced as my skin began to tingle and tremble as if touched.

Ridiculous, sense insisted, but I felt his gaze in the way one would a hand, trailing the sweeping neckline of my dance attire from shoulder to shoulder. I shivered and scanned more aggressively with my widened eyes.

Where was he? I had to see him and know if he felt what I did. Could he possibly share my surprise and equally my terror? Fear welled within my chest and carried out to my limbs, making me sway on my feet. This was...too much. I shouldn't feel such things. No, they were too heavy to bear, and certainly shouldn't be inspired by ghosts in masks. It wasn't right; it *had to be* evil. Did not the devil tempt with fire? Because I felt flames lick across my skin and climb up my ankles and calves exposed by my skirt, and shuddering so hard I could barely stay upright, I suddenly let fear overcome and ran for the wings on its inspiration.

Hastening toward the dormitory entrance, I never looked back and prayed ghosts were confined to the main building for their haunts.

Well, I'd learned two mandatory lessons in my first day as a member of an opera company. One: ballet could not be faked or accomplished with only knowledge of its vocabulary and steps; one also needed *talent*. And two: ghosts were *dangerous* even if intangible. He could *kill me* with a look alone, and I was undoubting that I'd die willingly.

Chapter Three

Erik~
   Chris-tine, Chris-tine, Chris-tine...
   The name pulsated through my body like a
reciprocated canon. I could barely take a single
breath without the torment of its eternal letters.
Chris-tine... Beating with my heart, becoming its
song, and echoing in my ears until I suffered.
   My God, what infection was this? It consumed
and overcame like a spreading disease, worsening
every second and anchoring its grasp a little firmer
within me. Deeper, extending groping fingers like
sharp-edged talons that sank into my living heart and
clawed its fragile build. I was ripped apart inside and
out by every emotion I'd thought dead or in my
control and a host of new ones I bore no logic for.
   Sense called it love, but I didn't pin all my faith
on the term. I *loved* music, but music did not try to
eat me alive in its possession. This was beyond
restraint. I preferred the concept of disease.
   From one unanticipated earthquake in a cellar,
my existence was forever altered. I couldn't form a
thought that did not have that infernal girl at its core.
I was a man possessed, creating fantasies day and
night of going to her, talking with her, being with her.
I *hated* the world and humanity; why was I now
entertaining notions of sharing my life with one of its
members? It sickened me because I felt *weak* against

23

this affliction.

I tried to play my music, to lose myself in the solace of cascading crescendoes and lush harmony, but *still, she* appeared. Her blue stare flamed behind the lids of my closed eyes, wide, innocent, such depth of color... I was the ghost, and I was the haunted one.

Chris-tine... My heart beat in her name over and over, torturing my waking and sleeping mind. I was only content when I had her in my line of vision, watching her from Box 5. As the Opera Ghost's designated box, it had been reconstructed for practicality. I couldn't very well make a visual appearance at every show, so I had altered its makeup, giving myself a seat within its shadows with curtains to obstruct the audience's view of my shape. I was as invisible to them as a specter, and I used that advantage now to watch rehearsals with a shrewd eye fixed on Christine.

Oh, that girl... What was it about her? Was it merely a fascination because she had not shrieked in terror at my image? ...No, more than that. I'd met her gaze in the cellar and *felt*, and that was enough to qualify her extraordinary makeup.

Emotions had spiraled out of my grasp in one shared look and had yet to be reigned back into equilibrium's sphere. Every glimpse of her had them swelling again and making giddy waves in my soul. Was it any wonder I surrendered to the sensations when they felt so delicious and euphoric?

I'd never known pleasant emotions, and to have them all created and written for one girl made me eternally grateful for her existence. I felt *alive* for the first time in my life and wondered what it would take to have these emotions permanently emblazoned in my heart. How could I have *her*?

The ballerinas were running their third act number again, and my gaze was riveted to Christine as always. Only *she* existed for me. Her dark curls were bound in a ribbon, tied behind her shoulders. From my constant observation, I'd been intrigued by their soft, thick mass. I could not reason how they'd ever make a smooth and sleek ballerina bun. They were destined to be loosed and free. I considered putting my opinion in with the management and insisting the ballerinas' hair be left unbound in the upcoming show, but...well, the Opera Ghost had never weighed in on hairstyles before. I wondered if such a detail would trivialize my reputation, but still... To see Christine's curls free and billowing about her shoulders as she moved... The idea raced ripples of longing through my body.

I was so inexperienced at these feelings! I felt ignorant! They came and went as they liked with desire as the worst of all. ...*Desire.* Dear God, what suffocation in a single emotion! It appeared and struck so hard, knocking my stability with its ferocious waves. I was *its* victim, and I detested the idea of defeat to anything.

Here was a prime example of unwilling possession. Christine made a pretty pirouette and then lifted one elegant leg straight toward the ceiling, and that leg could have *kicked* me with the reverberation desire gave. The curves, the alignment of perfect shapes. When she made such a motion, her tulle skirt bunched back and revealed more: hints of a perfect thigh just above the laced ties of her ballet slippers. And I burned to touch her! To run my bare hands up that elegant limb...only I would not stop where tulle rested. I would continue beneath its boundary...

I shuddered violently with my avid fantasy. Desire out of control like a raging wildfire, and I was as much its servant as my heart's. And what would beautiful, innocent Christine say to such salacious yearning?

Realism was a cruel voice in my head. It posed everything I'd rather have forgotten. The disfigured Opera Ghost wanted to put his hands all over her virginal body... I could not reason that request *ever* going over well.

But...eyes did not need excuses, and I could watch her dance and burn alone. It was pathetic, but if it was all I'd ever have, I was obliged to take it. I gazed at her lithe, little body and succumbed to the thrill, letting passion's fire smolder in my veins. It was tolerable alone when I had the distinct terror that if I ever touched *her*, I would be seared inside and out with a passion too great to hold in my hands.

I was mid-fantasy when Madame Giry's shrill voice shattered every picture in my head. I cringed merely with its splintering timbre and knew the intense urge to strangle her to silence for interrupting my erotic endeavors.

"Christine Daaé, pay attention! You came out of your pirouette too early!"

My fault... Her every distraction was *my* fault. I gazed at her in pure lust and knew *she* felt its echo. It was in the subtle tremble she'd suffer, the glances she'd cast out at the empty theatre seats as if searching for *me*.

My Christine wanted *me*... I was certainly no connoisseur of desire, but I could say that for certain because for all the fear in the searching of blue eyes, there was curiosity. She wanted knowledge and understanding, but she expected ghosts. I had no guarantee that a mortal man in its place would be accepted, ...let alone a mortal man that looked as if he'd climbed from a horror story into reality. What *acceptance* existed for that?

Rehearsal ended for the day, and as the ballet rats scurried offstage, Christine lingered, scanning the theatre again. A part of me ached to come into view, simply to gauge her reaction. Or...what if I appeared in Box 5 as a silhouette, nothing more? Would she give me that same pensive study she had in the cellar? Would she cower to fear this time?

Before I could make an attempt to learn, the

little Giry rushed to Christine and grabbed her arm for attention. My gaze was riveted to that unconsidered touch, and I was *jealous*. *I* wanted to touch Christine, but I would be subject to suspicion and scrutiny while the little Giry could act without a second thought. I wondered how soft Christine's skin was and cursed little Meg for the privilege to know. It didn't seem fair.

"Christine, are you coming? Jammes wants to play with your hair and see what we can do..." Meg lifted her touching hand to poke at Christine's disheveled curls, and my jealousy burst into an inferno beneath my skin. *I* wanted that touch as well, but I'd have been sensual and caressing when taking it. Meg was too busy making faces of doubt as she decided, "I consider Jammes brave if she thinks she's going to make a bun that will stay put on your head, but," Meg gave a bubbly giggle, "if she pulls your hair too hard, give me a sign and I'll elbow her. I'll pretend it was an accident."

Christine grinned back, and yet as always, I caught dark shadows in the background. That girl bore a sadness within her that I had little explanation for, save overheard snippets about a dead father. I'd never known attachment to a parent to sympathize with her loss, but...perhaps if love was the base, such sadness was justified. I couldn't help but wonder what happiness would look like instead. She'd probably be so brilliant if she were happy, a star eternally aglow.

"Tell Jammes that I will be there shortly," Christine decided, and I hung on her words. "I want to stay and practice a little longer. I know I can get that last section right."

Meg nodded understanding and bid, "All right, but if Jammes insists on using *me* as your substitute, *you* better be the one to elbow her. I didn't want to frighten you, but Jammes is *terrible* at styling hair. Last time she did mine, I ended up with *handfuls* lost.

I'll let you imagine how, but I vowed *never* to let her touch my head again. If I must act to preserve *you*, I expect retribution. Avenge my future bald spot, Christine."

A little laugh left Christine's lips, and I had an urge to thank the Giry girl because it was genuine. "If you think my boney elbows are good enough to avenge you, then I shall fulfill my duty."

"The bonier the better!" Meg excitedly declared. "Take a rib out if you can! Curse that Jammes and her ungentle hair-pulling!"

Another laugh and with a final wave, Meg ran offstage and left my Christine alone. Christine's blue gaze followed her friend before trailing the empty theatre again, ...searching for me.

But with a soft sigh, she turned away and began to dance. I could take no more. Lurking in Box 5 was tolerable when there was a stage full of tutus, but now...there was only Christine. I had to be closer.

With soundless stealth, I climbed down a hidden staircase in the wall and emerged at the back of an empty theatre, sticking to shadows as if they were a viable part of my essence. I couldn't let her see me, but...to see her, I would have done anything.

She danced the same routine they'd just ended, and to watch her, exposed and vulnerable on the stage, I was overwhelmed. She truly was a beautiful dancer. No, her technique did not equal a prima ballerina, but that did not matter when it was only her and a wooden floor. She moved with a grace I knew she did not realize she possessed; it was usually stifled when the other girls were on all sides of her, victim to her internal monologue of doubt. Now I saw its true splendor and was awed.

My passion-heavy eyes traced the contours of her body, heat building within me and tingling my fingertips with the need to feel and outline her curves in slow, languid caresses. Beauty sparked desire, but dance fanned the flame and left me hungry to taste. I wanted; how I wanted!

She spun and lifted her leg, and I ached to run my tongue from ankle to thigh, to learn the flavor of her skin and brand her cells into my mouth. I wanted something that would last forever, an eternal imprint of her upon my body. Every urge felt perverse to the rational side of my brain, but desire was so new. I didn't know how much to give, how much to take, how to fully feel it in a way that was morally standard. ...Instinct told me not to care about *moral* and just *possess*.

"Christine..." My heart beat the name in its pattern, and I dared to let it touch my lips and taint my tingling tongue.

So sudden that I was startled, she halted mid-step and raised wide eyes to my observing presence, and it seemed not even shadows chose to be my ally anymore. I knew she saw me, and her gasp resonated the theatre and burned my ears. I loved it despite its inception of surprise because it was *mine*. For the first time in days, some detail of her was solely my own to have and keep, and even a gasp was a treasure.

She stumbled back an awkward step, her ballet slippers whispering along the stage floor, but she made no move to flee, staring fixedly at me as if willing me to tempt our fate and push events on a path already deemed to happen. I'd known all along; I could leave and try hopelessly to forget *or* let things spin forward. Obviously, I no longer had a choice.

But I kept back, a theatre of seats away, and tried not to show her how completely she shook me. We were suspended in an uncomfortable moment, the same we'd suffered in the cellar where time halted its seconds and needed *something* to propel it forward. Bravery was the missing key, but we both were lacking its inherent strength. We both faltered.

Escape and freedom, and I was compelled to take an easy route and continue our ongoing game of cat and mouse. Appear, disappear, and nothing significant would change, and I might have traveled the simple road had *she* not surpassed my petrified power and appealed in a soft sound.

"Are you a ghost?"

I turned the inquiry over in my head and pondered a suitable reply. Yes, but I suddenly longed to be mortal? Yes, but in name only? Yes, but I could vow to be anything she wanted if only she'd grant me a window into her life?

Answers were fighting for supremacy on the tip of my tongue, but when words felt like they gave too much away, I recoiled and sought something to hide my sense of self behind. I couldn't show her a lusting heart and a damaged soul. So despite better judgment's argument, I picked up the façade I used as omnipotent Opera Ghost and strolled the aisles of seats closer to her wide-eyed shape with never a single waver in my step. No, I gave not even a tremble away.

"Perhaps," I replied with a nonchalant shrug. "Ghosts lurk in the dark shadows, don't they? And haunt the place that houses their eternal souls?"

"I wouldn't know such things," she insisted, and her small, white hands clasped and wrung before her with their restless unease. "I've never encountered one. ...Who are you then?"

I held my breath, creeping closer yet. I was still awestruck that my Christine was speaking to *me*. If I didn't know better with my nerves twisting my stomach as proof, I'd have assumed I was in fantasy's realm again. But apprehension had a distinct, unpleasant sensation and reminded me what I was beneath adapted bravado. No, this was *real*.

"Perhaps a ghost," I decided with another shrug, pretending much more control over this scene than I actually had. "Or perhaps...an angel." The idea had appeal; as soon as I said it, I found it a great improvement.

"I don't believe in angels," she stated, her blue gaze locked on mine as I lingered with rows of seats as my shield.

"No...?" I posed it doubtfully and surveyed her head to toe. "Isn't that quite a cynical viewpoint for one so young? You could tell me that you have no belief in God, and I'd wager it a choice with merit, but this... Angels are a fairytale story, something to give a promise of hope for the lost, and you speak with such conviction."

Christine blushed a soft pink, ducking her dark head as if a child being chastised, and I immediately regretted my matter-of-fact arrogance. Perhaps I needed to be softer, gentler. It was trial and error as my mind taunted how long it had been since my last legitimate conversation with a *living* human being. Not a piano's keys, not a figment of imagination, not a dead body at my feet. And this wasn't *just* a person; this was a young girl. She might not be shouting in terror at the appearance of a man in a mask, but that did not take away her naïveté or make her less innocent.

"Tell me," I encouraged in tender tones. "Why do you have no belief in angels?"

Dark curls rippled with the subtle shake of her head and a quiver that only grew with my chosen approach. Casting furtive glances up from her anxious stance, she timidly revealed, "When my father died, he promised to send an angel for me, ...to look after me, to keep me from being alone, but...it was a lie because angels don't exist."

"So certain." I surveyed her yet again at this close proximity, making out more details than I was typically granted from my box. So very sweet... Skin I'd deduced as white showed creamy undertones, warmer and richer, complimenting the petal pink of her lips. She was an absolute artist's rendition, and unable to stop myself before the words hit the air, I declared, "And what if I told you that *I* was the angel your father promised?"

Blue eyes met mine first with wonder. She

wanted to believe so much, to claim blind faith and have this...*me* as her proof that she was not forgotten. But to my dismay, skepticism relit and colored her initial joy as she concluded with somber unease, "Angels do not hurt others, and you..."

I would have cursed the little Giry, perhaps chosen her as the next worth 'hurting', but...none of it was a lie or exaggeration. I could truly only curse *myself* for every sin I'd had my hands within. Even justifiable murder was still murder. So I did the only thing I could to keep an open door without a lock: I lied.

"How ignorant of you to make assumptions!" I acted offended and sneered in my arrogant persona. "You who have been a part of this company barely a week seek to define my soul and its supposed faults! You know *nothing* of me, and yet you've chosen to judge. You cannot even reason if I am man or myth, ghost or angel, and yet you've named me murderer and found me guilty with no hope of reprieve. How is that just?"

Again that longing to believe like a pinprick of light in the center of her regret glowed vibrant. She wanted my soul to be as clean as hers, and for the first time in my existence, I wanted the same thing. "I...I'm sorry. All the talk in the ballet revolves about the ghost...and *you* are the Opera Ghost, aren't you?"

I gave an idle shrug. "To some. To others, I'm just a man. You may deem how you see me. Most choose horror without proper reasoning. They see the mask and make it their focal point, and I am not allowed to be anything more. But you...you saw me in the cellar and weren't afraid."

Blue eyes peeked up at me again with the slightest tug of a smile on her lips. It was subtle, but I took it as the greatest achievement of my days. Now if I could only make it bloom!

"You are not a *real* ghost," she concluded as explanation enough. "You've given me no valid need to fear you."

True, but I was accustomed to the reactions of the others, and to see Christine look at me, straight at my masked face, and give nothing but her sweetly innocent curiosity and intrigue, I was addicted. She was my drug, and I needed *her* forever.

"And," I continued, "I suppose that is why you chose to linger in an empty opera house alone. You weren't afraid a ghost would catch you."

"I have more to fear from Madame Giry's wrath than a ghost's haunting. I'll take my chances with ghosts if I can have extra practice time in between."

I forced my gaze to stay on hers even as it craved and pulled with a desire to wander. I'd grown used to perusing her body with boldness from the shadows and had to remind myself that I could not give such desire away while face to face. *That* would bring her unwanted fright.

So I held her eye as I haughtily decided, "You are as much a ballerina as I am a ghost. It is a veneer, a role to play. I watch you dance, and although you move beautifully, it is empty. You do not possess the passion that the other girls have for pirouettes and reveilles. ...No, no, don't blush and duck your eyes for being found out, Christine. In truth, I share your mentality. I believe the only redeeming part of the ballet is the music, but the rest..." I rolled my eyes and shook a doubtful head, pleased to see it earn an arc that was even closer to a smile. "I could do without the dance interludes and save ballet for the ballet, but some composers believe it an extra treat to fuse ballet into opera. Not everyone loves *both*, but try arguing that with an established composer *or* my management for that matter. They believe it draws a bigger audience; I'm unconvinced."

"So...the ghost *does* have a say on how things are run? That was no exaggeration of the ballerinas?"

I accepted that part with pride and my own hinted grin in return. "If I were an imbecile in the medium of music, then it would be a sin, but as it is, I have more knowledge than every buffoon in this theatre combined. My 'suggestions' are only meant to improve. I've considered pushing my clout and doing away with the ballet. One note, and I could have my way, but...since *you* arrived, I've developed a greater appreciation for it. Not a full-fledged passion or love, but...enough to want it to continue so that I may watch you dance."

How forward, and I grew anxious what her reaction would be and hurriedly went on before she could give one. "But in watching you, I have glimpsed that lack of passion I spoke of. Is it merely because you do not have the training the other girls do? ...No, I think this is something you've settled for when your heart lives elsewhere."

She was surprised I'd read her so well, but with *hours* of study on my side, I was doubtless in making such an assertion. And perhaps it was only because I was right that she deemed it fit to grace me with an answer. "My father's dream was to see me involved in the opera, but...to *sing*, not to dance."

My ear was intoxicated with the very word in her voice, and I eagerly pushed, "Then why not sing? Why settle for the ballet if there is something you could do with heart and passion? That is a life half-lived."

She shook her dark head, making curls bob and draw my stare as she distantly admitted, "I haven't sung a note since my father...since he died. Music was *his*, and to sing...it was for him, always for him."

So that was it. My little songbird had broken wings because of a father in the grave. She was *alone*, and I understood that so well. It inspired a deeper root in my heart because now I not only longed to adore her, but to protect her, to keep her untouchable by the true cruelty of the world. My Christine had no one and nothing as hers; I wanted to fill that void and draw myself into the holes in her being.

"Sing for *me*," I decided and savored the arch of her curious dark brows. "Let the music be *mine* instead. You wanted an angel; you were waiting for heavenly intervention. Well, ...perhaps that is what I am. Let me be the answer to your prayer, your angel, ...your angel of music."

I must have spoken it well because I saw no suspicion in my command. Or perhaps it was just that she wanted *something* so much. A means to heal, someone to prove she was not alone. I gave her all of that and more. I offered her the dreams she possessed and asked *nothing* in return. Not yet. How could I fathom being selfish when merely having her speak to me without fear was a gift?

But a flicker of uncertainty remained as she accused, "But you are no angel."

"I could be...for you. I could teach you, train your voice and give you the music. Music is *my* passion, my heart and soul, and I've never shared such things with anyone."

She seemed humbled by my admission and softly bid, "But you'd share such things with me?"

"You are alone in the world; I am as well. I have nothing but music to sustain me, and only music to offer you. I may not be a traditional angel, but music gives me wings and blessings. It makes me fly. Do you wish to fly as well, Christine? To let your heart and soul soar?"

I saw my words resonate with her, and she sighed as if I'd spoken her greatest desire. "Yes," she breathed, and in that instant, she started us on our fated path with one gentle command, "Be my angel of music."

I smiled. This was mine.

Chapter Four

Christine~
   God works in mysterious ways... I'd heard
that statement over and over again in my life, but I'd
never fully believed it. I was given its letters when my
mother died, again when my father joined her. As if
God's supposed 'mysterious ways' explained why I
was doomed to be abandoned by everyone I loved.
   When my father had promised an angel,
perhaps that would have been the 'mysterious' way,
but I'd never fully believed him. Maybe because I was
so young when I'd lost my mother and was given no
replacement in the form of heavenly spirits. One
would think a child without a mother *deserved* an
angel to stand in her place, but all I'd had was a
father, and for as much as he loved me, he was no
mother. I should have had my mother at least in
spirit, and since God had denied me as a little girl, I
highly doubted He'd listen to my dead father and send
an angel *now*. It was too sugarcoated of a wish, and
during his illness and passing, I'd grown up too much
to believe it.
   ...Or so I'd thought. Now...I had an *angel*, but
he was not designed in the traditional vein, not white-
winged or heaven sent, and yet an *angel* just the
same. *God works in mysterious ways...*
   My *angel* was a mortal man in hiding. To the
rest of the world, he was their ghost, a creature worthy

of fear and fabrication. To me, he was the blessing I'd longed for without ever making the wish. He was slowly growing to be my everything. Merely his existence healed my wounded heart, mending every sore spot with music as its sewing needle and giving it a new beat. I was...*changed*, and I could only credit him with my transformation.

Every day I suffered in the ballet, improving steadily, but only due to resolve and my newly constructed hopes. It was tolerable because I knew something better awaited me at rehearsal's end. Then once the other girls left and the theatre emptied, I met an angel and let music inside to make my heart and soul soar as promised.

The first time I sang for him, I was a mess. It was nerves and apprehension. What if he heard me and changed his mind? Saw my unproven talent as hopeless and another of my father's overdone exaggerations? For in truth, my father was the only one who'd ever heard me sing. I had no opinion but his in my inner ears. What if my angel was disappointed and took his music away already?

But I sang, and I watched his masked face with a critical eye as he loomed rows away in the theatre audience. And I saw something like that same surprise I'd been given in the cellars at our first meeting. I *felt* his pleasure, and even when he spoke with minimal praises and insisted we had much work to do, I took it as encouragement to know he would indeed teach me. I considered it a wonderful accomplishment and carried his existence like a brilliant secret in my soul.

As I said, I was not naïve enough to dub him a *real* angel, but...there were certain points that made me undoubting he was sent by God and His mysterious ways. From our very first lesson, I became aware that my angel teacher was some sort of prodigy.

As if desperate to keep propriety intact, he never came closer to me than with three rows of seats in between, occasionally strolling from one end of the theatre to the other as he listened, ever attentive but *careful*. He didn't even dare approach the instruments at the end of the stage, which left me wary how we would ever have pitches or accompaniment. But as we began to work with basic scales, *he* pulled the pitches he was after out of the air and his musician's ear. He hummed the exact scale he wanted me to repeat, and I stared agape at his moving masked shape, overcome by the sound of his voice. It was *exquisite*, and all I'd been granted of it thus far was a *hum*.

For that voice, I would have done anything. As my lessons progressed, I fought for every beautiful pitch he could make, often asking him to demonstrate what he was after simply for the sound. He never fully sang, as if shy by his talent, or perhaps as unaware as I had once been, but I was overcome and obsessed with the fantasy of what his full voice would sound like. Oh God, maybe he *was* an angel after all, for what human being could ever make such divine beauty with a voice alone!

I felt so close to him in the throes of music. He taught with gentle care and an intelligence that I felt privileged to know. And from his genius teachings, I felt my voice blossom in tones I'd never realized I could make.

He'd known from the beginning that ballet was not my passion; well, *here* was my passion, blatant and straightforward. It came through every pitch I sang for him and bubbled out from my soul. It was music, but it was also *him*. He was my inspiration and my guiding star. Music would have been a hollow shell without his essence to flesh it out.

A week of daily lessons, then two, and I counted minutes until I was in his presence again. When we were together and music our shared goal, I did not consider his alternate persona. I did not associate him with the same ghost the ballerinas still went on about. The girls liked to frighten each other, and the greatest threat was to tease that the ghost would take them away. I never once connected *their* ghost with *mine* because I perceived the girls as overdramatic and creating evil where none existed.

My angel teacher was *not* evil. I knew he wouldn't hurt anyone because I trusted the man I was with every night, alone in an empty theatre. He would *never* commit the crimes the girls pinned upon him. It made me angry merely to bear the suggestion.

But...some points had merit. I was no fool. I knew he wore the mask for a reason, and Meg's explanation of a mangled face kept coming back to the surface. I wondered if the stories held any weight of truth, but I couldn't reason asking. It seemed too much like rude prying. Perhaps he'd tell me in time, but for now, I let it go and made the mask just another part of him.

"Oh, they're at it again!"

Meg's exclamation dragged me out of my thoughts and back to ballet and a rehearsal I fervently wished was over.

"Who?" I asked, but she cocked her chin, and I followed its direction with my gaze.

In the far wing stood a group of male stagehands, leering at us with lustful eyes. Since rehearsals were moving forward for the new production, more and more of the cast and crew were on-hand and about daily. The stagehands were a vile sort when it came to ogling girls in form-fitting rehearsal attire. Most of the ballerinas considered it a point of flattery, for there existed a 'look but don't touch' rule unspoken through the corridors. They flaunted extra with the attention, but I felt violated with every stare and shrank behind some of the bolder ones.

Meg giggled at my unease. "Oh, Christine! You must get over these modesty issues now! Wait until the show! The patrons are just as bad, even with their wives sitting beside them!"

I cringed with the idea and cast anxious glances at our continued gawkers. One in particular made nervous goose bumps crawl along every inch of my exposed skin. Joseph Buquet was an old and overweight deviant who rarely came into the theatre without reeking of alcohol. The other ballerinas called him harmless and even humored his ill attempts at garnering female attention. Lately, I found his beady eyes always locked on my body, and it made my stomach turn to be his victim of choice. His gaze swept over my length, and I shuddered with disgust and recoiled further away as he licked his lips and sought to seem provocative. Teasing or not, I refused to condone his behavior.

"Oh, Christine," Meg gushed with a giggle as she hurried forward, never one to shy from such attentions.

As I shivered unconsciously, I turned away, preferring the empty theatre to the over-laden wings, but what I saw chilled me to my bones. My angel was visible in one of the boxes. Never before had I seen him freely out with others around, but he glared toward the wings, obviously having observed the scene of lewd conduct. And the look on his masked face...it frightened me. It was full of fire and fury, a seething rage that seemed to be boiling over in his mismatched eyes.

The breath fled my lungs and collapsed my posture as I contemplated that I never wanted to be on the opposite end of such wrath. But it shifted to me with his intent stare, and I buckled beneath the power. This was not a man to be toyed with or teased, tempted to sin, and for the first time, I was acutely aware of it.

His gaze lost its fire the longer it held mine, anger dwindling, but transforming into an adamant sense of possession. In one look, he made it vividly clear that I was *his*, and I wasn't sure I was allowed to argue.

At that night's lesson, all was forgotten, it seemed. Never was his appearance brought up, and without hesitation, we submerged ourselves into music and forgot the rest of the world existed. Reservations that I might have harbored drifted to nothing, and even when intuition wanted to keep skepticism alive, I didn't listen. Why would I? It was a more pleasant thought to consider his anger at the stagehands had been because he wanted to keep me safe and believed them disrespectful. That made him a protector and not sinister. I let that be my conclusion.

The next morning as I joined the other ballerinas, I could tell something was amiss from the first moment. Everything was too...quiet. None of the usual vivacity and exuberance, and wary for reasons I could not explain, I hurried to Meg and her wide green eyes and demanded, "Is something wrong?"

"You haven't heard?" she insisted as if my ignorance was a drastic mistake. "There was an accident first thing this morning. Joseph Buquet was working up in the rafters, and...he fell."

"Is he all right?" I urgently asked. In truth, I couldn't have cared less about the vile stagehand, but...I had other worries underneath.

"A broken leg, nothing too serious. He was lucky. But..." Meg lowered her voice to a cryptic whisper, "he's telling everyone that he was *pushed*...by the ghost."

My stomach knotted, heart pausing mid-beat, and while part of me immediately defended my angel ghost and disputed Buquet's accusation, another part just *knew*.

This should have been the moment intuition won out and took over. In a mission of self-preservation, it should have had me following the other girls out of the theatre at rehearsal's end and certainly not staying behind *alone*. But...wasn't it

41

unjust to condemn without giving my angel a chance to explain? I'd done that before when I'd accused him the first night of the ballerinas' gossip. I owed him the opportunity to dub Buquet a liar. Even a lie would be better than no words at all. ...Or maybe I just wanted to hear his voice so much.

From the instant he arrived, I could not keep my thoughts to myself or take the doubt from my expression. I wanted denials without ever having to cast blame, but he was stoic and seemingly apathetic as he stalked the back rows of the theatre, saying not a single word. If I *wanted* words, it was clear I'd have to give them first.

Pausing as I regarded his dark silhouette and that telling mask, I acted less apprehensive than I was. Following our usual routine, I sat upon the hard wood of the stage and deftly unlaced my toe shoes without much thought, moving by rote instead of concentration. One and then the other, and I gazed at his moving shape all the while. He paused only once as I tossed the shoes aside, and lifting his mismatched eyes to me, he let them wander from my set features down my stocking-clad calves and up again. This was not the leer the stagehands gave. There were too many whispers of sadness and guilt intermixed in the longing, and as he found my stare again, he abruptly broke it and began to stalk aisles.

I shivered in spite of better judgment, but as always, those eyes bore an element of touch. I *felt* them as one would fingertips, and to have them graze my legs in such an intimate manner inspired tremors that racked my entire body.

He was still silent, waiting for me to utter accusations we both knew I must, and finally as I rose on trembling knees, I let their sharp letters into the air. "One of the stagehands had an accident this morning at rehearsal. Joseph Buquet. Do you know who he is?"

Mismatched eyes glared a breath before he

paced onward, brusquely retorting, "Go on, Christine. Finish your tale and make it perfectly clear what you have dubbed me guilty for."

I cringed and swallowed hard, but there was no going back now. "He fell from the rafters, but he said...the Opera Ghost pushed him. Did you? Did you do it?"

"Of course I did!" he exclaimed as if my answer were obvious, and I was a fool even to ask. "Joseph Buquet is a repulsive creature. He deserved to be taught a lesson for his shameless behavior. I will *not* allow him to undress you with his eyes! It is demoralizing and certainly no right of his to even pretend to own."

Each sentence grew in aggression until I regretted ever posing the inquiry. For the first time, I longed to be free of this scene and out of my angel's presence. I didn't want to see this side of him or know it existed when it was so thick in hatred.

"So continue," he ordered, halting abruptly at the foot of the stage and staring bitterly at me. He'd never stood so close, but this was not the image of him I wanted as mine. "Condemn me for my rash behavior. I know you must. The good moral girl cannot condone violence done in her name. Tell me I was ignorant to lay a hand upon him, but never forget that I did it for *you*. He lusted after you as if the emotion were requited and put it on display for all to see. You do not deserve to have your reputation shredded to pieces for *his* desires."

I was thrown because he genuinely believed what he'd done was right. I didn't understand how anyone could hurt someone else and justify it to the point that remorse did not exist. He wasn't sorry at all, and how could I forgive someone who did not seek penance?

Shaking my head in confounded uncertainty, I stated back, "Please do not sin with my name on your lips. I do not want guilt upon my shoulders when I've done nothing to deserve it."

"Oh, haven't you? You certainly never stood up for yourself and commanded that bastard to cease his incessant ogling. You *let him* look at you."

"I...I didn't *want* him to," I explained, confused how blame had come around to me instead. What had I done so terribly to earn the growing fire in my angel's eyes? I didn't understand how *his* sin and the fault that went with it could be put upon me.

"But you never stopped him," he insisted again, biting and enraged. "He made his lust evident to every person who saw and proclaimed himself someone who could have you if he so wanted. And I...I hide in shadows, not even a *man* to you. My own desires cannot mold the role for me when you never look and see them."

He seemed so desperate, urgent for something I could not decipher, and taking the smallest step toward the stage's edge, I beseeched, "I don't understand what you mean. Please just tell me."

Even with a mask between, I read hurt in anger's center as its very core, and though he kept an unyielding glare, he demanded, "Do you look at me and see me as a man, Christine?"

"Yes, I-"

"*No*," he corrected, raising his hands in the air for silence. Sense bid that I should focus and see those hands as the same ones that had pushed Buquet out of the rafters, but I couldn't. They were just *his*.

"You *don't* see me as a man," he decided. "I am not allowed to *be* a man to you. I must cower in the dark and yearn alone, and it is hardly fair when a deviant like Joseph Buquet can look at you with lust in his eyes and *want* you as a man would, and all I am permitted is a voice and a fantasy."

"*Ange*, I-"

"*Angel*," he spat the term back at me. "I don't have a name to you. You've never asked for one because only men have names, people worthy to exist

44

in the living world."

"I...I'm sorry," I begged, and to my wide-eyed surprise, he began to approach the stairs leading onstage in slow, calculated steps. I didn't know how to react. Was this a threat? A danger? He'd *never* come so near, and though I staggered an unconsidered inch back, I forced my legs to halt escape and waited. If he meant to destroy me, so be it. I would not run from him.

He kept at the stage's edge, a good distance away, but the spotlights streamed light around him and gleamed along the material of his mask, illuminating and making it unavoidable. And yet...his gaze grew gentle, hopeful as he lifted defenseless hands that I saw tremble.

"Erik," he suddenly told me, "My name is Erik. Won't you say it and make it real? I've only dreamt its unworthy syllables in your voice. Will you speak it for me, Christine?"

My own name was an adoration when he gave it that soft and tender, and eager to return the token, I breathed, "Erik."

My angel had a mortal man's name, and even pretend couldn't be achieved anymore, not with that one, solitary fact.

He shuddered, and I couldn't believe *I* had that effect in return. He was always the one with power, and it shocked me to watch that shudder shake and crack his bravado with its racing possession. He broke before my eyes and slowly slid to his knees at the edge of the stage, watching me with tears in his gaze.

"Yes, and your Erik has disappointed you," he said with somber disdain. "But can you offer forgiveness? Can you look at the *man* before you and see that he is *nothing* without you? Look and see *me*, Christine, not the angel in your mind. You prefer illusions, but they aren't real... And the man is."

I'd known that all along even if I chose not to

dwell on reality's details, but now there were no denials that could equate. I looked and saw *Erik*, kneeling on the stage in supplication and reverence, his brilliant eyes rimmed in tears. The image shook me. How quickly he could go from a villain to a hero's heart! I didn't know how to accept it.

So with timid steps, I tiptoed nearer, grazing my stocking-clad feet along the wooden floor with every careful motion. What was I doing? Giving forgiveness as if it were my place to save his soul... Under the stage lights, he was real, a body with limbs and torso, tangible and solid, not the dark silhouette out in my audience. ...Alive, and I longed to comprehend verity.

Never speaking a word when none could validate my unbidden curiosity, I extended a quivering hand and shyly rested it upon his shoulder. He shuddered violently beneath my palm, and I curved fingertips into a very real suit jacket, holding tight when I knew he was unstable and falling apart with one touch. Real, he wanted me to see real, and yet he was as shaken by it as I was.

"Christine," he whimpered my name, and I adored the sound. It was as beautiful as a song.

So sudden that it went unanticipated, his arms darted out and caught my waist, weaving their lanky threads about my hips and entwining against the small of my back as I was pulled close. I went rigid and stiff, terrified for reasons I had yet to find, but his grip was fierce and unyielding as he pressed his one unmasked cheek against my abdomen.

I didn't know what to do, awkward in my own skin. Should I hold him back? Should I force him away, struggle and give him no choice but to release? But...he did nothing but clasp me to him, his fingers in fists against the small of my back as if to diminish their potential and steal the threat. I felt him breathe, a deep inhalation that opened the lungs pressed boldly to my legs, and it was exhaled as a sigh, so content that I feared destroying this moment. Would anger return if I pushed him away? Would the rift that had started forming its chasm in accusations return and extend like an abyss between us? I didn't want to take that chance. This was my angel teacher; *man* was second to that and the exhilaration that came in the music we shared. I couldn't lose it now.

Forcing numb limbs to comply, I rested my hands to both his shoulders, as much of an embrace as I could permit, and was oddly stirred with his next shiver as he delicately rubbed his cheek to the satin of my rehearsal attire.

"My God, you are so *soft,*" he hoarsely gasped, and I could not suppress the shiver such an impassioned admission ignited. It rushed through my body like a lit spark, flames that ran and licked at the confines of my veins *burning* their way out. I was afraid and wanted him to let go, but the command would not coagulate in my hazy head.

"Say you forgive me," he fervently begged against my stomach, and goose bumps arose beneath the thin material separating his mouth from my skin. "I cannot bear to consider this the *only* time I'll have this feeling, Christine. Don't let my rash behavior be the reason you deny me, not when this moment is *everything.*"

"Everything," I repeated in a whisper, only I could not decide if I agreed with him. An angel held me in his powerful arms... Only he wasn't an angel at all, and I didn't know what that meant.

He took my acquiescence as concurrence and rubbed his cheek again to my stomach as if longing to imprint the thin satin to his flesh. It didn't bring disgust, not the revulsion I'd known for Buquet and his leering desire, but...no, what it brought was indulgent and swelling, *terrifying* because it was beyond all control I'd ever believed I had. I was desperate for this to end.

"Do you forgive me?"

"Of course," I muttered, low and quiet and held my breath with a prayer for that to be enough.

And like God's resonant answer, his strong arms disengaged and released my quivering shape as I rooted my feet and tried to stand firm and not give away how much I missed his body the instant it was torn away from mine. Why? How could I want him and fear him at the same time? Every emotion seemed contradictory to one another until I had no idea *what* I felt.

My angel...Erik rose, arrogant demeanor back in place and mended at every crack, and striding the stage as if he hadn't just been *trembling* against me, he went to the piano and sat before its keys.

"Perhaps it will be an advantage to have accompaniment tonight," he decided as he ran quick scales up and down the keys, cringing at a few suspect pitches with flat intonation. "My managers *will* be receiving a note in the morning cursing their lackluster endeavors at keeping a tuner on hand. This is *opera* after all. It is an irony to let the cast suffer without correctly tuned instruments until the performance week!"

A tangent about instruments when my head was still swimming, and I tried to focus on the image of his proper posture at the piano when spotlights made the mask too prominent and noticeable.

He muttered onward about the wayward pitches, but I did not listen until a convicted assertion burst my haze. "The aria in the second act, you know it, don't you?"

Aria... "Carlotta's aria?"

"Do not credit *Carlotta* with any piece of real music," he sharply declared even as he nodded. "But yes, that piece. I'd like to hear you sing it now."

I felt the color leave my face. "I...I've never sung it before."

"I didn't ask if you'd ever *sung* it. I asked if you knew it, and you do. So *sing* it. Now."

I had no time to think. He played the introduction, and I jumped in with the first pitches. He never ceased playing as I was coerced to sing the entire aria, and though I knew it was not my best, he nodded after the last chord.

"Yes, this will be perfect," he concluded with the confidence I lacked.

"Perfect for what?"

"For *you*, of course. What did you think we were after with these lessons, Christine? *You* are to be the diva."

I went numb with his adamant decision. Diva... I'd *never* dreamed of such a future, and despite a temptation to argue with him over his supposed assessment of my talent and potential, I kept silent, staring at a masked face that loomed hauntingly over the piano's keys.

This angel...*man* had thrown another human being out of the rafters for *me*. What else was he capable of doing in my name? I was terrified to find out.

Chapter Five

Erik~

Obsession. I was obsessed, and I freely admitted it to myself and actually encouraged it onward. Christine... Her name might as well have meant the same thing as *obsession*, an identical definition, because that was what she was. And my current point of fixation was one semi-embrace on an empty stage.

Oh God, I'd touched the goddess... And weren't unworthy mortals automatically condemned to hell for such a sin? Well, I'd burn willingly if it meant I could have more. Another taste of the fire, another lick of the flame. I ached to *take* something greater, but hesitation came in an over-analytical mind.

I not only obsessed over my actions but *her* thoughts *about* my actions. Perhaps I'd pushed too hard and too far, and damn my infernal weaknesses! I'd given her a view of the vulnerable soul I yearned to hide, peeking out in desperation and *tears*. *Tears*! I'd cried genuine tears in front of her! It was a point I called pathetic. I needed to be strong and seem invincible because if she ever realized *she* could destroy the Opera Ghost, every game would be over and I'd fall for good.

So in un-validated fear that destruction was my imminent outcome, I did not make another attempt at *contact* despite how my body ached. I limited myself to angel teacher again, only now I resided on spot-lit stages instead of in the dark. It was a two-fold solution. I needed a piano to truly teach, and from the stage, I could watch more closely and condition her to seeing me as a man. After all, ghost or angel couldn't be a consideration when I was too near to forget my mortal makeup. Yes, she had to succumb to sharing the air with a *man*.

Obsession ran rampant through me, but when we worked, I put emotion aside. It was difficult but necessary when the talent I shaped was so pure and infinite in its potential. Christine was my muse and not just because I was infatuated with the girl. Her voice... It still stunned me that something so glorious passed her lips in every note and she was *unaware* that it was brilliant. With the right training and guidance, I knew she could rival every diva currently on an opera stage. Her gift bore no limit, and I knew *I* could make it flourish and continue growing forever if she let me.

But for now it was an intimate secret between only the two of us, as I watched her dance in the ballet and knew she was destined for something exceptional. Not a single tutu-ed brat had the promise Christine did; none of them realized they were dancing in the presence of greatness. Only she and I held that secret... In a way, it made me feel so special and close to her.

Obsession had stages that only worsened with chosen abstinence. Now that I knew what she felt like, smelled like, her softness, sweetness, beauty, obsession was an ache that shrieked in a shrill voice for satisfaction. *It* tempted me to more touches, promising I wouldn't regret it, that *she* wanted it, too, while sense argued the opposite.

I was doubtless what I felt for her was love, but...her heart was a mystery. There were times as we worked so diligently lost to music's consumption that I was sure she *must* feel *something* for me, something beyond mentor and confidante. She'd look at me with this glow in her eyes as if she couldn't get enough of my words to satisfy her. More praises that I purposely kept restrained, more instruction and guidance. I could tell that my company was cherished at those moments, but since I didn't push for more, I couldn't fathom how deep feeling ran.

Determined to give real purpose to our sordid relationship, I worked with her on the current leading role for the production. If she found such a thing odd, she did not let on of it after that first night and dutifully allowed my plans to prosper.

Unbeknownst to my rising diva, I had every intention that Christine would be the one to sing the lead on opening night. A talent of her caliber deserved to be heard, and when Carlotta was a screeching cat in comparison, it seemed a travesty to hand her leading roles simply because of reputation. No more. No matter what I had to do, *Christine* would sing.

While I was not above using sin and vice to my advantage, I was extra careful to keep my plan from Christine's knowledge. She'd never condone immorality, and her naïve sweetness couldn't reason the politics behind opera. She needed a contender on her side, someone to raise her up above the throng, and even if a bit of dishonesty was involved, that was the game. Only those wiling to play had a chance to win.

So while preparations were underway onstage and Christine spent her days as a mediocre ballerina, at night with me, she shone like the beacon star she was meant to be and took her rightful place as prima donna. It was a lot to put on her shoulders, but she seemed to be handling it with ease...all until one particular night.

I favored waiting until the theatre was empty to join her, most especially now that I allowed myself in view on the stage. I couldn't risk anyone else lingering and catching us mid-practice, so I always checked the vicinity first, locks in place, all bodies gone and not still in dressing rooms. It was tedious when my heart was racing ahead, eager to be with Christine, but my task was necessary for both of us.

As I finally deemed all satisfactory and joined her in the theatre, I found her once again practicing that dreaded Act Three routine on the stage. Her ballet improved by the day, and though she managed to blend well with the others in every other section, this Act Three number always left her berated by Madame Giry's eagle eye and perfectionist tendencies. I hated every time Christine was singled out for chastisement and perhaps if ballet were her only talent, I'd have found my own way to make the pompous Madame more lenient. But I couldn't truly care about ballet when opera was the greater passion in Christine's blood. For all I deemed, ballet was a temporary respite on the way to notoriety.

Onstage, Christine moved with too much heaviness. I noted that every time her mind was distracted, she overworked her motions, and now as she pirouetted, she pulled her leg out too early and stumbled off her toes with a discontented cry.

"You know this piece much better than you're giving yourself credit for," I called and discounted her startled response to my sudden appearance. Shock quickly relaxed to nothing but her frustration with ballet, and I took it as encouragement as I approached the stage and found no hesitation or apprehension in her stare. She didn't even question me, not anymore.

"Not according to Madame Giry," she countered, dropping her ballerina posture to a slouch. "Yet again, I was proven the worst dancer during her mid-rehearsal tirade on my every flaw. She says I lack grace."

"That is not true," I quickly insisted. "You have all the grace of a proper ballerina, but you spend too much effort second-guessing and comparing yourself to the others to notice."

"Have you *seen* the other ballerinas?" she retorted as if that were proof she was right.

"Not really," I admitted and did not shy from honesty this time. "I'm always too engrossed watching *you* to notice anyone else."

"Oh..." Pale skin quickly grew pink as she lowered anxious eyes, and I was intrigued by such a response. A blush... I'd caused her to *blush*, and I savored the achievement as her flesh tinted the same hue as her rehearsal attire. It was charming and delightful to behold.

Before I could consider every ramification that could come, I bid, "Come with me. I want to show you something."

She peeked up with curiously arched brows but never questioned as I gestured for her to follow. No, she obeyed with the softest whisper of her toe shoes behind my leading path. Ballet might not be a passion to either of us, but I needed her to realize that she was good at it. I wouldn't let tutus and toes shoes be the thing to shatter any confidence I was building because I needed a diva in the end. Confidence was a necessity.

Without a word of explanation, I led her into the wings and toward a darkened corridor, and though I heard the nervous skips in her breath, I did not turn to her or break our course. I was about to show her something *no one* knew about, and I bore faith in her to keep it as another secret only we shared.

At the far end of the corridor was a wall...only it was no wall at all. It opened to a passage, one of *many* I had about the opera house, and without a thought, I showed her its threshold and heard her follow me inside with nothing but a soft gasp to announce her fear.

I had a penchant for seeing in the dark. Too long living below the earth adjusted my eyes to shadows with barely a thought, but she would be lost without light. Thinking only of her and the fear I *felt* from her but did not look to observe, I lit a lantern I kept in the passage, and though the flickering flame was meager, I heard Christine's sigh of relief and only then regarded her. I hadn't wanted to see fear, knowing fear would hurt even if *I* were not its inspiration. Now...I saw a bit of anxiety but also a trust I adored her for.

"This way," I bid with the tinge of a grin and continued our path. Up a steep staircase, and when my chosen routes were usually down, this was foreign to both of us.

At the top of the narrow passage was a heavy door, heavy because on the opposite side, it looked like a stone wall. I pushed hard against its boundary and felt it give and part.

The rooftop. As we emerged into the cold night air, I savored the gasp of wonder she gave. Snowflakes were falling from the clouded sky, strikingly white against the dark of night. They had already formed a thin layer over the stone statues, masking their distinct features in white blankets. Being confined to rehearsal all day and as trapped indoors as I typically was, Christine wouldn't have known that it had started to snow, but I'd caught glimpses during my perusal of an empty opera house and knew I had to show her simply for the awe I now received.

Her gaze was transfixed on the tumble of white, lacey flakes, all the amazement of a child upon her beautiful face. She gazed at the snow as if it were all she longed to see, the same way *I* gazed at *her*.

Without a thought, Christine tiptoed out from under our rooftop awning until she could stand within the embrace of the snowfall, extending open palm and fingers as if she could catch a flake to keep forever. But as was inevitable, every one that touched her skin died a noble death, melting to nothing but droplets that trailed her fingertips and tumbled free.

In the midst of her enchantment, I gently commanded, "Dance, Christine."

"Dance? But I'll slip...and fall."

"No, you won't," I corrected with unwavering adamancy. "You need to find something passionate in the dance, and I'm giving it to you. Now every time you dance onstage amidst Madame Giry's chastisement and the other ballerinas' nonsense, you'll have this moment in your head: when you danced for me in the middle of a snowfall. It will be your muse of inspiration."

I could see how much my idea appealed to her as she cast glances between the cascade of white beauty and me. As she hesitated still, letting her fingers catch flakes and engulf her as another of their fragile brethren, I stepped behind her. One last detail to make this utter perfection. Never an explanation or request did I give; I slid my fingertips into her cloud of curls, feigning less nervousness than I felt as I found the clip holding them captive and released their curtain.

She'd gone stiff with my bold action, but she permitted with never even a dubious glance, certainly feeling the added weight upon her shoulders. I took such acquiescence as unspoken encouragement and dared to delicately caress her curls with shaking hands, thrilling as they coiled about my knuckles as if caressing me back.

But...this wasn't about me, and bending close to her ear, I again commanded, "Dance, Christine."

She shivered, and though sense longed to claim cold, I favored the idea that I affected her as much as she affected me. This time she obeyed, creeping more steps into the snow layer and imprinting its blanket.

Blue eyes closed as she took her first stance, and then to my mesmerized hypnosis, she began to dance. I thrilled with the first movement. It was beautiful and saturated in grace. She let go in that moment with no one to judge her but the man who adored her every breath, and she simply *felt*. Music was the silence of the snowfall, the peculiar stillness that came in a perfect moment, and as she spun, her curls echoed the dance, rippling and suspending upon the air as snowflakes caught in the web and lingered in their brief life.

Her eyes fluttered open, white tangled in her lashes. She was an integral part of the snow shower as though her motion propelled the cascade onward and made flakes giggle and skip in their typical pattern. I was riveted to the choreography in her body, the way she became as graceful and elegant as the flakes about her, their equal and sister, dancing *with* them in a portrait of purity. Beauty personified. Here it was, and it was *mine*.

Christine's pirouettes left twisted shapes in the snow bed beneath her toe shoes, every leftover imprint etching her dance into temporary permanence, and I scripted the connection of one move to the next, reading every footfall and equally every space between of untouched white. It felt like an evolving story, and as she lifted a graceful leg and snowflakes coated its curves and circled the crinoline of her tutu, I was unable to quiet a blaze of desire. It urged me to trail my hand from one murdered snowflake's remnants to the next, follow the path up the length of her calf and become as important to the scene as she was.

But...before I could give in with fingers that tingled and burned their yearning, I had to abandon every endeavor. Christine's foot came down to the snow, and I saw it slide. I never gave a second thought as I leapt forward and caught her tumbling shape in my arms before she ever grazed the ground.

She gave nothing but a whimper, but her hands grasped my forearms and dug tight in the material of my jacket while she sought to find balance.

"I suppose I was wrong," I gasped out, needing

words for concentration when her body so close was threatening to overwhelm. Instinct begged to press her to my length, to force every curve to the corresponding hard plane in my shape and mold her softness into me, but...I shivered and allowed nothing beyond the fists I'd formed in her curls.

"No," she breathlessly bid, and I was terrified it was a refusal of my unacceptable hold before she finished, "you were right. I didn't *fall*."

"I'd *never* let you fall."

"I know." She vowed it without hesitation, and I couldn't keep a smile from appearing.

"Your dance was exquisite, Christine," I told her as she met my gaze with that *blush* painting her skin. "I saw *passion* and *grace*, ...and my God are you beautiful!"

She lowered her eyes, hiding their telling orbs behind her snowflake-coated lashes, and without permission, I lifted her off her feet and cradled her to my chest. She did not refuse or struggle; no, she kept her fists within my jacket material and set her temple to my shoulder, and I had to stifle the urge to crack my walls and falter to tears. But to hold her like this... It was a blessing I'd never known.

I carried her back within my secret passageway, my attention fixed on the white flakes tangled in her loose curls and their immediate demise once we were back indoors. They transformed from something so beautiful and ethereal to something ordinary in water droplets and lost their magic because of my actions. There was some realism in that.

As the flakes on her bare arms melted as well, goose bumps were left behind, raising and reminding me that I'd been careless to have her outside without proper layers. For the first time, I was aware that she was as fragile as the snowflakes dying in her curls, and I must be delicate with her. ...Always delicate.

Her every breath was syncopated with mine, her heart a counterpoint with my own layered on top, so many rhythms that meant joined lives. I savored every detail as I brought her back into the theatre and to our usual place on the stage.

I longed to keep her, but memorizing in frantic desperation, I only paused a second longer before setting her upon her feet. I didn't want to lose this closeness yet, not when her eyes fluttered past mine as if to say the same. She gave *no* doubt in return, and I clung to that as permission as I slowly knelt before her.

My hands shook. I couldn't have stopped their quivering if I tried, so I let them tremble and give my insecurities away as I extended one and delicately caught her ankle in my palm. Oh God, I was so *careful* with her! Terrified a touch too intrepid and insistent would have her running. *No, not yet, Christine.*

I met the uncertainty in her blushing stare with my own, but I did not stop as I brought my free hand to the laces of her toe shoe just behind her knee. I'd never imagined a touch like this and couldn't know how it would overcome me with a tremor so vicious that I shuddered and nearly lost my grip. No, no, her shoes were wet with snow; I had to take care of my girl...

With attentive care, I untied and unwound, guiding the ribbon free and exposing the gentle shape of her calf as I'd enviously watched her do every night. This was much better than being the observer in the background; this was living the moment with her.

One shoe coaxed free, and then the other, and I glanced between my intimate task and her fear-fringed eyes. Fear... But what was I truly giving her to fear? I took no more than what I felt imperative.

...All right, that wasn't exactly true. I added two extra caresses: one to the delicate spot behind her knee and one to the arch of her foot, tender and overwhelmed. I ached for more, but...fear was not only hers. I was stoking desire's flame, and I didn't know how far I could steer it before it encompassed and swallowed me in its tidal wave.

As if I'd done nothing wrong, certainly nothing worthy of guilt, I drew away and rose on unstable legs that rushed me toward my preferred place at the piano before I could think better of it.

"Let us begin," I curtly decided, pounding out a ferocious chord with fingers that still tingled from stolen caresses. I couldn't look at her beyond a passing glance as regret began to well.

I'd pushed without a pull, and that was inconsiderable. One couldn't take without giving. It had to go both ways, and I'd *only* taken. Where was the *give*? I couldn't very well state it plainly and tell her that she was *allowed* to touch me in return if she so wanted. That was ridiculous, but...I felt *she* should have something, something in her control instead of mine, something to assuage fear I didn't want her to know. How could I give something back when I was still yet unsure she *wanted* anything from me?

My mind was tortured with thought, but I launched us into our lesson, hoping distraction would mend the broken threads in my head. It was not our best rehearsal, not by far, but when she seemed as shaken as I was, it was no wonder. She was addled and meditative. I had to call her attention back more than once, but I was no better. Every time my gaze landed on her, it inevitably was drawn to her legs with a magnetic pull and memories of an intimacy that I didn't want to call a sin. Was it a sin? ...It depended on her interpretation of the same scene.

As we both finally gave up a lackluster lesson and minutes wasted, I decided I could not bear to suffer the agony that would come once I was beyond blue eyes. Straightforward and blunt, I stated, "I need to give my apologies for my earlier brazen behavior. ...I should not have touched you. The last thing I wish is to establish fear between us, and...my actions were forward and improper. I will not breach etiquette again; you have my word."

I watched her brow ruffle and a nervous bit lip as she seemed to debate pressing the issue. Perhaps her own sense of guilt would convince her to take the blame on her shoulders and free me of its weight...or perhaps she was just relieved that it was over and done.

As I started to rise, she suddenly lifted stopping hands and bid, "Wait. Don't go yet, Erik. Please..."

I halted every motion and sat back upon the piano bench, still overcome every time she used my name. Another secret between us, only she would not see it as the same intimacy I did, not when in her world, names were commonplace. She couldn't know that I'd grown accustomed to 'Opera Ghost' and chose not to lower my semblance with a mortal title. But gods fell from their thrones only for *her*, and a mortal name no longer felt demoralizing when *she* spoke its letters.

As I gazed at her with an unspoken question, I saw her shift nervously on her feet before taking small step after small step closer to me. I froze, unable to breathe with her approach, anticipating and terrified at the same time. She'd *never* made a motion toward me, never anything I could fully misconstrue, but now her intention was wary but evident as she came to stand beside my piano bench.

"Please...don't make such vows," she softly bid. "I never asked for them, and if I hold no blame upon you, how can you ask forgiveness? Don't make it seem sinful because...it wasn't sinful."

"No?"

She shook her head, and loose dark curls bobbed with the motion and reminded me how they had flown free in a snow dance. It was the most beautiful image I'd ever seen on this earth.

Timidity gave that pink blush again, and as if eager to seem less shy, she asked, sweet and quiet, "Will you play something for me, *ange*?"

I nodded dully, still half-shocked every second in her willing presence. She made it seem she wanted the moment to extend as much as I did. Turning to the keys, I worried I'd falter when my hands shook as much as every part of me, but ivory keys were my native tongue. I was adept at their language so much more than this love speech I attempted with Christine, and as I began to play, I poured my heart through the piano's belly, letting it permeate the air and say everything I couldn't in words.

I knew she felt what I did, glancing at her every few measures of a made-up composition and glimpsing the wonder light her features and grow.

We lingered in that pool of pure emotion for a long while without words when words were limited in their capacity. Music spoke infinite and played about both our bodies like a ribbon weaving us together.

Eventually when we quit and I sent her off to bed like a child, I noticed the looks she cast back at every breath, full of realization and awareness. I was doubtless that in one serenade, I'd unwittingly professed my love, telling her the secrets I hadn't yet shared, and though she seemed awed such emotions existed, I still was unclear if they were returned from her corner.

Could she love me back? Even a hint of such emotion would be enough to settle my throbbing heart. But she was more guarded than I and had no outlet for wordless emotion as I did in a piano's timbre.

I made my heart a song when language had its faults and failures, and until she could find a way to do the same, I knew I'd have to wait and take only what *she gave* this time.

Chapter Six

Christine~

Emotion was addictive. It was a surprise to learn how much. One discounted the actual power emotions could hold when they were felt and indulged every single day. It was like they lost their sharpness with use and didn't overwhelm as they would if new. I had been privy to more of the bad sort since my father's death. Sadness, loss, loneliness, mourning. Happiness was a bittersweet memory and shut away when it brought only memories of what could never be again.

I was relearning happiness in singing and in my daily lessons with my angel teacher, and yet I was afraid to *feel* it to its deepest extent. I only let it graze the surface and never root inside. Except for the instant my lesson finished and Erik played his beautiful music for me. Then I let it free and savored its overwhelming possession.

It was our new pattern. Once work was done, he'd indulge my begged request and give me the key to my growing addiction in lyrical melodies and luscious harmonies. I was no fool. I knew my resurrected emotions were a reflection of *his*. He played what was in his heart, and I thrilled at its potency. It was so beautiful that I yearned to feel it the same.

In music's spell, it was easy. I could *love him* and just *feel* and not think of the consequences. It was almost *simple*. And while the idea of *truly* loving Erik terrified me, when melodies poured from his fingers, I was sure I could do it. ...I was sure I already did.

Erik likely perceived my newfound addiction as solely for his music, and I never let on the truth that it was actually his heart I craved more and its every deep-seeded adoration. When he played, love was pure and held nothing worthy of fear, not like a night he'd taken caresses on a stage as he'd discarded my shoes. *That* was something that only inspired terror. It was consuming and dark, and the memory alone made me tremble and left me unsure if I wanted to feel it again or not.

Perhaps that was petty. I wanted to *love* him but not *touch* him, but modesty kept me shy and unsure. Touch seemed heavy and real, and when he played his music instead, things were half a fairytale.

I wasn't naïve or completely ignorant on the subject. I knew we could not continue this peaceful sense of abeyance forever when it was sugarcoated and idealistic, but...a little longer couldn't hurt.

For the next few weeks, I was fortunate to stay in that rose-hued state, but then as was inevitable, the fragile bubble popped and thrust me back into the world.

Joseph Buquet returned to the opera. He hobbled about on shoddy crutches, but he seemed determined to do his job. I understood such adamancy when losing a position implied future starvation on the streets, more so for a man who needed to let his leg heal before he could search for another job.

It was not unfathomable that he'd endure the hardship to keep a cozy place in the opera crew, but from the moment he arrived back in the theatre, I was acutely aware that his focus was on me. This was not the same as the ogling, desirous leers he usually cast; this was ominous and rose anxious goose bumps on my skin. I had much worth worrying over, considering he and I both knew Erik was responsible for his accident. I wondered how accountable it made me if the sin was done in my name. I *felt* guilty.

I endured his looks all morning and tried to appear unaffected. Erik would be watching, and if he knew Buquet was up to his old games, there was no telling what he would do. I did not know Erik's basis for sin and reprieve. Where was the limit? I didn't want to learn.

As afternoon rehearsals began, the ballerinas awaited their Act Three entrance in the wings, and as I lingered back, I felt the lightest touch on my elbow. With a sharp gasp, I flipped about only to come face to face with Buquet's beady eyes. It felt like this meeting was inevitable, as if I'd been waiting all day for the instant accusations would find the light. I was more surprised by what I glimpsed in his eyes: *fear*.

He lifted a chubby finger to his lips for silence and then motioned that I follow, and though I hesitated a breath with an idle glance onstage to see that I still had time until my entrance, I obeyed. Let him try something immoral; I was confident his homemade crutches were not stable and could easily be kicked out from beneath him. The idea lessened my anxiety as I followed him into an empty dressing room.

"What do you want?" I immediately interrogated, on guard again as he closed the door before facing me. Alone in a room with a deviant man twice my size who lusted after me... I edged back anxious steps and locked my eyes on the base of his crutch. One swift kick, and I knew he'd tumble.

"Relax, girl," he snapped and made a face at me. "I'm not here to hurt you. Just the opposite actually."

His words were slurred and sloppy, and in the train of my thoughts, he took a flask from his back pocket and took a long swig before eyeing me again with a nonchalant shrug.

"Dulls the pain," he commented and waved the flask in the air. "Need something to take the edge off the damage your lover left behind."

I went stiff with the mention and feigned innocence. "I don't know what you mean. I have no lover."

"*He* would say otherwise. I'd watch that innocent body around him if I were you. *He* thinks it's *his* already."

Buquet's glazed eyes showed pinpricks of wisdom, and shaking my head, I refused to listen, muttering, "You don't know anything."

"Don't I? I was told none-so-gently by your masked suitor that I was not to even look at you again lest I find my death awaiting."

His words chilled me through flesh to the bones beneath because I knew he spoke true and I hated how much I didn't want to believe him. "And yet...here you are talking to me," I insisted instead. "If what you say is valid, why are you chancing your life?"

"Because I don't think any pretty young girl deserves the fate you have coming if you don't get out of this place. You've put yourself on the map of the almighty opera demon, and that is a place you don't want to be. Trust me. He is a murderer and a monster. The *devil*."

Buquet was straight-faced and solemn, his beady stare piercing me with its intensity, and although I listened, I kept doubts palpable between us. "I see no reason to believe you, monsieur. You are obviously inebriated, and-"

"Do you know why he wears a mask?" Buquet interrupted, and I went numb with the mere mention.

"That...isn't my business or yours either."

He ignored my unease and stated flatly, "Because he *is* the devil, mademoiselle. That mask hides what he truly is, the face of hell's own demon. He *is Satan* on earth looking to tempt the innocent to fall into fire and flame. The devil teases with pleasure and seeming bliss as he sucks your soul from your body. ...You don't believe me?"

Did I? I didn't *want* to, but I remembered one particular exchange and the way it had felt when he'd touched my leg... *Fire and flame.*

"Look at his face," Buquet ordered. "His *real* face, and you'll see I'm right. Do it before it's too late for you."

I shook my head, unable to find a clear thought as I pushed, "Why are you warning me? My presence is the reason you were hurt and why you have more threats on your head."

"As I said, I don't like to see pretty things destroyed for no good reason. He *wants* you. He isn't going to stop until he *has* you. If I were you, I'd take the warning for what it is and get out before that happens."

Buquet took another swig from his flask before deciding, "I'll say no more. It's *your* funeral and an eternity in hellfire if you refuse to listen. At least my conscience will be clear for trying." He was about to leave but added lowly, "I've heard the music, mademoiselle. He plays like an angel of God, isn't that so? But the devil was an angel once, too. Don't forget that."

And with such ill-omened overtones, he hobbled out of the room and left me with torturous musings that made my heart hurt with their pinch.

The devil... I already had suspicions about the crimes Erik claimed he did not commit, but...the *devil.* That was quite an accusation. I didn't want to put a single thought to it, but...I recalled the delicious way his music made me feel. Such exquisite sensation! And I *would* willingly fall to damnation in its spell. It was the perfect tool to claim my soul because I *wanted* its consummation.

If Erik were indeed the devil incarnate, I didn't care as much as I knew I should. Sense said to get proof and then make a choice. But...what proof existed except what lay concealed in a mask? ...Perhaps there was where my answer lay.

I carried on through the rest of rehearsal without a mind attached, but even when Madame Giry shouted at my lack of focus, I didn't fix the problem. I couldn't care about social humiliation with my *soul* on the line and potentially a step from hell's door. *That* seemed to hold more concern and eternal consequence than fumbling Act Three's routine!

When my lesson time arrived, I was yet a mess. I didn't know what I was going to do, having devised no possible solution in my contemplation. My meditation kept coming back to one point: that if an answer existed beneath the mask, I had to see and know. I never pondered what I would uncover except for a hope that it wasn't the *devil*. Would I even know the devil if I came face to face with him? Perhaps I'd find something ethereally beautiful and not realize what I saw was as much an illusion as his music...

My head twisted in a plethora of unanswered questions, and although Erik must have sensed my seeming insanity, as we began our lesson time, he made no mention of it. Unsurprising. He probably pinned it on my awful dancing and constant chastisement all afternoon. That made sense in reason's realm because *why* would I *ever* consider that I was taking music lessons with Lucifer himself? That was *absurd*!

Singing felt tedious when I kept wondering if perhaps I was a terrible singer and the devil was only humoring me because he wanted my soul. For all I knew, I could have no talent whatsoever. I'd clung to *his* assessments as fact without real proof. I had nothing, but...every time I met Erik's mismatched stare and garnered hints of his affection, I lost momentum and Buquet's warnings grew meaningless. I *knew* Erik, the important facets anyway, and everything else shouldn't matter. ...*Why did it matter?*

"Christine," he called with a sharp huff, "that's the third time you missed that entrance."

"I'm sorry," I beseeched and meant it. "I'm just...tired, I suppose."

What a pathetic excuse! I didn't believe myself and didn't think he would either, not when to him, being a musician came first and foremost. But...he didn't leap to temper or snap back at me. ...Perhaps that should have been a clue that something was unsettled, but I was so consumed in my own mind's traumas that I shrugged intuition off and rejected any musing that was not selfish.

"Will you just...play something for me, *ange*?" I begged, desperate for his music with a hunger I'd never known before. I ached for something beautiful, for the emotions he always gave in melodies, craving to my soul with a hope that I'd forget everything else when music took over.

He paused and regarded me a long moment, and I thought I saw sadness in those eyes and a despair I had no explanation for. But with a barely audible sigh, he conceded, and his hands created all the beauty I could ever require, spanning the keys and grazing with a delicate touch.

This was tender and fragile, a melody that evolved out of itself and wove its arms about my body as if to insist he longed to do the same. To comfort my fluctuating thoughts and smooth them to nonexistent with an embrace as his enticement. And as much as something inside craved his touch with a raw ferocity that ignited fear, I couldn't succumb to it. Not until I knew the truth...

I approached in tentative tiptoes, coming to the piano's siren call as I always did. It was the connective tissue between our hearts and solidified more fibers in its consuming melodies. This time I denied surrender and crept near, gazing at the graceful motion of his hands and every tender caress he granted a cold instrument in unacceptable envy. I shouldn't want the devil's touch, but though it bit in fire and flame, it stirred me to the depths of my being. I was already a victim falling to temptation, and even as I wanted answers, I knew they would change *nothing* if music were still his weapon of choice. I'd always falter and give in.

I came to stand behind him, and my hands tingled as I rested palms atop his shoulders, feeling him tense at my given touch when such a thing was so rare. A touch. I was about to deceive him with a touch and make something he'd consider a blessing into a manipulation.

I felt his body rise and fall with the music and an inhalation that savored this second...the second before I ruined it all.

Without a thought, my hand rose and went for his mask, and just as abrupt, music stopped, and his fierce grip had my wrist before my fingers ever found manmade material. I gave a small cry and cringed as all emotion I'd known seemed to spiral like a hurricane within me and lock in the one place he had me. His fingertips dug into the smooth skin of my wrist and bruised as I yanked and tried futilely to get free.

"I expect such merciless betrayal from everyone else in this abomination of a world, but not you. *Not you,*" he hissed, leaping up from the piano bench and jerking me with him to center-stage as his fiery gaze penetrated to my soul.

"I...I'm sorry," I whimpered, recoiling as far as I could as he twisted my wrist painfully in his grasp.

"You weren't supposed to fall to curiosity and doubt. You were supposed to be stronger than that, to *care* about your actions and their consequences. You were supposed to have a *heart*, Christine!"

His enraged insults drove like daggers into my flesh and pierced holes into my veins. What had I done? "Erik, *please.* I just...I wanted to see your face.

70

Have I not earned such trust?"

"*No!*" he shouted and spat back my word. "*Trust?* Trust is *not* seeing the horror beneath the mask. It is leaving me with my dignity and free will to show you in my own time. But you...you let that bastard Buquet tarnish every good moment between us with his vile lies."

"How...how did you know about that?" My heart halted and dropped in my chest. So he'd known all along... As I'd stood right in front of him, agonizing and debating a choice I knew would leave damage behind, he'd let me suffer instead of calling attention to a clandestine encounter. He *knew*, ...and he also concluded that I would fail. When he needed my loyalty most, I'd proven his lingering doubts. ...I *had* failed.

Tears filled my eyes and poured in rivers down my cheeks. "I'm sorry. *I'm sorry.*" I begged as if for my life, no longer fighting against his ferocious hold, and as he tightened until my fingers went numb, I welcomed the pain. It was superficial; it would fade and heal, but the pain I'd caused both our hearts would linger in scars forever. I'd broken us.

"Foolish, *foolish* girl," he spat coldly. "So quick to cast the first stone! The *devil*, Christine? Am I the devil to you? Have I *ever* treated you with evil or malice? Ever given *you* reason to condemn me? Ah yes, I pushed Buquet out of the rafters. I defended your honor and innocence with violence, and therefore I *must be* Satan on earth!"

Dragging me close by my held arm, he twisted it behind my back and pressed its capture to the curve of my spine. "Tell me, what did you hope to find beneath the mask? A demon face? A monster? A lie and *perfection* instead? How inconsiderate of you! To choose to steer our fate without ever giving my opinion pause. I cannot refuse and tell you no if you steal my mask away without permission granted. I can only react *after* the fact. Do you have any idea how often that has been the case in my pitiful life? I am humanity's victim, a monster shaped by its cruelty and spite, but *you* weren't supposed to know that. You were supposed to find that there was more to my being than a face. Selfish girl! You nearly destroyed everything!"

Anger then pain and back again, and I watched feelings fluctuate, and it didn't matter that a mask stood in the way to full depictions. I *heard* in his voice, and I *felt* in his grip. There was danger looming about his shape, that powerful threat that made my knees waver beneath my weight. I had no idea how far he would take retaliation, and I was afraid.

"Erik," I stammered and sought words, *any words* to appease, "you are *not* the devil. I know you would never hurt me."

With a fierce growl, he released my arm, and backing necessary steps away, he snapped, "You know *nothing*, Christine! You proved it tonight. Not my heart, not my soul, certainly not! Well...perhaps it will give my character some credit to admit that I've *never* entertained this sort of a relationship with anyone. I talk to no one. I humor no one. I certainly do not care for anyone. ...Only you." The rage hadn't calmed, but his heart shone through greater as he declared, "But then again perhaps my word is worthless. If you could denounce everything I ever said to you and let Buquet's abominable explanations mean more, then I am fooling myself and giving you more to doubt and mistrust, aren't I? Dear God, I am so *ignorant* when it comes to you. I never thought you would *act*, simple as that. Perhaps because in your presence, I forget what I am." A bitter laugh crossed his lips. "*Fool*! I *forget* that I wear a mask!" His sarcasm drew him back toward anger, and he suddenly shouted, "How dare I? How dare I see myself as just a man in your presence? I should be damned for that alone! But you never judged the mask, and it was easy to consider us equals. I should have known better."

Shame heated my cheeks, and as I lowered my head, I fixated on the fall of my tears as they broke free and struck my tulle skirt. It reminded me of a night in the snow as snowflakes had done the same. That night, I'd learned both emotions that humbled me and emotions that terrified me, but as I now considered I might know neither ever again, I cursed my naïveté and silently prayed for forgiveness.

"I just...wanted to see," I softly revealed because at curiosity's core, everything was simple and uncomplicated.

"Christine..."

He spoke my name with such desolation and yet such passion, and as I dared to lift my eyes and blink the blinding pool of tears away, I saw a mirror of my agony reflected back. To my surprise, he brought one hand to his mask, slow and quivering, and caught its edge at his jaw line. Lifting it ever so slightly, he exposed only his mouth, and I felt pain, raw and violent, attack my inner core.

"Oh..." It was the sigh of my deflated lungs as my eyes trailed anatomy so distorted that one could not even reason it a *mouth*, not when considered against its normal-looking counterpart. His upper lip swelled grotesquely above the bottom one, malformed and uneven in spots as if someone took thumbs and indented their shapes on the way up an abnormal arch.

My mind kept insisting it wasn't real. No, no, how could a voice so angelic and beautiful have such a demented casing? That seemed...ludicrous. The vessel containing it should be as exquisite as its brilliant timbre and not...ugly.

He showed me no more than his mouth, and as tears filled a mismatched stare always upon me, he jerked the mask back in place with fiercely shaking hands and ducked away from my continued observation.

"Who...did that to you?" I asked, shaking a stunned head too full of abnormalities to find reality.

"God."

God works in mysterious ways... The sentiment came back to haunt me with its sudden validity. It seemed the opposite of a blessing and utterly *unfair.*

"I...have to go." Erik abruptly made the decision, still not casting me a single look as he stalked toward the edge of the stage.

No... Never contemplating, I let impulse drive me and hurried after him, wrapping claiming arms about him and hugging my body to his back as he halted and shuddered in my embrace.

"No, no," I whimpered amidst tears that I buried against his suit jacket, pressing my forehead to his spine and holding him as if I couldn't let go. Sense insisted this was a product of compassion and a form of penance, seeking forgiveness for my earlier behavior, but...to *feel* him as he shivered and trembled, to inhale his scent and mold myself to his back as if I couldn't be close enough to satisfy some internal hunger, those details made the moment mean so much more.

I didn't care what else the mask hid. This was no *devil* I held together in my arms and no demon or monster. This was a man. For the first time, I understood what that meant and did not shy away or create angels or ghosts instead.

"Don't go," I pleaded and could not argue with instinct as I pressed flustered kisses to his back and felt him stiffen in surprise. "Don't leave me. I'm sorry, Erik. I'm so sorry..."

His tears choked his voice as he insisted in broken sounds, "There is a good reason I wear a mask, Christine, and it is *not* to hide the face of Satan. It is to hide something unworthy to exist, unworthy even to *be Satan's.*"

"I know," I whispered and pressed another

compassion-laced kiss to his spine. No...I *didn't* know, not the full extent, but I could imagine more horror and it only made me hold him tighter.

"Christine..." A gasp suddenly escaped him, but without a view of a masked face, I was unsure the trigger until his hand delicately caught one of mine and disentangled my hold. That was the wrist he had gripped in his anger, such a betrayer that I didn't even want to own it as mine, and although I had yet to survey it, the dull ache told me it was injured, perhaps bruising. I felt it was justly deserved.

He was silent as he held my wrist and inspected, and I could feel the self-loathing radiate in ripples from his tensed back.

I could never say if his next actions were to prove a point, perhaps that despite his deficiencies, he was no different than any other man, or if it was simply impulse fueling him as it fueled me. But his free hand lifted to his mask again. I was unsure what he was doing until my injured wrist was guided without struggle from me toward his face. Then his lips tasted me, and I stopped breathing.

He kept the mask held, certainly only exposing that distorted mouth again, but in all its abnormalities, it lavished healing adoration on my sore skin. Kisses, awkward and unsure at first, and I could make out the unnatural swell of his lip with every pressing through feeling alone. As he grew more confident, perhaps assured when I didn't try to pull free, he took more liberties. Slower, more languid, that misshapen mouth latched to my flesh, lips moving in devouring ravishment, and at their parted seam, his tongue was freed to lap gently at my veins.

I buried a cry in his shoulder blade and shivered. I was *terrified* as heat raced from the spot his mouth claimed to settle with a dull ache at my core, and yet for all my fear, I pressed firmer to him as if he were my savior at the same time. As much my protector as the one who could destroy me. With him, it was *everything*. Every emotion and sensation, good and bad, entwined in one package and weaving thorn-laced vines about our embracing bodies. I was so frightened *because* I wanted so much!

One more stolen taste as his tongue circled my inner wrist and made bruises ache inside and out, and so sudden that I mewed in disappointment, he lowered my arm and adjusted his mask. ...And I'd never gotten another view of that malformed mouth and regretted that fact.

Still delicately clasping my telltale injury, he softly insisted, "You deserve so much more than this, Christine, more than I could ever give you. You deserve a perfect prince, not a disfigured creature in the shadows."

"I like the shadows," I gave as a weak protest and rubbed my forehead against his back.

"I was under the impression that you did not favor the dark," he bid, but I caught the hint of a smile in his voice and savored it.

"When I'm alone," I corrected. "But when I'm with you, ...nothing frightens me more than losing your heart."

"Oh, Christine..." My name thick with that exact heart, and he lifted my held wrist again and pressed its injury to the bare half of his face, arching his cheek to my skin as he insisted, "You never need worry about that. It is *yours*, only *yours*."

I gave him hope because he deserved hope, because in spite of every trial in between, I *wanted* that heart and meant to be brave enough to have it.

This would be my greatest challenge: to follow my own heart and its emotions and stop letting the outside world in. The rest of humanity would dub the man in my arms as an ugly monster. I was determined not to allow such things to matter. I *knew* in my heart that he was no devil or demon, no monster, nothing worth fear, and I was adamant to cling to my own intuition.

With a soft sigh, Erik broke free of my hold, and I felt my soul go with him. A chill overtook my body where his had been and rattled me to my bones with a necessity to *feel him* again.

"Go in to bed, Christine," he commanded, meeting my stare, and though his tears were gone, I saw their dried remnants upon his one bare cheek and longed to *touch* them.

My gaze averted to the wrist he'd marked, and vibrant purple stared back in stark splotches. It didn't feel as guilty as it looked.

"I'm sorry," he whispered, wincing as I took in his damage, but I'd already shrugged it off to nothing. How could bruises matter when the kisses he left felt more lasting? "Will you...meet me tomorrow for your lesson?"

He asked a question he'd never asked before, but it was obvious he felt a need for assurance that I readily gave in a definite nod.

"Of course."

He still glanced at my wrist, and I thought it ridiculous to know such regret. I'd hurt him just as bad when I'd tried to unmask him. He only bore the disadvantage that his reprisal had evidence. "...Goodnight, Christine."

It was a dismissal, and though I hesitated a moment more, I obeyed and replied, "Goodnight, Erik."

My heart longed to stay, but my legs carried me off the stage and toward the entrance to the dormitories. I kept a lingering worry what the next night together would bring. He might put up walls, might hold back in fear of the damage he could cause. But I was adamant that I would be there waiting for him tomorrow and every day, and I'd prove his doubts unwarranted. Prove my heart, prove my soul, and prove that a mask didn't matter as much as my actions tonight made it seem. No, ...only the heart mattered, and his heart was *mine*.

Chapter Seven

Erik~

"Well done, Christine."

The praise might have been understated, but the awe in my voice made it hold more meaning, and I saw a reverberation of its colors upon her smiling lips. Her aria had been a source of brilliance tonight, lacking her usual tendency to second-guess and question sounds before letting them loose. Her training was coming along nicely, but I had no assurance that she would be ready for what I was about to throw in her path.

Gala night was quickly approaching, the launch into a season of opera, and I was determined that Christine would sing opening night and put herself in the forefront as a rising diva. *My* Christine... But it was difficult to look at her and see anything beyond a young girl still growing into the confidence she needed to possess.

So innocently exquisite, ...so desirous without even realizing it. I scolded my inevitable train of thought and tried to focus on talent alone. But...as she stood before me in her rehearsal attire, I allowed my gaze the right to roam her curves as if they were already mine, and I pondered her center-stage as the prima donna, lavished with attention and spotlights. To some degree, it was a disappointment and left me the bitter aftertaste of envy. I wasn't going to like sharing her with the world as much as I'd originally thought...

As I caught her blue stare again, I noted the blush upon her cheeks and wondered how blatant my musings were that she could read my wanting like an open book.

"Christine," I sighed, desperate not to show her how thrown I was, "it is late, and you sang beautifully tonight. Perhaps you should go in to bed."

"Must I?"

Was that disappointment to leave me? I wanted to change my mind, beg her to stay, to let me hold her, touch her, all the things I'd been longing for *days*, but with another heaved sigh, I concluded, "You need your rest. The show is approaching, and Madame Giry is working you to exhaustion. I am no better. I should be more conscious of your well-being."

"My well-being excels *only* in your presence," she declared with that *smile*. It was genuine and new in my company. Ever since the night I'd bruised her wrist and marked it as mine, she'd given me such smiles. I could not understand *why*, but I never questioned when every time pink lips arched, light twinkled in her blue eyes and illuminated happiness so pure that I yearned to have it forever.

"Then..." I hesitated before countering with a hint of apprehension, "Perhaps you should *always* be in my presence."

That smile again! What did it mean? Was she only humoring me, or did she agree? She never said so, as with a little shrug, she decided, "An angel is *always* with me, isn't that right, *ange*? So I will go in to bed now, but my angel will guard my every breath."

My gaze traced her features with a longing that tingled my fingertips. "I wish I were a *real* angel and could give your sentiment meaning."

"I don't." She shook her head, that smile ever-present as she tentatively approached my piano bench, swaying slightly on her feet at my side. "An angel would have to leave me for heaven, but you...you'll *never* leave me."

"Never."

She held her breath and lowered her eyes for a quick instant. ...*Shy*? I sought to read her but didn't have enough experience with *this* version of Christine. Smiles, blushes, coy...*like a girl in love.* The conclusion made me shiver and ache for it to be true.

"So I will go in to bed," she repeated with that grin, "but I have a promise for more moments like this to bring me sweet dreams."

"I am a sweet dream to you?" I inquired full of hope. "In spite of the unpleasant details in between? ...I hurt you last time I touched you."

She lifted the wrist I'd marked, a discolored bruise on its way to fading; she showed me without even a flash of condemnation. "When the mark is gone, will *you* then forget? Because I already have."

"Have you, Christine?"

I watched her timidly duck her eyes again before seeming to grasp conviction, and with a tremble to give her uncertainties away, she brought that lifted hand to my masked face. I stiffened with a lingering fear, recalling how she'd sought to steal my mask the last time we'd attempted touches, but I wanted so desperately to trust her that I forced myself to remain petrified in place and wait. If she wanted to unmask me, she need but do it. I'd be pliant as my own sweet dreams shattered, but perhaps that was our inevitable fate anyway.

I clenched my jaw to keep from lashing out in words and temper and glared fixedly at her approaching hand. But to my shocked surprise, she extended a single finger and brushed a languid caress along my exposed bottom lip. It was as if she hinted at our shared secret, the true distortion of my mouth, and validated the kisses it had taken the last time.

I stared at her beautiful face as she touched me,

and though she refused to meet my eye and only watched the progression of her touching finger, I saw no disgust or doubt. I saw emotions so gentle I could hardly believe they were mine.

As if timidity finally caught up, she withdrew with a brighter blush and bid, "Goodnight, Erik," with that sweet voice.

I couldn't even make a feasible reply, simply gaping as she turned and scurried off. Everything seemed to be falling exactly as I'd laid it out. ...Why then did I also know a terror for it to shatter before I could ever claim it? Curse my infernal pessimism!

But it hung like a dark cloud as I eventually gave up my staring vigil and retired to the shadows below. I tried to focus on the next step of my plan: ridding the stage of La Carlotta. An accident would be sufficient, a warning and a letter... I couldn't let Christine find out about the underlying deceptions to her push into the limelight. No, those had to remain my sins to bear in silence.

I was meticulously laying out the details in my head when I received my next shock of the evening. One of my alarms was resounding through the catacombs and calling me even at a distance, and with a heaved curse through the passages, I hurried my pace to seek out my intruder. I had traps and alarms at every point in the dark cellars for anyone who dared venture below, determined never to be taken unaware. I knew the deadliness of my traps before I even found the body, strangled by one of the ropes and dangling off the stone floor.

Joseph Buquet, meddling stagehand, his crutch was pinned between the rocks and likely set off the trap before he ever realized.

I felt no remorse for his death. He was at fault to seek out the Opera Ghost. What a fool! Transforming from lusting deviant to noble hero out to preserve Christine's innocence. Or perhaps he had been after simple revenge for a fall and a broken leg.

No matter. He'd have none of it now.

Making an annoyed face at his dangling, oversized body as I contemplated the effort it would take to rid me of his corpse, I chose to leave it until morning and walked onward. Ignorant bastard! And now when he went missing as all victims to my traps did, Christine might find reservations I'd hoped gone. Damn him! A nuisance in life *and* death!

I was muttering curses with every step, and perhaps my anger dulled my typically attuned senses because I did not gain my next, awaiting shock of the evening until I arrived outside the hidden door of my house. Someone was inside... I knew it before I ever set foot past the threshold, someone who'd managed to bypass traps and alarms and actually solved the riddle of the Opera Ghost's maze.

...There was only one person I could deduce with skills enough to anticipate my devices.

Scowling in growing aggravation, I burst through my door and greeted before suspicions were ever confirmed, "Daroga, you better have a very good reason for this unplanned visit and intrusion into my home without invitation."

Perhaps he had hoped for the element of surprise on his side, yet *he was* the surprised one as he leapt up from my couch and stammered, "Erik, ...it's been years."

I searched the daroga for hints of the exact number passed out of each other's presences, but he looked nearly the same. Small of stature, dark skin that insisted how out of place he was, simply gazing at him gave me the reminiscent sense of being in Persia, and I had to remind myself that was the past.

"A decade, give or take," I sharply filled in, "and yet your detective skills are obviously at their finest if you arrived at my home unharmed."

"Unlike your overweight friend?"

"Friend?" I spat. "The traps are for *enemies*, as should be implied by the dead body of a useless stagehand."

"More murders, Erik," the daroga tutted with disapproval.

"No, daroga," I curtly snapped. "Not this time. The traps are for my protection, and if someone *dies* in their grasp, I am not at fault. *Their* folly, not *mine*." Eyeing him snidely again, I added, "I have yet to reason why *you* are not dangling from one right now."

But the daroga shook his dark head and insisted matter-of-factly, "I know you too well, I suppose. Your traps were predictable."

"*Predictable!*"

"Did you not use a similar spread for the shah's palace?"

I sneered my perturbation. He was right, of course, but I'd never considered anyone from Persia finding me in the cellars of the Paris opera house, so repetition had been a matter of convenience.

"Damn you," I mumbled anyway and retorted, "I have worn out my patience with you already, so tell me why you have sought me out when you should be rotting away back in Persia. I have more important things to deal with than congenial visits from an old acquaintance."

"Acquaintance? I anticipated *friend* at least after all I did to help you escape the shah's dungeons."

More points I did not feel like reminiscing over tonight.

"What *things* could you possibly have to deal with?" the daroga questioned in his interrogative manner. Was it any wonder he'd been such a stellar law official for the shah's regime? His skills seemed just as pointed as ever as he surveyed my sitting room and awaited an answer.

Lying was futile; he knew all my tells. So I gave honesty instead, "I haunt the opera house."

"Ah yes, the resident ghost." He earned my glare of annoyance with his nonchalance. Asking questions he'd already researched answers to and then making my role inconsequential and a self-righteous crusade without value!

"And how long have you been spying on my life? Because none of it is your business anymore. We parted ways amicably. You cannot now come and preach on a moral high ground. It's too late for that. You knew what and who I was when you helped me escape."

"And look what I caused. I set you loose to terrorize another city."

"*Terrorize*, you bastard! I no longer kill without valid reason. I have more sophisticated tastes." I hesitated to reveal details, but gave one viable answer. "I play ghost to run the opera house in a better way than the ignorant management."

"*Better* way? *Your* way," he amended; he truly did know me too well.

"What does it matter to you? We're not in Persia anymore, daroga. I owe you *nothing* as far as I'm concerned. Now get out of my home."

The daroga shook his dark head doubtfully. "And...the young ballerina?"

I went numb and ground out, "She has *nothing* to do with you. Leave it be." How distracted did Christine make me that I hadn't noticed a presence spying on our lesson time?

"Will you lie and tell me that you are simply teaching her to sing?" He asked questions he'd already formed answers to, the *correct* answers.

"I *am* teaching her to sing."

"And?"

I cringed to make admissions. "Curse your interrogation! I'm in *love* with her! All right? Does that satisfy your exemplary detective skills? It is *not* a sin for me to fall in love."

But the daroga looked unconvinced about that. "Does she know the *real* sins on your head? ...Has she seen your face?"

"My face should not determine if she could love

me in return!" I roared.

"No, but...well, it does factor in, Erik," he somberly insisted. "A young and pretty girl might be thrown by its...distortions."

If he'd been anyone else, I would have strangled him for the remark, but considering he had indeed made it possible for me to be here and with Christine, I only scowled and ordered, "Get out. I'm done with this visit."

"Well, I'm not." The daroga took his previous seat on my couch, and unless I was to heave him out the door, I had no choice but to join him, dropping my heavy limbs into my chair and glaring unsuccessfully. "I'm actually not here to argue and judge your life, Erik. I...need your help."

"You sought *me* halfway across the world for help?"

"I had no other option," the daroga reported with a solemnity that I quieted to observe, only then noting the tenseness in his small shoulders, the age lines about his features, the weight of dread. "The shah...he knows *I* was the one to betray him and help you escape all those years back."

I scoffed in annoyance. "So he never gave up his quest for a scapegoat?"

"No, of course not. You were too valuable to him, Erik. When you were on his good side, helping him *murder*, he saw you as ally. Then you betrayed him and were set for execution for your folly, and he always knew one of his men had to have been involved in your escape. You weren't magician enough to poof out of his dungeon. He finally figured out that it was me, and never mind the loyalty I've shown since your exit from the kingdom..." He paused, and his desolation was etched into his frown as he revealed, "The shah has my wife and infant son locked in his jail. He says he will keep them as prisoners until I bring you back to fill their place."

I chuckled. I couldn't help it. "And your

platform to capture me into your clutches was to tell me the *truth*? How unoriginal! You forget that I don't know your so-called wife or child. Why should I care to help you by putting myself back in the shah's custody?"

"Because you *owe* me. I risked everything to save you. *And* because I'm not asking for your surrender; I'm asking for your help to free them without the shah's knowledge. You know the inner tunnels of the palace, the secret paths in and out. You *built* them! You could help me save my family *and* yourself!"

My mind flashed images of Christine. Her debut was about to be ours, and her heart was so close to my reach... "I can't go to Persia with you, daroga. I have responsibilities here."

"You have responsibilities to *me* as well," he countered and pleaded his desperation in his dark stare. "Is this about the girl? Because if she knows nothing of you, Erik, then you are deluding yourself to claim real love. My *wife* knows me and every flaw I possess and loves me still, and now she suffers for that love and because of *you*. Reality is more important than the fantasies you've built in your head."

"Christine *will* love me," I stated with conviction. "You don't know *us*, daroga. You don't know the hope she's given me."

"*Will* love you?" he repeated doubtfully. "And if she doesn't? If you tell her that you were once a murderer for the shah of Persia, that you have traps all over your underground kingdom to kill for you, that you hurt anyone who doesn't play by your rules, will she still love you? Will you force love upon her if she refuses? You're right, Erik; your face shouldn't matter, but your past *does*. And until she knows the truth, your little Christine can't truly *love you*." Rising with a huff, he concluded, "Tell her, Erik. Tell her everything. If she *loves* you as you wish, then she will understand why you *must* help me and return to

Persia. You need to fix *your* mistakes and atone for your soul. She will agree and wait for your return if she can love you through your truth."

"Damn you," I hissed. "I need not listen to a word you say. I may have owed you something a lifetime ago, but I don't now. And so help me God, if you put any thoughts in Christine's head, if you even speak to her, I'll renege our so-called acquaintanceship and you will end like that deviant stagehand in the passages. Show yourself out, daroga. I've nothing more to say to you."

He hesitated one last breath and replied, "You know the right thing to do, Erik. Somewhere beneath all of that arrogance, you have a conscience. It's what convinced you to leave the shah's service, and it still exists now. You like to pretend you are unfeeling, but that is the greatest lie of all. Tell your Christine the truth and see how she handles it, and then...I beg of you, help me save my family."

There were tears in his dark gaze, but he left my house without another pleading, and thank God for that! I was struck too deep. I knew the daroga; I knew he was a good man with an honorable soul, and as much as I wanted to be unmoved by his plight, it hit me violently. What if that were Christine in the shah's dungeons? *My* love taken away...

How this night had spiraled out of control I didn't know! It had gone from such hope to such despair in less than an hour. Now I had a dead body in my care and a loyalty I didn't like in my heart, and I hung my head in my hands and wondered what I was going to do.

Chapter Eight

Christine~
     From the moment I entered the theatre, I knew something was amiss. Whispers all around between cast and crew, among the ballerinas, the chorus, filling every direction like a low hum.
     Ducking beneath the drone and delving into its cloud, I searched for Meg and found her frantically exchanging gossip in a group. As soon as she saw me, she deserted the throng and caught my arm, pulling me into our own little chatter bubble.
     "What's happened?" I asked, still glancing about at stunned expressions and somber solemnity.
     "Joseph Buquet is *missing.* The managers refuse to say more, but we all know it was the ghost!"
     "Ghost..." I shook a doubtful head. "Ghosts don't exist, Meg. It's ridiculous!"
     "Christine, hush! If he hears you-"
     "I will go missing as well?" I finished for her and shook my head again. "Everyone is so keen to pin crimes on a figment of imagination and ignore that something sinister and evil could be the cause. There could be an abuser within the very cast or crew, and no one ventures for *reality* when the ghost is the more entertaining conclusion."
     "Someone in the cast or crew? That's...slander, Christine. You're making accusations."
     "As you do for a *ghost,*" I insisted and would

not back down. Always the ghost, and I refused to listen. The last time I'd hurt Erik with my doubts. I would not let that happen again and put credence to cries of 'Opera Ghost'. If Buquet disappeared, there were many more reasons than a crime of Erik's doing.

Meg was upset with my confrontation, and her green eyes shown with hurt as she replied, "Sometimes believing *is* reality, and if you can't see it, then you're going to get yourself into trouble. Ghosts *do* exist, Christine, and they are more dangerous than anyone ever suspects."

That was all she said, abandoning me for her more naïve friends ready to regard every tale of the Opera Ghost with wholehearted faith. As I surveyed the many others on edge and anxious as if anticipating ghosts to fly in overhead, I considered at least asking Erik about the disappearance. Not accusing, *never* accusing again. But a solitary inquiry couldn't hurt...

Rehearsal was relatively quiet and somber...like we were already a theatre in mourning, and after the main cast was released for the day, the ballerinas were kept and berated a little longer for our lackluster portrayal. It was expected; what wasn't expected was a summons from my managers.

"Mademoiselle Daaé?" Monsieur Firmin called and received a perturbed glare from Madame Giry to be interrupted mid-scolding.

I lifted nervous eyes to her, but though she scowled, she waved me away with Firmin without spoken protest. ...Insult would have been her retaliation, but it was uttered in stare alone as we left.

Firmin gave nothing away until we entered his office where his partner, Monsieur Andre, waited with an apprehensive expression. My stomach knotted at such attention as I devised every possible reason for such a summons. Every one was unpleasant. ...Could they know I was taking lessons with their own elusive Opera Ghost?

"Mademoiselle Daaé, is it?" Andre questioned,

and I gave a dutiful nod, not trusting my voice. "Well, mademoiselle, we are taking you out of the *corps de ballet*."

A gasp tore from my lungs, and without a thought, I dropped propriety and *begged* without shame. "Please, messieurs. I will do better; I promise. Don't cast me out."

"No, no," Andre bid with defenselessly raised hands. "Not cast out, mademoiselle. We have...another task for you." He cringed his distaste, and I assumed he was delaying bad news. "We need you to fill La Carlotta's role."

"W...what?" I was sure I'd heard him wrong, gaping with wide eyes while my brain replayed his words and could find no suitable variation. What name sounded *similar* to La Carlotta without *being* La Carlotta? Because if I'd heard correctly, then that meant... "I don't understand."

"Neither do we," Andre admitted, looking me up and down with a sneer of disdain.

"Andre, ...at least be polite to the girl," Firmin scolded and shifted focus to me with a sugarcoated smile I did not believe for an instant. "There was a little accident in La Carlotta's dressing room. As she changed her costume, her rather large and ornate mirror *fell* on her. We can't say how such a tragedy could have happened. It is not in our interest to run an environment without proper safety, but La Carlotta was so startled that she refuses to perform."

"Is she...all right?" I spoke but hardly realized my own words as my mind processed every detail in a whirlwind.

"A few cuts and bruises, nothing severe," Andre reported, "but the Gala night performance is two days away, and without anyone to sing her role, we are *ruined*. Every ticket is sold, every seat filled, and it is too late to cancel."

Gala night... I couldn't reason anything and tripped mercilessly over every letter past my lips.

"And...you are asking *me* to sing her role?"

"We were told you knew it," Firmin insisted. "Do you, mademoiselle?"

"Y...yes, but-"

"Done then! *You* will sing!" Andre exclaimed without ever asking me.

"Wait, Andre," Firmin spoke up. "Shouldn't we at least *hear* her sing first? What if she isn't...any good?"

He seemed to seek a courteous way to question my talent, and I quickly justified, "I take lessons."

"See!" Andre pointed out. "Lessons and all!"

"We should still test her out-"

"Why? You act as if our patrons attend to *hear* opera," Andre bid with a chuckle. "A pretty face that sings on pitch will do, and at least get us through the Gala. After that, we'll find a suitable replacement." Eyeing me again, he commanded, "Be ready to sing tomorrow morning, mademoiselle, and...don't come to rehearsal in that blasted tutu. You are not a ballerina anymore. Dress...like a *diva*," he instructed, tossing his hands out as if it were simple.

A diva...and how did a diva dress?

"Don't worry, mademoiselle," Firmin called to my growing agitation. "It's *dress* rehearsal. They'll fit you for costumes as soon as we begin."

"Oh..." I glanced between the two men, unsure I hadn't *dreamed* the last few minutes of conversation. Me...the diva. It never occurred to me to question their contention as I dazedly left the office and headed for the theatre.

My mind was a malaise of wandering thoughts. ...The theatre was empty; rehearsal was over; I'd bypassed Madame Giry's scolding; I wouldn't have to endure her scolding or belittlement again; I was no longer a ballerina; I was the diva...

Terror choked the back of my throat with that single thought. ...A diva, and I'd stand center-stage and sing in front of everyone...

"What did the managers want?"

Erik's question jolted me out of my head, and I stared at his masked shape on the stage as if I could not comprehend for a long pause. "I... They want me to sing."

"And?" he pushed with a flicker of impatience.

"I can't come to rehearsal in a tutu."

"Christine!"

"They want me to sing La Carlotta's role," I finally gave the answer he obviously wanted, and when he showed no legitimate surprise, I put the pieces together. "They knew I had the role learned. How did they know that? One of your notes?"

He shrugged innocently, making it seem not to matter. "La Carlotta stormed out, and they were as desperate for a lead as I was to thrust you into their spotlight. Do not be sore, Christine. Take opportunities when they arise and clasp with both hands. I placed something incredible at your feet; the correct response is gratitude, not suspicion. Even *I* know that."

"Thank you," I obediently replied yet still could not claim genuine gratitude when I was so overwhelmed.

"Come. We have much work to do, and with my managers still lolling about, we cannot work here."

I nodded acceptance and followed him into the wings, drifting in and out of neuroses. My fears attacked in waves as I cast one last glance out at the theatre before we left and imagined it full. ...A sold out audience, all eyes on me... Oh God, I couldn't do it!

"This is to be *your* dressing room," Erik called back over his shoulder.

Mine. I'd never had a dressing room, tripping over ballerinas at every costume change in our common room, and now...he opened the door and led us inside and I gasped onward.

"They had it cleaned out before the crew left.

Ready for your use," Erik told me as he turned up lamps, and I observed through wide-eyed bewilderment.

It was double the size of the room all the ballerinas were crammed into. Thick, soft carpet, brocade wallpaper of pink roses and lace, ...a full-length mirror that drew my nervous stare.

"The managers said Carlotta's mirror fell upon her," I distantly bid as I approached it and set timid fingers to my reflection.

"A freak accident," Erik replied, watching me through studious eyes I could glimpse in the mirror's glass. "You should have no worries over such absurd situations; this mirror is bolted to the wall. It cannot fall."

I walked to the edge of the frame, and as he said, there was no space between the gold trim and the wall...as if it were a part of the wall itself.

"We will run the entire role now."

I watched his masked reflection in the mirror, and though I nodded agreement, in a small whisper, I bid, "I can't do this, Erik."

He held my gaze with all the confidence I could not find and never wavered. "You were *born* to do this, Christine. What speaks now is only your inexperience, but once you are upon that stage where you were meant to be, you will sing and you will shine. Don't doubt me, *ange*."

"*Ange*," I repeated and could not suppress a touch of a smile. "I thought *you* were the angel between the two of us."

"I'll be an angel, and you be a diva," he gently concluded. "Neither of us fit those roles, not in actuality, but no one else needs to know that. Let it be a secret between the two of us, a secret that exists only within these walls and in our voices. To everyone else, play the role; be the diva, and I will carry the knowledge of your true self just as you carry mine."

I held his mismatched stare in the mirror and

94

wondered if it could be that easy. Pretend confidence, and breeze onto the stage like a veteran performer and not the ingénue I was. Trick the rest of the theatre and *myself* until it became natural.

As I breathed an uncertain sigh, Erik came up behind me, timidly setting his palms to my shoulders and making me regard the mirror's pictures.

"I do not see a diva," he said and tilted his masked face inquisitively above my shoulder. "No, not yet, but what I do see is a spark that not everyone possesses, Christine. A fire that can become an inferno if you let it out. I want to be *burned* by your blaze. Light it up and pour it into the music, and nothing else will matter."

I nodded; I wanted to do exactly as he requested, but I couldn't help but doubt my ambition. "They're going to hate me at rehearsal tomorrow. Moved from the ballet to a leading role practically overnight? When there are others who are probably more qualified and seasoned? I don't blame them."

"No more thoughts of *them*," Erik ordered with a sternness that had me biting my lip. "I only care about you and me. Let them insult and degrade you with their words. Words are *all* they have, and they only mean as much as *you* let them. Ignore every single syllable, and recall that they only wound if you drop your shield. And when rehearsal ends, *I* will raise you up again and fill your ears with the praises you deserve."

He still kept my gaze in the glass, but his hand rose from my shoulder and fingers brushed a caress down my cheek. I shivered in spite of every other heavy thought in my head and unconsciously leaned closer to those delicate fingers as they outlined my jaw.

"I look at you," he huskily breathed, "and I see such glorious perfection. Mine should be the only opinion to matter because I know your true heart, and they will only know your talent. Your voice is exquisite, and it will inspire jealousy and bitter envy at every turn. But it is only a piece of you. They will covet *its* beauty when really they should covet the beauty of your soul. You are extraordinary, Christine Daaé, and I am but another humble worshipper in your shadow."

I was in awe to have such praises as mine and know he meant every one as they illuminated blue and green eyes and made their glow twinkle. I knew without a doubt at that moment that I loved him.

"Now let us prepare for tomorrow," he decided and drew away with a reluctance I mimicked. But music had to take precedence, and there, in my new dressing room, we acted out an entire opera. We had no piano, so he plucked starting pitches out of the air and stood back as I walked the blocking with careful precision, imagining the rest of the cast as Erik hummed their lines and his golden timbre soothed any nerves that sought to arise. I did exactly as he'd said; I feigned diva and confidence and played the character with wholehearted conviction. Every glance at his observing approval made me undoubting I *could* do it.

And in the melee of our rehearsal and my growing fatigue, I forgot to ask Erik about Joseph Buquet's disappearance. The thought only returned as I entered my small room in the opera dormitories, but with memories of Erik's voice and adoration to comfort me, I found I didn't care about anything else. Only opera and music and a masked angel.

Chapter Nine

Erik~

Between Christine and me, I was the nervous one the next day as rehearsal began and the managers called a meeting to announce Christine's new role. I was so anxious that I could not keep still as I paced hidden in Box 5 and fisted urgent hands.

She looked so...*calm.* It was the façade I'd built her the previous night, and she accepted it and carried herself with grace and dignity as half-hearted accolades went about the cast for her new title. Just as predicted, they were jealous, many cold stares from other sopranos in minor roles who were more qualified than Christine for the lead. But to my pride, Christine never faltered, acting the diva persona as her shield. I had an urge to ring out with applause, for this role would be more difficult to maintain than the real staged one!

As rehearsal began, my pride swelled and exceeded its limits to overtake my every thought and feeling. She was...*exceptional.* She performed it precisely as she had in her dressing room the night before, and I was awestruck, hypnotized by her, *only her.*

This moment justified everything I'd done to put her in that place, and to glimpse the surprise all around from managers and cast was further proof. She quickly went from a suitable substitute to their little treasure in one glorious performance. ...No one would doubt her talent again.

Christine was rushed from place to place all day: the stage, the dressing room for costume fittings, back to the stage. She had no break, and that was the only part that worried me when she handled everything else to perfection. So as the cast was released, later than usual, I resigned myself not to work her further. No, tonight I would just settle with being in her company.

When she returned to her dressing room finally alone, I awaited her and delighted in the bright, even if fatigued smile she granted my masked intrusion. Before a word, she closed out the world and slid the lock into place, no chance for intrusions. It overwhelmed me when I pondered that no one in the rest of the useless world would *ever* lock themselves in a room with the fabled Opera Ghost and his disfigured face. But Christine...well, I already said she was extraordinary.

"*Ange?*" she questioned, and I saw doubts finally break through the diva façade and return the girl I loved to me.

I approached before I ever gave the praises she needed, and when I stood before her, literally within the shadow her body cast by lamplight, I knelt on the soft carpet and caught her hands in my shaking ones, bowing my head to graze my bottom lip to her knuckles in an attempted kiss.

"I would happily die in this place," I whispered and kept her hands in mine. "Reverently kneeling before your altar and adoring you. My God, Christine, you held an entire theatre in the palm of your hand and made everyone, including me, long to fall at your feet and beg for your favor."

To my surprise, she suddenly knelt on the carpet with me and slid her fingers between mine to make us unbreakable. "You are the *only one* I wanted to please, the *only one* I sang for."

"What a gift! I hardly deserve it, but I've never wanted anything so much," I admitted and stared mesmerized into her blue eyes. Such emotions! Tied deep to her very soul. Had I ever received their brilliance this unguarded and exposed? They made more than just her voice *mine*, and I refused to let them go.

"Erik," she whispered, and the reverberation of each syllable overcame me as they raced my spine and made me shiver. I was certain she meant to say more, but...sense knew this was the path to complications and the truths I did not want to reveal, truths she deserved to know...after the Gala night. Her debut and inevitable triumph had to come first.

So with a huff of my own chosen disappointment, I slowly drew away from her, rising on shaky knees. "You should go in to bed. We will forgo our lesson tonight. You need to rest."

She mirrored my disappointment. It was clearly etched now that her diva façade was gone, but with a reluctant nod, she rose, smoothing her skirts. I noticed that her hands trembled.

And so I made her the vow I'd given in my mind, "After the Gala performance." My gaze spoke the volumes I longed to tell, and I noted how it uplifted her spirit as she grinned at me and nodded.

"After the Gala performance," she repeated, and with great effort, she turned and abandoned me in her dressing room. I missed her from the first second she was gone, but I knew this was for the best. I couldn't chance putting too much upon her, not with the show but a day away. It would have been selfish.

I left through the mirror. I hadn't told her that *I* had also been the one to put her in this particular dressing room. Its mirror was attached to the wall for a reason; it was actually a secret doorway directly down to the catacombs. More than that, it was a window. I could watch her from the opposite side, and no one would know or catch my constant presence. It seemed the most logical option when so many others would be in and out of the room during the next days. Now I could always make sure she stayed strong.

A mirrored doorway, and as my thoughts hung heavy with a guilt I didn't want, I began to devise a plan to use it. After the performance... I'd bring her through the mirror and into my world, and I'd tell her *everything*.

Typically, I did not indulge keeping a conscience. I considered it a little masochistic voice inside meant to spoil living. Now that the daroga had been resurrected into my world, I had no choice. *He* became my external conscience and a nuisance I didn't know how to rid myself of.

From his first appearance, he paid me a visit every night. I grew to expect his presence before I entered my home, awaiting me after Christine's lesson with a weary, blame-filled expression. As much as I wanted to stay unmoved, he was *torturing* me into regret and guilt, filling my ears with stories of his wife, how he'd met her, how they'd fallen in love, his infant son, every detail I didn't want because they were so humanizing. As much as I denied his nightly requests for help, we both knew I was on the verge of succumbing. I hated to admit it, but this was *my* mess to clean. It killed me to consider that I was going to have to go back to Persia and fix this if I ever wanted peace...from my own mind *and* the aggravating daroga.

But where did that leave Christine? I loathed the idea of being separated from her, especially when she was the *only* bright spot in my life. I reasoned the solution was to tell her *everything* and beg her to wait for me, loyal and true, until I returned for her. ...It seemed like a death sentence.

After the Gala performance... And I was on pins and needles with its quick approach. When the day of the show finally arrived, I was adamant that I would not cower. I needed to make admissions as if in reconciliation for my soul, and I had faith that she would listen and accept me despite my sins. She had to; she'd already vowed herself as *mine*. The rest seemed simple.

The countdown to curtain and places had begun when I arrived on the opposite side of her mirror and peered inside. My heart halted its flustered beats with the very image put before me.

Her costume girl was helping her dress, and Christine wore only her flimsy undergarments. Through the lamplight, I could make out the silhouettes of her every curve in a far more provocative manner than her ballerina attire had once permitted. I did not scold my spying, not when desire struck so violent and abrupt that it startled morals into hiding. She was so *beautiful* and sensuous, and every thought of leaving *this* when it was so close to truly being mine made me ache inside and out. What if I lost her while I was away and returned to nothing...? No, I couldn't let that happen.

My hungry gaze traced the delicate curve of her hip, up its perfect arch, and lingered on the swell of her breasts, their peaks making enticing shadows against thin white material. My fingers tingled with the need to tear fabric away and steal a taste of their glorious sweetness.

She was just so *perfect*; it frightened me because surely sinners with ugly faces were not meant to belong with exquisiteness. The voice of sense somewhere in the recesses of my mind insisted she was a rising star. All Paris would see her tonight and want her attention; could I believe she'd indulge the thin cord between our hearts when so many greater offers would be tossed like flowers at her feet? Once again came that nagging twist of jealousy, making me regret this entire endeavor. I should have kept her for *myself*.

As I worried and pondered what the night

would bring, I watched her with a stab of bittersweet affection as she dressed and became the prima donna before my eyes. She never gave doubts away, but I glimpsed their reflection in the back of her gaze where no one else would spy them: anxiety, fear, nerves. But her posture was stoic and lovely, the queen about to take her throne. My Christine, and it was a bit of consolation to know she acted the part for *me*, because I had talked her into it, and it was just that: a role that would fall away when we were alone together. No one else would know that.

The costume girl scurried out to the call of two minutes to curtain, and as Christine was left alone, her shoulders sagged and the pretense peeled back its layers to give a glimpse of the flickering soul within.

"Christine," I breathed softly and set my fingers to the glass between us, and though she could not know my hiding place, I saw her react to my call just as she had the first time on that very first day we met. She shivered and started, but there was no apprehension, only a beaming smile because she knew *me*.

I was doubtless that would be my saving grace in the end. She read the secrets of my heart and had to realize that every evil I'd had a hand in committing did not alter its beat or its eternal devotion to hers. She had to know...

Gala night was a huge success. I watched from my box and savored every second as Christine assumed the diva role and triumphed over every battle in her path. She was fearless and graceful, and it was impossible to find the seam in her façade. Only I who loved the real girl beneath knew the truth and kept our intimate secret within the confines of my ribcage.

At final curtain call, Christine received a standing ovation, and I cheered as vivaciously as every other patron, noting the tremble in her limbs that she sought to conceal in her deep curtsy. The façade was cracking, and desperate to steal her before it evaporated to nothing, I ran through my passages to the mirror's doorway, impatient for her appearance.

I gave long enough for the costume girl to help her change into a dressing gown, observing her distant silence and dull smiles for the help. No, she needed *me* now. No one else could raise her up where she belonged like I could, but I had limitations and forced restraint until at last the costume girl left the room. *Finally...*

"Christine," I whispered her name and watched the spark within her reignite and gleam as she tilted her dark head inquisitively, seeking me out with an urgency I adored. She wanted *me*; I knew she'd always want *me*.

"Erik," she pleaded in a breathless whisper. "Please, *ange*."

I did not deny her. No, without preparation, I opened the mirror and saw her eyes grow wide as she leapt back before finding my shape and calming her fright.

"Erik! What is that?"

But I simply extended my hand through the threshold and held her gaze. She never hesitated. She set her hand in mine and wove our fingers together with a timid smile as I drew her into the darkness and shut out the rest of the world.

I had a lantern ready for her comfort, but the passages were no more than darkened stone tunnels. When one knew the correct path, there was no fear of traps or obscurity. It was all rather boring, and I found that my concentration preferred to lock on the girl following my gentle tugs without a single question. To my mind, she had made her choice already, and everything else I would spread before her tonight would not alter it. She'd given up her world to come with me; that alone spoke volumes.

"You have yet to tell me where we are going," she finally said after long minutes of only our echoing footfalls.

I glanced back at her and delighted in the fact that not even my masked face etched in shadows got a reaction, nothing but her continued curiosity. "My home. You did not think I lurked about the theatre day and night, did you?"

"And...does your concept of 'home' include rooms and furniture? It's not another damp, spider-infested cellar, is it?"

I actually chuckled at her light teasing, savoring the smile that never left her lips. She felt safe in my presence and *trusted* me; it was such a wonderful blessing.

"I cannot vouch for whether spiders inhabit its rooms or not," I returned with the same humor. "But it is *not* another cellar. I promise that you will be pleasantly surprised."

"We shall see."

I delighted in the challenge and only further when we finally arrived and I brought her through the front door. I'd left the fire dwindling in the hearth, and it gave a welcoming warmth that radiated about our bodies and chased away lingering chills. My home was exactly that, and as she observed the details of a sitting room not much different than one owned by any affluent man in the world above, I relished her surprise.

Releasing her hand as I moved to stoke the fire back to life, I kept half my attention on her observations as she wandered about, scanning furnishings, the thick rugs and covered walls that looked nothing like the stone outside, my piano resting in the corner, odds and ends. It was almost ordinary.

"Well?" I pushed from my place at the hearth. "Perhaps there is a random spider spinning a web in a corner, but for the most part, it *is* a home, isn't it?"

She grinned and nodded, and I memorized her image. My Christine in my sitting room and happy to be here with me. The newly beaming firelight illuminated her vision and made reddened hues in her dark, loose curls. How I ached to touch her! But first...

With a smile I could not restrain, I approached and knelt at her feet as I had after her first dress rehearsal performance, her awestruck worshipper. "Shall I now tell you how wonderful you were tonight?" She gave a nod with her feigned diva attitude, and I chuckled as I bid, "You *were* an angel, Christine. You surpassed mortal prima donna and became a heavenly being. I feel so certain I do not deserve you in my life. Angels belong in heaven and should know only wonders on earth, and I...I am no wonder."

"To me, you are."

I lifted a timid hand and dared to cup her cheek in my palm, astounded to see her delight in my touch. More blessings I did not deserve. "There are so many things I haven't told you. I...I've been afraid. You mean *everything*, and if I lose you..."

A furrow lined her brow, but she did not shrink away from my caress as she bid, "You won't lose me. How could you possibly? *You* are the very reason I sang tonight, Erik. You inspire me and make me *alive*. Nothing you tell me will change that."

Doubt whispered warnings in my head, but I put them to sleep and decided to trust her and the innocence in her eyes. ...Perhaps innocence wasn't stable enough to hold such credence.

Huffing a deep, forced inhalation, I let walls and guard crumble and admitted in genuine honesty, "I have not always been the man you have before you. My past...it is degrading and an abomination. I spent most of my life tormented."

"Because of your face," she concluded, somber and with hints of compassion.

Though it knotted my heart simply to recall or share such atrocity, I nodded and quickly went on, shying from a subject I did not want to broach. "And I retaliated. Pain for pain. I...hurt people, Christine, ...killed people."

The furrow deepened into a chasm full of questions, but all she managed was a soft, "Oh..."

"Yes, sometimes for my protection, ...sometimes for my pleasure. There were so many who wronged me and denounced my existence. I saw no grievance in revenge. I killed until killing became a talent. Others used it to their advantage. I became an assassin for the shah of Persia, killing his enemies, torturing without care or remorse..."

I hated admitting my sins; they made me weak and showed the true black stains on my soul. But Christine gave little away of her thoughts, keeping solemn and listening pensively with my hand still delicate against her cheek. I hoped touch anchored her to the Erik before her and not the one I was building memories of.

"Christine, ...say something."

"These things you're telling me," she softly beseeched, "they are your *past*." She was seeking assurances without the questions.

My nod was hesitant because...well, I had current skeletons in my closet, and regret only came with the fact that I must reveal them to her. "Killing for pleasure was addictive; it was easy to enjoy having such power and hurt for the injustices I'd suffered in my lifetime. But...at some point, it grew stale, and I didn't want a *killer* to be all I was. I needed to get out and find something better in the world. That was how I ended here at the opera."

"As their ghost..."

"Yes."

"You told me that you didn't hurt people."

"...Not for pleasure."

Betrayal flickered in her blue eyes; I saw it interspersed in hurt, and I could already conclude the train of her thoughts. *This* was my greatest fear. Not a past as a murderer in Persia, but a present as a vengeful ghost with unexplained accidents to account for.

"But...you hurt people?"

"Sometimes," I replied with a nonchalant shrug, and as she tensed, I pressed my hand firmer to her cheek, determined not to let go yet. "Sometimes it is unavoidable. I must protect myself and my secrets, and if others put me in jeopardy, I must react."

"With violence," she whispered, desolate and soft.

"How quickly you disregard the violence I have been on the other side of and endured as victim!" I justified. "I was beaten and tortured; even as a child, I was subject to ridicule, to fists, left for dead more times than I care to count."

"An eye for an eye?" she offered with a dubious shake of her head. "Hurt because you've been hurt? But what about forgiveness?"

"I am seeking forgiveness *from you*," I reminded with growing impatience when she again shook her head.

"No, I am not responsible for your soul and its sins. You do not seek forgiveness; you seek validation of your excuses, permission to hurt, and if I give it, then I am no better than you are."

Christine suddenly recoiled beyond my touch, and I grew urgent and terrified as she overflowed in reservations and suspicions built. "What about the stories of the ghost that circulate the opera? ...The stagehands that disappear? ...What about Joseph Buquet?"

She could have concluded answers on her own, and they would have been accurate. But I glimpsed a remaining ember of hope in her blue stare, a prayer that I would deny involvement. Though I contemplated lying, I knew I couldn't. I'd lie, and she'd know this time that it *was* a lie.

"Dead, but not of my own hands," I explained

as I hastily got to my feet. She thought I would touch her again; I knew it as she stepped further away, and I heaved a curse beneath my breath.

"What does that mean?"

"It means," I snapped, "that he ventured where he should not go and became victim to one of my traps. I must keep myself *protected*, as I said, and my traps may be deadly but they do their job well enough. And the other stagehands... Well, sometimes accidents happen and sometimes they are necessary. Those who see my mortal existence cannot very well go free to spread the tale and give a human fallibility to a supposed ghost! That would be suicide! Sometimes...I must *kill* to keep my secret."

Tears rimmed Christine's eyes, and I could not fathom why. Had I not explained it well enough? Surely she should see my point! One would think she'd want me protected!

"Why do you cry?" I snapped, and as I came close, she pulled back and lifted shaking hands to stop me. "I've done *nothing* to deserve your tears. I haven't been cruel or mean; I have barely *touched* you! All I've done is state the truth."

"I know your secret," she insisted in a choked voice. "I know you are only a man. Am I now another liability? Would it be just as simple for you to *kill me* and keep your secrets as your own?"

"Kill *you*?" I demanded, confused why she would deduce such a preposterous outcome. "Of course not! I *love* you!"

She whimpered with my words, and I felt sick to my stomach. I'd given a heart, and I wasn't sure I should have.

But with utter conviction, I stated, "And you love *me*."

"I don't *know you*," she retorted, tears falling faster and glistening in the firelight. "You told me that you didn't hurt others as everyone said, but you *do*. You lied to me, and now you want me to qualify your transgressions and dub murder forgivable. You aren't even *sorry* for what you've done. You think you have valid reasons to *kill* people."

Each sentence grew more hysterical until she was gasping breaths caught by sobs. But abrupt and unanticipated, she silenced, and realization flickered in wide eyes. "And...Carlotta? Did you...? Oh, please tell me that you didn't cause her accident."

"I did, but it was *for you*. It was the only way to get you onstage and heard." I could not reason where her gratitude was. I had given her *everything* she'd ever wanted, and she only sobbed harder and hugged her body with shaking arms. "Christine, this is ridiculous! I didn't *kill* Carlotta! I just startled her. I knew I'd cause no serious damage. And besides, her death would have had Gala night cancelled and your opportunity lost."

"And that is all that mattered to you!" she suddenly shrieked and surprised me with her aggression. I had never seen it from her and thought she was incapable of real rage and fire. ...Despite its inception, I liked it. It showed me that she was stronger than either of us realized. "Gala night would have been canceled, but Carlotta would have been *dead* by your hands and without remorse! Have you no regard for the worth of human life?"

"Human life is a cesspool of vindictive leeches and poisonous vipers. They bite and sting and know no remorse either! Why should I be the one to carry guilt when they have made me a monster without mercy?"

"Because you *kill* those who stand in your way, and...that isn't right, Erik," she said, soft amidst her cascading tears. "You are not a god." The statement seemed to ignite another realization, and in the center of a sob, she demanded, "You told me that you were no demon or devil, and yet every assessment of you screams otherwise. Perhaps that was a lie as well..."

Her words pierced into my body and left

wounds so deep within the marrow of my bones. *Demon, devil...* I'd endured such titles from a cruel world, but to Christine, I was supposed to be angel...

"How dare you?" I snapped back, and without thought, I lunged toward her before she could move away and caught her forearms in my hands, yanking them free of her solacing embrace and pinning them to her sides.

Love...I loved her, a voice in my heart tried to remind, but I did not *see* the girl I loved before me. I saw the same ugliness the world gave and a creature worthy of only *hate*.

"Erik, please!" she shouted and fought my hold, but I dragged both wrists to the small of her back and clasped them in one of my large hands, easily restraining her despite her struggles.

"Erik is dead," I declared coldly. "You killed him with your cruelty and arose the *devil* in his place. That is what you want, isn't it? A demon, Satan, a temptation you couldn't have refused and cannot be held accountable for. Because if you love a murderer who is *just* a murderer, that is an atrocity brought to life. So a devil you'll have, and your soul can stay pure. What kind of lover would I be if I condemned you to hell?"

I abhorred my threats and *her* for believing them, and with a grating chuckle and every word burning my throat, I spat, "*Devil*. You think beneath this mask is the face of Satan. Well, look and see if you find hellfire and brimstone in my eyes. Do you see the devil? Because I would have thought he'd be better looking and claim beauty as a weapon, but I...no, I'm ugly. Let me show you."

My free hand went for my mask, and knowing the horror I was about to reveal did not stop me. It was too late; I'd already lost. What difference did anything make anymore?

Fixing my glare on her tear-stained face, I took off my mask and unleashed hell.

Chapter Ten

Christine~

The term *devil* fell back and suffocated in a throng of other appellations that climbed over one another and fought for supremacy in my addled head.

God works in mysterious ways... This was its own mystery. A man or a corpse brought to life... I saw *dead,* and yet with a fury so great in its ugly planes that it *must be alive.*

My breaths were shallow gasps, resounding the air between our mouths, and I could not stop their hastening pace, so fast that I grew lightheaded and wondered if I was *creating* the horror I gazed upon in my hysteria. Perhaps it wasn't as bad, and my eyes were deceiving me. Perhaps *all of this* was a nightmare, and I was actually asleep in my bed awaiting the Gala night performance and over-laden in anxiety. What I saw...couldn't be real.

"Look at the *devil,* Christine!" Erik growled and pinched my arms tighter behind my back. I gave a cry at his fierceness and made myself focus and list the reasons this *wasn't* the devil.

There was no beauty here, nothing to entice temptations from his victims. He was half a skeleton, bones prevalent and uncovered every place flesh should exist to house their vulnerable state. No nose as if such an imperative structure had been ripped away along with the skin on that side, and an eyeball exposed in its socket without a fully formed lid to soften its spherical shape. I recalled every nuance of the malformed mouth, but alone, it hadn't been worthy of disgust. As part of the whole package of distortions, it bore a new wave of shock.

My tears blurred a damaged canvas, and even as I blinked and let them fall, they collected again and again over the surface of sight until I finally closed my eyes and stopped looking altogether. The Opera Ghost was a disfigured murderer, and I was ashamed because I loved him.

With a roar that seemed rooted at the core of his being, he shouted, "*Look at me*! Look at me, Christine! Damn you!"

And I sobbed and was afraid to open my eyes and see such anger, terrified I'd meet my end at hands I'd adored when they'd played music for me. Would they now appear just as beautiful as they strangled me?

Enraged further by my refusal, the hand squeezing my wrists forced my body forward until without consent or struggle, I was pressed to his length with nowhere to escape. I could feel his every heaved breath in lungs flush to mine, moving both our bodies while my shallow echoes never reached so deep.

And then...to my terror, I noted a detail that made my skin burn in pinks; he was...aroused, and I gave a choked gasp to feel it and know what he wanted. Those were the sensations that frightened me, ones that heated my lower belly and stirred my stability as they raced incessant tremors through the network of my veins. Desire... And it felt like a betrayal to my sense of morality to admit I felt it for a murderer.

"*Look at me!*" Erik commanded again, every consonant puffing against my jaw with his nearness, and though I didn't want *this* image of that horrible face, full of rage and animosity, I obeyed with a whimper.

A monster...this was a monster, forcing me to his body, lusting for me, devouring every good spot within me, and I could find no inkling of the Erik I'd loved within such insanity.

"Please," I whispered futilely to that mangled face and its soul-deep scars.

"Please? *You* beg *me*? Is death truly all you expect now? To be murdered by the man who adores you, who would move heaven and earth to possess you? That is all I've done, Christine. My sins and crimes, all for *you*, to be with you, to give you what you deserve. Even my sordid past. One could argue that it led me to this spot. *Destiny*, they call it! I was destined to be *yours*!"

Mine... and I wondered as I stared in horror at every word passing that malformed mouth if it was indeed destiny and I was *cursed* for the very thing I'd loved, ...but the man I'd loved was *not* a murderer willing to sacrifice my life for his own gain. I'd loved an illusion, and now the illusion was gone.

"But why do you still cry?" he demanded, his mismatched stare touching every feature of my face as if *searching*. "You're supposed to be *happy*. You...you *smiled* as you came with me tonight, *willingly* into my domain. You teased and grinned and held my hand, and now...you can barely look at me, only through the sheen of tears... You were supposed to hear my sins and *accept* them for the man they've made me, one eager to be with only you forever." Growing agitation painted his voice in hysteria as he accused, "You *knew* I was the Opera Ghost."

"But...you *lied* to me," I whispered, not trusting my voice to give anything but sobs.

"Logistics and minor details," he justified, shaking his head, and my gaze was riveted to those distorted features in motion. A corpse...but moving and breathing, animated when it should rest in the grave...like his victims. "The heart is the same and the soul beneath the sins. I am the *same* man who has spent weeks as your angel and ally, teaching you, *loving* you. I have not changed!"

"*Everything* has changed," I corrected, and the sob finally found a path out to echo around us.

He seemed confounded by my words, and it surprised me that he'd truly believed nothing he'd told me tonight would matter, that not a single letter would leave an imprint behind and make a difference to my heart.

And...to look into his eyes, I *wanted* to follow the dream again, to be naïve and gullible and let him rewrite every transgression he'd stated, but...the face before me was a *stranger*, and I remembered that *he* with his demented features had murdered the dream as brutally as every other life on his hands. My innocence was equally his casualty, and I'd never be the girl I'd been when I'd stepped through the mirror again.

"No...no," he muttered, and anger bore cracks that slowly shattered to the pain beneath as tears rimmed his eyes. "This wasn't *supposed* to happen. No, not like this. You were *supposed* to love *me*. You do! I know you do! ...You do..."

Pain drained with the fall of his tears, and with an exhausted cry, he slid to his knees before me again, still clutching my wrists behind my back. Perhaps I could have broken free if I'd fought, but I wasn't sure I *wanted* freedom. My heart felt twisted inside, constricted in its cage as part of me tried to hold it in and away from the ghost crumbled at my feet. It seemed a losing battle because he sobbed, and my heart sobbed with him.

That disfigured face was pointed toward the ground and out of my sight, but he slowly edged closer until he could set his brow to my stomach, a delicate pressure, never too much to shatter me. I gazed at his crown, making out the skull beneath a thin layer of hair, and as his shoulders shook with the power of his sobs, I ached to comfort him. If my hands had been free, I would have stroked his hair, but as we were, I was terrified one motion too fierce would destroy him.

He took my ability to touch, so I gave him the only other way I knew to comfort. Soft and timid, I began to hum the lullaby my father had played for me upon his violin years and years ago. And I ignored the voice of sense that said I was foolishly offering my solace to a *murderer*. For one moment, I yearned to forget that word and see only a despairing man crying before me, the man I *loved*.

Sobs halted their progression with my song; he seemed so desperate to *listen* as if in a soft melody, I gave him what he needed. ...Maybe I did.

As the song ended, he turned that bowed head so that his disfigured side was against the silk of my dressing gown, and tears smeared and soaked through until I felt their chill.

"I haven't asked much of you, Christine," he hoarsely bid, leftover tears tainting his angel's voice. "Not much at all, ...only your love. That is what I want, more than anything. Not even forgiveness accounts. Don't forgive me; hate me for the monster I was and still am, but give me your love at the same time. Please...I've built such dreams for *us*, a life... I never lived before you. I can't keep living with only shards of fantasy; they are sharp and serrated and will wound my heart until it scars."

"I...I don't know what to say...or to *feel*," I said as I battled the possession of contrasting sensations.

I longed to break away from him, and I longed to hold him just as much. My body betrayed and succumbed against judgment's reservations. But when the idea of his scarred cheek flush to my torso *should have* disgusted me, I suffered the perverse urge to feel it against my bare skin instead and hated myself for it. ...The layers of material in between felt scorched and uncomfortably thick, and skin would have been blissful...

"Just love me," he begged as if it were so simple. "Love me, Christine."

Something inside shouted that I already did.

Slowly, he tilted that face upward until only his chin rested on the wet stains his tears had left against my dressing gown. Despite its awful distortions, I did not even flinch to regard it. I studied its malformations so near and wondered how God could create something so hideous. Why would He? Why torture any creature in such a manner as if He *wanted* this man to suffer and bear the repercussions for *His* mistake? It seemed unjustly cruel.

Perhaps my compassion gave Erik hope. I did not show disgust when disgust was swallowed by too much pity. It was difficult to be repulsed when my heart ached simply to consider that corpse face constantly concealed by a mask's protection to keep it from ridicule and judgment. The mask was its own oddity, but it paled in horror to this damaged face, gazing at me with tears in its deeply-set eyes. ...He asked only for love, and my heart loved even if my mind doubted. Love thrived at the core of my being.

I felt Erik's free hand slowly snake a path up my spine, and I shivered and lost a gasp at the rippling sensation that chased his fingertips. ...Up until my curls claimed him and ensnared his caress, weaving about his knuckles and making the choice my heart wanted without my consent. His fingers found my bare nape, his palm cupping curls and skin as his fingertips pressed taut. Before reason could catch up and pierce the fog, his grip grew firm and he dragged me forward.

I never had the chance to struggle or refuse, granting only a tiny whimper as he forced my lips to his.

Oh God... This was awkward and unwanted, without permission or preparation. His mouth was fierce and demanding, his swollen lips puckered and intent against mine as if a kiss were only pressure and contact. I'd never known a kiss before, not to script its nuances, but this seemed too...aggressive. I went stiff against him, for the first time trying to escape, but my jerked motions only seemed to make him more desperate as he held tight like he wanted to bruise me everywhere at once.

My tears fell fresh and coated his disfigurement, pouring between our joined lips until I could taste their salty flavor and knew he must as well. He knew I cried and kissed me anyway.

Finally, my state penetrated his haze. I felt him sob against me as his grip loosened, and I was able to pull my lips free and *breathe*.

"No, no," I moaned and twisted out of his weak grasp, curling my limbs close and shrinking away. "No, ...you cannot *take* a love I haven't *given*."

He still knelt on the floor, staring at me with a malaise of shock and humiliation as he gasped, "I'm sorry."

Abruptly ducking his scarred face from my sight, he sought his discarded mask. I watched his trembling hands replace its barrier, and yet my mind could only wonder if they'd shaken in such a manner when they'd held me. Then they'd only felt strong and convicted.

"I...I'll take you back," he stammered, numb and distant, and part of me shrieked inside and longed for the man who'd only just acted with passion as his guide. I hated myself for seeking *that man*, but this one had taken his own love and buried it beneath abashment. I felt shut out, and for every overwhelming event of the night, I still ached for my angel. He felt lost to me.

I did not argue and returned to my world as willingly as I'd entered his. Our journey back was uncomfortable, as neither of us seemed able to process the fervent drama we'd just acted, more realistic than any the stage had shown tonight.

My mind spun in the silent chasm and replayed the scene over and over, sifting through the admissions he'd made to me, seeking which I found condemning, which erected walls between our hearts, and which meant little in the scheme of things. And when I looked at his dark shape before me, never a look cast back, never a touch offered, did I still see a man worthy of a heart I'd already given? ...I didn't know and bore too much confusion to sow such a life-altering path tonight. I needed time.

Erik left me in my dressing room without even a goodnight. He only gave me a hard, set look, devoid of the emotions that had earlier saturated through every crevice, and my heart thudded a resounding ache and longed to *beg* for their resurgence. But...no, I couldn't tonight. I needed to think clearly, and his presence was a weight unto itself.

He left me that night with the unspoken vow that I would see him the next night, and he'd seek another chance to win my acceptance. I was actually grateful in the promise of his return, knowing that he'd win in the end. I'd forget everything I should condemn if he were there to chase the shadows away. I loved him already, and I realized the moment he was gone that *nothing* had changed my heart.

*****

Erik~

I felt...addled inside, off my stable base as if I'd fallen and chipped my delicate corners. I could be fixed and repaired, but *she* was the one who bore that responsibility, and I had no guarantee that she would accept it.

My Christine... But was she truly *mine*? Would she *ever be* mine? Not like this, not with a gap in the middle of our hearts that was about to extend continents. In the midst of too much trauma, I hadn't set that revelation in place. She didn't know that come daybreak, I would be gone, and...I wondered if that was for the best.

As I prepared to leave, stalking my home and collecting random articles, my gaze kept drifting to the place she had stood. As if a spotlight shown on that speck of carpet, center-stage of our drama, I'd stolen a kiss right there like it was a scripted move in the libretto of our opera. For as blissful as that second had seemed in its action, it now bore as much regret and shame. She was right. I'd tried to take, ...but it had been with a fear I'd lost every chance and I'd never have another. I'd *taken*, and my lips, misshapen as they were, felt branded in her cells, as if I carried a piece of her with me permanently now. ...A piece wasn't enough.

Huffing a discontented breath, I abandoned my underground house the way an audience left a theatre after the final bow, still with scenes flickering in their heads but already moving on to reality. I had a task that now needed focus, a *redemption* of sorts. I was not a man worthy of Christine, not yet, but if I sought salvation for my soul, acted penance for my sins, ...perhaps I still had a chance. I would fix myself and the flaws she must loathe and return to her a better man, ...one she could love.

The daroga waited outside, but I had one stop to make. Though it was not my custom to wander into the sacred space of the dormitories, I needed one last image to cling to and recall in absence. Like the ghost I'd never been, I crept through the moonlit corridors and sought her out. She shared a small square room with the little Giry girl, and both were quite asleep as I snuck into the space and floated to Christine's bedside.

Dear God, she was so beautiful! Had I really kissed those perfect, pink lips tonight? How could I consider myself that fortunate? Perhaps I'd fabricated the entire episode merely out of my wanting, but no... I still *felt* their glorious, silken brand like a seal on my mouth, making me hers alone. *Always hers.*

Kneeling on the hard floor as if in bedtime prayer, I softly breathed, "I promise, Christine, that I will come back for you. Please don't forget your Erik... Oh, Christine..." Tears I didn't want to show filled my eyes and tumbled beneath my mask. "Your fallen angel tumbled into hell, but I will resurrect him and make him worthy of heaven *for you.* I vow it. ...My love will burn until I am with you again."

I yearned to touch her, to caress her cheek and wish myself into her dreams, but I didn't dare. Instead like the righteous soul I wanted to become, I lifted my eyes to a God I'd spent years cursing and begged with whole heart and soul, "Please...save this for me, this place, ...this heart. Please... I love her..."

That was all. I could manage no more words behind a sob, and I stole out of the room as silently as I'd entered without another glance.

"Are you ready, Erik?" the daroga asked as I met him on the dark street corner with the opera house towering in the background.

I didn't answer. I simply led our stalked pace toward the docks. I couldn't reason sharing my pains until their sharpness dulled. For now, I cried alone and only allowed the moon to know it.

Chapter Eleven

Erik~

Most people would dub torture as physical pain, and being a prisoner of the shah and locked in his dungeon, physical torture was a way of life. To my slight amusement, the shah had learned some new techniques since the last time I had been his victim. But not a single one, no matter the pain inflicted and wounding involved, compared to the torture in my heart. The ache, the loneliness, the reality that I had spent over a year loving Christine's memory with little hope of having love returned again.

Over a year...hundreds of days since the night I'd knelt at her bedside and begged her sleeping shape not to forget me. ...Maybe she had. Maybe now that nightmares of ghosts and fallen angels were gone, she'd moved on with her life. Why hold out hope for a monster's return? Perhaps my absence was a blessing.

In my endless weeks of confinement, I reasoned every scenario in existence. Sometimes I chose optimism and envisioned her waiting for me like the devoted pupil she'd once been, eager for my presence, yearning as desperately as I did with nothing but one forced kiss as compensation. Other times, masochism took over with a reign I could not dethrone and ignited visions of my Christine as someone else's bride, finding another to take my place and vowing a union before the eyes of God. That finale could mutate into so many variations: a marriage, a pregnancy, a child with another man's perfect face. Layer on top of layer until I was driven near insanity because I knew *nothing*.

I was allowed no contact with the outside world, and though some might call my sacrifice noble since I'd readily given *myself* in exchange for the daroga's family, I called it *foolish*. I truly believed I'd find a means of escape again. Oh, a day or two of jailed existence, maybe long enough for a bout of torture, but I would triumph in the end. I had too much waiting for me to lose.

Cursed arrogant attitude! That synopsis had been deemed realistic when our boat had docked in Persia after a three-week journey from France. Three hundred and ninety-four days later, and I berated my stupidity. I'd underestimated the shah and his craving for vengeance. But...*he* had underestimated my longing to return to Paris. It kept me strong enough to endure every obstacle put in my path. A weaker man would have given up and let death take him rather than suffer so uselessly, but I had images of blue eyes and dark curls to renew my fortitude and remind me that if I died, I'd never fulfill my promise of return. I couldn't disappoint her.

To anyone unfamiliar with the shah, his continuous passion for torturing those who'd wronged him would seem extreme. But I knew the man well, knew he took *pleasure* in causing as much damage as possible. I'd *been him* once before, without title and riches attached, of course, but *loving* the power of hurting and inflicting torments ordinary people could not fathom in their innocent minds. He was an opportunist who took anyone opposing him and made another victim. Since my return, I'd seen him numerous times to hear his gloated victories and spreading control over foreign territories. He loved to boast facts I was indifferent to hear and then hurt me for my continued apathy. It was a cycle that rotated around again and again, and I had little choice but to endure it.

With a frustrated huff, I stumbled about the inadequate accommodations of my cell. Stone walls on all sides, and considering I'd lived happily in the opera's catacombs, there was a familiarity in the damp darkness, but I'd had carpets and furniture, wallpaper to conceal the bleakness of rock. I'd *made* a home, but this was only a jail and could enjoy no such reprieve. I had nothing but imagination to change the desolate details, and though it worked for my surroundings, it was unfulfilling when it was applied to Christine. I could not conjure silken, warm skin in my mind or know the reverberation of ecstasy that came with her every smile. She'd shown me the importance of living and sharing contact with another human being. Here, I was alone again and lonelier than ever before.

A spider ran across the floor, and for an instant, memory saved me and gave pictures of the night I'd brought Christine to my home and she'd teased me, actually made me laugh when she'd wondered if I lived among such reprehensible creatures. She'd smiled and beamed like light in the dark; here I had none of that glow to caress my skin and radiate into my bones. Nothing but spiders and darkness and a dream I was afraid to consider might never come true.

Christine was my hope, and part of my enduring stamina against the shah was due to the fact that I *never* spoke of her, never a word even when I lurked the barred space without company. I was doubtless her memory would turn against me if I dared. I could hear the shah use it in his favor. Further torture. Play on doubt and insist any girl with a semblance of self-worth would never want a monster as ugly as I was. Tell me the same stories that tortured my head. When in my mind I had the power to believe or not, if the shah spoke them, my ears would hear and I'd falter.

The only person who knew the name of my guardian angel was the daroga, and I had seen *nothing* of him in three hundred and ninety-four days. I hoped he'd left Persia with his family; I actually held no grudge and encouraged it in prayers because this was *my* fault, *my* mess. As far as I was concerned, I deserved all the punishment I got and took it upon my fallible mortal body as God's penance. If I survived, I would be forgiven and worthy of Christine... That made this traumatic endeavor worth every affliction and-

My musings were cut off midway to salvation with the creak of an entrance and heavy footfalls.

Ah, my captor and persecutor. I'd already concluded he'd be back before nightfall. One round of torture this week couldn't be enough to please his insatiable appetite when the last time he'd actually gotten a whimper out of me.

I preferred to be unmoved, but he'd struck the sensitive damage of my face and won the whimper with low-grade behavior. One knew the rules. If one had a point of disadvantage beginning the game, it was a hollow win to use it instead of finding another. Obviously, the shah had grown tired of my complacency and chose victory any way he could get it.

"Good evening, my *friend*," the shah purred with his pernicious grin as the guards allowed him into my cell. He was a large man, overbearing in girth and jewelry as it was; every jewel glistened even without light.

I stayed back and aloof, stating with sarcasm, "Pleasantries before the entertainment? Is this new congeniality in its trial run? Because it is un-suiting to your authoritative demeanor. Why speak mundane formalities to those you mean to govern and squash beneath your shoe? It dulls your threat value."

The shah gave a condescending chuckle and lifted the whip he had beneath his lush sleeve to my inspection. "Here is your 'threat value'. The pleasantries were deceiving formalities."

"The whip again? How *original* of you!" I rolled my eyes and made my unimpressed reaction known. Without my mask, apathy was thickly cast, and I used it in my favor. *Never* did I give a single hint that my well-beaten torso throbbed in disdain with the mere idea of more.

"The technique might be overdone, but the method will be inspired tonight."

"Oh?" I posed doubtfully as the shah toyed idly with the whip and a conceited expression.

"Yes, I think you will find my portrayal ingenious." The shah arched a dark brow as if waiting for my curiosity to win out and questions to arrive, but I just shook my head and strode to the opposite wall, turning away. My steps were fluid despite the aches my muscles gave in reply. I had to act stoic, and even when every joint moaned a silent protest, I never revealed my pain and played the same omnipotent creature as the Opera Ghost.

"No interest or intrigue?" he prodded and chuckled an ugly sound. "Nothing from one who used to dote on the extent of his perverse forays? Whose vile streak for the macabre and provocative exceeded any creature I've ever known? Nothing?"

"I suffer ennui from your senseless prattle," I retorted. "Say what you wish, and get on with it. Your lead-in drags and seems redundant."

"Well, my *methods* won't be redundant. For you see, I have figured you out, Erik. You and your apathetic regard to even my most heinous of devices. Every creature in existence has an Achilles heel, and I know yours."

I was dubious and snickered beneath my breath as I faced him. "That's doubtful. Your skills at deducing are more lackluster than you grant credit."

"I needed no skills for this, only patience. *You* gave me the answer from your own repulsive lips." He pointed the whip in my direction. "You sing in your sleep, Erik; did you know that? Soft, barely audible, perhaps it is a coping device, but typically, it is just obscure melodies, but...last night, you spoke intelligible words, and your companion one cell over was more than happy to share the news for the right price. He is home with his family right now as we speak. *Freedom*. Such was the cost I was willing to pay for this particular tidbit."

It would have been a lie to say I was unshaken beneath my façade of surmised skepticism. Betrayed by my own subconscious. Perhaps *it* was tired of fighting even if *I* was not, and it had decided to end the battle when I was most vulnerable.

"I would put no credence to a single word spoken in sleep's realm," I determined and fisted my hands to hide their shaking.

"Oh? ...Then *Christine* means nothing to you." A sinister grin curved his lips. "I thought so."

I'd quivered! I'd given it away! My big secret of secrets, and one tremble, one miniscule motion caused simply by those letters filtering this accursed space as if resuscitated to life had undone three hundred and ninety-four days of armored protection. I'd shown the seam in its vest, the one soft spot where a sword could strike and hit home. Curse it all!

"So who is this *Christine*?" The shah dared to utter the name again, and even though this time I remained stable, it didn't matter. It was too late to take it back.

"A mirage." I shrugged the letters from my shoulders and pretended they were meaningless. "A fantasy I conjured to keep me company. Every lonely prisoner has his dreams, and Christine," the letters fell from the ceiling again and burned my tongue, "...she is my idealistic illusion. Perhaps women of warm bodies and soft flesh will not entertain notions of a monster's touch, but my fantasy girl does not stand on ceremony because I am an ugly freak."

I poured every skill I possessed as a master manipulator into that speech. Ah yes, don't let him realize Christine was real; let him believe I was prone to erotic illusions in the dark...

The shah chuckled, and the eerie quality made me shudder with dread. "So when you lay alone in your bed, you fantasize this Christine into existence and imagine she is with you, welcoming you with open arms despite your horrifying makeup?"

"Yes, exactly," I replied and hated myself for cheapening the value of love. "Now let's get on with that whipping you were so eager to give."

I carried it off and was certain he believed me...for about half a minute. Then it all fell apart. "I have spent the past decades seeking out weaknesses in the human race. What I've come to learn is a universal truth: that *love* is the primary factor in both triumphs and defeat. *Love*," he spat the word this time, "leaves a certain residue behind. When the heart has known it, it carries a fatal flaw in its valves that translates out to every detail. You should have bent and broken under my ministrations, but you've had love's hope as your ally to keep you in the battle. You live...for *her*. This *Christine*. How truly pathetic when any affection a monster feels must go unrequited!"

"How are you so certain in that?" I felt compelled to defend. "Love can also be unconditional and not even a demented face can break its root."

"Ah, so you admit it then! The girl is *real*, but unless she is blind, I will not concede to your argument. Look at that monstrosity of a face! I refuse to believe *any* creature with eyes could endure its sight, let alone *love* it."

"She does," I spoke and refused the incessant voice of doubt. I *knew* somewhere in the recesses of memory that she loved me, and I recalled one instant that last night we were together and one look that had glowed in affection even if words had never been applied. ...And then I'd shattered it by trying to seal it with a kiss.

The shah shook his head. "Impossible. Consider who you are, *what you are*. No one could love you, Erik. You told me once that not even your own mother could look upon your face."

Stupid admissions uttered flippantly to make myself more invincible and show no weakness. I hadn't *cared* when I'd said it; now it made me think of Christine and actually stung. Christine hadn't tolerated my face at first sight, but then...well, I was so sure she had lost some of that initial shock and derision. She *loved* me.

"A face does not make a man," I insisted and fought for detachment.

"No, *actions* do, and you are a *murderer*."

"Not lately," I remarked with a nonchalant shrug. "Not while locked in your little box. Now I am *atoning* for murder, and when the only person I still have violent urges toward is *you*, I'd say I'm on the road to redemption."

The slightest waver in his stance told me that the shah took the threat seriously, and he *should*! If not for guards lingering at my cell door watching the exchange and one decent chance, he *would be* a dead body at my feet, and I wouldn't care. But...as it was, he had the power. The second I could turn the game around, I would, and this murder would be justified.

"Your redemption will be your death," the shah snapped, "and now that I've found the right tie to sever, it will be soon. Realize, Erik, I am doing your Christine a favor. She doesn't want you to return. How could she? When there are so many *real* men in the world with *faces*? She has likely found something that equals perfection while you have been stuck in this cell. Have you pondered that, my friend? She has probably moved on and forgotten a monster was ever after her."

My fears stated from the one person I hated to my core, and the façade I fought to keep bore fractures.

The shah laughed again. "The little whore has probably had her share of men with perfect faces in her bed while you've only had a memory to feast on. She should owe *me* a turn for taking you out of her life!"

I felt anger fester and boil in my belly. The mighty Opera Ghost lived and breathed and would *never* be a victim. No, Christine wanted *me*, loved *me*, was waiting for *me*. I had to remember it and get back to her.

With a savage growl, I lunged at my haughty captor. One perfect grip, and I knew I could win. But I never had the chance. I'd barely grazed his arm before his guards were in the cell with us. If it had been only the shah and I, he would have been dead at my feet.

"Strip him!" the shah shouted, and without pause, the guards tore the tattered shirt I wore away and revealed the damage from the last beating. So much of my once white skin was covered in welts and blisters, tracks where a whip had struck before, burns that had taken the top layers and exposed the juicy center beneath. All of this was on its way to scarring. I would now not only have a horror for a face, but every bit of me was becoming an artist's distortion, a canvas of dementedness. I felt like a true freak show brought to life.

Fire burned in the shah's dark eyes as without warning, he gave the first strike. It was brutal and stung to the depth of my soul, but I didn't make a single sound. Strike after strike, and when he got tired of the already mutated flesh of my chest, he had me turned and held on the ground as he worked the same brutality on my equally damaged back.

Never a tear, never a sound, but as the shah

grunted and worked, *he* spoke and put Christine's name on his lips. I felt the reverberation of its syllables rattle my bones. Usually in the midst of torture, I fell into my head and heard *her* voice singing in my inner ear. A happy place and retreat out of my crumbling body. This time with her name present in the air, I had nowhere to go as if *she* loomed in the cell with us, and I couldn't leave her. I stayed aware and present and had to endure the full pain in every violent act.

I didn't know how long it went on. At some point, the shah tired and left, but my body was so abused that the incessant throbbing and burn convinced me that he was still mid-attack. I knew no peace until at some point unconsciousness came and swept like a comforting blanket over me, bringing heavy blackness and temporary reprieve.

I dreamt of her. Didn't I *always* dream of her? Subconscious had abducted that secret and gave me away in bitter betrayal, but I no longer cared. Let me speak her name in my sleep and at least have it as *mine* once more. Dream felt so real. I saw her smile and adore me in the deep manner she always gave when I played for her. *She loves me.* The tip of her finger caressed my bottom lip. A blush painted her cheeks. She said *my* name, ...called me *ange. Oh, Christine...*

Was this penance enough to prove my heart? Would she now accept my sins and love me through them? If I returned to her now, it would be as a mass of scars inside and out.

No, not *if* I returned! *When* I returned! Was hope already dwindling that *when's* became *if's* so quickly in the twilight of semi-awareness? No, *when* I returned, and this time, I would not be the pathetic monster kneeling at her feet, asking tolerance and permission to love her. I was through with that role. This time, no matter what it took, she would love me. I wouldn't accept refusal or doubt. Not when *she* was the only reason I wanted to live.

Her image kept me company, and though I couldn't feel her touch, I resigned myself with a portrait and the reality that I'd kissed her once, that her cells had coated my lips in that intimacy and soaked into my skin. Somewhere within the canals of my bloodstream, *she* existed in microscopic molecules, always with me, *mine* forever.

Christine... And when a hand touched my bare shoulder, for half a second, I believed it was she.

"Erik, wake up."

A voice I didn't recognize, and I forced consciousness to return. Pain came with it, and a moan left my lips in lieu of questions as my eyes fluttered open and observed an unfamiliar, foreign face hovering over me.

"Come on. We have to move quickly before the other guards return."

His words were gibberish to my jellied mind. All I reasoned was the *pain*, and as my companion, dressed like another of the shah's regime, slid an arm about my damaged torso to help me up, I tried to shrink away when contact seared as if another strike.

"I know it hurts, but if we don't move fast, there will be more pain for *both* of us. Come on, Erik. This is your one chance for freedom. Isn't that what you want?"

"Christine," I gasped out as the *only* thing I wanted.

"Well, here is your means to go to her. Fight through the pain and let's go." The man beside me was still attempting to lift me to my feet, and with his promise in mind, I suddenly found the compulsion to help, sliding my bare heels on the hard stone floor and seeking a stable stance.

Freedom. Christine. Such promises prevailed over every weakness in my being, and clasping my saving companion with arms that shook in their effort, I cringed my agony but stumbled out of the prison with him.

I did not recall our actual escape. Pain was so great that I had to concentrate on every step just to keep in motion. Obviously, the shah had been merciless this time, for I could recall no other beatings this debilitating. I didn't have time to know shame for my damaged body or the fact that I needed aid even to move; I simply clung to my companion and told my body to work with images of Christine on my inner lids.

My next memory was waking on a cot in a room I'd never seen before. Sunlight poured in from a high-set window, and I squinted to endure its brightness. Three hundred and ninety-four days without natural light. Of course I'd had small bouts when beneath the opera house cut off from the sun and moon, but to have suffered without choice and denied such natural gifts made everything feel different. I truly felt *changed*.

I was a free man, and even as I contemplated how and why, I took a deep breath as if I hadn't inhaled in over a year and let go of constricted muscles, sagging into the soft mattress and promising my body for the first time that it would never suffer such pains again. It throbbed and burned everywhere, but without the threat looming that *more* would come at the shah's whim, pain was strangely enjoyable. Because it *would end*.

"Ah, you're awake."

I knew *that* voice, and lifting my sore body to sit, I squinted and narrowed a glare on my grinning companion. "Daroga," I greeted stiffly, "you are supposed to be out of the country."

"As if I could leave you to rot in the shah's dungeon a second time!"

He shook his dark head doubtfully, and though I did not say it, I was so grateful to see him that I fought tears. Hundreds of days without kind emotion, without a pleasant expression, with *nothing* but pain, and the daroga was the greatest reality I could fathom in the midst of rescue.

"So...this was *your* plan?" I posed and noted the daroga's unhidden compassion as the wounds on my chest shrieked in vibrant colors. I hated bright hues, and to be covered in their smears and blatancy felt like too much attention.

"Erik, ...dear God he was ruthless with you! This is...*horrible.*"

"Oh, that's just my face, daroga. One would think the shock had worn off," I teased, and to hear him chuckle at my resolved sense of humor calmed us both despite the damage I could not deny. "Aren't you pleased to see I am still alive?"

"It is my greatest joy," he promised. "And you have no idea how wonderful it is to know you will *stay* that way. After all I've done these past months to have this moment with you, it truly is a blessing."

The daroga took a seat beside my bed and offered the meal waiting on the nearby table. In all my relief to be free, I'd forgotten about eating. When the past year had boasted only scraps, I was determined food would be another gift never taken for granted. As I chewed on a piece of bread, I motioned for him to speak, discontented with the way he still observed my beaten torso with self-blame. It wasn't *his* fault, and I saw no reason for guilt.

"Did you really believe I'd left Persia?" he asked, and I nodded matter-of-factly. "Of course not! I sent my wife and baby away somewhere safe, but I never left. My God, Erik, what you sacrificed for me, for my family! How could I leave you! But...it took longer than planned to get you out. The shah is being diligent to track every new guard he employs. So though I could get someone inside the palace, it took ages to feign loyalty and make an opportunity. I had three separate accomplices for the task; all are already out of the country. They knew the risks involved. And now once you are well, we will follow and leave this

God-forsaken place."

I nodded thoughtfully as I chewed and concluded, "I need a mask."

But he shrugged as if my deformity meant little. It terrified me to wonder if next to the beating my body had taken, my face was almost ordinary. Dear God, what would Christine say to all this? If my face had given her hesitation, what would she think of a distorted body to go along with it?

"I have to get back to Paris as soon as possible," I stated and reached for something more to eat. In truth, food was tasteless at present, but I knew a lack of nutrition in the shah's prison had taken its toll on my meager frame and left me to look like a skeleton, a skeleton covered in bloodied wounds and scars... I was disgusted with myself and knew I had to at least *try* to fix what I could before I made it home...to Christine.

"Paris? No, Erik, why?" the daroga pushed with an unhappy cringe. "There are so many other places in the world."

"But there is only *one* place Christine will be."

"Christine again," he retorted with a huff. "As we traveled to Persia, did you not make it clear that she'd been less than tolerant of your face *and* your sins? Is it really the best idea to return and be discarded all over again? It's been *months* since we left. Surely...she's moved onward with her life."

I narrowed eyes in a fierce glare and stated flatly, "You know, daroga, considering I came with you and sacrificed for *your* love, one would think you'd be a bit more encouraging for *mine*. This pessimism is unbecoming, and I don't favor it."

"And is *optimism* presenting your heart only to have it trampled upon again?"

"Yes, indubitably. And get your facts in order. It's been *four hundred and eighteen* days since I last saw her, since the second I stepped foot on a boat and out of Paris *for you*. If you are not going to encourage the growth of my relationship, stay here with the shah. I give you my leave. You saved my life, and we are even. I would happily have us part ways."

But he tutted softly and shook his head. "It would be a detriment to send you off alone after a stint of torture and exile. I think you need me yet, at least to get you safely home. A man in a mask is suspicious, and without the mask, even more so. If Paris is where you wish to go, then I won't argue the futility of happy-ending wishes with you. I will simply send you on your way when we arrive and bless your broken heart."

"As any decent friend would!" I concluded. "So it is settled. We return to Paris as soon as possible, and...I keep my promise."

My heart leapt a frantic beat in my chest with my spinning thoughts; I savored its pulsation. It reminded me for the first time in over a year that I was *alive*. And anticipation coiled and raced my veins, enticing the smile I felt tug my misshapen lips up to heaven. I was an angel redeemed, and I was convicted that Christine would know I was now worthy of her love.

Chapter Twelve

Christine~

"Flowers for you, Mademoiselle Daaé."

I knew that voice even as it attempted a higher pitch of disguise, but with the mountain of roses in the way as a makeshift barrier, I could not confirm identity and simply made a face back.

"Well, *that* was uncalled for," the voice went on as the walking-talking flowers took small steps nearer. "You know, this arrangement is quite heavy, and I don't catch even a whiff of gratitude."

"How could you? You've got your head stuck in the center of a rose bush, Raoul. I have a distinct feeling all you're inhaling is perfume." My feigned perturbation cracked into giggles as Raoul's dear face appeared through the middle of too many blooms with the dopey grin I always found so charming before it dissipated to a violent sneeze. I laughed harder and concluded, "Come on then. I suppose I'll add yet another bouquet to my dressing room's walls. It is beginning to look like a floral shop in there!"

The grin returned as if he'd won some exorbitant prize, and as he followed me amidst the bundle of roses down the backstage corridor, he decided, "The floral shop would be envious. You have a better selection. I've gotten you a little from *everywhere.*"

"I keep telling you to save the flowers for a

performance night. You cannot shower me with bouquets after *every* rehearsal. You're going to stir up even more gossip than you already have."

"To hell with the gossip!" he enthusiastically declared and made me giggle again. "Doesn't the prima donna deserve her accolades on a daily basis? Truly, Christine, the management should be just as generous as I choose to be and dote upon you for what you do. You are the *star*." He breathed the word dramatically and arched persuasive brows as he claimed his point.

But I shook my head. "I think they feel I am still earning the title."

"More than a year and countless shows as the diva, and they still hold a single reservation? How is that possible? You are *perfection*."

His compliment encouraged my smile, but I argued, "La Carlotta had the title for over a decade. By that standard, I am still an ingénue."

"Ridiculous!" Raoul and his rose collection followed at my heels into the confines of my dressing room. I was certain others spied us and watched as I improperly closed the door, but I didn't care. In that regard, I chose to *be* the diva and have my secrets. They would whisper and talk, but not a single letter would touch me. I was impenetrable.

Raoul found a solitary spot of space to fill with his flowers amidst dozens of other bouquets, all with his name on their affectionate cards, and I spun about and let the rainbow spread of colors and wafting array of perfumes swallow me whole. It was practically my own indoor garden. I'd never asked for such a thing, but I knew without a doubt that if the request ever even passed my lips, the man standing aside watching me would have fulfilled it without a qualm. He was just that devoted.

My gaze met his strikingly handsome features and sparking turquoise eyes, and I called myself lucky for the vast amount of adoration he vividly displayed.

Not every girl was so blessed, and this was not just a gentleman before me, but a Vicomte. What opera diva had a Vicomte as her endless admirer?

"Christine," he breathed with that smile and added with a sigh, "I want you to come to supper tonight and meet my parents."

"Dear boy, I've already met your parents."

"In prescribed roles. The opera diva meeting her patrons. You've met them as Mademoiselle Christine Daaé, prima donna of the stage, but not as Christine, their son's fiancée." His eyes shown with earnestness, and though I knew how much the engagement meant to him, I still felt uncomfortable with the words and averted my attention to flowers as I idly rearranged one set of blooms with another.

"We have to tell them sometime," he added, trying to recapture my focus. "We can't very well wait until the wedding, you know."

"They're not going to like it."

"I don't care. I love you. Let them chastise me, curse the musings of my rash heart and condemn my choice, but it won't change anything. I swear it. Is that your worry? That they will talk me into abandoning you? Because it is far too late for them to make even a dent in my resolve. I am doubtless what I want."

I still would not look at him, pulling a purple bloom from one spray and adding it to another to make a clashing chaos of color. It was more interesting than matching tones.

"They can't approve," I reminded. "You are a Vicomte. No matter what we feel, I am so far below your status. They must assume I am after your title and wealth. It is just the way of things. Did we not agree from the first point that we would not even tell them I was the same little Daaé girl you used to play with on your beach holidays? It would have seemed convenient and would only add more suspicions. And now...they're going to think I am a fame-hungry leech, desperate to latch onto your name."

"Let them!" Raoul was fervent as he caught my shoulders and made me cease my pointless motions and face him. "I don't care what they say. I am marrying *you*. But I think it is better to spring this on them now rather than later. Let them get used to it a little before we start wedding plans." His fingers set gently to my chin and grazed along my jaw. "Come to supper, and we'll take the challenge together. Whatever they say, I am in this with you. If they're upset, we'll leave and escape. Run off, marry on a tropical beach somewhere, sail away from titles and parents and every restriction the world tries to put upon us. What do you say?"

It was a tempting offer, but with a disappointed sigh, I reminded, "The opera. I am under contract. We can't just run away...at least not until the end of the season." I said it because I knew it would inspire the beam of hope in his turquoise eyes. I could never tire of that optimistic look; it was something I envied him for.

"All right. Then we have an option if my parents choose an insane and irrational course," he replied, and his flawlessly sculpted lips curved into that charming grin. "So, supper?"

"You know I can't. I have to practice. We have our first musical rehearsal for *Faust* tomorrow, and I can leave no space for judgment in error."

"You know that role forward and back."

"I'd rather be over-prepared than make a silly mistake. Perhaps between shows, we could attempt a supper with your parents, but now...I'm under contract," I reminded again. "And there are always those ready to take my place the second I falter."

He huffed his discontent but cupped my cheek with understanding. He was *always* understanding. Maybe because he could never fully gauge the pressure I was constantly under, and he was pacifying me the best way he knew how.

"I could tell you that you are the best by far," he said with a new smile, "but you will call me biased."

"Yes, I will."

"So I will go to supper alone with my parents, but I'm going to hint that I have someone special in my life. Maybe it will dull the shock a bit when we reveal *you* as my mystery lady."

I was skeptical of that. This entire relationship was a huge impropriety and a faux pas by society's standards. No softening of the ultimate blow would matter once my name was presented into their aristocratic bubble. I didn't belong, and every person on the cusp of society's top hierarchy would make certain I knew it.

"Practice well," Raoul bid, and clasping my face between his palms, he gave a teasing expression, playful and silly.

"What are you doing?" I demanded and lost to a smile.

"Ah, it worked! I rid you of that pensive brow!" He accepted his triumph by imitating the expression I'd previously worn, all knitted forehead and solemn air before cracking to a chuckle. "No more serious face! You are already in your focused musician's mode, and this is a role you already know. Go easier on yourself. Have fun with it for a change."

Even his most well-intentioned encouragement made no impression on me. Raoul thought performing was easy. Get onstage and sing. He could never seem to grasp the mechanics of singing, no matter how often we'd had the conversation. He claimed I was making it more complicated than it should be.

Still making faces in hopes for more smiles, he leaned close mid-game and pressed his lips sweetly to mine. A quick, chaste kiss, but he knew me well enough to conclude my mind had moved forward to the task ahead of me and was unable to savor tender tokens of affection in its current state.

"I love you," he bid with one more kiss to my furrowed brow.

"I love you, too."

And with that oath and a playfully grinned wink, he was gone, escaping the cage of musical hypnosis I would now fall victim to. Music called, and I never ignored its possession. I needed it on my side to take up my battles alone. It was quite a challenge when aside from a Vicomte with no knowledge of the arts beyond what he enjoyed hearing, I had no ally or guide. My reign as prima donna was still too new to leave up to chance and talent; I didn't have enough of a reputation yet. Hard work was still the only means to success.

I scampered to lock my dressing room door after Raoul. I knew others would see him leave and could not endure an interrogation by an overly-exuberant Meg eager to analyze every word spoken and every action indulged. She did not know that we were engaged, and I had no intention of telling her. The second she had that information, the entire *corps de ballet* would be abuzz and onward through the tiers until *everyone* at the opera was aware of my personal situations. I was careful to keep walls and doors with privacy intact for exactly that reason.

Oh, they all knew Raoul was my avid admirer, maybe assumed we were courting, but that was all they could assert with any sort of conviction. It was imperative because Raoul had more to lose than I did, and he was not averse to burying his love in flowers and closed doors around the opera's corridors. Maybe others dubbed us lovers, but they'd never guess Raoul's intentions were far more honorable than that. I had a proposal, and most girls in my place would never be so lucky.

Casting one more look about my quiet, flower-infested dressing room, I deemed it safe to embrace my biggest secret of all. My knees used to shake when I approached my full-length mirror; they used to quiver as I unhinged the latch to a hidden doorway and sway my balance as I wandered the dark alone away from my world of light and into a place I should have been shut out of forever. Nerves used to coil in my belly with a fear of being found out for this indiscretion by managers or ballerinas, worse yet by the one person who could validly call it an intrusion to his home and property, but...no one ever had any idea that I spent as much time in dark catacombs as my world above.

Finding the mirror's secret had been a challenge, but as the first days without Erik had dragged endless minutes and my worry had grown, I had become desperate to figure it out. There was a trick latch on my side, well-concealed by the ornate, gold frame; it was more difficult to locate on the opposite side, a detail I had learned only once I'd managed to trap myself in the threshold and couldn't get back. Acute terror had built to hysteria to be looking through a mirror like a window and know *no one* could save me but my own self. Three hours I had endured stuck between worlds, and I was determined such a trauma would never happen again. Learning every detail in the mirror's construction and how to master its magic had been a necessity, difficult but not impossible.

That had been the first in a string of challenges, but I triumphed over every one presented. Finding the particular path through the dark passages without folly or death when Erik's devices were horrors unto themselves, deciphering the door of the underground house in a wall of pure stone, bypassing a rigged entrance to get inside. I'd taken every test, and adamancy helped me win, ...adamancy *and* a wounded heart.

These trips into the depths below all began because of an internal bruise and a need to heal its scathing pain. I'd been so certain that Erik was just avoiding me, hurt after a confrontation that had shaken our stability with strikes from both our respective corners. He had opened his soul, given me secrets I truly didn't want to know, put his deformity on display, ...stolen a kiss I'd never consented to give. He'd leapt every boundary between us in one night, and choosing distance at first was not inconsiderable. I could imagine that he bore regret, guilt, pain, and I had allowed what I dubbed penance for a few days. Then loneliness had consumed, my heart aching merely to beat beneath a purple and blue wound inside, and I'd grown urgent with a fear he'd never return to me. ...Maybe that fear wasn't entirely unfounded.

As I expertly wandered the dark catacombs and arrived at the hidden entrance to his house, I knew the familiar hope my heart always inflicted at this point in the trip. It had appeared on my very first journey below and was resurrected on every sojourn, a prayer and held breath to find my Erik inside, awaiting my presence, perhaps missing me, loving me. I called myself a fool for entertaining its possession as if a chance could still exist. He was gone. It was past time to accept that. I'd hurt him that night, and he couldn't forgive me and had abandoned me for it.

Stepping out of the damp catacombs, I made myself at home, lighting a fire in the hearth and treating this as my secret place. My first nights spent within these walls, I'd felt awkward, like an intruder, but as time passed and Erik did not return, I had begun to explore the small rooms and found a contentment here that I did not have in the world above. Perhaps it was because Erik's aura lingered, and I *felt* him still when I was in his chambers, ...like I was still a part of his life and he a part of mine. ...Perhaps it was because he'd left his things behind: furniture and accessories, clothes in the armoire. All hints he could come back...

With a desolate sigh, I forced the idea away and crept to his piano. I was the one to play it now. Not

143

like him, of course. I did not possess such a virtuosic talent, but I used its pitches and keys to practice within these walls, far away from eavesdroppers. I knew I was safe here and could work with a spark of Erik as inspiration.

No one dared wander the lower cellars. Their Opera Ghost might have taken a hiatus, but with his traps still active, the threat was alive. Perhaps some came close enough to catch echoes of my voice when I sang within the stone walls and maybe they scripted a tale of love for their dormant Opera Ghost, as if he'd locked himself below to savor music with his lady love. ...If only such a dream were true!

For hours, I worked and filled the silence of the underground with my voice and music to chase any other idling ghosts away. I almost didn't want to leave the house when I'd finally given up singing for the night.

A few times under the spell of urging, I'd conceded to creep into Erik's bedchamber and lay my head down upon his pillow, curling up in his bed. How pleasant it would have been to sleep there, molded to the imprint his body had left in the mattress, but... I couldn't risk doing any more damage to my heart. It grieved beneath so many layers of fake facades. It had been ripped apart with Erik's absence, a wound that clotted and began to heal only to be torn open again and again every time I came down here with my hope on my sleeve. I didn't want it to hope anymore or to *feel*. So I'd let it go numb and bundled it in blankets full of fake smiles and a delight in my life that I did not actually possess. I *hurt*, and I tried to make it unimportant.

One last look over the empty house, and I returned the way I'd come through damp passages to a world I didn't feel I belonged in. Of course my dressing room said differently, over-laden in the perfumed petals of another man's love. Raoul did not know my secret hideaway or that I'd given my heart to an angel ghost only to have it as damaged as a corpse's face. Raoul was a good man who did not deserve a woman who only spoke love but never let it touch a shrouded heart, but...his presence made me feel *wanted* and ordinary, ...*loved*.

Raoul was a part of a past I'd almost forgotten. We'd played together as gawky children, the sort of friend one made because he was the only person in the vicinity. For one summer at the beach, we were inseparable, and that was it. I'd barely recalled him in the patterned scheme of my life, but he had been present that fated Gala night to see my performance and *he* remembered. For months, he'd pursued my attention, recanting tales of our juvenile games as he'd chased me about the corridors backstage, but I'd kept trying to shrug him off. I hadn't wanted his focus or his affections. I was mourning and hoping so hard that nothing else had mattered. But eventually, I had to make myself grow up. Erik wasn't coming back; it took time to be able to state it aloud and believe it. I *still* carried that damn, undying flicker of hope's fire, but I'd made myself move on even without a heart attached.

The diva... I was the diva now, and if I couldn't have love, I'd at least have the music as my heart's companion. Music filled a particular void inside, and even though I held back a piece of myself, the piece that had been solely Erik's, I *sang* and it meant something.

I was dead inside to leave for my apartment that night, dead during a hollow, dreamless sleep, dead to return to the opera the next morning. The only time life flowed anew in my veins was when I stepped on the stage and sang Marguerite's role in our musical rehearsal. Then I became *her*; I was no longer Christine with an un-beating, frozen heart, and I could breathe, however briefly.

For one instant in a day of endless rehearsal, I felt the music creep inside and tap a vulnerable spot in my protected heart. As I sang Marguerite's spinning wheel aria, I felt a reverberation of my own loss. '*Il ne revient pas*', no, he does not return. *He is gone.*

That resonant echo pounded my body, and before I could rebuild my armor, it threatened with tears and a lump I had to frantically swallow against. Iron had to be reconstructed and impenetrable as I told myself I was Marguerite, not Christine. My lost love would return in the next act, and even a tragic ending meant an *ending*. Marguerite would not be left in this suspension of an un-healing wound within. No, *she* had finality, and I had to live on with that persistent swell of hope that still *felt* Erik. Erik was gone. *Stop dwelling...*

My mind debated an internal war during the remainder of rehearsal, but my will was stronger now and won out every time. It mended my veneer to perfection so that when the Vicomte arrived to gush over rehearsal and take me to lunch, he never saw a single fracture in its shield. I smiled at him and caressed his cheek, held his hand tight in mine, and though I never *felt* a single touch, my gaze showed a fabricated affection, and he believed I did.

Chapter Thirteen

Erik~
"Christine, you were exquisite! My God, the way you sang! Every glorious pitch! You are amazing!"

"Oh, Raoul, you spoil me with such compliments, dear boy!" Christine's smile lit every feature of her face in its glow as she caressed the boy's flawless cheek with delicate fingers in gratitude.

"And I'll spoil you further over lunch. Come on, darling. You must be famished." He held out a hand, and she took it with nary a hesitation to be found, weaving fingers, inseparable and tight as she giggled and let him pull her toward the door.

It felt like a play being acted out in front of me, each line delivered with the correct emotion of characters onstage, each motion like pre-planned blocking. *His lines, her lines and a touch to the cheek, his lines of exit, join hands, end scene.* I watched life, and I would have dubbed it fictional if not for the backlash of pain that struck in a brutal wave as soon as they were gone. The lovely little couple, hand in hand like conspiring children...

My body shook and shuddered with the violent attack upon my vulnerable heart, and I shrank back against the curtains in Box 5 and gasped a necessary inhalation to recover before asphyxia set in.

Pain and then anger. It started as a spark,

stone striking stone in the perfect spot to catch and ignite fire, and the flame traveled from its origin through my veins and out to every extremity. So while I'd been rotting and festering in the shah's prison, beaten and tortured nearly to my death with *her* name as the hope upon my lips, she'd found herself the perfect prince charming to take my place and turn a nightmare into a dream. *Boil onward*, and the fire bubbled in my belly and seared my insides.

I knew that boy. As a fixture in the opera, I'd made it a point to learn every patron and every person who contributed financially to our resources. A *Vicomte* whose parents made a sizable donation twice a year and required their son's attendance only *once* for the season's opening.

...Ah, the Gala night. The pieces fell in place. So the young milksop Vicomte had been in his annual attendance, had seen *my* Christine sing, and had been enamored with her.

I grew sick on the spinning of my thoughts. Had this relationship been going on that long? How many days...*seconds* had passed before she had chosen a replacement for her angel? She'd obviously struck a fortune to not only capture a handsome face, but a *Vicomte's* title besides! *Oh...* My heart leapt and throbbed a bleeding, blinding agony within my ribcage. *No.* This was *not* how things were meant to happen.

With a ferocious growl, I raced into my passageways out of the world, away from life, stalking a fitful pace into the darkness and actually praying some of my rage evaporated into steam around me. It was potent and poisonous, and I feared what I'd do in its grip.

My mind fluctuated rationality and processed the details I'd gained since my return. Someone had been in my home. That had been an immediate realization, someone who knew the path well enough to avoid injury. I hadn't wanted to assume it could be

Christine, but she'd left music scattered on the piano. *Her* music. Christine in my home. I took all such facets as good signs. My God, I'd had such hope that only blossomed to learn Christine was the leading prima donna. It was my dream for her, and it had come to pass in my absence. I considered myself a key reason for her promotion, all the molding I'd done with her talent as my sculpting clay.

Christine, a prima donna, and yet... I'd watched the entire rehearsal from Box 5, so eager to see her sing, to hear that voice as I'd carried it in my inner ears in echoes for almost a year and a half. But...I was disappointed.

Of course her voice was beautiful; there was no denying that, but...it was devoid of its true essence. She sang vocal acrobatics, high notes, legato lines, all *empty*, passion-less. She sang like a wind-up doll, cranked, released and let go, with nothing behind porcelain eyes. And it *infuriated* me because I knew she was better than that.

Christine... I felt just as haunted as ever, once again watching from outside of her life and terrified to get too close. But no, I would not fall to pathetic, heartsick admirer. I'd endured *hell* in a quest for redemption. I was through being patient to gain her affections and backing off in fear of pushing too hard. *No more.* She'd been my saving grace, my only thought of peace during every trial I'd endured. I would not lose her to a flawless Vicomte when *I* was supposed to stand in that place beside her, caressed by her fingers, holding her hand, smiled upon. That was *my* designated role, and to hell with being a gentleman! To have it back, I would do what I must and *take* this time without regret.

As I paced my home, refusing to acknowledge the lingering aches of my tortured body, I searched for an answer. Through suffering and recovery, returning to Christine had been my sole thought. I hadn't considered what would come after that. Now to have her, I had to think on a larger scale, outside the little bubble we had once spent our precious moments confined to alone. Now there was a *Vicomte* to add into the equation, and if the affection I'd witnessed said anything, it was that I needed a greater power than love to win. ...I knew the exact angle to play.

Buried in a secret compartment in my armoire was a small chest filled to its brim with jewels in every color of the rainbow. Obviously, the shah had had many reasons for the revenge he'd inflicted, and one was the sum stolen from his private treasury during my first stint in his court, back when I'd had his favor. It was about to be worth the blood spilled to gain it. Wealth put me on the same level as a Vicomte even without the formality of a title, but then again I already had wealth. The Opera Ghost got a pension of sorts; this jewel-filled treasure would notch me above pathetic Vicomtes and buy me the means to Christine's soul.

A meeting with the managers would have been unfeasible a year and a half ago. I would have done everything by notes and haunting, but this time I needed credibility. Even if they'd heard their Ghost was a masked man, and they probably *had,* seeing as how they stared awkwardly at the mask during the entire interview, they had no proof when I also had a flesh and blood body and ghosts had limits, like being unable to purchase property. The managers had no collateral against me, and with the treasure I placed before them, they could not argue or resist. And it was done, simple as that. I was the new owner of the opera house.

Interaction with the bumbling previous managers was one thing, but I was about to readily put myself in the lion's den. As the cast was called together after lunch, I lingered out of sight for the announcement.

I was not obligated to make an appearance. I could have let the news of a new manager be shared and leave them speculating until I was ready, running the ship without ever coming face to face with the crew, but...I *wanted* Christine to know.

From the shadows, I gazed upon her, granted no more than a view of silken dark curls at this angle. I could not read her expression, but I *could* read her arrogant Vicomte as he sat idly in the back of the theatre as if he had a right to be on the premises.

Oh, that would be my first rule put into law! No outside visitors observing rehearsals. My previous managers had been too lenient for fear of upsetting the balance and losing a monetary contribution. I didn't care. Let his family pull their funds. I'd find others. This need to please compromised the very integrity of the opera, and for what? To keep spoiled, rich boys from having temper tantrums? *Oh please, throw a fit, Monsieur Vicomte, and show Christine your true colors!*

Andre and Firmin elongated their goodbyes with tears and melodrama suited for another theatre production before introducing me onto the stage with them. More melodrama about to erupt from the pits of disgrace, and I actually trembled as I stepped into the spotlight for the first time.

Gasps all around, but they were expected. The ballet rats had an accurate depiction of their prior Opera Ghost, and their wide eyes spoke volumes of shock and terror. I let them gawk and choke on their fear in their seats and settled my gaze on Christine's equally wide eyes.

She wasn't breathing. I only knew because when she finally inhaled, it quaked her entire frame and pierced in its gasp over the rest. I played unmoved and apathetic to her stare and dragged my reluctant attention over the rest of the cast instead.

"Let's have this clear and understood," I spoke over mumbled whispers all around. "You are under *my* employment now, and I expect obedience and hard work. What I observed in your rehearsal this morning was sloppy. I will not tolerate *Faust* performed like a two-bit street show. We are the pride of Paris, and if you do not want to live up to that standard, there is the door. Get out."

I gestured, cold and haughty, and ran my eyes over the jittering ballerinas. If it were fully up to me, I'd have cut the ballet out entirely. Let them find their own theatre. I was tired of little girls with weak spirits, but...I did have an audience to consider and had to ponder the situation like a businessman now. The laypeople of Paris favored the ballet. *Ignorant fools.* I'd have to keep the little pigeons...for now.

"Know that I speak for the good of the company," I added with forced congeniality, but it was difficult to be the focus of so many sets of eyes and remember *I* had the authority. I was not acting it as a ghost. I was above them because I had paid my way to the spot, and no matter what I did or said, what awkwardness plagued me as I played a role so new, they had to be subservient, little peons. *I* was their employer. It was a pleasant rush of power. "Now get to work. I will be watching when you least expect, and if I catch any unsavory detail, there will be consequences. Every single one of you is replaceable whether you are dancer, crew, ...or even prima donna."

I shot that right at Christine, finally capturing her in my stare. I played bitter, but I saw the faintest glisten of tears before she ducked her head. Crying, ...was she? But why? Perhaps she'd hoped I'd stay gone, and now I'd put a definite crick in her plans. *Power, Christine, who has the real power now?*

I observed my shell-shocked cast one more moment and almost chuckled at the fear hanging thick in the air. I had brought that upon myself. They likely thought 'replaceable' did not mean turned out of their jobs so much as disappeared and *dead.* Stupid children. I'd atoned for murder; I wasn't about to add more and make the penance I'd done worthless.

Ending on the threat, I stalked toward the end of the stage and put rehearsal in the musical director's hands as he called attention for Act One. Almost immediately, I heard footfalls follow me into the wings and shivered from head to toe. No, no, I had to be strong, *invincible*, and not break.

"You...you're back."

Oh, that sweet voice... I shivered again and forced my spine stiff and muscles rigid so that natural responses did not give me away as I finally turned and set eyes on Christine's uncertain expression. Her stare ran over me, but did not halt on my mask like the others in the petty audience. She took in *every* detail as if desperate to *see*.

"Yes," I replied with detachment and refused to let my guard waver. "I couldn't stay away from the opera. The music called me home."

"Oh... The music." She lowered her flustered expression, and I wondered if I created the flicker of disappointment I thought I observed.

"I see you have achieved your dreams," I offered, still without real emotion attached even as I took the opportunity to regard her unnoticed and rake my gaze over every nuance, seeking changes with an urgency to interpret and define her again. ...We had once been so close. "And yet from what I earlier heard, you are far from your potential."

Blue eyes darted back up with a flash of defensiveness. "What do you-"

"Oh, you sang the correct pitches and rhythms, but I found your interpretation...uninspiring at best." I was blunt, but I was also hurt. I would have softened the blow a year and a half ago, but now...she had someone else to pick up the pieces when she fell apart.

As if on cue, prince charming came rushing into the wings, and catching my last line, he leapt to Christine's rescue. "Excuse me, monsieur. I hate to intrude and contradict, but I considered her rendition exceptional. Of course, I am no connoisseur of opera, but I *do* know what I enjoy and she was superb."

I narrowed a glare upon him, shooting daggers with poisoned tips in eyes alone as I spat, "Yes, exactly. You are no *connoisseur* of opera; you know *nothing*. She was mediocre, and as the prima donna, she needs to *shine*."

"It was just a rehearsal-"

I cut him off with a raised hand first, every joint taut with my rage as I spat, "Precisely! You prove your ignorance, monsieur, and Christine knows better. Even a rehearsal should be treated with the same care as a performance. She is the prima donna, but there are a dozen sopranos in that theatre ready to rip her to shreds and take her place. She must *never* give them a reason to find fault, and if she were truly a slave to the music *as she was taught*, there would be *no* fault."

Christine would not lift humiliated eyes. I caught hints of her fierce blush and wondered if there were tears to accompany. I hoped there were! I considered how many I'd shed to contemplate her *alone* here *without me* this entire time, all in vain!

"She was amazing-"

"Monsieur *Vicomte*, is it?" I spat the title at him. "You have no place in this theatre during a *closed* rehearsal."

"My parents are prime contributors-"

"Money buys you a seat on opening night, not free run over the theatre. I will only ask politely *once* for your departure. Next time...well, simply hope there is *no* next time."

A threat gelled in the propriety of a stoic posture and calm expression. I never spoke anything dangerous, but Christine's attention darted up as if she heard 'murder', and grabbing at the boy's arm, she pleaded in desperation that said *she* took me seriously even if he didn't.

"Raoul, please go. He is right, and he is the

manager now." The label was laced in a spite I gave her credit for. "I will see you later."

But the Vicomte clasped her hand, and my glare settled and locked on the contact. So he felt soft fingers and palm, *skin*, and I had empty hands, un-allowed to *touch* her? *Damn him.*

"I have a right to be here," the Vicomte pointlessly argued, and I rolled my eyes purposely to his regard. "This is a public place."

"Not during rehearsals!" I insisted back. "I will not tolerate my prima donna casting moony eyes back and forth with you when she should be concentrating on her performance. *Music* is her *only* lover when she is under *my* roof."

"I never distract her-"

"Raoul!" Christine's irritation was obvious to all of us, and I prayed to God that it lasted. "Please *go*. He's right. I need to be focused, and...you shouldn't be here. It isn't your place."

Exactly! I wanted to shout the word. Not *his* place! *Mine!*

The dejected Vicomte conceded only because *she* was the one insisting this time, but he did not go without a final caress to her cheek and soft words I plainly overhead. "I can meet you as soon as you are finished for the day. We'll go to supper."

She nodded in appeasement before shooting me a glare that clearly said she'd obeyed and done as I wanted.

"Sing well as always," the Vicomte added with a grin for her and then a sneer for me before he abandoned us entirely.

Christine and I both watched him go in chosen silence, and even after he was beyond sight, we lingered before I broke the moment. "Get back to rehearsal. If you miss your entrance, I will find you a decent understudy. And...your young man may be good at keeping proper pretenses, but his suspicion is transparent. ...So help you God, Christine, if you tell him what lies beneath this mask."

That was all. It was half a threat for the girl I longed and ached to embrace instead. But with it in place, I stalked back toward the shadows and felt her eyes follow my retreat.

So this was to be our relationship now. It was disappointing, but...I wasn't sure hope had a heartbeat anyway. Once again, God had smote me. I'd prayed for her to stay mine, went off to find retribution for a damaged soul, suffered and remained true, and now...cruelty was my blessing in return. If I was not meant to know her love, then I preferred her hate to something in between. Love and hate were polar opposites, but both were felt with fervency and vehemence. I would accept hate and carry it proudly.

Chapter Fourteen

Christine~

If my morning rehearsal was 'mediocre', then my afternoon was pathetic. I had *no* concentration for notes and melodies when my head was a vortex of musings and questions.

Erik was back. I couldn't quite wrap my mind about that fact when I'd felt abandoned for so long and had surrounded my heart in brick walls and iron bars in his absence. I had tried so desperately to give up an anticipation for any sort of return, and now... My God, what was I to do? What was I to *feel*?

Singing was a chore I didn't want to be doing when I was eager for answers, and every scene I was not a part of thrust me back into visions from the past. He'd loved me once, and then he'd left me without explanation or choice. He'd run away when things imploded and hadn't stayed to fix them with me. I *hated* him for that.

The more I pondered our situation, the more my anger grew. I owed him *nothing*, not now with his prodigal resurrection, not when my heart had meant so little that he'd left it behind. I would have been content never to set eyes on his masked face again, but *no*. He'd flipped my world upside down. He had *no* right. I was the prima donna, and he'd chastised me like a child. I was *engaged*, and he'd tossed my fiancé out of the theatre. Infuriating, arrogant Opera

Ghost! He was convicted to controlling my existence once again, and I wasn't about to stand for it. He'd surrendered the spot already.

As I sang my final scenes, they were supposed to be laden in love and then salvation, but I filled every note with an aggression I couldn't keep to myself and noted the many confused expressions turned in my direction. Oh, I hoped Erik was listening! He'd threatened me with an understudy. Well, let him hear my fire and rage and know I was not defeated so easily!

Rehearsal ended with frantic comments from the musical director. Typically, he let little mistakes go, but now under Erik's management and push to excellence, every faulty detail was mentioned along with an insistence to have each fixed by the morning in case our manager stopped in to observe. Only *I* knew that he'd likely never left and had certainly overheard every error with his analytical musician's ear. He was going to be the hardest to please of anyone, and the first manager we'd ever had unafraid to put his opinion first. It was a terrifying possibility.

The second we were released, Meg came rushing to my side. "Christine! Oh my goodness! Our new manager is...the *Opera Ghost!*" she gasped the words quiet and yet resonant as if I hadn't realized that point myself and would give a shock I had no energy even to pretend.

"I don't believe in ghosts," I insisted as I had during the ghost's former reign. "Our new manager is a mortal man, Meg. He only has the power to frighten if *you* give it to him. Stop believing, and he will fall from his pedestal. I promise that."

She arched dubious golden brows, but I was not about to elaborate. I had a prior engagement awaiting my attention.

Sense wrote the play of events and flashed pictures of the Vicomte arriving at my new apartment, probably there already, waiting on my doorstep like a loyal kitten, presuming my imminent return with another bouquet of flowers and dozens of sweet words to comfort the harsh ones he'd witnessed our new manager heave at me. And *that* was the scene I belonged in, accepting every token and clinging to Raoul's arm as we strolled off to supper and let treasured moments together soothe every ugliness the world sought to offer.

Yes, that was how the evening *should have gone.* So why had I chosen instead to linger after the cast departed and wander back onto the empty stage alone? The lights had been turned out, but moon-glow streaked the wooden floor and illuminated in pale hues. I felt it bathe my silhouette and paint my features incandescent, and I tilted my face to welcome the sweet caress and sought the presence I knew would join me.

"How reminiscent of days past!" His voice came first before a shape in the shadowed theatre and that white mask always taunting even when he'd once sought tenderness. "It's simple to forget any voids in between when you stand so willing before me, eager... You were *always* eager for my presence, as if I couldn't get here to you fast enough. Do you remember, Christine?"

"I was naïve," I stated back, unshaken on the outside but a mess within as every past sensation re-grew its broken wings. He'd appear, and I'd tingle from head to toe. I *still* tingled and didn't want him to know he possessed such power.

"No," Erik corrected as he strode up the aisle. "You wore your heart open to me and brimming over in passion. It was in the music we made together and in the air surrounding us. You never held it away from my grasp even when you should have."

"And then you trampled upon it," I accused without fault. "The girl you speak of was a *fool*. She should have been more careful with her misguided compassion and 'open' heart, as you call it."

"Ah, and is that why I now find *none* of it left in you? I damaged it, and you cut off its blood supply and let it shrivel to nothing."

His words stung. He made me sound unfeeling and heart*less*, and considering the pain I *always* suffered beneath the surface, it was an insult. "You are ignorant," I snapped back, "and *wrong*. I didn't kill my heart; I gave it to someone else in your stead."

Mismatched eyes searched my face in the moonlight, obviously dubious to my claims, but I kept resolve firm, even as he climbed the stairs to join me on the stage. ...So close I trembled and fought not to show it.

"So you will argue *he* possesses your heart," Erik stated coldly. "The milksop fool with his title and money. And for such worthless trinkets, you denounce me as well as the music."

"Denounce? You *left*."

He shrugged as if such an imperative point meant *nothing*. "A reality now remedied, but what have I returned to? Not the girl whose talent I molded and brought into existence. Where is *that* girl? You sucked the life out of her and walk about in her empty shell!" he retorted in a shout, and I cringed at how completely he could tear me apart.

"How dare you?" I replied with equaled fervor. "Just because I am no longer the weak pupil adoring at your musical temple, it does not mean I am undeserving of my place. I *earned* the leading spot of prima donna, and I've spent over a year carrying it *alone*, learning what I must to retain it when my *teacher* abandoned me. I have done quite well for myself, and I refuse to listen to you shred it to pieces when *you* are the reason I had no allies and no one to push me to my potential. You *left*," I reminded again. "You gave up your place in my life, and there is no room for you to return now and take it up again. I do not need you."

Hurt appeared so quick and vibrant that I had

only a split second to regret every assertion before he skipped ahead to anger and the rage I recalled in nightmares of that last night together. I fueled the fire because it was just so *easy* to push him toward anger's grasp. It was the emotion he always chose first.

"How wrong you are! You don't *need me*? And yet the performance you gave today was a travesty and a murdering of music's soul. For all Carlotta's flaws and there were *many*, she never would have sung like an automaton with *nothing* inside. You shut every window within, barred every entranceway, and now you stand before me and speak of hearts and accusations? You say you *gave* your heart to your pathetic Vicomte. What heart, Christine? I've yet to see even an inkling of it!"

Closing the remaining gap between us, he glared solely into my eyes, and I fought to cling to my faltering strength with clawed fingertips. *No.* He would not shatter me, would not decipher me, would not pick apart the nuances he favored from those he didn't, would not construct a new Christine to his liking. Not again.

"You look at me and seek a heart you perceive nonexistent," I blamed and glared back. "But you forget that hearts can feel *hate* as passionately as *love*. Look for *hate*, and maybe you'll find it."

He gave a grating chuckle, so close that its reverberation played on my skin and made me shiver. "Hate? I cannot find even hatred in your little guise. Give me hatred, Christine. Give me *anything* that constitutes passion, and I will be satisfied. Hate me to your core, but *show me*! Because all I see are walls inside, an inability to feel. You *don't want* to feel, and you can spout words of hate and rage at me all you like, but not a single emotion you've given is more than a façade. You've disconnected your heart from the world, and *that* is why I won't accept anything you wish to put before me. Hatred, *love* for a worthless peacock, music in your voice. *All* of it is hollow and

161

dead."

"I *hate* you," I hissed and was certain I meant it no matter his assessment.

"No," he replied, shaking a doubtful head. "You don't."

His arrogance infuriated me. He was so convinced he was right that hope twinkled in his mismatched stare as if he was but waiting for me to fall and embrace him, to be *his* when I refused even the idea.

"You *left*," I bid again. It was my excuse and reason and equally reminded the heart hidden somewhere inside why walls were a necessity.

"And did you pray I'd never return?" he questioned, and before I could interpret his intent, he caught my shoulders in pinching hands and dragged me closer than I wished to go.

"Stop," I pleaded and tried to squirm free.

"Did you beg for my presence even once, Christine? One wish from your lips that I would come back to you?"

To my horror, his arms wove about my struggling body and forced me against him, and in spite of every sensation I sought to hold from cresting, I lost a soft cry and felt yanked beneath a tidal wave I didn't want to feel. *No.* No more feeling *anything* for this man. No, ...he'd use every emotion to destroy me all over again if I let him.

"My God, how can you keep up these pretenses even in my arms?" he demanded, clutching me flush to his torso. "Do you not feel how perfect and *right* this is? ...You are *mine*. I feel it; why can't you?"

His. The word left a bitter taste in my mouth even though I had yet to speak it. And *his* evidently meant he'd leave at inopportune times and inflict *hurt* at his choosing.

"I'm *not* yours," I shrieked in indignation and struggled with more vigor. "Let me go, Erik!"

But my arms were pinned in his grasp, and I

could do little more than wriggle tense muscles and gasp shallow breaths that left me dizzy. He would *destroy* me...

"No," I muttered and felt tears threatening to break through the dam.

"Yes, Christine. Oh God, how I've *ached* for this!" Every word was husky and breathed against my ear, encouraging the tears to rim my eyes and blur moon-glow and its silhouettes.

"No..."

Ignoring my half-hearted protests, he released one arm, but before I could gather conviction and dart, he lifted the edge of his mask from his misshapen lips. My eyes grew wide as they fixed on the abnormal contours I'd only recalled in dreams, and in my hazed distraction, the hand at my lower back forced me upward until those distorted lips were upon mine.

His kiss was harsh and branding, possessively fierce the same as it had been that last night. I contemplated for one second that perhaps he did not know *gentle* could exist in the realm of kisses, ignorant to the shades and variations of such an intimacy. I'd grown experienced in his absence, but there were not other kisses and ventures in my head, only an urging to *show him* what a kiss could truly mean. I hated myself with the thought because it meant that I felt something and that was unacceptable.

I couldn't breathe. His mouth was firm against mine, his body so crushing that I felt suffocated. ...Suffocated in his love; wasn't that our very relationship put into phrase? I tried to shrink back, but he moaned deep in his chest and pushed his hips against mine, proclaiming his wanting so vividly that I shook all over as cascades of sensation attacked my unprepared body.

My body wanted, but my heart shouted a desperate *no* and begged me to get free.

His tongue plunged between my lips, and for a second, I was so astonished that I quit all struggles. He seemed urgent to taste, devouring voracious as if he longed to cover every taste bud in my flavor.

Another delirious moan, and it was *beautiful* as it tickled my eardrums. The sound, the timbre of something laden in such arousal, the knowledge that such a guttural instinct meant he wanted *me*. ...And if I forgot all else but his misshapen lips, soft against mine even amidst a hard kiss that flattened their swollen shapes, this was *ecstasy*, craved and shaking me to my core. But...that was if I forgot, and I didn't want to forget.

Recovering scant wits, I acted. I bit his lip, not hard enough to be a valid injury, but it rattled him and the spell of desire he was lost within. As he jerked away, I broke free and recoiled, glaring at him in spite.

"Don't touch me!" I commanded and suffered residual shudders that would not cease. It was too much. He was the reason I'd burrowed my heart and sealed it in iron, and he was also the reason it beat violently in its cage and ached for freedom to beat *for him*.

Erik's mismatched eyes flared in fire, and I fisted my small hands against my chest and considered myself a decent threat right back. But he touched his bit lip, glaring blamefully, and quickly put his mask back in place.

"I am not *yours*," I insisted before adamancy could fade. "I will *never* be yours again. I am the Vicomte's. We are *engaged*." It was the cruelest weapon in my arsenal, and I heaved it at him, knowing the damage it would cause before I even said it. I watched the word swing through the air and strike straight to the mark, debilitating his fury and exposing the hurt beneath.

"Engaged...?"

"No one knows yet," I felt compelled to add in my quick-rising grief.

"Indeed... Then let me be the first to congratulate you," he sarcastically retorted. "I know how rare an occurrence it is for a Vicomte to *marry* an opera tart. ...Rare, no, *nonexistent*. Vicomtes *don't* marry opera tarts."

"Raoul loves me."

"You? Or is it just your pretty face? Your desirous body maybe? I cannot reason your boy is ignorant enough to perceive *marriage* as the only way into your bed, ...but I could be wrong."

"How dare you?" I snapped, but I knew we both did not mean our anger, not on this point. He was hurt. I'd attacked with words, and he was attacking back. "Raoul is a good man. We knew each other in childhood."

"And *that* makes him worthy of your hand?"

"No, his *heart* does. He is honorable and noble; he's never taken a life because it stood in his way." More accusation...

"Oh, go on, Christine. List me more stellar attributes. Don't forget that he is also *handsome*, flawless, never mistaken for the devil out to steal your soul, a prime candidate for every *blessing* God could offer a single person." His bitterness made me cringe. I'd never intended to speak a word against his face; that was too low for me. "But," he went on and leaned close, "don't you dare lie and tell me that you *love* him."

"I...I do."

"*Love* is impossible for one with an un-beating heart," he accused and grabbed the wrists of my fisted hands, jerking me close even as I fought to hold my ground. "And your heart, *my love*, is a vindictive void right now. Oh, I will take the blame. *I* did this; I made you cold and killed you inside. I *murdered* your heart. The crime is fitting, wouldn't you say? I *made* this cold-hearted diva before me who can feel *nothing*, not even the music. Now I have to fix you."

"No," I insisted and twisted in his hold. "Leave

me be. I told you that I am not yours."

He scoffed disbelief. "Say what you like, but until the end of the season, you are *legally mine* by contract signed in your own hand. I cannot risk destroying the production, so I suppose I will take the challenge."

"What challenge?" I retorted, narrowing my glare when his grip would not loosen. "Let go. You're hurting me."

"And *God forbid* I leave marks. If the dearest Vicomte sees, he might assume a *monster* touched your precious skin and tarnished your innocence. He can't have that, not when he'll expect a pure virgin on his wedding night."

"Stop," I commanded, but his anger was ground out in hurt and made me stop battling and allow his hold. "Erik, you *left*." It was my greatest argument. "And I couldn't wait for you forever. You are not *allowed* to put guilt upon me for not wanting to be alone anymore."

Tears appeared again with my admission, and as it struck him and made anger fizzle out of existence, he dropped my wrists and turned away from my stare. "Get out. Go to your supper with the Vicomte."

"And you won't even tell me *why* you left or where you went?" I pleaded and gave him one chance to amend things. A chance he didn't take.

"It is none of your concern," he replied, desolate and solemn.

"But, Erik-"

"It had *nothing* to do with you, and I am disinclined to share. Assume more crimes; it's what I'm best at. Isn't that so? I murder and damage; I take everything good and taint it in blackness. Think that if it justifies your broken heart. I don't care." I didn't believe him for a single word. "But the opera, Christine, that means something to us both. And whatever it takes, I expect you to meet your potential.

Hate me if you must. For, as you said, hate is as tied to the heart as love. Hate, but *feel,* damn you. Find your passion for the music and *sing.* I will not tolerate mediocrity from you when I know better than anyone what you are capable of. Hate me, or *love* your Vicomte," he spat, "but do it with your heart."

I wanted to find an argument, anything to keep his attention, but he was already escaping into the shadows. I couldn't see him beyond the dimness of moonlight, and I wondered if he left entirely or if he lingered, watching me like a ghost.

An absurd terror built that he would vanish again for years at a time, and it was such a surprising sense of fear because it tapped deep inside against the heart I'd kept caged. Evidently, *fear* could touch the heart as well, and when this particular swell was bound to love, it was no wonder. I *felt...* And that terrified me just as much as losing him again.

Chapter Fifteen

Erik~

　　Running an opera was not as easy as I'd imagined it would be. Maybe it was because I was determined to have my hands in every facet from finances to management to production details. The stage director did not favor my intrusion, but I didn't care, reminding who was in charge and paid for *his* services.

　　More interactions, more confrontations, but I was not about to do things halfway. I'd put myself and my mask right into their faces. The hell if I'd back down when I'd been making these decisions for years before as the Ghost. Oddly enough, I'd had a bigger say when I'd threatened with accidents and haunted them. Now as a mortal man with straightforward demands, I had to deal with protests and contradictory opinions. I contemplated resurrecting the Ghost and his notes and insisting my mortal hands were tied, but...too many of the cast had drawn connections already between me and their missing spirit. I wasn't sure playing the role would prove to earn me much fright value anymore.

　　I wanted to spy *every* rehearsal hidden in Box 5, but other tasks in my new *office* had me in and out of eavesdropping range. A ghost with an office? It was humorous in its way, or it would have been if this venture into the living world earned me what I was truly after. But...thus far, Christine seemed eager to avoid my presence as much as she could, rushing out of the opera house the instant the cast was released, never lingering alone in her dressing room, always observant to the shadowed corners around her. I would have taken it badly if not for the reality that she was *afraid* to be alone with me. I knew it without doubt. Ah yes, because she had a fiancé to worry about betraying, the pompous Vicomte who had wisely taken my hints and stayed away from the theatre. Foolish fop! I would make sure he lost in the end, but for now...curse it all! I had an opera to run! What had I gotten myself into?

The stage director Reyer had just called an end to rehearsal, and as I lingered like a warning in the theatre, ignoring the constant wide eyes my cast dared to throw in my direction, I noted that Christine paused one breath on the stage, holding my gaze in hers.

She was so beautiful: hope, salvation, and ecstasy in one body, and I *wanted* her to the depths of my being. Why could she not see that all I'd done had been for *her*? Even leaving Paris all those months ago had roots in a need to become a better man *for her love*. But she still looked and saw the same one that had deceived her and covered his crimes. Not even separation had rebuilt trust. She'd claimed hatred, but I didn't see evidence of that. I didn't see anything in blue eyes but denial. But if the denial was directed toward me or her heart, I had yet to learn.

Before I could request her company as too many others still hovered near, she darted for the wings and away, ...running from me probably with a Vicomte eager to absorb every smile and laugh she'd grant him instead.

Heaving a vile curse that observing ballerinas gasped to overhear, I fled their wretched world and embraced the shadows of the underground. This plan was not working. I needed *more*. I'd vowed not to stand back and wait for her heart; well, it was time to put it into action.

Before I even entered my home, I felt a presence, and for the moment of a single held breath, I thought it might be Christine. ...Oh God, maybe as I'd cursed her, she'd been coming along this path, coming *to me*. Maybe she was proving she was *mine* always...

But disappointment was a lance to the gut when I opened the door with anticipation only to have it suspend mid-air and crash back down. "Daroga... Make yourself at home."

He was seated upon my couch, freshly-brewed tea laid out on the end table and cup in hand, and he merely shrugged as if his intrusion meant little. "I wasn't sure how long you'd be. ...If you were giving any *lessons* after rehearsal's end."

He was fishing for information about Christine that I was hesitant to share. I instead snapped, "You know I appreciate that you rescued me from torture and accompanied me from Persia, all liberties which were my due since I was only in Persia again *because* of you, but I deem your gratitude excessive. Get out of my house."

With a light chuckle, he shook his dark head and contended, "As soon as I conclude all is right with you and an angry mob won't be chasing you down and dubbing you their previous ghost. An opera house, Erik? You used the shah's stolen riches to buy an opera company?"

I gave an idle shrug and reluctantly joined him, pouring myself a cup of tea as I muttered, "It seemed a feasible investment. I perceived you'd commend me. Instead of pitching accidents and threats to have my way, I now can employ my commands with a clean conscience and legality on my side."

But the daroga eyed me suspiciously, intuitively reading what I hadn't said. "And is this purchase about owning an opera house or owning a certain young mademoiselle?"

"Owning her voice. I have a contract," I snidely remarked with a smirk. "*Legally*, the voice is mine until season's end."

"Ah, I see. So she was not as enthusiastic with your return as you'd hoped."

"If enthusiasm now includes hostility and a newly named fiancé whom I incidentally threw out of my theatre and probably lost his family's generous patronage leading to eventual bankruptcy, then yes, enthusiasm to the utmost degree."

"Erik..." The daroga shook a somber head. "I tried to pose once before that maybe this particular girl is not capable of giving you what you want. She *is* young and innocent."

"And I am an infection as toxic as the plague," I added for him with a cold glare. "Yes, you made such peace for your conscience more than once now, but you forget that she *loves* me. Beneath every obstacle she wants to put between us, including her noble fiancé, she loves me."

Doubt never hidden, he inquired, "Did you tell the young lady *why* you left her all this time? At least give yourself excuse and a quest equally as noble as her other suitor?"

I chuckled into my teacup and swallowed before I replied, "And you truly consider tales of torture in the shah's dungeon will have her embracing me with open arms?"

"Women favor such fairytale triumphs of good versus evil."

"It's never that black and white. You forget that to tell this story, I'd have to include that I *was* the evil in our first round in Persia, hence *why* I was wanted for torture. My sacrifice wasn't noble so much as repenting my evil deeds. It's difficult to argue that one is the good hero when one has also been the evil villain."

"Repenting graduates you to hero," the daroga

decided. "And I can vouch for that when I was the one to gain by your sacrifice. You saved my wife and child. Tell your young lady *that*."

But I shook my head and insisted, "You don't know Christine, daroga. She's going through a selfish phase right now. I daresay such details won't make an impression upon her."

"I disagree, but...handle it your way, Erik."

"I have walls to break through with her first. I did it once with music as my key. I will do it again the same. She doesn't need to know the rest of the story."

But the daroga silently observed my masked face as he sipped his tea, and I shifted uncomfortably to be so analyzed. "Is this because you think she can't accept your past...or your more recent present? That *is* it, isn't it, Erik? You don't want to tell her of the torture because you consider it a humiliation."

Humiliation, degradation, repulsive, a horror, but I was not prepared to admit it aloud and shrugged off his surmised conclusion as if it meant little. "Christine likes heroes with flawless faces and physiques. If I have neither of those things to give her, I have to find something to be the equivalent. She loves the music. I will give her that. Being in charge of the opera means she can be my diva as long as she wishes. It isn't much, but for now...it will suffice."

"You bought the opera to keep her in your company then," he reasoned. "Because her fiancé doesn't have scars from head to toe, and...you think the music is compensation for the things you can't change to appease her."

I hated hearing it stated blunt and straightforward and snapped back, "I do not need your psychoanalysis. I love Christine; she *will* love me back, and that rests the case. I appreciate your continued meddling in my life and your wish to see I am well, but it is futile. Go off and be with your wife and child. Wasn't that the point of all this to begin with? And yet you've spent more time in my presence than theirs."

"I just...want to be sure you are well first," he insisted, but I knew there was more to it. He felt guilty for taking me away to Persia and getting me stuck beneath the bonds of torture. He took the blame upon himself despite my hand in the start of this game, and now he was making his own penance by choosing to stay until he deemed I was happy and well-adjusted. I didn't have the heart to tell him that his quest would likely be wasted and any peace he hoped I'd gain was a fool's wish. I had learned how important it was to atone and the reconciliation of the soul, but I'd had it easier. I'd been tortured, and he had no such simple path to his own enlightenment.

The daroga kept in my company the rest of a dull, quiet evening. I doubted he had anywhere else to go. In public, he was as much an outcast as I was, and what kind of acquaintance and semi-friend would I have been to toss him out? I had the distinct feeling that until I either fixed things with Christine or gave her up, I'd have a small, foreign man coming and going in my underground home, putting in his opinion whether I wanted it or not. *Damn.*

In the spirit of such a conclusion, I decided it was time to stop waiting for Fate to wake up and do her job. Time to play on my terms.

As Reyer gave the final notes to a cast I dubbed lackluster after my afternoon's observations, I called before dismissal could be announced, "Mademoiselle Daaé, will you please stay behind? I need to have a word with you."

I saw *fear*. It leapt like mad in her eyes, but beneath a frown, she nodded consent as concern permeated the rest of our audience. Yes, because they perceived their new manager as the demon Opera Ghost with a distorted, devil face beneath the mask and the potential to devour souls. *Christine* knew better, but her obvious unease only fueled the gossiping wildfire as the others were dismissed and rushed out.

I waited in the back of the theatre until the stage cleared and minutes after to be certain everyone had gone, and as I stood, I stared fixedly at Christine's ducked head and trembling shape. When had she ever been *this* afraid of me? Not even our first meeting when she'd expected a ghost or when I'd shown my true face. This was...odd.

My gaze traveled through dark curls drawn loosely back in a ribbon, onward to soft shoulders and the scant bits of skin exposed at her neckline, lower over her curves...

Since I'd returned, I hadn't fully appreciated desire's consummation. No, because Christine felt so out of my reach that desire fell second to a love I was desperate to reclaim. But...no one was about anymore, only she and I, and for a year and a half, desire had been a fantasy I couldn't touch. Now...she was practically at my fingertips and in my care.

Silent as the preying wolf, I stalked the empty aisle and approached her shape on the stage. I gave not a single footfall away, and yet I saw her stiffen before I ever arrived at her level, her every breath quivering with its inhale-exhale motion.

"Christine," I breathed in husky letters that gave wanting a name.

She never looked up, quickly replying, "If you intend to scold my performance at rehearsal and insist you've made good on your threat and arranged an understudy, then be done with it. Raoul is waiting."

I hated his name, hated the sound of its syllables in her voice. As far as desire stretched its fingers, *mine* was the only name I ached to hear, and though I fisted hands that tingled with their need to grab and hold her, I did not disguise my annoyance as I snapped, "And I'm sure a Vicomte would not understand if you chose your career over his company. He'd believe your so-called job was

completed and over at rehearsal's end. Never mind
the fact that real musicians devoted to their talent
need *practice* and *lessons*; they need to commit
themselves to what they truly love and make it their
greatest passion in life."

Still, she kept eyes downcast as she muttered,
"And do you mean the music, or do you mean *you*?"

I shrugged idly. "If *I* can bring the passion out
of you, then a little of both perchance. You have been
a distant stranger to both the music *and* me since my
return, and I can only be disappointed." My gaze
traveled her curves again, now close enough to see the
goose bumps upraised on her bare forearms and every
revealed speck of flesh. Did they make layers beneath
as well, coat her skin in telltale secrets?

"You ask for too much."

"I ask for what I *know* you can give. You're
afraid," I accused exactly what I read, "and I cannot
decide if it is a fear of me or of what I make you feel. I
force you to look within and pour your soul out to the
music...to *me*. You never put up such walls before,
and when you tried, I destroyed them from their base.
Remember the ballet, Christine. I have no magical
snowfall this time to grant you portraits of passionate
interludes, but I will inspire you just the same."

"How?"

I contemplated because I truly had no idea
what the answer was. How could I reach her soul
when she *wanted* to keep it from me? But music was
the key; I was doubtless, and with the slightest smile
upon my lips, I gently commanded, "Marguerite's
fourth act aria. Sing it now for me. Close your eyes
and just sing, Christine. No matter what happens,
don't stop singing."

Her blue gaze finally lifted laden in wariness, a
dark brow arching in a question mark, but with a
reluctant sigh, she slowly let lashes flutter closed and
obeyed.

The recitative passed her lips and resonated

out into the vacant theatre in the same restrained manner I'd been subject to at her earlier rehearsals. Emotion but reined so tight that she felt *nothing*, and what she showed seemed trite and contrived. A beautiful voice was *only* a beautiful voice and nothing worth a second listen without a spark to show its true excellence. That spark came from interpreting, and beyond that, it came from *feeling* and letting the music flow through the veins. It meant becoming a willing servant to music's mastery, and Christine was too determined to control every emotion she ever felt again to realize she wasn't feeling *anything* at all.

She came to the aria, "*Il ne revient pas...*"

As she sang with rounded tone and precision, I wandered around her postured shape, softly speaking near her ear. "What are you singing? 'He does not return'. Surely, you *know* what it feels like to be abandoned. Your father left you; *I* left you." I cringed to use the trauma in my favor, but I could hear her steady tone waver with the reverberation of emotion I was seeking.

"I left you," I repeated it as she had accused at our last encounter, "and hurt you, didn't I? I took a piece of your heart with me."

Ever studious, she kept her song sounding, but every miniscule tremble shook her vibrato and spoke to the place I sought to reach. Shaking with my own uncertainties unavoidably present, I edged close until her back was only inches from my chest, so near that I saw her sway on her feet as she sensed my boldness. Her curls were a cloud before me; I longed to press my face into their soft caress, but...not yet.

"Keep singing," I reminded in a whisper above her ear and shared her shudder. She never denied me; closed eyes stole the vividness of reality, and so as my arms delicately snaked about her waist, she shivered but did not draw away.

"He does not return," I repeated her lyrics and fitted her body snugly to my chest so that her every deep inhalation was half-mine by default. "And you will never have *this* again; only in dreams can you feel him, and it is disappointing, a hollow embrace when touch is but a memory. Oh God, Christine, *feel me*," I begged it and finally surrendered to her curls, letting their coils envelop my face and breathing in her scent. "Imagine it. Being so utterly alone with only fantasies for comfort. ...I couldn't *feel you*," I hissed the words as tears gathered in my eyes and I permitted their tumble into her hair.

Her voice was in pianissimos, barely beyond a whisper, and though real singing was choked away, I never cared. I felt the quivers in her breaths and heard the catches in her tone, and it was exactly what I wanted. Emotion, raw and pure. Her small hands lifted and timidly rested on my forearms, her grip growing firmer with every second that she tested my tangibility.

As her aria ended, I whispered thickly against her ear, "*Feel me*, Christine. I am not a ghost haunting your dreams. I am *real* and *alive*, here with you. No one will take you from me, not your Vicomte, not the rest of this world. *This* is where you belong, only in my arms."

"No," she suddenly muttered, and even though she tried to break free, I tightened my grip and kept her against me.

"No? You'd dare deny me after everything I have endured to be in this place with you again? I *won't* accept it. I may not be your milksop Vicomte, but I had you first. You were *supposed to be* here waiting for *me*." Pleasant peace quickly mutated to pent-up pain and anger, and on its heels, I molded my body flush to her back and pressed my desire against her, half a threat and half *proof* that I spoke the truth, that I'd never stopped wanting.

"Forever?" she gasped out and squirmed, and I could not suppress a moan at that tempting gesture. She wanted freedom; I was too aroused to even consider her agitation. Another struggle, and my head swam until she shouted, "I wasn't even worth a *goodbye* to you! And you dare to insist that I am *yours*! Would you have had me await a hopeless dream for the rest of my life? As far as I knew, you were *gone*, and I was *alone*. Erik... Let go. I'm tired of these games when *Raoul* will be the one hurt in the end. He has done nothing but *love me*. That is more than you could manage."

"I have *always* loved you!" I yelled back.

"You *left*!" she shrieked and struggled harder. "I hate you! I hate you!"

I felt her break. That was the second the walls collapsed, and a sob ripped from the recesses of her innermost soul. *There* was my girl, and as she cried, her little hands struck at my grasping arms in a need to hurt as I'd hurt. She couldn't possibly, and I knew that disappointed her.

"Yes, yes, put it all on me, Christine," I crooned tenderly and pressed my masked face to her silken crown. "Give me all your hate, *ange*. Let me feel it. Let it go."

A year and a half of separation, a year and a half mourning, grieving, aching, of loneliness and longing. I deserved eternal damnation for what I'd done to this girl. I loved her, and she suffered because of it.

"Let go," she whimpered amidst another sob.

"Never."

"I am not yours!" she cried. "You gave me up when you left and broke my heart." Weak became saturated in fury as she suddenly shouted, "Monster! You're a monster without a heart! Selfish, *selfish* man!" Struggles grew fierce again as this time, she whimpered, "You can't keep doing this, Erik! *You* deserve pain and torture with a bleeding heart, but why do *I* deserve such agony? I have done nothing worthy of it! Your love has been my punishment!"

Her accusation was sharp enough to delve

within my soul. Punishment... Was my love something so vile? I hadn't realized... But as I held the struggling girl sobbing telling tears, for the first time, I *did* consider myself selfish. Just because *she* had been my hope in the shah's dungeons, my saving grace and fantasy, didn't mean that *I* was *hers*. And wasn't it ignorant of me to *assume*?

With a reluctance that made muscles stiff and inflexible, I released her from my embrace and watched her stumble and stagger to stand on her own two feet. She flipped tear-filled blue eyes to mine, their hue so vibrant, brighter than usual. Funny how tears had such an effect. Making pain prettier than even happiness. My eyes were probably just as luminescent, but I was not privileged enough for them to be dubbed 'pretty'. No, they'd seem to clash their blue against green more than usual and be *ugly*.

"You don't deserve punishment," I muttered with realization, "but neither do I, and that's *all* I've ever had. Christine, I..."

I considered filling her ears with my story; the daroga had pushed as much. Tell the truth, no matter its degrading reality, but...I looked at her hurt eyes and could not reason using her inevitable sympathy to win her. That would never be enough.

"You...have an awaiting supper companion, don't you?" I pushed and gestured to the stage exit. I took it as a victory that though she carried pain, I was granted views of it now. No more stone heart and guarded shields. It was so deep that it took my breath away, and as much as I hated the idea, I considered that the *Vicomte* would be the one to mend its chasm. He'd heal her every wound, and I would be nothing but the villain who'd caused injury and bruises inside.

She seemed for a second like she would protest my offered escape, lingering before me with those accursed tears lighting blue eyes so brilliant that I was enamored with their contours. But then with a gasped inhalation, she spun on her heel and ran. I did not pursue. Why *punish* her further?

For the first time, I regretted my choices, every single one I'd made with her love in mind. I'd left her with love in my heart; I'd suffered with its ever-present solace as my salvation; I'd returned desperate to kindle the spark. She was right. I was a selfish man. I'd never once considered *her* love.

Curse it all! I'd *atoned* and *still* God condemned me! It wasn't fair! Even monsters deserved forgiveness if they were penitent. How much more would it take? Or would redemption only come if I were sacrificed on the proverbial cross, a *symbol* of pure, unconditional love for all ages?

But even in death, I wouldn't have what I truly wanted: Christine, her heart and soul, her body, every bit of her in my life, in my arms forever. ...Monsters also deserved love, and I was denied its possession from every angle but my own. Torture had been whips and pain, burns, chains, beatings to blood and broken bones, but its agony was endurable when placed beside the aches of the human heart. I'd had hope to get me through, and now...hope was gone.

Chapter Sixteen

Christine~
I ran. Tears blinded every step and smeared the amber and pink hues of sunset like paint splattered on a canvas, a mess of nothing definitive, only color. It felt too bright and exposing, and I longed for night and its dim shades to hide me again.

Dear God, it was as if every wound inside had their scabbed surfaces ripped wide open again, and I could not stop the blood flow as it pooled out of me. I ached from the inside out with emotions I'd thought dead, suffocated at their source of breath. Now they were born anew, thriving, beating into me and taking their share. I didn't want to *feel*, but Erik had found a trigger within and used the music to penetrate my defenses. Every one of these *feelings* were *his*, good and bad, from inspiration to consumption, and I didn't *want* their possession.

My footfalls echoed in my ears as my boots clanked the cobblestone walkway to my apartment. I thought only to be alone, to sob into my pillow and pray the poignancy wore away and trickled out with tears, but...

"Christine! My God, what's happened?"

Dear, sweet Raoul. He was at my side within half a breath and dragging me into his arms without awaiting explanation. I never had to tell him that my tears were out of love for another man; I could just take the comfort he offered and cling to him as if *he* would save my soul from its downfall.

It was so ironic. I'd once wondered if Erik could be the devil, and in the end, he might not have Satan's lures, but he was after my soul just the same. He'd already won it, and even as I tried my best to protect it and keep it as mine, it was falling.

"Darling, ...did you have a poor rehearsal?" Raoul worriedly asked as he gently stroked my hair.

Yes, to him, that would be the only thing to bring such tears. He'd *never* seen me cry. I'd been so careful to appear put together and *whole* for him, not the true damaged creature within. Why would he ever think my hurt ran deeper when I'd given him no impression that anything but he and the music mattered to me? *Music...Erik...*

"No, no," I whimpered in reply to my heart's frantic whispers.

"Then what happened, darling?"

I drew back to meet his kind eyes, and the *truth* fluttered on my tongue. Raoul deserved its secrets. He *loved* me, even if it was only the version I'd presented to him and not the extent of my real, broken self. He should know... But the words were so heavy that my mouth could not form them all.

"The new manager...he upset me."

"That man with the mask?"

I nodded, dull and empty as tears still silently fell. "You've heard Meg speak tales of the Opera Ghost. *He* is the Opera Ghost."

Raoul's handsome features creased with doubt. "Those are stories, Christine, and Meg is dramatic. Did she talk you into believing her frivolous fairytales and frighten you? Ghosts aren't real."

"No, they're not, but evil men with sins on their souls are. The title 'ghost' just makes them immortal in their infamy."

"Evil men? Christine, ...did this masked man hurt you?"

I saw the mixture of fear and anger build in the Vicomte as he leapt to assumptions that very well might have been true, but I couldn't tell him *that part* of the truth. "No, ...not like that, Raoul. He...wants so much from me...in the music, and I can't give it to him. He was...disappointed with my performance today."

"Oh!" I saw relief as Raoul clasped my shoulders and grinned with encouragement. "You have such a tender heart, Christine! You cannot let his *opinion* mean anything. Mine is far more important, and I think you are extraordinary and amazing, a diva to rival all divas of the stage. This manager of yours has rubbed every member of your company the wrong way with his condescending temperament. Let me speak on your behalf and remind him who funds his business."

"No!" I immediately exclaimed, shaking a frantic head. "You mustn't dare!"

"What's the worst he'll do? Turn you out of your job?" Raoul scoffed his disregard. "Let him! You don't need to worry over money or salary. I'll take care of you until we're married and then none of this will matter."

"Raoul!" I snapped and forced his attention. "He *is* the Opera Ghost, and the tales Meg tells are true. ...He could *kill* you."

The word only rattled him a bit, not nearly as much as I believed it should, but he obviously didn't give much credence to Erik's power. "You sound as melodramatic as Meg."

"It's *not* melodrama. He is a *murderer*. I know it to be true; he told me."

"Did he threaten you, Christine?" But as I desolately shook my head, the Vicomte presumed the worst again and I couldn't deny it. "What has this...*Opera Ghost* been to *you* that he makes such admissions? ...Is there something more you should be telling me?"

"He...was my teacher once. He...he's in love with me." Speaking it was enough of a betrayal, and I saw it bruise the Vicomte as his grip unconsciously tightened on my shoulders.

"And...you?"

"I want to be with you," I said before I even contemplated. Oh Lord, I was not about to crush the Vicomte's heart as violently as my own. Perhaps I loved Erik; perhaps my heart still felt tied to his, but I knew being with him was destructive. He'd hurt me again and again, but Raoul...his love was *safe*.

The Vicomte took that as assurance enough, and with a relieved sigh, he cupped my cheek adoringly in his palm and decided, "Then I want you nowhere near this masked man, especially if he has the potential to hurt you if you do not give him what he's after. Christine, ...you must understand my concern. If what you say is true, then this is a dangerous situation. Perhaps you *should* leave the opera."

"I can't. I signed a contract." It was an excuse. Maybe there were ways beyond such limitations, but I wanted to sing. And for as terrible as things seemed, I couldn't reason *never* seeing Erik again.

"Then...*I* will attend rehearsals with you again." Before I could argue, Raoul shook his head against me and concluded, "Let him be angry and threaten! I have a right to be present and observe what my family's money funds. If he argues, I'll take my case to the *gendarme*. Don't worry. I will not leave you alone with that man, ghost or not."

I swallowed back another protest. What could truly be said? I'd given Raoul too many details to make his own retort impenetrable.

As his gaze roamed my tear-stained face, he slowly clung to one point I had not given him. "If, as you say, Meg's Opera Ghost tales are true, does that mean his face is...?" he trailed off with a wince as though he could not even fathom something so unsavory, and it bothered me.

"It's...a deformity," I was compelled to defend, "and it's cruel to judge something he had no hand in creating. *God* is responsible."

"God works in mysterious ways. Have you ever heard that phrase, Christine? Perhaps God was marking him so the world would see his evil makeup. A warning to those with good souls."

I went numb as he took a saying I myself had uttered in sincerity and turned it into a travesty. I'd seen optimism in its words; he saw the opposite. "A warning?"

"Yes, to keep pure souls like yours safe and turn you away from malevolence. If the stories are true, it certainly makes sense. God would want to keep you protected and make sure you know evil when it appears. I refuse to believe a man with a deformed face is *coincidentally* a murderer. Fate carves our path from the beginning, so if this Ghost is evil, he was *destined* to be evil."

"But...you don't reason the world could make him such a way?" I posed with a dubious shake of my head.

"Of course not! What a flimsy excuse! We as mortal beings with souls know right from wrong. God gave this creature a monster's face instead of a soul, and *fate* scripted his path to evil before he ever took his first breath. That's all there is to it, and he will be held accountable for his sins. Oh, Christine, thank God you told me! What if I'd stayed ignorant of such horror and *lost you*?"

Raoul hugged me to his chest, and I went willingly even as my head reeled with his remarks. I *knew* Erik better than anyone, and Raoul's quick assessment made me angry. How could he judge something as life-altering as a disfigured face? I saw *no* compassion in the Vicomte for Erik's plight; maybe that was due to jealousy, but I saw it as *cruel*.

For the first time in months, my musings felt

tied to my center, and it *hurt* me to know Raoul could condemn Erik without truly analyzing him, without knowing his love and passion for the music, ...his love and passion for *me*. Such things were redeeming qualities in my eyes.

We went to supper, but I kept quiet most of the minutes, unable to escape my mind's caverns as the details of the evening played in an incessant loop. Thankfully, Raoul did not push and left me at my apartment later with nothing more than a kiss and a promise to be there in the morning.

The next day passed in an unending pattern. Raoul was my anchor and rock, keeping me grounded in the world when my mind and heart yearned to drag me other places. He went to rehearsal with me and lingered in the back, and if Erik cared, he made no appearance to argue otherwise. Hour to hour ticked their minutes, and he never came, not even to check our progress. It hurt me because my immediate terror was that he'd disappeared again.

Oh God... What if my rejection had frightened him off like the last time? Sense said I should be grateful if that were so, but I couldn't reason beneath a newfound swell of agony in my chest. It throbbed with my heartbeat and did not subside as the day wore on. I still saw no sign of Erik's presence, and the bleeding wound in my soul oozed its wares onto the stage and another lackluster performance. *Erik, where was Erik?*

The instant Reyer dismissed us, I was halfway down the aisle. I would go straight to his office, to the underground, whatever it took to find him, drag him out by bare hands and knuckled fists if need be!

"Christine!" Raoul assumed my projected path was to *him* and caught my arm with a welcoming grin. "You sang wonderfully."

I shot him a glare of annoyance, only to find that he meant the sentiment. Suddenly, Erik's assertions held weight. The Vicomte obviously knew *nothing* of music because my performance was most definitely mediocre and subdued.

"Christine..." All thought fled with that voice, and I spun wide eyes about to catch the mismatched ones watching the Vicomte and me in solemn somberness.

Raoul leapt to attention and darted between my body and our masked companion like a guard dog on alert. "If you intend to chastise her or speak threats because I am in attendance, do not bother, monsieur. I can have the *gendarme* here to speak our rights in mere minutes."

"By all means, make yourself comfortable in *my* theatre," Erik snapped with a condescending sneer. "If it keeps the Vicomte *and* the *gendarme* happy, then I suppose I'll have to allow this disrespectful impropriety to continue."

The Vicomte cast a glance about to find we were the only ones left in the theatre, and with a cold glare, he retorted, "I am here to see that Christine remains protected, Monsieur *Ghost*. I will not stand idly by and let you hurt her."

I met Erik's enraged stare over Raoul's shoulder and could say *nothing* in conciliation. He *blamed*, but I deserved it and the guilt that erupted.

"Hurt her...?" Erik distantly bid. "If she truly believes that is my intent, then perhaps it is a blessing she has *you* to keep her safe, Monsieur Vicomte." Every word was sharp and directed solely at me as he added, "I only sought you out to tell you that you sang well today."

"My performance was-"

"Not performance," he hastily interrupted. "Performance was shoddy, and you know that. But for the first time since rehearsals began, I heard *you*, your soul and heart in your voice, and if hating me is what brought it back, then please *hate* me to every extreme of the word. But keep singing as you did. Why do anything if there is no passion in it? What a meaningless waste if you don't *feel*."

Music...or marrying a Vicomte who didn't even know the shades of my heart...

That was all he said. With one more glare at the Vicomte, he left, but I watched him stalk down the corridor toward his office until he disappeared from sight.

"I think you were right about everything, Christine," Raoul was saying, but I barely heard a word. "He *is* your Opera Ghost, and only God knows what he is capable of. A madman!"

This began a string of speeches from the Vicomte about how best to protect ourselves from the Opera Ghost's diabolical plans. I ignored the majority of his ideas and instead silently dubbed him a fool to ever consider posing battle with the almighty ghost. It seemed like a child's game of pretend: Erik as the Opera Ghost, wailing and moaning as he haunted the opera corridors, Raoul as the hero in a miniature cape and crown with paper sword in hand ready to duel to a fake death scene, and me the damsel in distress. I didn't want to *be* the damsel in distress.

The situation was taxing, and as the next week slipped by and I saw Erik only as he headed between office and theatre, I grew bored with the entire world and my place in it. I was angry and hurt; the emotions were broken out of my self-made boundaries and more powerful than ever in their attack, but I was also *longing* inside for the man I'd once known and loved, the *angel* I'd never wanted to be without. Since his return, I missed him still, and though rifts were un-mended and hearts bore scars, I could take no more of this separation.

Raoul awaited me at rehearsal's end, and though he offered a late supper, I claimed fatigue and was grateful when he brought me home. By his standards, I was *safe*, locked in my little apartment for the night and secure until he came for me in the morning. Tonight would not follow his protocol.

As soon as I saw his silhouette disappear, I emerged from the front door and rushed back through the city, chasing the final rays of sun until I arrived at the opera. I was quick to enter the building, gliding through empty corridors to my dressing room, past the secret doorway in my mirror and onward to the network of underground catacombs.

I couldn't say what I hoped would come of this or what I thought I was doing, only that I had to hear Erik's voice, any words, even angered outbursts to calm my wayward spirit.

Thin slits of light escaped into the darkness from Erik's hidden doorway, announcing a presence within, and with a racing of my heart, I hurried the final distance, my footsteps echoing off the stone before I burst into Erik's house.

"Erik," I breathed his name in anticipation, but though a fire burned in the hearth and welcomed me, there was no masked angel leaping to his feet with my intrusion. No, instead I came face to face with a small, dark-skinned man in foreign attire, tossing his teacup on an end table and gaping at me with wide eyes.

"Mademoiselle...Christine, is it? You gave me quite a fright. I was expecting Erik," he said in thick accent and forced a chuckle to cover his obvious unease.

"You...know who I am," I stated with my own discomfort as we both studied each other and sought to read our characters. I had no idea if I regarded friend or foe.

"Yes, Erik's spoken of you...quite often in fact," he replied with a kind grin and sat back upon the couch cushions. "Let's move beyond formalities. I am...a friend of sorts. Erik might not use that term, but then again, I'm not sure he knows its definition. He tends to treat everybody as failing and falling into the category of *enemies* no matter their intentions. Tea?"

189

I shook my head but cautiously took a seat in the chair across from him, still unsure if my guard should waver and drop. "And...where is Erik exactly?"

"He hasn't returned yet. This past week he's been dallying above. At first, I thought he was back to teaching *you*. Your lessons used to delay his appearances, but that was in days of old. Now...well, I think he's just unsettled and doesn't want my company. I try to make him talk about it, and lately, his burdens are too heavy to share, it seems." He eyed me as he sipped from his teacup, and though I didn't want to share either, I knew my guilt was evident upon my face. Walls were no longer my specialty or working in my favor.

"You know," the foreign stranger continued as he scrutinized me with a shrewd eye, "the days when Erik was teacher to you, that was the most lighthearted I'd ever seen him. Take it from a man who has witnessed some of the worst parts of Erik's existence. Teaching you was something that gave him hope."

"Hope..."

"Yes, and it was quite lucky that he continued carrying that hope the entire time we were away. It was the inspiration for his survival, you know."

My ear caught on details that intrigued, things that were mysteries Erik was disinclined to reveal, but the stranger before me seemed eager to talk. Even as I wondered how much I could trust, I was anxious for every word.

"Erik...refuses to speak of such things," I murmured as if we were exchanging secrets.

The foreign man sighed and rolled his eyes. "Stubborn one, he is. I tried to push him into it. I think you *should* be told, but..."

His expression grew solemn, and I wondered what I was getting into, suddenly apprehensive. Perhaps Erik wouldn't speak of his time away for good reason, but as my mind created its own interpretations, I grew frantic and impatient. I *needed* to know with an urgency that tore at my heart.

Choosing the point I could argue with the most proof, I demanded beneath a furrowed brow, "Was he...hurting people again? Or...killing?"

"No, no, by Allah, no," the foreign man assured, hasty and adamant. "Just the opposite, mademoiselle. Erik was not the assailant this time; ...he was the victim."

"What?" I gasped the word and felt my stomach drop without even a solid explanation to hold. "What do you mean, monsieur? Now you *must* tell me."

He huffed indecisively at my wide eyes and desperation. "Erik is going to heave me unceremoniously out of his life for this betrayal. You really should ask *him* to tell you, now that you know there is something worth telling."

"Your deduction of his stubborn nature should also include his dire need to seem invincible and in control," I retorted. "If you know him at all, then you realize that he will deny me any such story."

The stranger shook his dark head. "This time there's more to it than his need to play god. This time...it's *shaming* to him, mademoiselle, and...it's *my* fault he was ever put in such a position. He left Paris to help *me*."

"He never told me, not why or how or a single valid point. *Please* tell me, monsieur. He accuses me of walls, but he has done the same, and...I can't bear it."

He still seemed hesitant, glancing at the sealed door as if gauging how much time we had undisturbed before Erik returned, but with a sigh, he nodded consent.

"All right, but only because if you don't hear it and know what he would rather keep alone, he's going to lose you. I told him as much, but he refused to listen. You deem him unforgiveable for abandoning you when really he sacrificed everything he loved and was *punished* for it left and right."

Punished... I'd dubbed his love as my punishment and hated myself for speaking in the heat of the moment and regretting only later.

"We were in Persia for the last year and a half, mademoiselle," the small man said, holding my gaze with utter honesty. "Did Erik ever speak to you about his past in Persia?"

I pondered and muttered, "He said he once worked as an assassin for the shah...and killed for him."

He nodded. "Those were his *real* dark days, not these Opera Ghost pranks and mischief. He was merciless in the shah's court, but the job required it. Such a cruel state was not a stretch for a man who had spent his life as humanity's mockery. I daresay he took out decades of being weak and victimized by victimizing others. It is no excuse, but...I don't think any of us can truly sympathize with Erik's plight. To spend one's entire existence rejected and abhorred for something he couldn't fix or change... That is a lonely life, and I'd imagine the base for quite a lot of hostility and anger, ...a need to retaliate.

"And the shah gave it to him. For a time, Erik was the shah's golden boy, obeying every command, torturing at will, never questioning. But any man with even a flicker of decent emotion in his heart must eventually tire of such brutality. Erik wanted to quit the shah's service, but he knew too many secrets. He was invaluable and was ordered to stay or die, so he made his own third option and tried escape. I helped him. Call it pity for his case; call it a hope that he *would* seek something better when his life had been a tragedy thus far. I made sure he got free unscathed and thought we'd never encounter each other again. But the shah is no fool, mademoiselle. He knew *someone* aided Erik's departure. He was on the hunt for years. To him, it was a disgrace to his rule that mutiny could abound. Once he learned *I* was the one responsible, he took my wife and infant child, jailed them for treason, and I came here in search of Erik."

My mind envisioned his tale with deft precision and could already predict the path it would take. To me, it felt like fiction. A shah upon his throne in a foreign land, tormenting women and children with his vindictive ways, but surely a *hero* would save in the end...

The foreign man smiled at me gently as he continued, "I arrived in Paris only to find my once reclusive and desolate friend had found a sudden purpose and meaning for his life. *You*, mademoiselle. He was your teacher, and...he loved you. He didn't want to leave you, but he opted to come to Persia and help my plight. We both thought it would be a quick trip there and back. How could we have guessed the shah would put Erik in an impenetrable dungeon that took quite a bit longer to find a means out of again?"

"Dungeon..." The word conjured images of stone encasements and *bars*. Trapped like a caged bird, unable to fly free.

Growing darkly somber, the foreign stranger replied, "He was jailed for over a year in a solitary cell, ...and he was tortured, mademoiselle."

Tears filled my eyes and poured rapidly down my paled cheeks. "What...what does that mean? I don't understand."

His nod was thick in his reluctance to elaborate, and I felt sick to my stomach as I fictionalized the story again. No, no, it couldn't be reality. I'd *seen* Erik since his return, *felt* him. I knew he was here and *all right*, and torture seemed...severe and savage, ugly. Surely it was an exaggeration.

"*Tell me*," I begged in desperation, leaning closer in my seat and fisting my shaking hands in my lap. "What does *torture* mean?"

"Beaten," he revealed, and my heart reverberated and echoed every hard consonant in throbs as he stated, plain and blunt, "Struck, whipped, burned. Only Allah knows what else; Erik won't tell me the extent, but every horror you can imagine. The shah is a sick sadist, and he had *years* to devise a fitting punishment for what he saw as his greatest enemy. He'd trusted Erik once and is not a man to betray."

A sob passed my lips, and I pressed it into my fisted hand, my entire body lost to uncontrollable shivers. My God! And Erik would never have told me!

I wasn't sure if my sudden burst of anger was truly *anger* or just the pain of knowing I had no control over any of this. It had already happened, and I'd never been included in a single detail, a part of his life he'd shielded me out of and couldn't even share it now that it was over. Impulse was the swell in my heart that longed for Erik's presence to assure myself that he was *here* and then the necessary need to wrap my arms about his body and never let another blow even graze him. But...reality was that he didn't want that.

As I continued to cry into my fisted hands, the Persian man offered a solace that cut even deeper, "But *you* saved him, mademoiselle. *You*, fantasies of returning to you. He made you his only hope and survived what would have killed any other man. If he hadn't had *your* memory as his salvation, he would have given up. ...When we were finally able to get him out, he was...in bad shape. The shah had been vicious in the last beating he endured, but all Erik could speak of was coming back to Paris for you. No matter the pain and injury, you were all he wanted to make him well. He saw his confinement as penance and the transformation he needed to become a man worthy of your heart."

Oh no...what had I done? I'd called Erik *selfish*, selfish for trying to step in and reclaim a heart he'd given up. ...He'd *never* given up. *I* had, and I was the selfish one between us to have never considered anything but the hurt I'd suffered without him. I'd never even given a thought that perhaps he'd had a reason to go, a reason that exceeded both of our hearts, or that he hadn't returned because he *couldn't*. All that time, he'd loved me and wanted me even as he'd endured agonies I couldn't even imagine, and at the same time, I'd spent a year and a half cursing him and lamenting my broken heart, building walls so I wouldn't have to feel it as it beat with a split down its center. ...What had I done?

"Why didn't he tell me?" I cried in the middle of my sobs. "Why did *he* decide I was not allowed to know and hurt *with* him? That is *unfair*."

The foreign stranger shook his head again, tears suspended in his dark eyes as they watched me carefully, and with a waver in his voice, he replied, "To him, it truly *is* a humiliation. He wants to seem so strong all the time, to never fully expose the vulnerable spirit within." He scoffed as if the idea were ridiculous. "And he would rather have given you up to your Vicomte suitor than seem a broken man in your eyes."

"But he *isn't* a broken man," I insisted, vehement and crying into my shaking knuckles. "He *isn't*, but he wouldn't have let me say so. He took a hatred I'd fabricated over a love I could have granted. ...He told me to put it upon him...all my hatred for what he'd done to *me*. Oh my God, what have I done?"

Finally un-fisting my taut fingers, I buried my sobs into my shaking hands and felt them tear me apart inside.

"I'm sorry...sorry," I gasped between sobs that seemed endless. They were the residual outpouring of a year and a half of loneliness and a love I'd been so sure had been lost to me. Every disappointment, every hopeless second, every instant I could only have memory when I wanted the man attached. It all streamed out in the wake of revelation. I was tempted to crash to pieces, but I couldn't. Not when I needed to fix things.

"Mademoiselle?" The Persian man reached between our seats and set a gentle hand upon mine. "Life isn't about our mistakes in the past. It is about how we mend their ill-doings in the present. I never believed a man like Erik could find anyone to love him for who and what he is. But...if *love* is what you carry in your heart for him and I mean a love that exceeds compassion and pity, a love that can forgive as well as grow, then chances are not lost. Have hope."

But hope was coated in self-guilt, so much that I couldn't bear to stay in that underground house and await Erik's return, too terrified I'd anticipate and he'd *never* appear again. It was just retribution if now after every secret learned, I lost him for my foolish behavior. So on the tide of regret, I rushed home with barely a muttered goodbye to my foreign companion and a head too full to know reason.

My dreams that night were laden in depictions of the trials Erik had endured. I couldn't seem to get out of Persia as nightmare led to nightmare, and I heard *his* voice in my ears proclaiming love and pleading for mine in return even as he suffered.

I awoke at dawn and burrowed my cheek into my tear-soaked pillow; it was wet with every pained ache of my heart. I could barely carry its weight, heavy and laden within the cavity of my chest, crushing my bones at every thudding pulsation.

And how was I to lighten this burgeoning beat? I wasn't supposed to know the truths I'd been given; *Erik* had not told me, and it was almost a betrayal to have their pictures in the back of my mind. The Persian man had made it clear that Erik was embarrassed by his abuses. *I* saw no source of abashment; I saw strength and resilience, a soul too powerful to be fractured, but...*I wasn't supposed to know*.

I was solemn as the Vicomte arrived and

walked with me to the theatre, and when he worried and asked why, I claimed nerves for the show and insomnia. Lies, lies, more lies, and I didn't *care* that I could form their falsehood so easily to the man I'd vowed my loyalty to. I was *not* loyal. I loved another man; I was already condemned, and lies seemed frivolous in comparison.

Rehearsal was going on, and I was mid-scene when Erik strode across the stage to speak to the director. My gaze was drawn to him as if I'd been compelled by longing, tugged from the core of my being, and though I resisted following in step and touch, eyes could travel for me and observe his nuances as if I only now *saw him* since his return.

My breath choked in my chest as knowledge opened my eyes and showed me what I hadn't realized before. Oh God... He moved, and there was a new stumble in his walk, a hesitation that interrupted his typically smooth grace. He'd always been an extension of a legato melody; now I glimpsed miniscule staccatos, never anything too obtrusive. No one else would have taken a second glance, but I *knew* him. How had I disregarded that telltale sign? He moved like a man with pains to hide.

Of course there was no blatant evidence, but his suit hid his body like a second skin and gave a *flawless* precision. More clues for me alone. He wore the mask to mimic a perfect face when his own was anything but, and as the pieces fell into their designated spots, I realized that since his return, his suits had grown more distinguished and formal, the sort one chose for the highest events, not day to day wear. Why had I attributed all such changes to his new post in society's world? His suit was as much a shield as the mask on his face; *perfection* when it couldn't exist for him...

He never regarded my spying presence, not even on his exit, and I hid my disappointment when I considered the Vicomte in the audience. No one could know.

But as the day dwindled its prescribed hours, my heart's aching suffocated my every breath. No matter what outcome it brought, I had to fix this; only then would my heart beat free and light again. I merely had to figure out how to win everything from nothing.

Chapter Seventeen

Erik~
    I was tired. That was a typical occurrence of late. Evidently, running a theatre *and* directing in my subtle, opinionated way in combination with sleeplessness and an unsettled heart took a toll even on the omnipotent Opera Ghost. I was starting to regret my hasty decisions made with a rash rush of impulse and love. Buy an opera house, run the show from the frontlines instead of behind the scenes, all in hopes of second chances and regaining a heart I'd never had as mine. *...My love was a punishment.*
    I had to remind myself every occasion that I yearned for one iota of Christine's attention that *she* did not want me. Initial plans to *take* seemed pointless and wasted efforts now, and perhaps this new sense of maturity was a product of my Persian confinement. I was angry and hurt, but I wasn't dead or in a cage any longer. Perhaps I needed to appreciate small blessings.
    The extent of my so-called maturity was limited in its scope. In my effort to give Christine what she wanted, I *ignored* her and avoided being in her presence. That was all I could manage. Leaving the opera completely was beyond my capabilities...yet. Little steps. Disentangle my heart before severing its necessary artery. Then I might bleed, but I wouldn't perish. I'd continue on...alone again. Why did that

seem my doomed fate?

As I walked across a crowded stage with more side notes for the director from my constant, unobserved spying, I *felt* Christine's gaze upon me, branding me to the marrow of my bones, but I never once broke my stoicism. Why would I want to look back and see suspicion and hatred, candid and vividly cast? I'd *asked* for hatred in hope of finding love. How that had blown apart in my grasp!

I ignored Christine; I ignored a cast and crew full of vicious leers and cruelty. I did my job because I loved the music above everything else, and that had to come first. Curse every nay-saying fool in the backdrop!

Confining myself to my office and a pile of paperwork was futile when I had to *breathe*. Breathing made my heart continue to beat, and my beating heart *hurt* with a physical ache in my chest. I wanted *Christine*; I loved *Christine*. Why did love exist in the world when if it wasn't requited, it became *agony* instead?

Regret and longing were a bitter combination, and work became impossible within their possession. I paced a fitful path about my office like a caged tiger, stalking its cell with a need to be free. But I was also my own jailer and couldn't let myself wander for fear of tempting temptation.

Christine was too close, and as rehearsal continued and echoes of music poured through the cracks to tease my ears, I fisted desperate fingers and insisted this self-denial was for the best. Separation, tying off the poisoning valve within my heart so it would wilt and shrivel away. This was the route to preserving my integrity. I'd fallen weak beneath love's spell, but I would rise again.

Through walls and doors, I had little beyond vibrato and high notes to judge, but as Christine's Act Four aria began, I halted my stalking pace and felt a shudder rack my spine. *Oh God... That* was the voice

I'd been after for weeks. I heard...her heart, and mesmerized, I crept out of my cage and wandered toward the theatre door, needing to see and hear more as if it were for imminent survival.

Without a single telltale sound, I lingered in the furthest shadows and ran starved eyes over her as she sang from center-stage.

He does not return...

Her heart saturated every pitch past her lips, lacing the tone and giving a new depth that stretched to her very soul. Thick and oozing pure, raw emotion so vivid that I caught the glimmer of tears in her eyes, glinting like diamonds in the stage lights. Tears... A genuine heart open for the taking, and I felt my soul reaching to her, extending from the core of my body and stretching its sinewy embers toward the only place I ached to be. She sang, and it was difficult to consider anything but that she was *mine*.

Her voice rose and blossomed upon a high note that tore into my body and made a violent wound on my heart. I prayed it scarred and remained with me forever. I'd hurt her... I never wanted to forget it. It would be the most beautiful scar I owned.

The aria dwindled back to a wispy pianissimo, and as blue eyes fluttered closed with her last held pitch, tears tumbled free from her lashes. They made thin streaks along her reddened cheeks that beamed blindingly and proclaimed to every one watching, especially me, that she was vulnerable and exposed at that moment, a bare soul on the stage.

My God, that had always been my greatest desire for her. She was one with the music; even if *I* would never have her, she had given herself over to music's consumption and let it flow through her instead of around her. It was a meager compensation, but at least, it showed that my teaching had stained an imprint on her existence. It meant in some way, I'd mattered.

I abandoned my hiding spot before her eyes

ever fluttered open. I couldn't bear to watch them land on the enamored Vicomte sitting on the opposite side of the theatre, watching her with echoes of *my* adoration in his stare. No... I didn't need to be masochistic at the moment. It could only end poorly, and my heart had already taken its beating.

Once again, I tried self-confinement, and it worked long enough for rehearsal in the theatre to end. I heard the bustle of departing bodies, the laughter and chatter as they wandered the corridor beyond my office door, and inevitably, I found myself wondering if Christine were among them, perhaps on her way to her doting Vicomte, who'd be ready to lavish her in well-deserved praise. I hated myself for fantasizing it and believing it to be fact.

Oh, how my heart *hurt*! It was such a burden to bear, and later as I finally emerged from confinement and strolled the darkened corridors, it weighted my steps and called all my attention and focus. I could not reason a path beyond *pain*, and I was so consumed in its possession that when my ear first caught the tinkering of random pitches on a piano, I thought nothing of it. Perhaps I'd lived among music too long and had songs and instruments in my inner mind's caverns because it took a concentrated effort for me to recall that everyone had left and the theatre was supposed to be empty. ...Perhaps we had ghosts...

Following the path of siren pitches like a sleepwalker, I crept back into the theatre and conjured Christine. Another fantasy, another ghost in my memory, ...or so I thought until she stopped tapping keys and blue eyes rose and halted upon my observing presence. Oh God, this had to be another creation of my hungry head! Because she looked at me and I saw *so much* in her eyes that it scared me. I got stuck in those blue orbs and didn't want to emerge again.

Seconds stopped moving for that riveting

infiltration. We were no longer two bodies, seeing
skin and bone, hair, face, tangible creation; we saw
soul to soul in that paused abeyance. A look through
infinity's chasm to a place with no corners or walls.
We were revealed to each other, and I was so
astounded that I could not find the will to question.
No, I only longed to stare and see *this* image forever.

She spoke first and rattled me back to reality.
"Am I intruding?"

"No...no," I stammered and forced my legs to
carry me down the aisle toward her with feigned
control. "Is your Vicomte lurking somewhere in the
wings, ready to purge the world of the dastardly Opera
Ghost at first chance?"

It was half an accusation when it seemed my
secrets were shared among the three of us. I'd given
her too much credit to believe she'd remain loyal to
me.

But though guilt flashed, she did not let it sway
her as she admitted, "I told him that I was staying in
the dormitories with Meg tonight for some quality
time with my prior dancing comrades."

"Oh?" My mind spun webs of hope, and I
hated how quickly it consumed me in an unqualified
optimism, ensnaring my gullible soul in its sticky
threads and strangling every suspicion that *should
have* existed.

She shrugged with idle innocence, but her gaze
remained unguarded and light. Dear God, it
reminded me of my little ballerina! The anticipation
for *my* presence, the playfulness I'd never shared with
anyone, the meeting of hearts on an empty stage...

"I couldn't tell him the truth," she added.

"Which is?" I pushed, impatient for knowledge
she possessed.

"That I have been mediocre in rehearsals and
need help to reach my true potential," she reported
without the defensiveness she'd previously held on the
subject. "I was hoping...*you* could fix that."

"Indeed..." I didn't tell her that I'd witnessed glorious perfection earlier, terrified praise would lead to changed minds. "I suppose I could teach you again. Maybe a lesson or two, ...help you find your inspiration."

We eyed each other, ever tentative and uncertain as we carefully built one bridge at a time for fear it would all collapse and drop us. Cautious in my steps, I joined her onstage and shivered beneath her gaze as it followed my every motion. A strange malaise of emotion churned in those blue depths, and I could not reason the source or why she frowned when I sat at the piano bench, closer to her than I'd been in long, unendurable days. She'd asked for this shared moment, hadn't she? And yet she seemed...hesitant and somber and gave no explanation as she moved into the piano's bow and took her place, but I had no intention of asking and ruining the most pleasant exchange we'd indulged since I'd returned. Better not to know...

Our lesson was *bliss*, a window backwards into our past where everything faded to the outer divides but the music. We shared passion and love beneath music's blanket and forgot the pain hands and words could inflict when melody did not sugarcoat life. We belonged to each other, and souls met and merged, wrapped inextricably about one another's. If I'd earlier perceived to disentangle from *her* possession, this proved such an extraction was impossible. I was hers, maybe more than she'd ever be mine, but even bits were better than nothing at all.

She gave me everything, no walls or constrained heartbeats. She was the Christine I'd always known she'd be since the first melody she'd ever sung for me. Confident prima donna, gleaming from the inside out with a charisma not every singer possessed, alive and alight and extraordinarily beautiful in her pure essence. I adored her to the deepest recesses of my being, but when declarations tickled the tip of my tongue and longed to meet air, I bit them back and refused to let them fly the space between us. No, ...she had a fiancé to consider, and I had a heart full of scars.

As our precious time drew to its inevitable end, I mourned her loss even as she stood before me, terrified of the first minute I would have to breathe without her. But *she* was the one to prolong when I dreaded letting go.

"Will you play for me, *ange*?" she softly pleaded, and I felt tears collect in my back of my throat at that longed-for request.

I never hesitated, leaping heart-first into a sonata that spanned the length of the keys and rode around my body in its circumference. I played and watched the music envelop and embrace her as my arms ached to. How often did it get to love *for me*? And when she closed her eyes and shivered with a tinge of a smile, I was in heaven.

This was half a dream because I knew eventually, we'd have to wake up, and what then? When I was unsure what had sparked this flame into existence, I was afraid to question and lose every second. So I simply played as if we'd fallen back through time's line and were a year and a half in the past where Vicomtes had no faces, only titles and strangers, where we'd barely hurt each other beyond loving too fiercely.

And just like those past pleasures, she tentatively approached my piano bench. Confidence had evaporated, prima donna deflated and put away for her next showing, and the girl at my side was *my* Christine, blushes and innocence, uncertain to bear her heart so open, pinned to her bodice and exposed for the world to see.

This was what I'd spent countless hours in the shah's prison imagining, and as the scene pulsed with life, I prayed I wasn't lost in imagination again. Maybe all this was a fantasy, and in reality, my tangible body stood at the back of the theatre, envisioning and mourning what was forever gone.

But she rested small palms upon my shoulders, and the breath fled my lungs as if I'd endured a punch to the gut, dropping my poised posture to a slouch. Oh, she had such power in those tiny hands! Bending reality into an arc and my will with it. One touch, her palms delicately set with never a hint of pressure, and I felt *crushed* by sensation's wave. It swallowed me whole in its devouring bite.

I never ceased pounding my fingers to the ivory keys, so rapacious that the joints ached, and the piano's belly vibrated with the ferocity. It was a song of *need* and longing, of the desperation I suffered to have *her*. ...Why couldn't I have her? Just *this* for always?

Her fingertips curled within my jacket material, a determined grip from a girl that I knew swayed with an unstable core. It surprised me, but not as much as what followed. One hand relaxed; I felt it ease out of material and lighten upon my shoulder. I never stopped my melody, not even when that hand set to my mask and deftly removed its barrier as if it meant nothing at all.

My face was exposed, and though I felt her gaze roam its ugliness, I never looked. I didn't want to destroy when I could pretend, and in my spinning slideshow, there was no disgust or hesitation. ...I liked that version better.

But she released a breath in a soft sigh as if she were *content* to see my hideous features, and before I could collect a courage I wasn't sure I possessed, she leaned over my shoulder and pressed her smooth cheek to my damaged one.

"Oh God...," I whimpered and shuddered the length of my spine as my fingers attacked a piano's keys in compensation for the need that plundered my unprepared body. And she was so *steady*! I couldn't understand *when* she'd grown such conviction. My little Christine had been a shy creature, a violet one wrong step from being trampled by the vehemence in my heart. Now...*I* was the weakened, timid one between us, a mass of shaking limbs and fear that gnawed my insides. She was so soft, so warm, and to feel *skin* against my deformity and know she'd put it there of her own free will... Those condemning tears trickled down my cheeks, wetting hers by default.

"Erik," she whispered gently when she felt it, and her arms entwined about my neck as she hugged her bent body to my back, flush to my concave spine, keeping me in one piece with *her* strength as anchor.

I shook my head, but the motion nuzzled my cheek against hers and smeared my tears between our flesh. "No, no," I moaned, and my body quaked with the violence of a sob. "No, stop. Please, God stop! What are you doing, Christine?"

Playing would have been a welcome diversion, but my hands trembled too harsh and gave wrong notes and dissonance that bellowed its cacophony and made me cringe. I hated to play like a novice; I was better than that. Emotion should exist through the music and the body, not become so jarring that it made music something suddenly unappealing.

I broke free of her loosened hold and darted a safe distance, glaring with my naked face to utter threats I felt valid. Our last battles had put her in firing position, and I'd allowed her to make anger mean something. This time I had no regret to heave it right back.

Fisting taut fingers before me, I pressed my face against my sleeves and swiped tears away, determined that I'd shed no more for her.

"What are you hoping to accomplish?" I demanded in a growl. "Last I was aware, we were in opposite corners with no hope of crossing the abyss, and now...tonight... What *is* this, Christine? Are you seeking only to unravel me? If *my love* is *your punishment*, is this to be mine? An existence where

207

you use my heart against me in your revenge? You know *exactly* how to wind me about your little fingers; you know every weakness in my armor and how to poke through and spear the flesh within. Is that your intent?"

She looked so hurt that I almost recanted my harshness and pleaded forgiveness. But tears overflowed from the corners of her blue eyes, and she begged in a rush, "Condemn me! Please, Erik, I deserve your hatred! What I've done..."

"Christine... I don't understand."

Before I could pursue explanations, she dove toward me and hugged her little body to mine, and I was so shocked that I didn't hold her back. My arms still bore fists as their punctuation, extended in mid-air at my sides and unable to flex and break. If they shattered their whole to five separate fingers, I worried my heart would do the same, come apart to shards and imbed in my skin. Cut me, bruise me, I'd been damaged and exiled, refuted and reviled, a man un-allowed to *live* his life. I'd endured every violence the world had to offer, but here was the point that would equal my demise. Christine, holding me with fingers fisted in my jacket and her tear-stained face against my sternum, ...embracing me as if it were all she wanted.

"I don't hate you," she cried, rubbing her nose against my bones and engraving its shape. "I've *never* hated you. I thought you left me so easily, as if my heart meant *nothing* to you. You took away my choice to love you or say goodbye, and I was destroyed. I couldn't reason what I'd done so terrible to convince you to go and abandon me. And I hoped and prayed like a gullible child for you to come back." Her voice cracked with her frantic words, and in the exhalation of a sob, she cried, "How could I have known that you *couldn't* come back?"

Couldn't. That word spoke it all, and with a sharp intake of air, I caught her shoulders and forced her away. I looked in her tear-filled eyes, and I *knew* what I saw now. How could I have not deciphered it clearly before? Sympathy, pity, compassion. They were not my usual spread of emotions to behold. That was my excuse for my failure.

"Of course," I sarcastically retorted. "Pity the freak. Humor his desires because he's endured more pain than the rest of the world will ever know. Dear God, I am such a *fool*! And your good heart is eager to appease and qualify your regrets, to wipe guilt out of existence! This is *exactly* why I wasn't inclined to share my traumas with you! They are *mine* to carry alone because I *know* how to deal with their reverberation. But you are naïve to such things. You hear and think your compassion will change the world and mend every horror you cannot fathom." Gathering rage in a tight ball, I heaved it at her. "You weren't to know without *my* permission! Who told you? ...Or do I already know? The daroga is a meddling bastard!"

She flinched at my vile curse but stood her ground. "*You* should have told me! All this time, I thought you ran away to bruise my heart as viciously as I'd bruised yours. And instead you were...beaten." The word imploded with a sob that seemed rooted to her core.

I felt my skin flush red. Anger, humiliation. I was a man meant to be revered. I'd carved that niche for myself in the title of Opera Ghost. But this travesty dropped me below the level of humanity, a creature whose claim to emotion was molded in commiseration.

With a roar from the deepest well of my pain, I shouted at her, "I want *love*! *Love*, Christine! Not this pathetic offering of empathy and futile attempts at understanding. You *can't* understand! Watch the hero fall; watch him drop into the pit and be ripped to shreds by their clawed talons! Ah, your heart aches. Any human being with a sense of morality would bear

an aching heart because violence is just that
horrendous and repugnant. It is a commonly shared
reaction of gut instinct and a compassionate heart. I
was *beaten!*" I yelled the crime and heard it echo the
theatre; it was as ugly as music was beautiful. The
letters came back in their resonation, and it felt as if I
heard as well as *said* and lived it again, so I added
more abominations, each to cover the last. "I was
whipped until I bled, burned through each layer of
skin, marked and scarred until my body was as much
a revolting abomination as my disfigured face. I was
beaten into submission like a worthless animal, and I
endured it all because of *you!* I anticipated every pain
and every brutality done to me because each put me
closer to your heart. One more whipping, another
crime atoned for, another inkling of forgiveness, and if
God cleansed my soul, if He made me pure again, then
I was sure I could have *you* as my blessing."

Aggression faded into each sentence, and to
watch her body shake with sobs, her eyes full of horror
that had *nothing* to do with my face, I yearned to ask
why. Humanity was vindictive and malicious; I'd
thought she'd already learned that.

Her shaking arms lifted with rigid muscles as
she buried her sobs against her forearms. Perhaps she
didn't want me to realize how violent her cries were,
but her entire torso convulsed with their power, so I
dubbed her attempt for naught.

Crying...for something over and done. Yes, it
was brutal. I was depreciating how much I'd survived,
but...well, I wanted to forget just as much. I wasn't
going to tell her that the pictures still haunted me, the
pain that returned in tingles along my skin as if my
body couldn't fully pretend as I wished. No, ...it still
expected more pain to come. But whenever the horror
peeked out, I forced thoughts to *this* place, to lessons
upon the stage with Christine smiling at me, and I
found something better. I'd been horror's inflictor
and then its victim, and I preferred to think I was

enlightened and knew that something better could
come from pain.

"Christine," I said, softer and yet unable to
conceal my desolation, "I realize it was ridiculous to
wish such things. You are not mine, but it was the
hope you *could be* that got me through. Will you
condemn me for it? It was a harmless endeavor. For
every time I've considered taking and making *my*
desire all that matters, I can't. I love you too much for
such dramatics. Let it exist now as the futile prayer
that played on my lips during my imprisonment, and
nothing more. You are not mine," I repeated and
shook my head as I turned from her crying shape and
sought my mask. It had fallen from her fingers,
useless then, imperative now, and I bent to retrieve it
and stared bitterly at its stark formation. How I hated
the man it made me! I'd let it be my costume too long,
and what was I without it?

"And what now?" Her question was coldly
demanded as her arms dropped to hold her trembling
body. "Will you leave me again?"

I heaved a breath as I replaced my mask,
keeping my back to her until the persona was back in
place. "I never should have returned. I should have
known better. ...I am too damaged even for the
beauty music provides. I'd hoped to do good in some
way, to absolve every abhorrent memory I wear
written on my body and *create* something exquisite
instead. The music..." I said it even as my eyes trailed
her features. *She* was my something exquisite, but I
couldn't have her. Music fell short in that regard.

"And that will be all?" she demanded, shaking a
defiant head. "You will leave me again without a
goodbye and vanish from my life?"

"You have a fiancé to tend to you," I reminded.
"I am sure *he* will be accommodating."

"No, ...no," she whispered. A handful of timid
steps crossed the gap between us, and I didn't scurry
away as sense argued I should. She quivered and

hesitated, searching my masked face, but her small hands lifted. I watched with unuttered intrigue, curious to her intentions as her palms fitted to my cheeks, one to skin, one to mask, her joints fluttering in their intrepid pulsations.

So near that her eyes burned as they dove into mine, and with tears wavering her voice, she spoke everything I was terrified to hear. "You were beaten," again, a crack over that word, "and you were tortured, and the whole time, I was here, *loving* you…"

Chapter Eighteen

Christine~

"You were beaten," my voice broke over that horrible word, "and you were tortured, and the whole time, I was here, *loving* you..."

It was a liberation to say the words and drive them into his doubting mind with a stare that shone from my very soul.

"Love, Christine...," he muttered, the desire to believe prominent and beaming so powerful that I had to allow my gaze to wander the masked face I clasped between my shaking hands instead of soul-stealing eyes. "I returned seeking love and found that it had been given to another man."

"I don't love Raoul." I hated even bringing up his name and forming its letters when the air felt sacred in this place, the spot I'd fallen in love with an angel.

My attention was riveted to his exposed bottom lip, and when it moved with spoken words, I was hypnotized on its changing shapes. For all his flaws, that detail was perfection.

"No? But you expect me to accept that you love this damaged carcass instead?" he queried and shook his head against my hands. His tears wet my fingers, and I longed to kiss them away... "I was ignorant to come to you and expect what I have left to be enough... What good is a saved soul in an ugly vessel?

My face is a burden, but my body...it is a *degradation*. I'd sought to forget how deep the scars ran. I could play for you as I just did and make you *beauty* instead.

"...There were no pianos in that prison, no music, nothing but memory, and so often I'd devise compositions in my head for you, sing them in my sleep. They were compensation for the things I was losing in that hell. I'd return with a million more scars, but I thought if I gave you music and beauty through its sphere, it would suffice. I considered myself *lucky*," he spat the word, "that the shah never touched my hands. He did not break fingers when ribs seemed a more integral hit. ...I never cared about ribs; what good could they do me? But my hands were important *for you*, and that meant something at the time. Now...I denounce those saving thoughts and call them ridiculous. You have someone else to love you who can give you the physical perfection I never could. Even without new scars, my face was always a *horror*. You have better than that as yours now."

I listened in tears and shook my head at every point I thought wrong, and when he finished, I vowed in utter urgency, "But I *want* the horror. Have I not proven that your face doesn't matter? My God, Erik, I took off your mask but moments ago and was *relieved* to find its scars unchanged. I was *terrified* that...they'd hurt your face as well."

"Only once," he admitted. "That's cheating in the realm of torture, and the shah prefers to make *new* marks, ones he can call *his* and not *God's*."

"Show me," I bid and knew how blatantly my heart was in my eyes as I reached for his mask again. "Don't hide, Erik," I begged as I drew it free and watched in fascination as his scars filled my view. "Please, not from *me*. I may have built invisible walls to my heart, but you use the mask as a tangible one, and I can't bear that anymore." My eyes traced his face as I let the mask fall from my fingers a second time, and in soft whispers, I beseeched, "Show me where he hurt your face."

He was trembling before me, and the hand that lifted was racked in violent tremors as he brought it to the base of an exposed eye socket. I noted that he never touched his own face, as if he couldn't bear to endure any *feeling* in that tender space. I was not as easily deterred, and as he lowered that hand again with a defiant denial in his shaking head, I brought my own fingers to the place and did not obey.

"I won't hurt you," I vowed, seeing him flinch before I ever even grazed a caress. "I promise, there is no pain in my hands."

"Yes, there is. You can *destroy* me with those hands," he insisted, but I was desperate to prove that wasn't my only talent. My quivering fingers brushed delicately along the defined sculpture of bone about his green eye, and he shuddered and moaned at first contact. "Oh God," he breathed, "your touch *burns*."

I would have worried the burn was atop the skin instead of below, but he closed his eyes and arched toward my fingers, encouraging more with a soft whimper that tingled my ears. Unable to help myself, I made a firmer touch, full pads of fingers outlining the cavernous shape and studying his reactions with my hesitations piquing. "Is this all right? May I touch you this way, Erik?"

A cry passed his misshapen lips from merely my words before he collected thoughts and muttered, "Don't stop *please*, Christine. No one...has ever touched me gently before."

His admission made my heart ache in my chest, and with a rush of tears, I obeyed impulse and leaned close to press my mouth to the spot instead. He whimpered and went rigid against me, and I felt him fight the urgent instinct to pull away. His whole body pulsated as if a battle raged within, but I kept unmoved, lips in place, conditioning him to tenderness and waiting for him to calm.

"Christine…" My name was an adoration on his tongue and made me shiver and edge closer to his body. My God, this was *mine*. I wouldn't ever lose it again…

My hand cupped the almost perfect half of his face; my lips on one side, my palm to the other, and it was practically an embrace for something that he called a *horror*. Let me claim it and make it mine, and his opinion couldn't matter if *I* stamped the impression of *my* lips upon its distortions.

Ever gentle, I moved my mouth against his abused bones from the corner of his closed eyelid along a defined cheek's contour and lingering against his temple. Kiss after kiss, one to the next in a seamless legato melody that bore no audible music, and as I followed my devised path again, I kept my lips soft and pliant and tasted him with the timid tip of my tongue, flicking licks across that un-encased bone. I tasted his bone because there was no flesh there to stop me, and it was such a blatant intimacy that his hands finally broke free of fists and clasped my waist as if he needed stability to bear it. His frame shook with tremors, and as tears escaped his closed eyes and spilled in my path, I caught them between my lips and let their salt coat my taste buds.

My eyes were open, studying that face and its telling reactions, and with the tinge of a smile I could not deny, I kissed a feather-light trail to the bloated arch of his upper lip. A kiss at his will had harsh tendencies; I was about to write him a new definition. With my heart in every gesture, I grazed my mouth to his and caught his overcome cry in my next breath.

He never took control, never too fierce; he let me kiss *him*, and I moved my mouth with utter delicacy against his misshapen lips. Dear God…I'd never known a kiss like the one I was creating for Erik. Kisses I'd granted Raoul were chaste and shallow, superficial, never delving within. This one felt embedded in my soul and stirred embers deep within like the ash in an eternal fireplace, every motion bringing a new flame to burst into existence and scorch my inner being.

I never gave too much pressure, never too much ferocity; I savored gentleness and spoke every devoted adoration in the movement of my mouth. He allowed, and when he shyly imitated my motion, I felt a jolt to my core and gave an unconscious cry that vibrated joined lips.

Oh God, to know he could do *that* much in a single, tender contact both terrified and excited me. Why had I wanted a heart behind cold walls when feeling *this* was so deliciously overwhelming?

I *ached*, and my only coherent thought was that I wanted *more*. Gentle still, I let my tongue part his lips, grazing the swollen shape of his upper one on a path within the cavern of his mouth. I shuddered from head to toe, and gentle faltered to hungry as I tasted him and felt the reverberation of his moan. His hands were tight on my waist, fingertips curled and sunken into my hipbones. Perhaps they'd make marks even through layers. ...I *hoped* they'd mark.

My tongue teased the inner contours of his mouth, tingling with his flavor and craving more. I felt like I couldn't plunge deep enough, taste enough, kiss enough to truly display the longing engraved on my bones. I wanted *this*, and I prayed to God that Erik believed it.

As I drew back to glide my tongue along the bloated swell of his upper lip, he shuddered violently and recoiled beyond my caress.

"Oh, Christine... What you're doing to me! ...You cannot realize!" The hands at my hips molded me to his hardened length and to feel it throb and pulse its desire made my knees tremble. "This *must be* a transgression, and sin is rewriting itself upon my soul! But you kiss me, and I *ache*. Such a perversion, isn't it? To grow so aroused because I know you kiss something revolting and disgusting. It is practically taboo. The beautiful, innocent girl laying her perfect lips upon a *monster's*. It's wicked and vile, a deviance that will send me to hell all over again, and I don't care! I will burn alive without regret, but...I am *terrified* to corrupt *you* with me. It's less damning to desire a perfect man than a freak of nature."

His self-abhorrence was so profound, like a bottomless schism in his center, and I was determined to be the reason it found a base and fill it with my love instead.

"If it is a sin, then let me burn alive with you," I pleaded and ran rampant caresses along his scarred face, unable to cease touching him. "I'd choose condemnation without regret, but what sin can truly exist if I *love* you?"

"Love..." He murmured the word again in the minor gap between our mouths, and savoring its syllable in his voice, I brushed a kiss to his deformed lips and set my forehead to his, breathing his breaths, so close that I brushed my nose to the place his should have been. *This was mine.*

"But what will that mean?" he demanded even as he mimicked my gentle nuzzle and rubbed the empty gap from which he breathed against me. He might have considered it another perverse act, but I smiled and shivered as I edged closer to him. "You have a fiancé by your own vow. You speak of *love*, but does that mean *I* am the choice of your heart? And will you break *his* heart to be mine?"

"I'm already yours," I insisted. "I've *always been* yours. Telling Raoul will be unpleasant, but it must be done." Cringing as my mind rushed ahead and envisioned the scene and the Vicomte's reaction, I clutched courage with both hands, desperate not to let it falter. "He won't like it. He'll want to protect me from the evil Opera Ghost. It will be inconceivable to him that I could *want* the Opera Ghost."

"And...do you? Do you *want* me, Christine?" He asked it with fear thickly ingrained in every letter.

"Even damaged and scarred? I can give you nothing better. I ache so much with a fire in my veins that has never been extinguished, but...I wear scars that tell a story of *weakness* and *degradation*. They mask my omnipotence and make me fallible; I went away to be deserving of you but came back worthless even to be a man."

"That's not what I see when I look at you," I promised with lips so close to his that their surface felt charged with sensation. "I see an angel."

"I've never been an angel."

"Perhaps not in your perception, but in mine, you were an angel from the first moment we met in the cellar. Angels don't need white wings and haloes to exist. Angels are those who put us upon our path, who guard and guide, a heavenly *blessing*. You've *always* been mine."

He shook his head, but I caught hints of a wry grin as he posed, "Even as I lusted after you from the shadows? I doubt angels know such voracious, mortal desires...not to *this* extent." His hands clasped my hips fitfully between them as he pressed against me. "Please tell me that you want this, Christine. I cannot burn alone any longer, not after feeling your lips upon mine, your tongue in my mouth..." A moan vibrated his chest and rippled through my torso with his. "Christine... Please tell me that you want more."

I did, but I felt my cheeks flame red to admit it. "Yes, ...of course."

But he misinterpreted my hesitation and quickly assured, "The scars...are permanent, but I will make it so they never matter. Desire has no eyes. I will make you its victim and so overcome that you can consider nothing but an ecstasy so great that it steals senses. I will bury you in pleasure, make your body sing with its intensity."

I felt so awkward and uncultured at that moment, closing my eyes to hide my abashment as I muttered, "How do you know such things?"

"I've been victim to pleasure, victim to pain, but I've never poured adoration upon another human being. Never a lover, never even a creature I've desired. Is that what you're asking, Christine? You want to know that you are the only one, and how irrelevant! *You* have had a *fiancé*." It was half an accusation when he spoke it this time, and I quickly shook my head. "No? But surely to know the nuances of a kiss, you also know the facets of desire. I was gone for so long..."

But I shook my head again, stumbling for words on a topic where I felt like an ignorant novice. "No, I couldn't... I didn't want... I wanted *you*. The long spans of empty minutes that I suffered without you, and all I had was *one* kiss to sustain my mind and convince me that you wanted me, too, when your absence spoke so differently. And Raoul... I could never give him a heart already inscribed in another's name. It was yours, and any kiss he gave could never touch it. Can *you* forgive the betrayal of chaste kisses if *yours* were the only lips I truly wanted upon mine?"

"My *misshapen* lips?" He added words I didn't consider important and made them prevalent by leaning closer to brush said *misshapen* lips to mine. It made me shiver deliciously. "*This* is what you fantasized all the time I was away?"

"Yes, yes, God, yes," I murmured and slid restless fingers along his nape and into the thin coating of hair lining his skull.

Perhaps any other girl *would* consider such details unsavory. My lover looked like a corpse with a corpse's features and elements, but I loved him harder and fiercer because those were the things he couldn't change and every other unsettling point he *had* changed *for me*. *God works in mysterious ways...* Well, *He* had created both of us and gave *me* the capacity to love and desire something anyone else might find repellent and obscene, and if I were wrong and sinning as Erik wanted to consider it, then God was unfair and I'd take this path anyway.

"I fantasized *you*," he admitted in a sigh, and he smiled as he brushed my lips again. "Every minute in that prison, I envisioned your face and your body, you wanting me, loving me, aching and begging me to take you. Oh God, Christine, my imagination was so torrid and provocative; maybe because I held a fear it would be all I'd have, that I'd die in that cell before ever seeing you again."

Hearing such a horrific fate that *wasn't* ours made me grip tighter as I cupped his nape in my palm and dug fingertips into his skin, desperate to steer us both from dark thoughts. "But now you *have* me, and it is *real* and *yours*. ...And what will you now do to me, *ange*?"

He shuddered and arched his desire tellingly against my body as his gaze burned fervently into mine and insisted for him. One hand clung to my hip as the other teased with fingers that outlined an ascent along my spine and slid temptingly into my hair, fisting within the blanket of my curls.

It amazed me that every part of my being seemed to intrigue and intoxicate him further. I'd never concluded any of my features as special or exemplary, but *he* seemed overcome in their simplicity. His hand was in my hair, and that morning I'd pinned it with little consideration beyond the nuisance of curls dangling about my face. *I* never proclaimed it extraordinary, but *he* tangled his fingers within its mass as if they never wanted to emerge again and curls were astonishing.

With a soft moan that hovered the air surrounding our embrace, he held my stare one more second before dragging eager lips to my jaw. Slow and as gentle as I'd been with him, he laid kisses across its line and onward, lingering on the place below my ear before continuing down the column of my throat.

His moan was drowned out by my cry. It

disentangled from my vocal cords and slid past my lips without my consent as fire engulfed my yielding body. I'd never known such consummation, and all inspired with delicacy as his chosen tactic. He brushed that disfigured mouth along my neck and formed more kisses, and I whimpered and shifted anxiously against his hard body. Nothing existed but the need pulsing my veins, and I suddenly understood his assertion that desire had no eyes. I wanted *him*; scars were never even a consideration.

His mouth rested in the crease of my throat, and I *felt* the smile he indulged, obviously pleased he could produce such an unbridled reaction. I arched closer to that tempting kiss and shuddered as he parted lips and licked my skin in languid undulations. Had anything ever felt so frightening and craved at the same time? I cried out my desperation and curled taut fingers against his crown, moving with him when he arched his hips and teased me with his wanting.

"Christine," he breathed my name, and the letters breezed the cool wetness his mouth had left upon my skin and created goose bumps that spanned my entire body.

"Don't stop," I gasped without voice and delighted in the light chuckle he gave me back.

"I have to, or I might take you right here. Dear Lord, how I burn, *ange*!"

Words were as arousing as kisses and *that voice*! It had only sounded in my dreams for so long, and now I hung upon its timbre and heard music even when it didn't exist. His mouth stole one more taste of my neck before he reluctantly drew back to find my hazy eyes.

"Erik," I muttered the only letters I wanted upon my tongue and kneaded my fingers restlessly in his hair, eager for him to succumb when I could barely speak what I wanted.

"I *ache* to make love to you," he insisted, and the hand in my curls emerged and outlined the features of my face. "But I will not put sins upon your soul. Rid yourself of your fiancé first, Christine. You are *mine*; you have always been *mine* as much as I am *yours*. But I will not play games for you to dally in breaking his heart. End this engagement because I refuse to kiss you in shadows any longer and watch you run to him."

It was fair. I knew he was right...even though my hips writhed against his hardness and purposely tempted him. He shuddered so violently that I shook in the aftermath and then glared at me in a mix of blame and contempt.

"Don't," he commanded, stern and inarguable, the almighty Opera Ghost giving orders that I deliberately ignored, pressing to him and grazing more kisses to his lips. "Christine," he muttered in warning and yet gave in long enough to slide his tongue deep and claiming before he collected strength and shrank free of my hold. Piercing me with the passion in his stare, he revealed, "Now your taste will be inside my mouth all night, your flavor on my tongue, reminding me this scene on the stage was *real* and not another fantasy."

I shivered with the power in his words and vowed, "I'm *yours*, Erik."

"Make sure the Vicomte knows that. And I..." He cringed with a look of annoyance that creased vividly without the mask to stifle it. "I have a daroga to rid *myself* of. His nightly visits are about to become an aggravation, but hopefully, when he hears all is well and right, he will quit his guilt quest and return to his wife and child."

"He's worried about you. Don't be angry with him for telling me about Persia," I pleaded and reached out to caress his cheek and reinstate the good that had come from it.

"I can't," he decided in a sigh and captured my hand, holding it to his cheek as he turned to set a kiss to my palm. "But I intend to prolong informing him that his meddling worked. I can't give him the satisfaction upfront, or he'll claim he was right all along and I should have told you from the start."

"You should have," I agreed, and yet I could not stop smiling at the disfigured face of the man I loved.

"Yes, but *he* doesn't need to know that."

One last kiss shook my knees as he gave it, a subtle brush of lips to lips before he sought his mask, hastily reminding, "Get rid of your other suitor lest I grow jealous and do it for you."

There was still a little voice in my mind that worried what his version of 'getting rid' of the Vicomte entailed. I couldn't fully silence it, but I believed him when he'd said he'd atoned for me. I preferred to think that meant he'd keep morality on his side, but...well, only time would tell that.

"I love you," he added, and I wondered if he suspected my doubts because it was abruptly given.

"And I love you," I vowed back with a smile and watched him vanish into the shadows. The Opera Ghost had just kissed me and made me ache. The Opera Ghost wanted to make love to me... Those factual statements were the unsettling part because when Erik was there with me, I rarely considered his Opera Ghost reputation. Then he was just Erik, my love. I needed to make certain it was always that way.

Still moving upon wobbly knees, I rushed from the opera house with sunset tinting the sky in color. Faster, quicker with purpose to every step, and I never let myself think it through or second-guess as I wound up on the Vicomte's doorstep.

I knocked frantically and spoke just as agitated to the maid to gain Raoul's presence, determined not to let cowardice catch up.

The instant Raoul appeared in the doorway before he could even speak a greeting or give a smile, I blurted out, "I'm in love with the Opera Ghost."

Chapter Nineteen

Erik~

No matter what I'd told Christine, from the moment I left her presence, I was convinced every second had been a dream. Even as I gave scant details to the daroga, enough to insist I didn't want him loitering about in my home anymore every night, I didn't fully believe it. *He* even regarded me suspiciously, perhaps because of my lackluster telling of news that should have made me exuberant. But I was just so afraid to *hope* and then learn I was wrong and alone again.

But...dear God, I could still *feel* her pressed against me, her soft curves and warmth, her hair in my hand, her kisses branding my ugly mouth and making it worthy to be hers. I could *taste* her all over my lips and upon my tongue, and yet I doubted my senses and refused to put full credence. It felt gullible and ignorant when fantasies in the shah's prison had been equally as lifelike, convincing me of her presence in my arms before I'd learn I was alone and disappointed again.

I *loved* her, and my God, if every detail of the previous night *had* been a masochistic fantasy, then my soul was now working against me, and suicide might be a viable option. How could one live as an enemy to oneself? *That* was insanity, and I was adamant that madness would not be my path. Death had more promise.

In a sudden need for control of a floundering existence, I chose to stay away as rehearsals started the next day. If it were a fantasy, it was better than reality, and if I saw the Vicomte in the back of the theatre, the fantasy would burst and show its fairytale makeup. *Let me have the dream a little longer.*

I caged myself in my office, trying to focus but faltering at every endeavor. All I could do was think of Christine: her body in my arms, her mouth atop mine, her little sounds of desire brandishing a path into my ear canals as sweetly devised as a melody line...

And then her voice poured through the walls and doors from rehearsal, and I shuddered to my core and felt thrown and struck against a rocky shore. My body ached; I wanted and yearned, and tears gathered in my eyes in a sudden terror that I *had* concocted the whole scene and she wasn't mine. Oh God, if she wasn't, I longed to die!

The morning dragged to afternoon, and no matter what I did, I was haunted. *Christine...* She was all I obsessed over. And then my prayers suddenly received an unanticipated answer.

A soft rapping on my office door shook me from imagination, and shouting a terse, "Come in," I expected another intervention from an unhappy crewmember, maybe Reyer with a list of complaints for my integrated changes. Being in charge meant *no one* was happy. I could have caved to their every wish, and *still* they'd find *something* suitable for their grumbling resignations.

One could envision my astounded and aghast expression when *Christine* opened the door and scurried inside, blue eyes wide and yet glowing with light. She smiled when she regarded my rigid posture at my desk and darted to my chair with a soft laugh. Just like a dream... But with only a trembling hesitation in her extended hands, she lifted my mask away from my stunned features and found the horror beneath as if it were the greatest treasure in the known world.

Her little hands fitted gently to my cheeks, her skin so warm and *real* that it *burned*, and I shivered and lost a soft, unrealized moan merely at the tangibility.

"Christine," I sighed, and my hands shook in the air as I opened fingers and slid them along the curves of her hips, gradually *feeling* her. As I tested her solid form and found its concreteness, I cried out and drew her to me until I could burrow my face to her belly and infect my lungs with her scent.

"Oh God, you feel so real!" I exclaimed and pressed kiss after kiss to the bodice of her gown. "If this is insanity, let me never emerge from its possession! I will willingly choose a fabricated reality if I can have even a fragment of my Christine to touch and hold. ...Are you real, *ange*? Tell me that I'm not dreaming you."

She never paused, wrapping eager arms about my neck and lighting upon my lap as if it were a known intimacy between us. I met her gaze with surprised delight in my own and found such a smile that it stilled my heart.

"I'm *real, ange*," she vowed back, and I couldn't help myself. I covered her elated face in frantic kisses, one after another, cherishing every tiny feature of her beautiful visage. She took each with a giggle and clutched me tighter with nimble fingers. "Shall I always acquire such a favorable reception? If so, I will escape rehearsal more often!"

"Rehearsal?" I halted mid-kiss at her temple and listened long enough to hear Mephistopheles bellowing out his lines. "Isn't your scene approaching?"

"Perhaps," she decided with an idle shrug. "But I have an imperative meeting with my manager that I would not dare disregard. They will have to carry on without me until *you* have given dismissal."

"Indeed?" I fisted my hands in her dress, my knuckles bearing into her back as I fathomed one unanswered detail. "And...what did the Vicomte say to this clandestine meeting? Or is he awaiting just outside the door?"

"Of course not!" she exclaimed and set an appeasing kiss to my jaw. "He's gone, Erik. I saw him last night and told him that my heart beats for the Opera Ghost alone."

I wanted to believe her so much that my voice wavered in tensed hesitation and an excitement I couldn't let myself find. "And...? What did he say? Is he out for blood and retribution?"

A fluttered laugh poured past her lips and tickled the skin of my disfigured cheek. "Raoul is not the sort for guns and blades. Yes, his heart was broken, and he tried to reason with me in his analytical, caring manner, but in the end, it is *my* choice. I don't favor being the cause of such dramatics, you know that, but in this instance, it could not be avoided."

"Thank God," I breathed, and every muscle seemed to relax and drain of fear to know it was over. I wasn't accustomed to winning and getting what *I* wanted in the end, and maybe I would have kept doubting if not for Christine's soft body on my lap, proving at every breath that she was mine and *wanted to be* mine of her free will.

"So...what now?" she asked sweetly with the slightest wobble to remind her trepidations.

I had no intention of forcing anything upon her, but she timidly scooted closer to my telling desire, her shy eyes half-closed above her tentative smile. My God, she could tempt true angels to leap from the heavens in their final fall from grace to have her!

"I have no daroga waiting below," I reported with the tinge of asked permission. "But tell me what *you* want, *ange.* ...I could carry you away, make love to you with every ounce of passion in my body. ...Is that what you wish, Christine?"

I couldn't help but pose my yearnings when she squirmed against my aching hardness and stole my breath. I would argue *she* enticed blatancy.

But she ducked her eyes with her nod, and though I wondered if I pushed too hard, she shocked me to a shudder as her sweet lips met mine, urgent and demanding, firm in their pressure and deliberately sensual motion. How could I resist!

I barely hesitated as I lifted her into my arms. *This* was all I wanted from the world. Let it collapse and decay in our absence, and I wouldn't mourn a single thing. I took what was important with me as I brought her into another secret passageway hidden in a back closet of my office. She looked about with fascination and then cast me a dubious, arched brow.

"You have your own way around the entire opera house, don't you?" she asked, her amazement in a contented grin.

"How do you think I delivered my Opera Ghost notes into the *locked* management's office? I would call my labyrinth of pathways necessary and conducive to any intelligent ghost's way of life," I teased with the words and savored the little giggle I got in reply. Oh, such bliss! She was happy; *I* was making her happy. There was nothing as wondrous.

The trip below was a test of patience, most especially when this stretch of my maze was laden in numerous traps. God forbid the typical bumbling managers ever found the hidden entrance. I'd taken extra precautions and had plenty of avenues to avoid with Christine warm and persuasive in my arms. The last thing I needed was to trap us in one of my many torture chambers.

My modicum of concentrated efforts kept me silent as I rushed us along, but she was equally quiet. I wondered over her thoughts and tormented my inner confidence with a terror that she didn't truly want this. Perhaps she only consented because she knew how desperately I ached...

Dear God, the thought would not weaken its intensity despite my resolve to avoid distraction and pay attention to traps and corridors in the dark.

...Well, if it *were* true, I was adamant to adore her so vehemently that she never regretted her choice. She was handing over her virginity to a monster composed of scars and damage, and even if the soul within was whole and penitent, the facts remained the same.

So much pressure to please when I'd never been in this position. Abuse was the only foundation in my mind, and that entailed pain and degradation. This was the first time desire was a pure thing, and I was so grateful to her for this gift that I was overcome.

With anticipation tingling my skin, I carried her inside my hidden house and straightway to the bedroom, experiencing her nervous tremors with her. "Have you been in this room before?" I asked. "In your exploration of my house during my absence, I mean."

She glanced to my gaze with a secretive grin and revealed with a blush, "I laid in your bed a few times."

"What?" I stuttered, mimicking her grin. Such an intimate detail, and how had I not realized as I'd slept in that bed that her aura lurked? My God, her cheek could have been in the same spot on my pillow where mine rested!

"Pathetic, I know." Her smile deepened her blush. "But...your scent lingered upon the pillow and within the covers, and...I'd lie there and close my eyes and pretend you were with me. That was at the beginning when I was so certain you'd come back, but then more and more time passed and hope felt foolish."

"I'm sorry," I couldn't stop the apology from pouring forth as I set her upon her feet. But she scurried to the bedside without a word or even a shared gaze that I could read. Kicking off her shoes, she lifted the covers and slid within my bed, nuzzling her face into my pillow in the same place I'd restlessly shifted the entire night before, suffering insomnia with my musings of *her*. It was a paradox because my mind's eye could bend time back and convince me that *I* lay in the bed, not her, and she was another fantasy. I hated the thought as soon as it appeared and quickly sought to shatter disillusionment as I followed her path.

Looming beside the mattress, I watched her curl on her side, facing me, her eyes finally upon mine with more hesitation than I wanted to see. "Do you think I'm foolish?" she asked, and I nearly chuckled at such an unexpected inquiry.

"Why would I ever think that?"

"Because I loved you so much that I went to such childish extremes to capture even a piece of you. You left, and I didn't know if you'd come back. Did you realize that you were *everything* to me, Erik? That when you left, I was *alone*?"

I nodded. I knew it *now*. With delicate fingertips, I stroked her brow and admired the curls strewn across my pillowcase. "And I consider it an absolute wonder that you loved me so much. That last night before I left, I hurt you with truths I should have told from the beginning, and...I used *this* face to frighten you further, to punish you because I thought I'd lost you. Christine, ...I can't fix that, but I can make sure that for all its horror, it meant something and isn't forgotten."

The pads of my fingers marveled over her soft cheek, and as she lifted the edge of the covers in a timid invitation, I went eagerly and lay on my side facing her, tracing her features and half-afraid to do more than touch her face.

She was the one to reach for the clasps of her gown and expertly unhooked them, holding my eyes apprehensively at each parting inch of material. She asked without words if that was what I wanted, and I hoped the hunger in my returned stare gave her an answer when I could form nothing beyond the hoarse breaths passing my lips.

Her gown was discarded; she tossed it off the bed, and I shuddered as the sound of falling material echoed back. It was like a prelude, setting the mood before the first strains of a romantic symphony. Her corset was the next series of chords, modulating toward a lush melody whose arched shape was drawn along the gorgeous curves of her feminine body. *She* was music's muse, molded in harmonies and dynamics, and my body reacted to listen to her symphony, crescendoing with her brilliant forte and swelling with the intense passion that poured free.

"Oh my God," I breathed and extended shaking hands, fingers splayed wide to touch as much of her as I could at once. My grasp clasped either side of her ribcage and dug into the lingering cotton of her chemise, pulling it so taut that the shadows of her breasts deepened their hue to press flush and strain to be loose.

She wasn't breathing; I felt no stir in the lungs beneath my palms, and to glimpse the widening of blue eyes, her fear felt like my own trial to overcome. I had to replace it with something glorious instead. Meeting her gaze one last second, I suddenly bent and pressed my mouth to one silhouetted nipple, savoring her sharp cry as it filled the air.

I carried a nervousness that I'd be awkward. Fantasizing what I wanted to do to her and actually *doing* it were two different things. Now I had *substance* between my hands, not imagined beauty but real beauty that was far more exquisite and yet fragile. I took care with every motion; kisses first, my misshapen mouth gentle in every affection, and through that flimsy chemise barrier, I felt her nipple harden and extend to meet me and considered it a great and humbling achievement. Her cries were soft whimpers, and I kept glancing at her face, only to find her gaze riveted to my actions. Oh, I thrilled to push her onward! And parting my lips, I found that yearning nipple with my tongue, lapping at intruding cotton and impatient to tear it free and taste *skin*. But...for her, I would take my time.

She burned my ears with her desperate moan, and I smiled against her breast and circled the tip with my tongue, shuddering when her hand darted out and clung to my hair. How overwhelming it was to be *wanted*! She scooted closer until her legs could overlap mine and arched nearer to my throbbing manhood, tempting more when I was already aching too much.

My hand slid beneath her chemise to find her other breast and learn its soft weight, and I groaned to my deepest depths to cup it in my bare palm, its tip just as pronounced and leaving its stamp behind. Never before had my hands known anything so flawlessly constructed as Christine's body; every detail made me further certain she was more than any other mortal woman in existence. She was the true *angel*, and how fortunate I was that she arched and writhed against me, longing for *my* touch, garnering pleasure from *my* ministrations and no one else. It felt like a cruel joke of Fate, as if the second I surrendered and fully believed, she'd vanish and remind me I was worthless and not allowed such blessings.

But...reality was in every unexpected detail *she* created, surpassing my lackluster imagination. She shimmied out of my hold, but not to sever contact. No, she yanked her chemise over her head, threw it aside, and invited *more* contact.

I moaned my delirious delight and ran rampant eyes over her breasts, never hesitating to cup them in my hands and gently stroke their softness, teasing the tips with my fingers and savoring her immediate cry. Oh, that cry! Like music! And I wanted to swallow its beauty as I covered her mouth with mine and kissed every sound away.

Desire was such a fickle fire, consuming but more demanding than the control I preferred to keep. I wanted to spend forever in its suspended state, but I knew I had to have more before it betrayed me and soared to its eager culmination. No more waiting or trepidation, I slid one hand down her silken torso, following its baited path within every other layer. Skin was my guide and led me to her center.

Christine went stiff against me, dragging lips free and shivering, but she never spoke a refusal as my fingers slid along her womanhood. In truth, I was as afraid as she was. Had I ever had something so fragile in my care? I harbored a fear of touching her incorrectly or causing pain when pleasure was all I sought. But though she stayed all rigid muscles and tremors, she parted shaking thighs and encouraged with wide eyes locked on my face.

My fingertips grazed before daring to slip within, and our cries echoed off the headboard and permeated the air at the intensity of contact. "Christine," I gasped and set desperate kisses to her temple as I stroked her and coated my fingers in her wetness. My touch was curious, intrigued, fevered, all emotions growing one out of the other. "You're so wet... I want to drown in you!"

My impassioned declarations were returned in her gasps, and as I dared to probe deeper with a delicate thrust from an audacious finger, she shouted so beautifully that I memorized the timbre to play over and over in my mind.

"Oh, Christine, I'm going to be scorched in the heat of you, and I pray to God that you leave your own scars upon my body. Mark me as *yours*! Burn me to my core! I want to be *yours*, only yours for eternity."

I meant every word. I'd been tortured by the shah to pointless scars, and what did they mean? Nothing but things I longed to *forget*. This moment with Christine was something I wanted to remember forever, but scars on the inside were not visible. I'd have permanent marks only in my veins.

My caresses were more certain with every second, and as she arched her hips to meet my thrusting finger, I shuddered and knew I had to have her. I freed my hands from the flames of her flesh, but before I could finish disrobing her, already grabbing for her petticoat, she extended determined hands to my shirt buttons, and I went numb and stiff with a terror that surprised me in its powerful devastation. It fractured desire with narrow cracks.

"No," I gasped and shrank beyond her reach, reading hurt in her knit brow.

"Erik, please...let me undress you and see..."

I could tell she fought for an accurate word: *damage*, *scars*, *horror*, all were unpleasant in their connotation and were only uttered in our heads. "I...I can turn out the lights first," I offered brusquely. "It can be dark as a tomb down here, no revealing sunshine or daylight. The dark can be our ally, and then...it will make things easier."

She shook her head, curls cascading along her pale skin and dancing across her breasts. I could not help but be entranced in every rippled motion. "I want to see you, Erik. ...Please."

"But...it's an abomination. I undress you and uncover ethereal perfection, but if you undress me, you will not be so fortunate. It's a shame really. You have to look upon not only this horrific face but a repellent body besides and still find reasons to desire. That...might be an impossible feat, and now that I've felt your arousal, ...what if you cease desiring me?"

She shook her head more adamantly, her eyes overflowing in a compassion I wasn't sure was enough to confirm for her. "I want *you*, Erik. Please trust my love. Scars are superficial; they can't reach beneath the surface, but *love* does. ...It's just *skin*, *ange*."

"And...is my face just *skin* to you?" I pushed

doubtfully.

"No, it's *you*, yours and mine just as much. But *God* made your face. You consider it tragic, but God works in mysterious ways..." A smile touched her lips with the sentiment before she finished, "He made that face so I could love it. He wanted to be sure I would see you for the extraordinary man you are."

I had to touch her, so overcome with her words, and I delicately brushed my knuckles in a caress along her cheekbone as I reminded, "God didn't create those on my body."

"No, but they mean something just as important. They show your heart in blatant display. They are strength and self-sacrifice-"

"They are reparation for my dastardly existence."

"No," she spoke with inarguable certainty and held my shame-filled gaze without waver. "God does not punish in pain or seek penance through torture. This was not in God's hands, nor was it just atonement for your sins. This was undeserved, Erik. You did not deserve to be brutalized when your heart was already penitent. It is not an eye for an eye. Forgiveness comes with selfless acts and righteous deeds. This was the devil's abuse, and every scar left behind is nothing worth odium or reproach. I will script them in honor and courage and more love than most mankind could ever feel. Please...let me prove it to you."

It was difficult for me to conceive anything but evidence of a time I was weak, and how could the omnipotent Opera Ghost ever be anyone's victim? I was not supposed to fall, and here was a permanent inscription of 'coward' upon my body. But as Christine reached for buttons again, I kept hands diligently fisted at my sides and permitted, desperately holding back a rise of tears and a need for a shield.

I fixated on her face, and as button after button

gave way and whispered my Persian enslavement in every revelation, I saw the true horror of it furrow her brow and bring the same tears I restrained to her stare.

I didn't look down at my body; I'd seen enough to know it was horrendous and rarely regarded it since my return. I knew there were deep grooves of missing flesh and healing patches from brutal burns. The shah had a penchant for hot pokers, and scattered about were upraised brandings in his crest, as if I were marked property, a stamped animal in his stables. The leftover evidence from the whips was the worst because each lashing was recorded, criss-crossed strips in pale pinks that were vibrant on my white skin. There was still more healing to be done, but I doubted they'd be less prominent, ...maybe less pink if I were lucky.

Christine's shoulders shook with silent sobs as her blue gaze wandered the length of my torso to the waistband of my pants and up again, taking it all in as one complete picture and then my horrific face on top of it all. I feared it was all too much for her, feeling the violent tremors of her hands as they fisted in the material of my open shirt and could not seem to un-flex their joints.

So abrupt that she jumped, I clasped her chin in curled fingers and forced her eyes to hold mine as I snapped, "No pity. I don't want pity, not from you, Christine. Please, I can't bear that!"

I spoke harsh, but the words were so deeply embedded in my heartache that her tears fell faster, and she suddenly hugged her body to mine, pressing her bare breasts against my damaged torso. It was a more overwhelming caress than hands could have ever given, and I shuddered and moaned when my body expected pain to exist in every contact and received softness and warmth instead.

"I love you," she insisted in a whimper and burrowed her face in the hollow of my throat. I didn't know what to *feel*. Should I be angry? Was this her way of blocking the horror from her line of view and beseeching forgiveness? Or was this solace? My temper had the urge to pop and erupt, but her tumbling tears struck my skin and trickled down my chest, stinging in some places that were still a bit raw, and impulse said to comfort *her*.

"Christine...," I moaned desolately as I slid my arms about her shape and clutched her to me, but fear lurked in my ignorance, and I added with ferocity, "I won't let you go. You already chose me. If disgust lives in these scars, so be it. You came to my bed willingly, and no matter what, I mean to have you."

It was cruel on my part to lay such terms, but desperation took control and insisted how easy it would be for her to reconstruct her broken walls and drag her heart within their protection.

I would have ripped off remaining clothing and taken her right then, but her hands caught my interest as they finally released material and slid to my waist. Ever delicate and unsure, they made a timid path and found the bare, equally-damaged skin of my back. The whip marks were worse across that expanse of muscle, and I felt my bones shifting within my skin to endure a touch that was gentle. She gasped at what she felt, but no more loudly than I did to know the heated pressure of tender fingers graze up and down my spine, slow and learning every scar's variation.

She was thorough and ever attentive, brushing finger pads and then full hands in their mediocre scope, caressing as if they could repair damage. Every scar seemed to have a voice all its own, and as she touched and enticed it to surrender its secrets, it told its story of mutilation to her in whispers. As I writhed and moaned with her unceasing endeavors, I could only consider that if disgust were present, it was well-hidden.

But no...no, would disgust have her arching her hips against my hardness at every breath and rocking her body so sweetly to mine? Tears were still careening along my chest, but little sounds were passing her lips and blazing a path to my ears, mews of *wanting*; they could mean nothing else. And to me, this was the best acceptance in existence. She did not need to utter fancy, flowery sentiments or fabrications that the damage wasn't as terrible as I knew it was. Her desire was enough to conquer my sense of humiliation and remind me that though imperfect, I was a man still and finally worthy of love, ...*her* love.

The healing power of touch was almost *too* much to endure. When my body recalled that hands could hurt just as easily as they could be gentle, it was an ongoing challenge to calm beneath her sweet fingers. She pressed little kisses to my collarbone, finding its distinct shape between two burnt patches, and as her tongue emerged to touch and taste, I shuddered and fisted my hands in her petticoat.

"This body is a travesty," I muttered as I rubbed my scarred cheek against her silken crown. "I wish I had something better to give you, something worth desiring. Christine, you deserve perfection."

"I want *you*," she vowed without waver and arched against me again.

It was nearly impossible to find coherent thought beyond the thrumming throb of my ache. I refused regret, guilt, or any emotion that went against what I yearned to take, and abruptly capturing one of her hands from beneath my shirt, I dragged it between our bodies and pressed it boldly to my erection. I wanted it clear and evident, the blatant insistence of desire's threshold, and I watched her eyes widen to truly gauge my size and shape, her fingers shaking as they encircled the shaft and cupped with a palm that burned through every layer still present.

Her caresses were flustered and apprehensive, timid as her gaze held mine and continuously asked for her if she was pleasing me. I longed to assure her that there was no way she *couldn't* please me, but words failed to a hoarse moan that I prayed said enough.

I couldn't let it go on long, too overheated and desperate not to find completion in a touch alone. Not yet. Not when an absolute treasure awaited my claim.

Disentangling from her, I jerked away clothing at every fluid motion, holding her stare with my hunger prominently displayed. She blushed in reds and pinks as she slid her petticoat down her narrow hips but watched my body come into view all the while. I knew the scars were brutal and saw their reflection in blue eyes that seemed to be etching every one into her mind, as if tapping their shapes into the tin sheets of memory's wall and leaving a flawed, uneven palette behind.

As I unclasped my pants and yanked every other layer away, I was the one wearing a blush but mine was exuded from a shame I could not fully denounce. My thighs and legs were as brutally devastated as my torso; one particular marking from the whip ran from my hipbone down to my inner thigh, still pink and ugly in its recovery, and her attention fixed to its savage horror with a soft cry. Shaking fingertips grazed its length, and I shuddered in an aggressive combination of pleasure *and* pain.

"Erik," she whispered laden in empathy, but this was different. It was like through that touch, she *felt* my pain and shared it with me, not sympathized it into a contrived existence.

The wound drew focus first, but as her fingers ascended their path again, they continued across my hip and more scars on their way to my eagerly swollen manhood. I could barely stand it, shuddering before her bare fingers ever closed around me, and as her touch left its own lasting imprint and learned the secrets of the male body, I drew her pantaloons down her hips and out of my way.

I *needed* to touch her, half-afraid her desire would be vanished now that she'd seen the portrait of my wounds, but as my fingers grazed and found her slick wetness, I could not stop myself from plunging them deep and moaning my desperation to take their place.

"*Please*," she gasped, and I took that as permission. I did not hesitate even a breath, guiding her back and parting her thighs. She clasped my shoulders, making flustered caresses to more marks, but as I thrust deep, she abruptly cried out and went stiff and frozen in place.

"Sshh," I cooed, one hand upon her hip to keep her from pulling away and the other cradling her cheek. I swiped a flood of sudden tears with my fingertips and tilted her chin to force her gaze to mine, searching blue orbs for love beneath the overlying blanket of pain. I'd *hurt* her. I hated knowing guilt for it because it felt like another sin had just been engraved upon my soul when all I'd wanted was to give her pleasure.

"I'm sorry," I was compelled to murmur, but for as much as I regretted hurting her, I did not regret taking her virginity. Was that what her pain was supposed to inspire? She'd claimed God did not punish with pain, but perhaps she was wrong. Perhaps *she* regretted, but I was sheathed in a heated wetness so amazingly delicious that my entire body trembled and felt at peace for the first time in my existence.

She was still unyielding beneath me, as if terrified to move and make pain swell, so in soft tones, I whispered tenderly against her ear, "I suppose I gave you a permanent scar of your own now even if it is inside where no one will see. And yet it's forever, Christine, a branding that makes you mine. You're mine... Please tell me this means something extraordinary when to me, this is the most wonderful moment I've ever lived."

She hesitated, and my terror built until she finally spoke. "You're wrong. You gave me a permanent scar from the first moment, and that meant *forever* as much as this does. For as extraordinary as this is, I've always been yours."

I adored her words and pressed grateful kisses to her trembling lips. I didn't expect more than that. It was *love* and made this instant that we were one body, one heart and soul into a blessing.

I was afraid to move and hurt onward, and as I slowly shifted my hips, desperate to feel more, she gave a cry and drew my wide, worried stare.

But with shallow breaths heaving from her lungs, she gasped, "Do that again."

I groaned with relieved yearning and eagerly obeyed, always careful. Small motions, gentle and yet slightly deeper with each penetration, and though whimpered cries left her lips, *she* was the one to arch and meet me and encourage.

I was humbled in my amazement to watch her, to gaze at her desire-clouded features, knowing she wanted *me*, and then to feel her innocent body learning passion and testing its powerful pull. She was discovering *with me*, and I was as riveted to her as my own body's responses.

Her skin was flush to mine everywhere, her legs entwining with my own in the restless pursuit of wanting, and it astounded me the second I stopped caring about scars and knew she did, too. She dug taut fingers into my hair and raced fitful caresses along my skull as her cheek rubbed my scars. I *felt* her blush, the heat poured out of her skin the instant before she softly muttered, "You can...move harder."

The word alone in her voice made me shudder, and I quickly insisted, "Tell me everything *you* want, Christine. Please I beg of you. I want to please you. Don't be afraid or shy, not here with me like this. Tell me what you want of me, *ange*."

She hesitated still but finally breathed against

my ear, "Harder," and I shuddered again as I eagerly complied.

Like a sudden allegro, I shifted tempos and obeyed, thrusting deep and hard as she clutched me and buried her cries against my throat. I would have feared it was too much, but I felt her find pleasure, my name fleeing her lungs in a shout that sent me up the peak after her.

It was *glorious*; I couldn't have staved off ecstasy if I wanted to. Losing her name just as fervently, I was overcome, clinging to her with arms I wished could mold into her skin and become fixed, ...never let her go.

Ripples of shivers racked my body as the air in the room chilled and cooled my heated flesh, stinging the convalescent injuries down my spine with a pleasant sort of pain I hoped would never fade. I lifted my head to meet Christine's stare, desperate for acceptance in a way that exceeded even baring my body. I needed it as if I'd perish without it. *Oh God, please let her know no regret...*

But she immediately pressed her mouth to mine, catching my sigh of relief in her kiss and breathing into me something better. Acceptance, love, desire, the lingering traces of her climax. I felt it all, and finally, the tears I'd fought rimmed my eyes as I kissed her back and hoped she felt as much returned from me.

"I love you," I sobbed the instant we broke a kiss and savored her adoring smile. Whatever I'd done to deserve this, I was in awe and was determined to keep it forever. Every horror was suddenly worth its scars and agony if all was forgiven and in its rightful place. Christine in my arms, in my bed, open heart and soul, *mine...*

God works in mysterious ways...

Chapter Twenty

Christine~

Oh, to be in love! I could reason that nothing was as remarkable and awe-inspiring as loving the person one was meant to. I felt *complete* inside, like a human being suddenly made whole and given the very purpose for living all in one glorious emotion. *Love...*

That first week, I functioned half in a haze. One thought, one random stimulus, and I could be dragged into memories of Erik and our overwhelmingly passionate endeavors so quick that a disgruntled Reyer frequently had to call me to attention. It was just too easy!

And God forbid if Erik walked into rehearsal at any point, for his gaze *always* sought my shape and turned me into a gelled pool of anticipation. It was quite obvious to cast and crew and anyone with eyes that I was having a torrid love affair with the Opera Ghost, and I didn't care that they knew it! I was too enamored, blinded to anything I did not wish to see.

Erik was all I breathed for, but opera had its place next in line. As *Faust* quickly approached, an amount of serious effort went into perfecting my role. Every day a lesson at rehearsal's end was our top priority. We had to let music do the touching first and embrace each other through melodies inextricably entwined.

To my wonderment, Erik actually conceded to

sing parts with me, playing Faust opposite my Marguerite and acting out the scenes as if we *were* the real show. How amazing such a rendition would have been! Erik's angel voice sung Faust in a way I'd never heard, perhaps a way only heavenly creatures were meant to behold. It would have stunned Paris to hear such exquisiteness upon the stage, but I never asked him for such a thing. I kept it all for myself and savored every second spent in harmony almost as much as every second making love. Both were their own unions and equally as beautiful.

Erik was my muse for love, passion, desire, every detail of living in general, and eager to be the same for him, I threw myself wholeheartedly into love's arms and fell harder this time than the first time a year and a half before. Now I knew that if he left for any reason at all, it would *kill* me.

As another endless span of rehearsal finally closed its minutes, I watched the cast leave and dallied on the stage, awaiting an angel, *my* angel, and I had so much to anticipate: music and then being carried off into the shadows and allowing them to devour me whole. I could hardly hope to keep patience intact, but as it was, I had little choice but to await Erik's presence, mentally willing the ambling ballerinas off to their dormitories.

Meg caught my eye and gave me a little wave as she scurried after the others. She'd kept her distance ever since it became noticeable that I'd abandoned a Vicomte for the resident Opera Ghost. She didn't trust Erik or his intentions, and although it stung to lose a friend, I understood her point as much as Erik's. He had made it his mission to torment for too long, and then add in the deaths and the accidents... It was no wonder.

Finally, all were cleared out, and I lifted myself up onto my toes in makeshift ballet motion as I scanned the empty theatre for a mask. Mere moments later, he appeared, striding down the aisle with the new confidence my love had given him. Now doubt was dead and hesitation suffocated, and mismatched eyes burned me in their silent adoration and insisted he had memory just as close to the surface.

"Erik," I bid with the hint of a smile. Our secrets were exchanged in every glance, candid and genuinely bestowed but so blatant in the telling that my knees shook beneath my weight.

"Shy blushes!" he accused with a chuckle that thrilled me. "Truly, Christine? After nights of voracious lust and groping hands to bare skin, you *still* blush so charmingly innocent!"

"It's an impulse," I justified, "and understandable considering the sort of things we did last night..." Merely the mention deepened my hue until I felt the fire coming out of my flesh and guessed red was my color of choice. But last night...oh, his mouth had been *everywhere*, and the blush was half in abashment and half in longing for him to do it again!

"The sort of things we'll perform as an encore to our lesson...if you are willing, of course." His returned grin whispered more secrets and made me duck a coy smile. "Are you willing, Christine? Because I am. Dear God, you are delicious! I could taste you all night on my tongue, and yet it was unsatisfying when I didn't have your heated body against me, ...your legs wrapped around my shoulders..." He reminded the salacious details, and no matter my determination, I could not drag the corners of my lips down or stop the shiver that racked me with its fierce intensity.

"Erik," I chided, halfhearted when I wouldn't have truly minded skipping a lesson and going straight for the finale. "Ridiculous man! If I am now faltering pitches and lyrics, it is solely your distracting fault!"

"Shy again," he accused, approaching in calculated steps. "Or wanton beneath a façade of

246

modesty and terrified to admit it. You *want* my mouth all over intimate places, ...but it's more proper not to readily admit it."

I laughed as he closed the gap between us and sought to prove him wrong. "I want your mouth all over my body," I boldly revealed despite the betraying blush. "Your tongue teasing my deepest, most intimate places. If it's wanton to admit it, then that's what I'll be."

My bluntness had the desired effect as Erik shuddered and lost his breath in a soft gasp. "Yes, love, be wanton. I adore it."

His arms slid about my waist and drew me into him, and I was as eager as he, pressing my body to his hard planes and arching against the insistent proof of his wanting. It was such bliss to be engulfed in his embrace, a place I'd already made my own and carved out in my imprint; I was adamant that no one else would ever fit in my alcove or steal what was mine.

Curling tighter to him, I tempted, "Can we forgo our lesson tonight so I may practice my wanton role instead?"

A chuckle vibrated the chest against me and stirred in its motion as he bent and pressed his masked face into my hair. "I wish I could concede, but one surrender on my part will lead to a million more requests. I would be a fool to let you realize that *you* are my inherent weakness."

"Well, now that you've told me, perhaps I should use such knowledge to my advantage! What sort of promises would it take to destroy your will, *ange*?" I arched suggestive brows as he met my eye and showed me fire in return.

"Only one in particular," Erik decided, but flames smoldered in embers behind a sudden solemnity that inspired my worry.

"What, *ange*? I'll promise *anything* you want." But provocative implications had lost their luster and fell to the background of concern.

He hesitated, and I feared the worst. Everything was *perfect*; what could he possibly still see lacking when I gave him *everything* at every chance?

"Well, ...you've had a fiancé before..." As soon as he started with an awkward shrug, I felt my heart lighten and my soul bubble within me. "But I hoped for only a brief engagement. *Faust* opens in two weeks, and I considered that once the performances were over, we could marry. I know that is very soon and leaves little time for preparations, but I cannot reason waiting longer...if you agree, of course."

It astounded me because he'd obviously plotted the details and kept from sharing them with an abiding fear that I'd refuse him. How ridiculous when the suggestion alone made my heart skip in urgent excitement. Although I was sure he felt its flip, I pursed contemplative lips and posed, "And does that mean we may tell everyone of our engagement and make it abundantly clear that you are *my* fiancé?"

I loved surprising him and surrounding him in comments of my unending attraction, and to watch him arch dubious brows and snicker softly, I savored such responses. "Do you truly wish that, Christine? When the cast and crew already share whispers and look down upon you for your involvement with the Opera Ghost? Marriage is a bit more arrant than simple rumors, you realize."

"Undoubtedly. And I only consent to marriage if it can be public knowledge. I want the world to know I love you."

"Indeed?" His incredulous grin spoke his delight. "I feared you were adverse to revealing personal affairs considering no one but I knew of your so-called engagement to the Vicomte."

I made a face at him. "I never truly wanted Raoul. Why do you think I was the adamant one to keep it a secret? It never felt...*right*. But with you, it's what I've *always* wanted, and I want to shout it from the opera house rooftop."

My dramatics brightened his grin. "Then you *do* consent? You will be my wife?"

"Yes, yes!" I covered the unmasked side of his face in elated kisses that muttered more devotions. And as he chuckled his bliss, I considered that all was as it should be, finally in accord and on its designated path. This was *perfection*.

...And how quickly it was shattered.

I'd harbored an ominous terror to accept that we'd reached our happy ending, half-afraid of an unrealized evil lurking on the outskirts. I had pinned reservations on the Vicomte. I hadn't told Erik the extent of our heated argument the night I'd broken the Vicomte's heart. Raoul had let me go but not without filling my ears with *his* conjured fears, naming Erik a monster and swearing I'd regret my choices. He'd been devastated, so I hadn't taken valid threats away from him that night, but I kept a trepidation that he'd reappear when I least expected.

How wrong I was to dub Raoul our villain! Evidently, we had a more powerful force working against us, but neither Erik nor I knew it, not until a certain moment while embracing on the stage and celebrating our newly-acquired engagement...

I was a comment away from reminding Erik that he'd vowed we'd skip my lesson if I agreed to marriage, and perhaps if we'd acted the entire scene five minutes earlier than we now were, we would have bypassed the threat altogether. But as it was, Erik suddenly stiffened against me, and I lifted worried eyes. I saw that he was *listening* for something. I could practically glimpse the eruption of his Opera Ghost stealth and skill set.

"What?" I breathed without sound to interrupt.

"Someone is in the opera house," he reported steadily as he released me and scanned the empty theatre. I had no idea how he could tell such things when I found not a single clue, but he was on guard and nervous in a manner I did not think he'd employ if our intruder were a lingering ballerina or crewmember. He seemed to *know* the situation was worse than that even before an unfamiliar voice made its presence known.

"Erik! How are you, old friend?"

I fixed my confusion on the man striding down the aisle. Another foreigner like the one I'd encountered in Erik's home, but this one was *no* friend. It was in the air of malevolence surrounding him. He was a forbearing presence, large and rather round at the same time, clothed in lush silks and satins, far finer than any I'd ever seen. Wealthy, affluent, and yet subdued in the telling, for only the fabric choices gave it away, nothing too ostentatious, but looming at the theatre doors were two tall, muscled men. ...Guards. Why would anyone walk about Paris guarded?

I shifted my focus to Erik, standing but steps from the stage edge, and I noted his unease immediately. His back was stiff, every muscle pulled taut and hands fisted at the ends of tense arms. I could not read if this was anger...or fear.

Nerves twisted my gut for no confirmed reason, and with feet that barely brushed the stage floor, I crept behind his shape and set a shaking palm to his shoulder blade. He leapt beneath my attempt and shot me a glare as if he suddenly recalled my presence. *Fear...* It was definitely fear.

With a breath that shook his entire body, he clamped a firm hold on my arm and drew me behind him, forcing my hand against the small of his back as if trapping me there before he replied to our intruder in his arrogant Opera Ghost tone, "Shah, what are you doing out of Persia? Sightseeing? Vacationing? I thought you were not welcome in much of the free world because of your extremist tendencies and merciless militia tactics."

Shah... I felt as if the air were knocked out of

me, and shivering hard, I curled closer to Erik's spine. The shah of Persia, the one who had hurt my love with scars inside and out...

The shah chuckled coldly and retorted, "Intelligently, I play middle class when out of my own country. Visiting tourist from a foreign land. No one questions as long as I'm careful."

"And if you're not, would they haul you into their prisons to stand trial for your war crimes, or would you just be deported with a slap on the wrist? How far does your jurisdiction run?"

I admired Erik's haughtiness more than ever because I felt how rapidly his heartbeat raced, how intense it pulsed. But he never showed even a hint of it, retaining the façade effortlessly in the face of genuine terror, and ducking my head against his back, I pressed my lips to his shoulder blade and held an eternal kiss to a spot I knew was covered in horrific scars.

Oh God, and *this* was the demon man responsible! I had the urge to attack on my own, to *hurt* someone. I thought I'd never understand such hostile sensations, but suddenly, I was no better than a sinner eager to commit crimes.

"Concerned for my welfare?" the shah posed doubtfully.

Erik gave an idle shrug. "Eager to get you heaved out of my country."

"Oh, I don't intend for a long trip. Usually in these instances, I depend on my regime to get jobs done for me, but we had it with such certainty that you would be here that I decided to take this task myself and make sure it was done right. You really are a fool. Escape the Persian dungeons, but put yourself out in the public eye? It seems everyone in this damnable country knows of a masked man who purchased the opera house with precious jewels as his remittance. Jewels, Erik? And those wouldn't be the same jewels you stole from my care the first time you fled Persia like a common criminal, would they?"

"Well, of course, but *stolen* is such an ugly word. I considered it compensation for services rendered. I took quite a few lives for your entertainment and made death into another amusement. You owed me."

"Not *that* much, dear *friend*, and twice now, you've had accomplices aid your pilgrimage out of Persia. *My* people have deceived me to preserve your worthless existence." Each word grew in aggression, and I could feel the shah's malevolence exuding over both of us like a cloud of pestilence. "It *astounds* me. You are a monster and a murderer; I can respect such traits when I share your love for depravity, but *you* are worth dramatic resurrection and rescue while I am the one reviled and betrayed. *You* and your face of death! How is that fair?"

"If you are only here to pout like a petulant child, then get out of my opera house. I have no patience to put up with imperial rulers and their temperaments. I have a cast full of divas that would rival your every tantrum. Go back to Persia where you belong."

"Oh, I intend to, but not without your company. You have not finished your sentence; it ends in death, and you escaped before its culmination."

I felt Erik shudder with the recollection, and I shared it with him, as tremors racked my frame and revealed my growing terror. No, *no*, I would *not* let such a thing happen. Sense posed back, who was I to stop it? I was small and fragile compared to the auras of power coming off both men in the room, and even if I bore my own strength in my heart and soul, if it didn't translate to physical superiority, I was nothing more than the tantruming diva Erik spoke of.

"Be gone with you and your sentence," Erik shouted back as if unaffected. "You do not have the law on your side in this country to help enforce your authority. Go back to Persia, and stew in your anger; I am finished with this conversation."

Another grating chuckle resounded and brought goose bumps to my skin. "And leave you here to your opera because *you* see no benefit in being dragged back to Persia like the animal you are? What awaits you? More torture? Death? But what does it say of my rule if I let insurgents go free and bear no consequence for their wrongdoing against their leader?" His gaze spanned the length of the theatre, and he remarked as if music meant something to him, "You're to perform *Faust*, isn't that so? The story of a man who signs his soul to the devil. Such truth in life! What a remarkable tale that is! I hope your cast does it justice! And...may I assume the little waif behind your back is the prima donna star? Ah, *Christine*, your sweetheart!"

"Don't you dare speak her name," Erik hissed, and the grip he had upon my arm tightened to a pinch. "She has *nothing* to do with this."

"She *could* if I deem it so. How much more pleasant to take out your punishment on *her* in your stead!"

The growl I felt vibrate Erik's chest stretched to his core, and half a step from assault and attack, I clamped my free arm about his waist and prayed he wouldn't act rash and throw me aside in his need to retaliate. "Erik, please," I gasped softly and knew he heard as he yielded back into my hold.

"If you touch even the floor beneath her feet, you will be dead where you stand," Erik hissed coldly, and for the first time, I was grateful for threats of murder in his voice. "You forget that this is *my* opera house, and I have the upper hand this time. Get out before I use it."

I peeked over Erik's shoulder at the enraged shah, hating the man so much in his arrogant pose as if he possessed the right and everyone else must therefore be wrong.

"For now," the shah decided with a sinister grin that he directed right at my spying gaze. "As you said, I don't have the authoritics on my side and can't very well *haul* you back to Persia. But...this is *not* over. I will see you soon." His focus set upon me again. "And you, too, Christine. I look forward to getting to know you better. What a surprise to find a lovely creature such as yourself at the mercy of a monster. You can do better."

"Better?" Erik spat viciously. "Like *you*? A man who *rapes* and *tortures* with just as much innocent female blood on his hands as male warriors?"

"Oh, don't be a hypocrite! We are two of a kind, and you, my *friend*, have retribution coming for you. You shall see." He turned to go before adding over his shoulder, "And if I were you, I'd warn your comrade the daroga that if we cross paths, he's dead without prolonged torture attached this time. I'm finished playing games with that one."

I could feel the rage running down Erik's spine in ripples, but he kept frozen in place until the shah finally took his leave with his guards right behind.

"Stay here," he commanded sharply as he released the viselike hold he'd had on my arm.

"Where are you going?"

"To make sure he's really gone and lock up," he snapped as he was already stalking a path into the theatre with never a single look back at me.

I was terrified what that meant and just as much what would happen if the shah or his men still lingered. But Erik was right to say he had the advantage and every trick and trap he'd set about the opera. He no longer seemed paranoid in my mind to go to such an extreme. Some circumstances called for it, and here was a prime example.

Never a sound echoed the theatre to meet me, and without Erik's intuitive sense of danger, I was ignorant to what was happening, anxious and shaking all over. This was the worst scenario I could imagine being thrown into our happiness. The shah of Persia wandering Paris out for Erik's blood and demise… Raoul's broken heart seemed childishly immature in comparison.

My frantically roaming eyes landed and locked on my arm, still extended in midair suspension. Where Erik had gripped, fierce marks remained, nothing severe; perhaps a bruise would be left in the wake, but here was proof that Erik still had violence in him. For the first time, I was actually grateful for it.

When he strode back into the theatre minutes later, I could not decipher his feral expression, nothing but the rage still un-cooled on the surface. He kept his real musings hidden, refusing to meet my stare as he joined me onstage. Without a word, he swept me off my feet, clasping me tight to his body as he headed for one of his secret entrances and escape in the solace and safety of shadows.

I kept quiet and pliant, but his heartbeat was erratic and uneven against mine and told more than he willingly wanted. Not even when we were securely contained in the dark did it slow its rapid throb, and I wondered how much of this was fear of the future and how much was actually fear of the past chasing our heels.

We arrived, and as soon as he set me on my feet, he was at his piano, attacking with a vengeance. Ugly dissonance, pounding chords that bellowed against the walls and likely poured all the way back up the path we'd descended, such was anger's possession. Fire and fury, and I shook on my feet to watch him.

His fingers hit the keys with such force that I knew they must hurt, but this was a peculiar onset. Typically, music would have given escape and release, but this time as he launched into a fitful melody, he fumbled and mistakes resounded. It was completely atypical for a man obsessed with perfection to be out of sorts.

More erroneous pitches cut shrill and blatant through my body, and I watched him grow more and more aggravated with each. Music became a stranger when he seemed most in need of its comfort, and with a growl so ferocious that I jumped to overhear, he swiped the notated pages of music resting before him to the floor and leapt to his feet in surrender.

"Erik…" I knew *I* had to be the one to calm him if music had failed, and I shook with a new sense of trepidation. Oh God, what if I failed as well?

"This was supposed to be *over*!" he roared, and vocal cords were abused as harsh as piano keys in his aggression. "I suffered and rotted in that cell and performed my penance to God and mankind already. How much more am I expected to give?"

"I told you before, God does not take penance in pain-"

"Naïve!" he snapped at me. "Of course God does! He has you blinded to His true nature. The dutiful Catholic girl comforted in the promise of heaven after death and eternal rest for her doting father. But *none* of it is true! Death is *death*, and God is a master manipulator, deceiving the entire human race with futile vows of an afterlife of paradise. Don't you see that such ideas are sugarcoated illusions? They are not real, and God is truly a sadist who loves to look down from His high pedestal and watch the *agony* of living."

I put no credence in a single one of his fiery arguments, knowing the underlying factors fueling debate. With the danger now lurking and threats of more torture, Erik saw this as God's revenge, pulling happiness from his fingers again. It was wrong to assume such things, but I couldn't find a strong enough point that would change his mind, not in this state anyway.

Lifting defenseless hands, I made a timid approach, half-expecting him to lash out and pounce like a wild animal. Every breath he heaved shook his entire frame and played hoarse and harsh in the room, stirring violence in its subtle boil.

"You are *not* going back to that prison," I vowed the words I knew he ached to hear and yet was terrified to believe. His shoulders trembled, and as I stared, still afraid to touch him, his arrogant façade showed its stitches as they slowly frayed and split his persona in two.

A sob ripped from his chest, and I was there to catch him in my suddenly strong embrace, weaving my arms about his body as it creaked and moaned and gave its true weakness away. This wasn't the omnipotent Opera Ghost; this was a man with scars as vivid on his soul as on his body, and I was content simply to feel him hold me back and let me be his stability.

His face pressed its tears into my hair, and without a second thought, I reached for his mask, freeing his distorted features and sliding my hand up his nape to cradle that beloved head in the crease of my neck. I loved him so much at that moment that I feared my heart would burst.

There were no more words spoken that night. I held him for a long time, and then when tears subsided and I knew he needed more, I undressed him with steady fingers, revealing his damage to my adoring eyes with an appreciation for every abnormality that he wouldn't understand but was desperate for just the same.

Oh, that body... It had been through so much trauma. The first time I'd uncovered it, I had been overwhelmed in compassion and *his* pain, shocked to tears in the revelations of a story that had seemed fiction until I had proof. Every other uncovering the past week had been in the heat of desire, and the true heinousness had worn away and barely been acknowledged. Tonight, there were new feelings altogether, an acceptance I hadn't fully grasped and a sudden gratitude that this was *all* there was. He was *alive*, and to hear the shah insist death was the goal to such unnecessary suffering, I suddenly adored every telling scar and sought to show it.

Hands with tender fingers and then lips and tongue, and I lavished oaths of my affection upon every inch of his skin. Such an artist's canvas... At first view, the colors and textures had been jarring; now they were all a part of the whole. Pinks in many hues, tans and even whites paler than his skin tone, and it was the spots that were *not* marked that seemed odd and out of place.

My tongue laved attention up and down the path a whip had taken along his chest, languid and with a core of heated aching that I felt him reflect. Desire was a gradual build and inevitably constructed when he arched toward my ministrations and lost breathless moans above me.

Burn marks still looked raw in some places, and I was overly careful to kiss their center and upraised branding. The shah's crests upon the body of *my* lover. I felt compelled to make my own seals, only mine would be created with my mouth and run far deeper. The manner in which Erik grasped my hair and encouraged told me that even if invisible, he *felt* them and wanted more; yes, *my* marks brought pleasure, never pain.

Dragging his pants down his hips and out of my way, I knelt before his trembling frame and devoted efforts to the vicious injury from hip to inner thigh. This one was the pinkest of the bunch; even though it healed, it would stay prominent forever, so harshly granted. I kissed its length, lingering purposely at its ending point on the otherwise soft flesh of his inner thigh. He groaned, desperate and wild as I moved my mouth with delicate seduction, my curls tickling his legs and the thick hardness of his erection, protruding not far above my chosen spot.

This was all deliberate on my part. I wanted him to feel cherished, but more than that, I wanted

him to *want* and know desire from skin otherwise
wounded and victim to too much pain. I didn't kiss
the details that did not bear marks tonight, not his
elegant hands or his God-created face. I kissed
manmade damage and made it clear that I was
aroused to delirious heights by the same things he
dubbed a humiliation.

But I broke my own protocol for a quick minute
to indulge his boldly brazen manhood, taking him into
my mouth and shivering at the uninhibited cry such
voraciousness brought from an angel's voice. The
hand in my hair fisted and tangled, but he let me do as
I pleased and tease him with the tip of my tongue and
soft, brushed kisses that made him thrust urgent hips,
never taking the reins, never asking more than I gave.

One more time, I parted my lips and took him
inside before I felt the frenzy build, and catching his
hands, I coaxed him to the carpeted floor with me and
let him undress me with abrupt tugs and a search for
the skin beneath. It was vehement and necessary.

Once bare, I fitted myself upon his lap and took
him with quick, hasty motions, straddling his hips and
urging him deeper with every uncontrolled cry from
my lungs. I knew how much *he* needed this, to feel
that I desired him just as much despite the things he
viewed with shame, but I wanted him to realize that *I*
needed this just the same. Beyond desire's hunger, I
needed this intimate closeness with him, this baring
of souls through scars and skin. I pressed my chest
flush to his, heartbeats echoing each other in their
flustered patterns, breaths in harsh unison and
moving our motion along a tidal wave. We were so
close at that instant, one in every way we could be,
and I prayed it would last forever.

When pleasure came, I burrowed my cries
against his disfigured cheek and tasted the tears
falling unconsciously from his mismatched eyes.
Their presence made my clutch him tighter, running
fevered caresses from adoring hands up and down his

259

scarred back as if we were fused forever.

"I love you... I love you so much," I vowed in gasps as he thrust harder, clasping my hips and rocking me with his ferocity. Deeper, almost *frantic*, and when his ecstasy came, I covered his face in kisses and swallowed his guttural cry in my mouth, stealing it as mine.

Pleasure brought renewed terror, it seemed, and his arms locked around me and wouldn't release as he begged against my ear, "Don't let me go. Oh God, Christine, *please*. Don't let go."

"I won't," I vowed and mirrored his pose, clinging with limbs that trembled in their yearning necessity to stay strong. No, I *couldn't* falter. No matter my own fears and the swelling compassion that made his pain mine by default. I couldn't show a single crack, and even if I was weak beneath the veneer, I stroked his hair and back and never let him realize my hands actually shook. No, I played steady well enough to calm him and only cried my own tears when he slept peaceful in my arms.

Chapter Twenty-One

Erik~

  I had to hunt out the daroga. He'd been absent from my underground home since we'd both learned Christine's love was real and soldered, not a fabricated product of my imagination. I hoped he'd left Paris and went off to join his family, but I checked hotels anyway, always on guard in case I encountered the shah instead.

  Oh, let us cross paths! I was armed with a noose, which I preferred in struggles, *and* a dagger just in case. But certainly, the shah chose affluent accommodations, and I sought the daroga in the shoddy parts of town.

  I wasn't pleased to find him almost easily at a hotel near the river. No pseudonym in the hotel registry, no decent attempt to hide himself. He even opened the door after I gave but one knock!

  "Fool!" I spat as I pushed past him and entered the meager confines of his hotel room. "You could be *dead* right now because you did not take half a second to ask *who* knocked first!"

  "Dead?" he scoffed with a roll of eyes. "Here to *kill* me, Erik? Have things gone awry and sour already with the fair Christine, and now you blame *me* for freeing you from captivity? Because that is ludicrous reasoning, and I refuse to die for your rash heart."

Teasing! He dared to tease at a time like this! I had an urge to free my noose if only to inspire some modicum of fright in him. "Maybe you *deserve* what's coming for you if you so carelessly jest when I am here with *your* welfare in mind."

"What are you talking about?"

His continued flippancy irritated me, and I snapped, "The shah of Persia is traipsing about Paris, eager for *both* our heads. If I were you, I'd give proper seriousness to the situation, seeing as how *you* betrayed his supposed merciful graces to get *me* out of that infernal dungeon. You have as much of a target on your back as I do."

"The...shah?" the daroga stammered, and I saw the somberness I was after finally settling in. "But...how? Why? He *never* leaves Persia."

"Double-cross him enough times, and it seems he does! We, my friend, have committed treason, mutiny, and any other crime that makes us insurgents to his insidious rule, and he is eager for revenge at any cost."

"You...saw him?"

"Oh, he came right to me!" I revealed as I idly wandered the meager space, scanning pathetic surroundings with a grimace of distaste. "And worst of all, the bastard laid eyes on Christine and threatened with his brand of torment."

"What are you going to do?"

With a nonchalant shrug, I concluded, "Kill him."

"And how do you intend such a feat? I'm sure he's heavily guarded." The daroga spoke the minor details I would rather have forgotten when vengeance was on my mind.

"Perhaps, but given the option, I'll take the chance. The bastard will *not* touch Christine."

I glimpsed the solemn agreement in his dark stare and assumed he considered his wife's entrapment. God only knew what she'd gone through;

I hadn't the heart or strength to ask when my mind would have immediately put Christine in the situation and driven me to insanity imagining her tortured.

But all of a sudden, as reality seemed to intrude, his stare grew wide, and he demanded, "Where is Christine now?"

"Rehearsal. I paid that fool director Reyer a little something extra to keep her always within his gaze. I daresay that he now presumes I am jealous and controlling, but I couldn't very well give him why and have him add insanity to the list. You must admit, telling others that the shah of Persia is lurking about Paris out for vengeance and blood sounds like another tale fit for the stage!"

The daroga nodded, but as he contemplated my admissions, he somberly stated, "You're assuming Christine is safe amidst her peers, but...my wife was taken from a public place amidst other people..."

I went numb with his words as my mind raced ahead and envisioned a scene of the dastardly shah stealing Christine right from the stage as his guards threatened death to anyone who tried to stop him. I could see every detail as if it were indeed fact, and without another thought, I rushed for the door with the daroga two steps behind.

We ran to the theatre through the city streets in broad daylight, and I did not consider twice that my masked face was illuminated by sunlight and receiving odd stares all around. Christine was the impetus for this display; the crowds could gawk at the masked man and the dark-skinned foreigner chasing at his heels, and if it meant they paused their treks to point and make a clear path for us to get by in our haste, then our eccentricities were doing us a favor.

I burst into my own opera house as if on a rampage and raced straightway to the theatre. Before I even passed the doorway, her brilliant soprano embraced me in its aria, but even as my ears *heard* her presence, I was an anxious mess. I halted at the doorframe and stared with ravenous eyes that couldn't get enough, desperate to assure my doubting mind that *she was real* and the scenes I had concocted of public kidnapping were not. A difficult feat even with her image in my line of view. Until I was touching her, I was sure I wouldn't believe. I'd been haunted by too many realistic figments with her image in the shah's dungeon to ever trust my eyes or ears again.

"Well, isn't she amazing!" the daroga softly exclaimed beside me, and I shot him a glare that clearly insisted I'd forgotten his company. But...if *he* saw her, too, she *must be* real.

"My cast is gossiping about *you* even as we speak," I snapped. "They probably think you're a foreign investor looking to purchase their sorry little jobs."

With a huff, I noted that my assumption wasn't far off. Eyes all around. Even Christine mid-aria onstage was arching a dark brow at our spying, and all I could do was offer her a blameless shrug in return.

"You wear a mask, and *I* am the one gossiped about?" the daroga muttered. "Well, that is certainly a new twist."

I ignored him and strode right through the web of penetrating gazes with never a care to the sting they gave as I halted rehearsal with a raised hand and stalked onstage. Reyer looked annoyed to be interrupted, everyone ceasing in an indefinite pause as if time itself had suspended its progression, but that was fairytale time, not real life.

With no explanation, I went straight to Christine as blue eyes read me quizzically, and never giving my intentions away, I caught her hand in mine. *Real, solid, warm.* I pulled her after me into the wings, calling over my shoulder to Reyer, "Continue."

"Erik!" Christine snapped, but I was unyielding as I drew her through the busy corridors with the daroga a handful of steps behind us. We received more anxious stares and hushed whispers, but none slowed my frustrated pace as I pulled her into her dressing room.

One of the young costume girls was inside, waiting for Christine, costume in hand for a fitting, and with never a care to play congenial, I ordered, "Out."

"Erik!" Christine warned again, but with a frustrated sigh, she gave the costume girl the kind smile I could not have managed if I tried and watched the girl scamper toward the door, recoiling past the threshold and into the hall with the daroga's entrance.

"She didn't like you," I told my Persian companion as he closed us inside with a relieved exhalation.

"I noticed! Your antics are evidently expected and acceptable, but a visitor from a foreign country is the suspicious one. How ironic!"

Christine found no humor in our banter, and jerking her hand free of my hold, she demanded, "What was that all about? You just stole me off the stage mid-scene!"

"And my impulsiveness is not endearing to you in some way?" I offered in appeasement. My worry had simmered back to a grateful sort of elation, and ruffling her feathers made her adorable when I now had her solely in my care.

Her irritation fractured to a bit of a smile even as she sought to keep a straight face. "It *would be* if this wasn't two weeks to opening night."

"Considering that you can sing the role forwards, backwards, and sideways, I am not concerned."

"Erik-"

"I'm allowed to play overprotective and the stifling fiancé when we have a validly dangerous threat hanging over our heads."

"Fiancé?" The daroga latched onto the word with pleasant surprise in his arched brows.

"Yes," I sharply told him before returning focus to Christine, "and *as such*, your welfare is my priority. If you don't believe my paranoia, will you trust the daroga's? The shah is not a threat to take lightly."

Her expression sobered, and her hand pressed to my chest, searing my scars even through layers with her natural heat. "I know that already. I am not taking it lightly. I just don't see what can be done against it."

I covered her sweet hand, keeping it to my heartbeat. "We could leave Paris, leave the entire country even. Hide away for awhile. It might be the best course for now."

"But the opera-"

"Curse the opera!" I exclaimed with vehement aggression, and when she sought to pull her hand away, I trapped it in a fist. "The opera means *nothing*. *You do*! I would happily give up *all music* for the rest of my existence if it meant you'd be safe and mine. Nothing compares."

"Mademoiselle," the daroga spoke up and broke into our bubble, "you should trust Erik. When it comes to the shah, evil bears no limit. He knows no mercy and has no heart for compassion. He is truly a vile creature who does not follow the rules. If *you* are his chosen target, he will not stop until he has you."

My fears, and to hear them in the air made me shake and hold her hand tighter even as she met my gaze and insisted back, "Why are you so concerned over *me*? *You* are my worry when he threatened your death."

"He wants to hurt me in the worst way imaginable," I corrected and lifted my free hand to her cheek, marveling over its delicate softness. "And that is only a relevant reality if he hurts *you*. Nothing would give me more agony."

She doubted my words. I could tell as her gaze lingered on my chest and fantasized the scars underneath. I'd watched her memorize their layout in our lovemaking the previous night for exactly this reason, to be able to call upon their picture and acquire strength.

"Abandoning our lives is not the answer," she concluded with a shake of her dark head. "The shah is just a mortal man; he is not a god or invincible, and he can be conquered."

"Yes, if I *kill him* before he does any viable damage."

"Erik, I didn't mean-"

"No? I may have atoned for my past sins, but this is one I can justify committing, and I would do it without a qualm," I insisted. "It would be ridding the world of a monster."

"Erik, don't-"

"If *you* don't want us to leave Paris, then I will do what I must for our safety, even if that is *murder*, Christine. Do you understand? I don't *want* to be a killer, but if it comes to that, you cannot pass judgment. I will take the consequences before God, but you are not allowed to call me a monster and break away as you did once before. Promise it to me, Christine."

"But murder is-"

"*Promise* it," I commanded and knew I was being cruel, but with the idea of losing her to my own actions as great a possibility as losing her to the shah, I was adamant in my fear.

She held my stare with somber concern but conceded, "You will not lose me; I promise that. But...please keep murder as a *last* option."

A minor victory. I felt I had her permission in some obscure manner, but if attack came, I needed to protect us both, and that was my best defense.

It was in painful reluctance that I allowed Christine to return to rehearsal, and that was only with the condition that I would be in constant watch over her. She might not have favored the terms or my avid paranoia, but this was a point I refused to argue.

She was fortunate I didn't push it further when eyes were unreliable and I preferred touch. But I resigned myself to the audience and watched like an over-attentive hawk every second of every rehearsal during the final runs before the opening.

With days' passage, one to the next, and no sign of imminent danger, one would have thought I'd have relaxed my guard, but I knew the shah too well. He'd wait for an opportune moment to pounce and destroy, and I refused to let him find one, bustling Christine between the underground and rehearsals with never a spare second in between. If my turbulent distress upset her, she never said so; she acquiesced and actually held me a little tighter whenever we embraced, wove fingers unbreakable with mine on our treks between worlds, stayed to my side at every chance. It was for *my* piece of mind, and I loved her for such unqualified understanding.

The night before the opening of *Faust*, I was as anxious as one of my cast. I kept a terror that the shah would find a way into my show. After all, he had made mention of its performance as if he wanted to add his own drama. And so I had taken care to position guards during final dress rehearsal, ready for any danger that could erupt in a theatre full of people. My employees had spied me giving my new armed employees instructions and obviously considered I'd lost my mind, and perhaps they weren't far off. Anxiety had such an effect, and I was a tightly-wound ball of it, leaping at every sound that wasn't the background of *Faust*'s score, terrified the second I calmed would be the second my world altered.

Perhaps that was why when Christine came home with me that night, she dove at me with wild abandon, tearing at clothes with fingers urgent for the scarred flesh beneath and pressing fervent lips to every feature of my face to steal the very words of protest from my mouth. She seemed tenaciously set in her plan to distract me, and it was so well-executed that I forgot everything for as long as desire held.

Hands and mouths, tongue plunging deep and tasting inch after inch of heated skin; we both burned alive in the wanting, coming to each other at the cusp of its waves and riding out each undulation to its fulfillment. Our bodies entwined and made a music more glorious than the stage could hold, moving as one in that choreographed dance as old as time itself, and love was the sacred shroud spread atop us, blocking out any evil that tried to graze our hearts.

Afterward as I lay curled behind her, still so deeply embedded in her heated wetness, she whispered into the comfort of shadows, "I'm nervous about the opening."

It was almost humorous that in all the drama with the shah and potential imprisonment, I hadn't considered such a thing. "Nervous? But you've done this before and often."

"Yes, but every performance since that first Gala night has been contrived and hollow. You said it yourself: I was an automaton whose wind-up key was turned, but now...you took the walls down and it will just be *me* on the stage, exposed and vulnerable and with my harshest critic to please."

Kissing her temple, I vowed adamantly, "You've *already* pleased me...quite well, in fact." My teasing earned me the little giggle I was after, and I eagerly added, "You forget that this heart-revealing sort of performance is what you were born to do. You will shine and sparkle upon that stage tomorrow night; I've no doubt of it."

"If I do, it will be for you, *ange*, all for you." She took a trembling breath; I felt it lift the arm I had fitted about her torso. "Erik, ...I know you're afraid for both of us, but I cannot stand to see how heavily it weighs upon your thoughts. I beg you to remember that you love the music, that that is why we take risks and chances. Music always meant so much to you, and now..."

"There is no music in a dungeon cell, Christine," I reminded solemnly. "Only what plays in memory, and it is disappointing at best. I would rather put protecting you above loving the music for the moment. I can appreciate such things when I know I'm free."

She peeked back over her shoulder at me and shook her head, stirring disheveled dark curls upon her pillowcase. "Have I taught you nothing? Foolish man. What good is there in living if we cannot appreciate our blessings? You will fixate on the risks and chances not taken instead of savor the ones right before you, and tomorrow night will be a blurred haze in your memory. You love music; don't let fear for what may or may not come to pass steal that from you." Her little hand cupped my scarred cheek and lovingly trailed its deformations. "There will always be situations where we cannot predict the outcome, but if you allow the fear to outweigh the pleasure, then...life is empty. I know it's true because I lived a year and a half dead inside and unable to see the world beyond my pains and trepidations. And now...don't waste our bliss together with your own terrors in between us."

I wanted to argue that what I did had merit, that obsessing over her well-being was necessary, but at the heart of every contention, I knew she was right. Since the shah's appearance, I felt as if I'd been grasping happiness with slipping fingers, and my zeal to cling to it meant suffocation. I was more concerned with *keeping* happiness than *feeling* it. I vowed to myself at that second with her in my embrace, her heartbeat practically aligned with mine, that I would listen to her, and tomorrow night when she triumphed, I would share her joy with her. *Joy* not terror of what could be. The present should mean *more* than the future.

With that new mindset, I went about final details for the opening the next day, bustling about my office while the performers were tended to in their dressing rooms. I was even lighthearted and humming Faust's final duet to myself as I went through a stack of bills upon my desk, sharing a bit of Christine's performance excitement. I could hardly wait to see her upon the stage!

A knock at the door jarred me from my fantasies of her voice, and as I called, "Come in," I harbored a hope to find her beaming smile behind the door. It was a meager disappointment to find the daroga instead.

"Yes?" I tersely snapped as he closed himself inside. "If you can't tell by the bustle about the opera, it's opening night, and I am quite busy."

"Too busy for a report on our old acquaintance, the shah?" the daroga asked with suspicious, arched brows.

"I don't want to worry about him today. I have guards about, ready to attack if necessary, and it will be left at that. I'm tired of fighting an invisible battle. Christine is right to say I've been obsessing over imaginary evils instead of living my life. So any news you have can wait until after the opening."

"But...I know where the shah has been staying."

"Oh?" I didn't want to care, but his comment piqued my interest when I longed to stay two steps ahead.

The daroga's snide look seemed to insist he knew I'd falter to revenge's curiosity, and he obliged me. "Using my sleuth skills, a bit rusty for lack of employment, I found that he and his men rented a rather large, luxurious room at one of the most elite hotels in the city. And...well, this doesn't say much for my detective tactics, but they haven't really been hiding such information. They've been spending and gambling all over the city. It's almost as if the shah *wanted* us to find him. Why do you imagine that would be?"

I shrugged with feigned apathy. "I'll analyze it

with you tomorrow, but I'm not supposed to care tonight, remember?"

I meant it now that I had the information, and I would have extradited him from my office if not for the *next* knock at my door. All my assertions were null and void in one sentence from a flustered costume girl.

"Mademoiselle Daaé is gone."

Gone... Gone... Gone... The word whirled in a vortex, repeating its solitary syllable in my mind a dozen times before I comprehended what it meant. *Gone... Christine was gone.*

I ran to her dressing room without a word, the daroga chasing behind. I couldn't breathe; breathing felt like it would stir the earth too much, and stagnant air burned my lungs and choked me as I searched even the corners of the small confines. No Christine...

"Perhaps she's lingering about with some of her comrades," the daroga offered, but I heard his voice tremble and knew he had the same thoughts I did. No, she wasn't with friends or the obnoxious ballerinas. She was *taken*. I *knew* it, intuitive and undoubting, and the note the daroga found upon her vanity was no surprise.

" '*Her or you*'," he read aloud and then glanced at me with solemn, anxious eyes. "Erik, what are we going to do?"

I felt sick on a potent tonic of rage and fear, but in the midst, I gasped out, "It's opening night. She *cannot* miss curtain."

"I think we have larger problems than a botched show-"

"No, that is just *one more* problem. I'm doubtless it's an extra feather in the shah's turban to destroy my theatre as well as my life. Bastard! And so help me God, if he lays one *finger* upon Christine, I will cut it off!" As emotion spiraled, I hung my head in my hands for a long inhalation and sought the path to rational *sense*. It was there, buried somewhere beneath hysteria, and when I found it, I chided my own stupidity not to have realized right away. "I know what to do."

"What?"

"Come on."

We rushed out of the opera house and onto the Paris streets. I was fueled with the pulsation of retribution. The shah would pay for this. *No one* touched what was *mine.*

"Erik, where are we going?"

"There is only one person who can help me," I insisted and picked up my pace until the daroga had to jog to keep up.

"Who?"

But I gave him no answer as the houses grew larger and more *expensive* in this part of the city. I did not explain or hesitate. I found the one I wanted and hurried up the walkway to the front door, pounding furiously on its surface without an inkling of patience left.

A frazzled maid answered, her eyes widening to survey a masked man and a foreigner on the doorstep, but as she gasped, the very presence I sought joined her at the threshold and gripped the door in a fierce hand.

"What do you want? You are not welcome here," the Vicomte de Chagny snapped, hatred in his turquoise gaze.

But I was not above swallowing my pride, and with as much earnestness as I could muster, I bid, "I need your help."

Chapter Twenty-Two

Christine~
The most terrifying moment of my life was emerging from a delightful dream of soaring with angels and finding myself in an entirely strange and unknown room. With an inaudible gasp, I scanned the opulent surroundings and desperately sought to recall my last memories.

I'd been at the opera, waiting in my dressing room for my costume girl... *Oh God...* They'd come through the door almost kindly as if they hadn't wanted to cause panic and damage. The shah's guards...and they must have drugged me. The last I could remember was falling to darkness.

As I abruptly sat up on a chaise, my head gave a pirouette, and I pressed my hand to my brow and sought to hold it in one position. *Drugged definitely.* In the center of the haze came one doubtless thought: I was ruining opening night, and Erik was going to fly into a rage in my absence.

"Ah good, you're awake."

I went stiff with that voice and peeked through my fingers at the hated, smiling face of the shah of Persia.

"You...you took me from the opera house," I stated as I weakly lowered my hands to my lap and fixed him in my stare, seeking to sound less affected by such news than I was. "It's opening night. How dare you?"

The shah chuckled, and his beady eyes raked over me and made me shudder in anxious disgust. "What obstinacy in you! If I were you, I'd be a bit more worried about your well-being than a silly stage show."

"Silly?" I posed and narrowed my glare.

"Well, of course! Children playing pretend before an audience. I respect the talent, but I consider the medium overdone. Now if I put my pretty nightingale in a golden cage and had her sing for me alone in my bedchamber, *that* would be something far more valuable."

My arms wove protectively about my body as I tried to shield myself from his penetrating stare. "You had no right to take me," I insisted and sought to keep a waver from my voice. "Erik is going to kill you."

"Your disfigured lover has been an absolute humiliation to my rule. Did he tell you?" The shah plopped into an armchair facing me and acted as if this conversation was casually ordinary. "Once the pride of my regime, a killer with a heart of stone and a penchant for perverse suffering to rival mine. He built me torture chambers in his genius, sent insurgents to suffer, murdered on my whim. But...when it grew stale, he double-crossed me, fled the country with a nice sum from my treasury in his pockets. He made me look a fool, and *no one* makes me look a fool without consequence and punishment."

"So you tortured him," I spat back and did not regret my aggression.

"In every heinous way imaginable," the shah confirmed without a flicker of remorse. "It was justly deserved. He *should have* died, but he had this unending hope of returning to you. *You* were his saving grace. How pathetic! He wouldn't let go of an existence full of unfathomable pain and degradation because he longed for you. And now I've taken you away, and we shall see how fast he crumbles and resigns to further torment to save you."

I didn't speak, afraid he was right. Erik would do anything for me, but I'd rather not verify that to the evil mastermind devising torturous deaths.

"So now, dear Christine, we simply wait for the moth to come to the flame. I expect him at anytime; he isn't a patient one. And then we'll see what happens. Perhaps I'll take you both back to Persia with me. I have quite the harem, but fair-skinned beauties are a delicacy in my country. They're not nearly tough enough to last. The few I've had in my services chose suicide after only one excursion in my bed. Evidently, they were not accustomed to the derision of pleasure from pain. ...I feel sure *you* could learn. If you let a revolting freak with the face of a demon between your legs, surely you have some dark layers to you."

He licked his lips, slow and provocative, and I fought tears that threatened to give my real terror away.

"...Perhaps I should offer you a taste now."

He started to rise, and I contemplated the struggle I was determined to put forth. He was a large man; I feared I had no hope of triumph when in comparison, I looked like a little girl. Thankfully, I never had to test my abilities. A knock at the door had the shah huffing his annoyance and rushing to answer.

I knew we both assumed it would be Erik, and I felt my chest constrict in anticipation and terror. But one of the guards stood uncomfortably before his master, glancing to my observing eyes before making his report.

"Sire, ...we have a visitor I think you will want to see."

The shah sneered but nodded consent, and a gasp fled my lips as our 'guest' entered the room with eyes that sought mine first, perusing my shape as if in desperate need to make certain I was well. I wasn't sure if I should be grateful or completely confused, but it felt so wonderful to see a familiar face, even if not the malformed one I wanted.

"Excuse my intrusion, my good sir," Raoul stated, flat and with a haughtiness I'd never heard from him. "I don't know how things are run in your country, but here we do not carry off claimed women against their will. It is uncouth and unacceptable. I demand the release of Mademoiselle Daaé this instant, or you will have the *gendarme* banging down your door and hauling you to prison for kidnapping!"

The shah looked Raoul over, obviously finding nothing worthy of worry in the threat. "And who are *you* to speak with such authority? I see nothing but a pathetic boy."

Narrowing his glare, Raoul replied, "I am the *Vicomte de Chagny.* Perhaps titles below *shah* mean nothing in your country. But here I have the law on my side, especially considering that you have *my fiancée* under your locked guard."

My gaze widened a bit with his assertion, but I offered no protest, not a single word. I just prayed Erik knew what he was doing with this plan.

"*Your* fiancée?" the shah inquired, scrutinizing me in his dubiousness. "I was under the distinct impression that the young lady was involved with the one you call the Opera Ghost."

Raoul scoffed against him. "Are you out of your mind? The 'Opera Ghost' is *obsessed* with Christine; we barely escaped his dastardly plot to force her hand. He has had her in his eye of infatuation for years and will not accept the truth: that Christine does not want him back. She chose *me.*"

"But…I saw them together. He was protecting her." Every argument the shah made was met with a denial from Raoul, every query constructed with an answer, and I would have been astounded if I could have broken character.

"No, that was another pathetic attempt to win

her heart," the Vicomte arrogantly stated. "Don't you see? The 'Opera Ghost' is as much a thorn in my side as yours. He tried to *kill me* to gain Christine willingly as his once. He put an ultimatum at her feet to be his wife or watch me die. So I have no qualms against your vendetta. Take him back to Persia to fester in your jails, but you will *not* enact your war with Christine as bait and prize. She is *mine*, and if you think you can come in and carry her off no better than that madman, I will have every branch of law enforcement in France pursue you."

The shah seemed to be weighing Raoul's fabricated words; I was half-amazed by the details devised in a makeshift story about kidnapping and ultimatums, but as I met the Vicomte's steady stare and saw his worried affection, it hurt because I knew the motive behind it was real. He genuinely loved me still and would face shahs and officials to attempt to be my hero. But...considering Erik was the genius behind the curtain, it was hard to dub only one of the two as hero-worthy.

"Vicomte, your presence takes me by surprise," the shah sneered in his thick accent. "This girl may be your fiancée, but she's also the key to Erik's destruction. If I simply let her go, I am doing a great disservice to my cause. He didn't break under the worst tortures imaginable with *this girl* in his heart. Handing her back to you means *nothing* for me."

The Vicomte looked livid as he strode to my side and grabbed my hand, pulling me off the chaise and to my feet. "So burn him alive, stick a sword in his gut, drown him. I don't care! This monster has done his damnedest to ruin our future; I will not let him win. You can find your own methods to the demon's end, but Christine will *not* be a part of it. Come on, darling."

I curled tight to Raoul's side and played the role of damsel in distress, for the first time grateful for its facets and my supposed savior.

Perhaps we would have made it out without consequence, but the door suddenly opened again. I felt the air knocked out of my lungs to see the shah's guards drag into the chamber an enraged Erik and his stumbling Persian friend, the daroga.

"Monsieur Vicomte!" Erik snapped before even regarding the shah's presence. "How fortunate to cross paths with *you* again!"

"I came for *my* fiancée," Raoul shouted back and tightened his hold on my hand. "She will *not* be the one to pay for your sins! Damn you, ugly fiend! Does it make no impression on you that Christine was *kidnapped* because of *your* involvement in her life?"

That was a brutal blow, and though I longed to give assurances to Erik, I cast him no more than an emotionless glance and stayed against Raoul's side.

"Does it truly make a difference when she has *you* to play her hero?" Erik sneered, and his stare was bitter when it hit me. It roamed my frame and glowed in contempt and animosity, but I knew beneath the façade he was checking for injury in unending concern. Yes, I *knew* the man I loved, and I *knew* the Opera Ghost. He might act the role flawlessly, but I would still *know* his heart.

"Erik," the shah finally intruded, passing attention between the two rivals in skepticism. "How good of you to join us!"

"I was *invited*," Erik stated, cold and biting. "Her or me? Weren't those your terms? Of course, I couldn't have realized she'd already have a champion on her side, ready to fight to the death for her." His focus went from me to Raoul as he prodded, "Would you, Vicomte? To the death? Because I presented such endearments only to have them trampled by her callousness. Be wary of her fickle heart, Monsieur Vicomte. Pain, torture, and the imminence of death. I faced it all with her name on my lips only to have hope crushed in her wake. Damn you, Christine. I may be your casualty, but *my opera* will *not* be. You are under contract, and now you've ruined opening night!"

"Oh, all this grumbling of hearts and love and opera!" the shah exclaimed with a grunt. "I am at my wit's end! Such drama and for what? You fight over *one* woman in a world of millions! It's futile!" Lifting his stare to the Vicomte with only a glance at my silent observation, he commanded, "Get out, Monsieur...*Vicomte*," he made a disgusted face over the title. "I already have what I came for anyway."

Raoul did not wait to be told twice, and tucking me to his side, he guided us toward the door. I had nothing but one quick, pleading stare with Erik before it was stolen, and he granted me nothing in reply but apathy. Oh God, I prayed he knew what he was doing.

Raoul quickened our pace once we were in the hotel corridor, clutching me as if we were lovers who belonged in such an affluent hotel. *He* did, and that made our escape easy.

"Hurry. Let's get out of here," Raoul muttered as we emerged into the fading glow of evening, and I gulped fresh air.

"That was planned? But what is Erik doing? How does he intend to get *himself* out?"

"I don't know. I was only given my part in the ploy, and that was to get you as far from this place as possible."

"But the opening-"

"Erik *cancelled* the opening," Raoul reported and ushered me toward an awaiting carriage.

The revelation struck me straight to the heart. "Then...he doesn't plan on getting free." I spoke my desperate thoughts without feeling words on my lips, numb and only continuing to walk with the Vicomte's urging.

"You don't know that."

But I felt hysteria grow and choke my throat as I shouted, "The shah gave him a choice: him or me, and he obviously made it! An ultimatum, and sending me off with you means *I* stay safe!"

"Christine-"

"We have to go back!" I concluded and sought to twist free of his grip, planting my heels on the pavement and refusing to move onward. But he was stronger and tugged against me.

"No, I promised to take care of you!"

"I'm not going to let him return to that torture chamber and die at the shah's hands! Raoul, let go!"

"No! You need to trust Erik. Whatever he's doing, he is doing it *for you*. Whether it's sacrificing himself or simply getting you free and clear before he poses battle. Trust him, Christine, and stop this insanity!"

I would have continued, but he lifted me up, unceremonious and awkward. As bystanders stared and whispered on the street corners, he hauled me into his carriage, tapping the driver to go.

Silence extended, and behind my somber stare, my mind created every explanation and fantasized their details. Erik with a plan underway to get free... Erik without a plan and intending to be the shah's prisoner again... None felt settled or correct when I had no proof or whispered encouragement. He'd given me nothing but that final, apathetic stare. What did it mean?

"Erik said you'd be safest back at the opera house," Raoul reported as he attempted uncomfortable conversation. "He said you knew the way below."

I nodded, but shadows seemed like cold strangers when Erik was beyond my reach. Instead of dwelling and obsessing more scenarios, I shook my head and dared to push, "You hate Erik. You made that clear that last night we saw each other. Why did you concede to help him?"

The Vicomte shifted his gaze about the tight quarters before finally replying, "He said *you* were in trouble, and I didn't hesitate. ...I know I'm not the one you chose to love, but that doesn't mean everything between us was a lie. My heart was real, and...the very thought of you at that shah's mercy..." He shook a somber head. "I'd have done *anything* to get you free. I'd imagine your Erik feels the same or he wouldn't have shown up on my doorstep."

It was true, but I didn't agree aloud as the carriage veered forward and brought us to the opera house.

It was deserted, which was so odd when I recalled the earlier chaos and jitters of opening night. This wasn't the same as an empty opera house after rehearsal; it was as if I could feel the shattered hopes and dreams hovering invisible in the air. So much hard work, anticipation, exhilaration, and all for naught.

"There will be other opening nights, Christine," the Vicomte said as if reading my agitated thoughts.

"Were you planning to attend tonight?" I asked in lieu of heartbroken renderings for lost music and the love of my life.

"Of course! I had to show my support, and if I didn't... Well, that would have made me pathetic to every person aware that you broke my heart. A Vicomte needs a better reputation than that. However else would I find your substitute?"

He meant it as a light joke, and I would have laughed if my heart weren't so heavily weighed down with ominous dread. But as it was, I managed only a weak smile and led the way to one of the hidden entrances below.

It was odd to show such secrets to Raoul, but when I pondered all he'd done for me this night, I concluded I owed him my confidence. I could interpret the discomfort he tried not to show as we wandered the dark passages, but also a level of amazement to witness this product of Erik's genius, a morbid fascination that kept him peeking ahead to glimpse what we'd encounter next.

"A place like this would have been treasured when we were children," he softly said, jumping when even whispers reverberated the stone walls and back around again. He lowered his voice even more and hissed, "Imagine, Christine. Playing our games through these passages. It might have been fun to pretend ghosts and wail our way through the dark corridors."

"Yes, if the corridors weren't equipped with deadly traps for intruders who don't know the way."

The Vicomte silenced with that information, and a glance over my shoulder showed me his wide-eyed surveillance of the stone openings in random directions. And the amazement wore off.

It was a strange evening to be sure. I didn't know what was happening with Erik and the shah, and desperate to distract me, the Vicomte told stories he made up on the spot, some ridiculous and some laden in joked humor. He sat in Erik's chair and kept me company as I curled on the couch with anxiety tight in my belly. And every time he saw me look blankly at the door, he halted whatever story he was telling and started anew to recapture my attention.

It was the most unorthodox opening night I'd ever endured as instead of playing a part to an audience, I played a part to Raoul and never let him see how my heart ached on the inside. No, he didn't need to know that.

Chapter Twenty-Three

Erik~
     Jealousy was a blazing fire in my gut that was not extinguished even well after Christine left with the Vicomte. It was *my* plan, and yet I was sick with every consideration of my Christine pressed to the Vicomte's side. It haunted me even as the shah's ignorant guards tied my hands behind my back and made me a prisoner again.
     "Are you sure about this?" the daroga muttered beside me, equally captive with genuine fear in his eyes.
     "Quite. Don't doubt me, daroga. You should know better than that."
     "Usually, I do, but we are currently restrained. Can you untie those knots?"
     "I *can*, but I won't need to," I spoke with a confidence that exceeded fake Opera Ghost roles. "You worry only about how I'm going to get rid of the Vicomte's infuriating presence now that I've let him into our lives, and I will take care of everything else."
     "Erik," the shah called as he stalked before us and tilted a haughty head. "What a relief to have you back where you belong! You really should know better than to make attempts at a *normal* existence. You aren't built for it! Your dalliance with the little opera diva should be proof. Trying to *force* your love? That is a further abomination on your soul." He

chuckled and concluded, "I like you *evil* and malevolent. Why did you ever leave my employment to begin with? You could have been one of the most highly regarded assassins in the world."

"Exactly!" I snapped. "But I figured out there was more to life than *killing*."

"Yes," he agreed with another laugh, "*forcing* love on a young, innocent girl. So how far did this little scheme of yours go? Did you force her to your bed as well?"

That one stung when I had the truth in fragments of confined memories. Forced... When I pondered it, it sickened my stomach. Imagine! Forcing such things of Christine and cheapening what had been freely given! It would have been empty lust.

"I do not rape the undeserving," I spat back at him. "It may be a shock for you to hear that *love* runs deeper than *desire*."

"And you knew she'd be disgusted with the very concept," the shah pushed onward. "Sharing the bed of a man scarred from the inside out... Well, that *is* a repulsive scene to be sure."

"Ignore him," the daroga spoke up, and I gave him credit considering how frightened I knew he was. "You speak to a man who uses desire as a weapon and punishment. He doesn't know what *love* means."

"Ah, daroga," the shah crooned, coming to stand but inches away, "you are going to boast greater scars than your friend here before I'm through with you. I will have you begging for death."

The threats shook the daroga's collected bravery, but he sought a poised posture and replied, "Maybe, but through it all, I'll know I'm *loved*, and that is something you cannot take from me."

"Spoken by a man full of fear," the shah retorted. "And what of you, Erik? Eager to return to the dungeons and inevitable death? I am not sensing the same break in you that I did that last night I tortured you. I suppose we'll have to find it again."

"I'm not afraid of you," I declared without waver, and I wasn't. Not anymore. I wasn't even escaping my bindings when I could have because I had already won with intelligence as my sword this time. I even smirked at the shah as I concluded, "I'm not going back to your Persian torture chamber and neither is the daroga."

"Oh?" he scoffed. "You are outnumbered and restrained, but go ahead and attempt a struggle if you wish. Perhaps we'll start your torture here."

A chuckle left my lips as I fixed him in my stare and stated, plain and blunt, "You are a pompous, arrogant bastard with a falling regime. Violence is not the way to people's hearts, and making them your victims is a sin that God will judge you for when you lose it all and end upon his doorstep. You will see. The tides will turn, and *you* will be the victim."

I spoke from concrete knowledge of the subject, and glaring at the shah, I noted that that could have been *me* if I'd continued on a murderous path of cruelty. A heartless, merciless monster in nuances that exceeded ugliness and scars. Thank God for Christine! She was my salvation. As she said, *God works in mysterious ways...*

The shah was about to launch into a tirade, perhaps attack in his aggression, but a fierce knock at the door had him darting his stare to its threshold. "Who is it now?"

"That will be the Paris *gendarme*," I stated, resolved and without emotion. "You see, my *friend*, the Vicomte reminded me that cancelling opening night was going to upset our many wealthy patrons who already paid for their tickets with heavy donations. And it did! I was hauled in as manger and questioned if I'd stolen funds to which I had to report that we couldn't hold our opening because my star soprano had been kidnapped by a foreign ambassador to sing for him in his private suite. You can imagine the reaction I received to such news! The *gendarme* were eager to investigate, and...well, if they figure out you are the *shah* of Persia, God knows what they will do to you."

"Ingenious," the daroga commented beside me with a glowing grin as the shah backed toward the windows in a fear I was pleased to cause. Yes, a violent ruler of a foreign land known for the blood on his hands would not be well-regarded in this country, especially with two victims tied in his room.

The *gendarme* pounded against the door. It would be mere moments until it broke apart, and as the shah and his guards climbed out the window, he yelled back, "This isn't over!"

"Yes, it is. Come back, and you'll be *dead* the next time we cross paths." My threat followed him out the window, and when the door finally gave, it was the first place I pointed the uniformed policemen with a tilted head.

All I could think about was returning home to Christine, but we had questions to answer first. More half-truths: I'd come to rescue my soprano, and the foreign ambassadors were angry they did not get their private concert and took it out upon me as manager. The lies flowed just as smooth as honesty as I dubbed the daroga my chauffeur and met his glare with a blameless smile. We were about to be free men; might as well take advantage and add some jest to the mix.

When we were finally allowed to leave, I abandoned the daroga with fire beneath my feet, rushing through the now dark city streets back to the opera. Oh, I did not doubt I still bore danger upon my shoulders. The shah was a powerful enemy to have, but for now, I'd take my victory for what it was, knowing the *gendarme* would pursue and woe to him if he were caught!

Faster, and I harbored an irrational fear I'd find an empty house and Christine off with the Vicomte, as if the hero truly earned the spoils, and I would have nothing. The idea made me rush at a ferocious pace and travel the dark corridors like a shadow demon, floating and flying with feet that barely touched the ground. I didn't stop until I burst through my front door, and gasping shallow breaths, I frantically surveyed the scene.

Christine...curled on my couch asleep. It was a dream come to life.

"She tried to wait up for you," the Vicomte softly reported as he rose from my chair. "But...we didn't know when you'd return, and she fell asleep. I kept her safe...for you."

I could tell it hurt him to say it, but he gave a solemn nod at my presence.

"I'm glad you aren't dead," he insisted, half-hearted, but as he cast a glance at Christine's peaceful shape, his expression softened. "It would have tormented her if you were gone...again. She may have believed that all the time we were together I didn't know some part of her was missing, but...she wasn't as good at hiding it as she thought. I knew, and...it tortures me that it was *you*. She suffered because her heart was *yours*. No matter what I did to try and earn it, I never could come close. I just hope you realize what a gift you have."

But I did, and I adored her one more instant in my stare, trailing the fine porcelain sculpt of her features and savoring the knowledge that they were mine.

"Come on," I suddenly bid to the Vicomte, who was also adoring her in his stare, "I'll take you up. I don't trust you to walk the path alone and not get yourself killed, and...though I cannot condone your attachment to Christine, I do owe you my gratitude for what you did tonight. Your death wouldn't be polite compensation. ...Thank you."

I hoped he realized how hard it was for me to utter those words. They stiffened my tongue and did not want to come loose without effort. But he took them with another nod and glance at Christine before he followed me out of the underground.

This part was just as torturous as awaiting the *gendarme*'s questions. I wanted to be back with Christine, but first I had to rid us of the Vicomte and lock up securely, patrolling the entire building in my paranoia before *finally*, I could return to her.

She was still asleep on the couch, such a beautiful portrait, and with a contented sigh, I knelt on the carpet and set my cheek on the cushion beside hers, studying her so close that her every breath tickled my skin. Oh, to feel it uninhibited! I had the thought and ripped my mask away in my eagerness, knowing when her eyes opened and she saw my scarred face, she would be elated and not horrified that a monster watched her sleep.

Desperate for that exact look, I gently bid, "Christine, love, wake up." My hand cupped her cheek and brushed fingertips along her hairline, encouraging a ripple-less return to consciousness and dreams that carried over with her.

Blue eyes fluttered, and as they found mine, a soul-deep sigh left her lips. "Erik..."

"Yes, love, I'm here and real and *yours*." Anyone else would have blanched to see a corpse's head with bloated lips speaking such vows, but my Christine beamed a brilliant smile and lifted her hand to imitate my pose and caress my disfigurement as if it was all she longed for.

"How did you get away?"

"Intelligence and wit. You'd be surprised how much better such things work over violence." I trailed my fingers along her cheekbone and nose, onward to outline her full, pink lips, every facet dearer to me than anything I owned. "I will fill your head with every detail tomorrow. But right now, I ache to carry you to bed and sleep in your arms."

"Yes, please."

That night after she found the haven of sleep

again, I stayed awake and uttered prayers. For so long, doors to God and reconciliation had felt closed to me, but now to have escaped the shah and be home with Christine as my future, I felt redeemed. I prayed for us both that night and thanked God for putting her in my life to save me. My very own angel...

*****

It was *Faust*'s opening night...again. The patrons were not pleased with the delay, and as compensation, I vowed to host a Masquerade Ball at the season's end. Ah, the upper class and their parties! It was accepted with positive responses all around, and I was suddenly the greatest manager the opera had ever had.

As I finalized details in my office, listening to the bustle outside in the corridor, a visitor came with a knock at the door. I was pleased to find it was the daroga, smiling his greeting. "I was nearly trampled on my way inside. Is this how every performance day goes?"

"Oh, they're just over-exhilarated with pent-up anxiety from the first time we attempted to open. And every department has their own superstitions as well. The ballerinas used to perform some sort of chanted séance to the Opera Ghost as good luck before every show. Now that the Opera Ghost is their manager, they stood outside my office door this morning and chanted like cloistered monks at noonday prayer." My report had the daroga snickering beneath his breath, but I got all-out laughter when I added, "They wanted to do it inside around my desk, but I banished them to the hall. Those girls are the most irrational little brats in existence. If they'd put as much effort into their dancing as they do endorsing each other's fears and drama, I might actually start to find ballet favorable and worthy to grace the opera stage."

"And didn't Christine used to be one of them?"

"Yes, but *she* is the exception to every rule, and watching her dance in a tutu was an exercise in self-control. The Opera Ghost couldn't haunt the ballerinas when he was too aroused with the concept of being anywhere near Christine. She tamed the ghost."

"And the man," the daroga added with another chuckle. "Or so it seems now that you are a husband."

The title was still so new and odd to hear. Every time Christine said it, I felt my heart ache as much as when she spoke her love. Now to hear the daroga speak it, I fathomed its letters a privilege I was fortunate to own.

"Was this rash little ceremony a response to having to hear that Vicomte call her *his* fiancée?" the daroga posed, and I shrugged.

Rash *and* hasty. I'd practically dragged Christine to a church the day after our drama with the shah, but...well, dragged was a harsh word. Dragged but *willingly* so. She'd laughed most of the way there as she fought to keep up with my hurried pace.

"I didn't want to wait a second longer. Near separation experiences have such an effect." I eyed him with suspiciously arched brows that he only saw in half with my mask in the way. "And on the topic, when are you off to join your family?"

"Tomorrow morning. I wanted to see your opera first, so that I might fill my wife's ears with its tale...albeit without the singing. If I imitate the melodies, she's likely to throw a shoe at me and wish for my continued absence! Ah, it will be heaven to see her!"

I knew that feeling so well, enduring prison and torture with it in my heart, and all I could think as I watched the glisten of love in the daroga's eyes was that I longed for Christine so that I could show her the same look.

"Well," the daroga muttered, "actually, I also came to tell you that I have it on good authority that the shah boarded a ship back to Persia. His guards were caught, but he escaped to return to his evil ways."

That was no surprise, but I'd heard that the caught guards were revealed as the shah's men and sentenced to death. "The shah would be a *fool* ever to return to France," I concluded. "He can hide behind his crimes in *his* country, but there is no mercy for such sins here."

"I truly pray you are right because you and Christine deserve a blessed future without threat lingering."

"A threat lingering? Oh, we have one of those!" I exclaimed with a smirk. "It's called the Vicomte. It seems even a marriage does not rid us of his presence. He's our new best friend, do you know? He comes to supper and lavishes attention on my wife. I would wring his throat, but my darling wife takes pity on his case and continuously poses the argument that dearest Raoul has no one else and would *I* really want to be so alone if I were in his place?" I rolled my eyes at the melodrama.

"And where is jealous Erik in all of this?" the daroga questioned with obvious skepticism.

"He is sustaining himself on Christine's new seemingly brilliant idea of matching the lamenting, lovelorn Vicomte with her dear friend Meg Giry, one of those tutued brats. We just have to get Meg beyond her fear of the former Opera Ghost so that she may join us for supper, and then once darling Raoul is happy, we may *all* be happy."

The daroga laughed and clapped his hands. "It's practically its own opera show."

"Oh, I know it, and I live it," I reported sarcastically. "Hence what happens when one spends too much time in an opera house."

"And why I will be getting out before you all corrupt me to be equally dramatic." His grin held an element of melancholy as he deemed, "I shall miss you, my friend. We've endured hell together on more than one occasion now. It would be nice to share some pleasant memories at some point."

"I'd call this one pleasant, and if you require more, then you need to collect your wife and child and bring them to Paris on a lengthy vacation trip."

The daroga pondered such an idea with a slow nod. "Perhaps I shall. Besides, what would you do if I weren't here to check in on you every now and again? I fear you'd miss me."

I acted arrogant, even though his words rang true and commented sarcastically, "And the opera melodrama is already wearing off on you. Get out while you still can. Lest you start with tears and gushing eternal devotion to the Opera Ghost!"

I received a chuckle in return, and he decided, "Christine is quite good for your temperament. I don't recall you ever being so droll. Give her my regards and thanks, will you?"

"Most definitely."

He gave one last grin and a fond nod before finally taking his leave, and I was truly sorry to see him go. Certainly, he reminded me of the times in my life I'd rather forget, but he was also one of the only people I could call 'friend' and mean it. His presence would be missed.

I had five minutes of semi-peace with only the buzz of conversations in the corridor as company, and then another knock arrived. This time I knew who it was before she even opened the door and slipped inside.

I was in the middle of signing a paper, and before I glanced up at her, I demanded, "You are not a part of that chatter in the hall, are you? You best be preserving your voice for later."

But all thought fled my brain and with it any care for vocal welfare or the show in general as I regarded her. She wore her frilly dressing gown, no layers or corsets, nothing but her curves highlighted by its fitted shape.

"Lock that door," I ordered distantly, unable to

tear my eyes from her body as she giggled and obeyed.

Never a hesitation, and once we were confined, she hurried to my seated posture and lighted upon my lap with a bold smile. "I missed you."

"Oh? ...I thought you'd be engrossed in preparations and crazy rituals like the ballerinas."

She considered with arching brows as my hand lifted and trailed the smooth column of her throat. "Perhaps I am starting my own ritual, and now before every performance, I will steal away with my husband the Opera Ghost and be voraciously devoured for good luck."

"Voraciously devoured?" I quoted with a thrilled chuckle, and as she removed my mask, I did not hesitate to comply, burying my misshapen mouth along that tempting throat and lavishing skin with kisses. "Is this what you had in mind?" I asked and felt her shiver and lose her breath against me.

"Yes, yes, more," she muttered and eagerly straddled my hips as my hand roamed the partition in her dressing gown and found her bare beneath.

"Vixen!" I scolded. "Maneuvering the crowded corridors in nothing but this silk wrap! How utterly brazen of you!"

She scoffed her disagreement and slid her hand to the buckle of my pants. "As far as everyone but *you* knows, I am wearing every proper undergarment beneath like the perfect lady and Opera Ghost wife."

"Oh, and stealing into my office and locking the door behind you isn't telling anyway?"

"No, but once I have you moaning and crying out, it will be," she proudly concluded as her hand found its path into my clothing and eagerly stroked my erection without gentleness. And the little tart! She got just what she wanted as I shuddered and lost a fitful moan to be her willing victim.

"You are shameless!" I gasped with the hint of a chuckle. "And how lucky I am to have you!"

"So very lucky." Her blue eyes glistened in

impish delight and the bit of mischief I'd been starting to drag out of her. As such, she played no games with what she wanted, and lifting her hips over me, she took me inside in one quick thrust that made us both cry out.

It was fevered and quick, her body moving over mine with remaining articles of clothing rubbing in friction. I could feel the scars beneath sting and burn, and I didn't care. I was equally as urgent. Let her tear open every wound in her vehemence, and I'd simply call myself blessed to be her victim.

I didn't doubt we were overheard, neither of us bothering to keep the arrival of our pleasure silent, but I concluded it wasn't a bad thing. Love and passion combined, and when everyone else perceived me as only the masked Opera Ghost, perhaps I *should* make it known that I was also a man worthy of Christine. I wanted us to seem as close to ordinary as we could get and strangle gossip and cruelty at the source, never to touch us again.

Entirely spent, she dropped weakened limbs and sagged against my chest, her body melting into mine as if bone and muscle lost tenacity and buckled. I had a sudden wish for clothing's loss when her skin was such a delicious texture and temptation to mine. But I settled for remaining sheathed in her wetness and wrapped her up in my trembling arms.

"Now how are you ever going to have the strength to be the diva after that?" I questioned as I set random kisses to her hairline and temple.

"Oh, I have no worries about that," she muttered back. "Give me five minutes to recover, and I will exceed your every expectation."

"You already did," I teased and nipped her earlobe with my teeth, savoring her delighted gasp and the way she arched her hips and made me stir within her. "Little diva, and you will have them all as eager to kneel in your shadow as I am."

"And later, may I also be the diva *with you* and

have you as I wish, succumbing to my every whim and command?"

I moaned my agreement before I could make words. "Yes, most definitely, my diva. Bend me to *your* will."

She laughed her anticipation and wove her arms about my neck, pressing her face to my jaw as she whispered, "Can we spend forever this way, Erik?"

"That is my intention," I promised and kissed her dark crown. "Forever, my beautiful wife."

I felt her smile against my skin, lips pulled taut in the arched shape, and it was as savored as language. I wanted to keep it...*forever*.

Opening night was a rampant success, and Christine sang with more passion and vibrancy than I'd ever heard her. I watched from Box 5, out in the open where she could see me, never giving any regard to the glances cast up from the audience every time the lights brightened between acts. Let them stare and speak; nothing grazed me. I was more invincible as a man in love than I'd ever been as Opera Ghost. Because *Christine* lifted blue eyes solely to me during final bows, the diva with accolades all around and thunderous applause as her appreciation, and she blew me a kiss and made her love evident to every person in that theatre.

My greatest achievement. For all the agony we'd both suffered, we'd reached the happy ending where we could just *love* without any intrusions or fears. And as I blew a kiss back to her and gave her a supplicating bow from my box, she beamed with adoration, and I knew this, *this love* was what life was all about.

Love had given me a bruise at its first stirring, a bruise that never healed; no, it progressed its possession upon my heart until it flowed my bloodstream with its essence. A bruise became a deep and permanent scar, prominent and always on display, and I wore it proudly. It was a branded mark every person could see, vulnerable in its exposure, and yet it was the most beautiful scar I owned. I prayed love marked me again and again in scar after scar and showed the world that I belonged to Christine. Now and forever, I was *hers*.

Also available from Michelle Rodriguez:

Opera Macabre
Daydreaming Roses and Fairytale Monsters

The Angel and Demon Chronicles
The Devil's Galley, book one
The Pirouettes that Angels Spin, book two
And Angels Will Fall, book three
Imprinted on a Demon's Heart, book four

Manifestations of a Phantom's Soul, volume one
Manifestations of a Phantom's Soul, volume two
Manifestations of a Phantom's Soul, volume three

Manifestations of a Phantom's Soul:
The Untold Darkness
(available exclusively from Createspace.com)

The Opera Ghost Unraveled

ABOUT THE AUTHOR

Michelle Gliottoni-Rodriguez wrote her first novel in high school. Fifteen years later, she's up to 29 and still counting. Fascinated with Gothic romances, she calls her greatest influences the works of the Brontë sisters and adds in an adoration for "The Phantom of the Opera" and Buffy the Vampire Slayer. In August 2011, she published her first novel, a Gothic vampire romance titled *Opera Macabre*. Over the past three years, she has published another vampire romance and the first four novels in her series *The Angel and Demon Chronicles*. In addition to writing about vampires, angels and demons, she posts Phantom of the Opera stories online and has even had the honor of having them translated into German and Russian for worldwide fans. Due to the wonderful support of her Phantom "phans", she published her Phantom novel, *The Opera Ghost Unraveled*, and three collections of Phantom short stories titled *Manifestations of a Phantom's Soul*. This past fall, she also released a collection of dark stories called *Manifestations of a Phantom's Soul: The Untold Darkness*, available exclusively on Createspace.com.

The other side of her life is a passion for music; she's also a trained opera singer with a Bachelor of Music from Saint Xavier University in Chicago. She's won various awards and accolades in the Chicagoland area and has portrayed such roles as Rosalinde in *Die Fledermaus*, the Countess in *The Marriage of Figaro*, Yum-Yum in *The Mikado*, the Queen of the Night in *The Magic Flute*, and Isabel in *El Capitan*.

From writing at 4AM to practicing for her next performances at 7AM and then onward to being a full time wife and mom with an 8 year old, a 5 year old, and an almost 2 year old, one would call her life crazy, but she likes to think of it as "full" and blessed.

For more information on Michelle's Phantom stories and original works, check out her website:

www.michellegliottonirodriguez.webs.com

or

Michelle Gliottoni Rodriguez
on Facebook.

Made in the USA
Middletown, DE
20 July 2015